THE NAPLES PREDICTION

G. D. MATHESON

D'ÉLAN PUBLISHING

© 2014 by G. D. Matheson.

All rights reserved. Use of any part of this publication reproduced, transmitted in any form or by any means, electronic, mechanical, photocopying, recording or otherwise, or stored in a retrieval system, without the prior written consent of the publisher is an infringement of copyright law.

This is a work of fiction. While many of the places and historical events are real, some have been fictionalized. The characters are pure invention. Any resemblance to persons living or dead is entirely coincidental.

ISBN 978-0-9688583-5-6

Published in Canada by d'Élan Publishing
754 Toronto Avenue
Penticton, British Columbia, Canada V2A 2P9

For Norma

With special thanks to my children, Catherine, Murray, Owen and Ian, for their encouragement to write this story; to Bill Gaynor and Viviene Calder for their thoughtful critique; and to Dawn Renaud, who helped me commit this adventure to print.

Prologue

Kristin Stefsdotir lay on the cabin roof, gazing out at the lights of Naples twinkling in the darkness. The June night was hot and humid, but a slight breeze through the *Challenger's* rigging made it easier to sleep up here than in the yacht's stateroom below. Across the water, Vesuvius's towering hulk rose like a sentinel against a pale night sky, providing a sobering backdrop to the sleeping city while surrounding the huge volcano's base, a band of shimmering city lights coiled like a snake around its prey.

But here, the prey was by far the greater threat: Vesuvius and its big daddy Campi Flegrei, the supervolcano that lurked beneath the Gulf of Pozzuoli, made this one of the most dangerous places on Earth.

Today, though, it had become a little safer. Kristin and her colleague, Dr. Reginald Pyper, had just finished installing their newly developed volcano monitoring software, VolcanoWatch. As of this afternoon, both volcanoes were being heavily scrutinized by the most advanced system in existence. Replacing a time-consuming hands-on analysis method, VolcanoWatch would speed summarized information to scientists by instantly and simultaneously interpreting data from dozens of instruments spread throughout the volcanic danger area.

The full moon reappeared from behind the clouds. Kristin glanced down at her son, asleep on the mat next to hers. Heph had turned nine today. Yes, she thought with satisfaction, it had been a very good day. The anxiety that was keeping her awake was a holdover from that strange argument with Hilda Marsh and Antonio Camponolo the previous evening.

The meeting with the two Naples scientists, here on the yacht, had been cordial yet tense. Kristin and Reg shouldn't have had to defend their expectation to continue as consultants, visiting regularly to oversee the operation the new system. It was standard procedure. VolcanoWatch was already successfully monitoring Popocatéptl in Mexico, Pavlov in Alaska and the Taupo caldera in New Zealand. But Hilda and Antonio had vigorously resisted signing the consulting support contract.

Why had they been so difficult?

Kristin had been particularly surprised that her old colleague Hilda insisted she and Reg should back down. Maybe Hilda felt she had to agree with the other scientist. After all, Camponolo was not only influential and politically connected, he was also her boss. But what was *his* problem? It could not be a budget matter; ample funds were available. Why was he so insistent? At one point, Hilda almost seemed—afraid. What was it she'd said? "Kristin, it would be in your best interest to cooperate. You and Dr. Pyper don't know what..."

A look from Camponolo had silenced her.

Well, she'd soon be working with Hilda again in the African Congo. That would provide an opportunity to find out what was going on.

Still musing, Kristin drifted off.

She woke and instinctively glanced over at Heph, who was still sleeping. A muffled thud below deck brought her fully awake. Reg was sleeping in the stateroom; he had probably just used the bathroom. She sensed movement and watched his half-naked figure come on deck and walk across to the rail. Was he preparing to dive over? The clouds parted and the moon lit up the deck, and she gasped. It wasn't Reg.

Blood seeped down the side of his face. He was sheathing a knife, and his hand against his pale torso glowed crimson.

"Mom?" Heph sat up.

The man at the rail looked back at her and teetered, trying to abort the dive, but he lost his balance and went overboard with a splash.

Kristin placed a finger over her young son's mouth. "We're in terrible danger," she whispered. "Be quiet and follow me." Pulling him with her, she descended a ladder to the opposite deck. They hurried aft, climbed over the side and slipped into the dark water of the bay. There, she whispered in his ear, "Let's play dolphins. Ready?"

He nodded.

Swimming under water, she kept the boy close, every few yards bobbing up for air. When they were fifty yards out she treaded water and spoke softly to him. "Okay, now let's race to that buoy over there—" All the lights of the *Challenger* came on. "Down!" The yacht's searchlight panned over the water above them, then moved on.

They came up for air. "Dolphins again," Kristin said.

Finally reaching the buoy, they hung on and rested. "Good thing you are a water-baby," she told him as the searchlight continued to scan the water. "For a nine-year-old, you're an excellent swimmer."

"What's happening, Mom?"

"A very bad man is after us, Heph. Think you can swim all the way to the shore?"

The boy looked at the lights of a distant wharf. "I can make it easy, Mom."

"Rest here for a bit," she said, watching the yacht.

"Is Uncle Reg okay?"

Kristin pulled him close. "I don't think so," she said.

"Did the bad man hurt him?"

Kristin nodded.

"But why?"

She kissed the top of his head. "I don't know." Was this just a random act of violence, theft? If so, why was the man back on the yacht, looking for them? Remembering Camponolo's sudden brusque capitulation last night, and Hilda's fear, Kristin shuddered.

"Heph, when the bad man leaves the yacht, I'll have to go back and get our passports. We can't leave Italy without them."

"Why don't we just have Uncle Reg take us to Spain on his yacht?"

She looked at the boy. "Because, dear, I think Uncle Reg is dead."

She could sense him trying to comprehend. "Dead?"

"Yes. I think the bad man murdered him."

The boy was silent, thinking. "Then you could drive the yacht."

She shook her head. "I can't. I don't know how."

They waited. Finally, the yacht's lights turned off. Moments later, clouds obscured the moon. Kristin put her watch on the boy's wrist. "It is 2:20. If I am not back by 2:40, swim for that wharf, find a policeman and tell him what happened. Okay?"

"Okay. But be careful, Mom."

Swimming in the warm water of the bay was easy, yet she was experiencing cold shivers. The adrenalin rush was gone. Only a sickening fear for her child remained. In this part of Italy, Mafia were rumored to have murdered thousands. She must get out of the country with her son, and do it quickly.

She struck out fast, watching for movement on deck, and reached the yacht before the moon peeked out from behind the clouds. Waiting a moment, treading water, she listened for any sound up there—nothing. Hauling herself up, she crouched on the deck and watched.

All clear. Climbing the ladder to the roof of the cabin she found her flashlight. She crawled down and, holding the flashlight like a club, entered the salon. Was he waiting for her? Hurrying to the galley she stuffed two seal-tight plastic bags in her pocket and grabbed a butcher knife.

Stifling her fear and holding the knife at ready, she crept down a passageway and descended the stairway. She entered her stateroom, placed her wallet, her journal and the passports in sealed plastic bags, then selected light clothing for herself and for Heph and stuffed everything in her shoulder bag. Back out in the hallway she hesitated; the door to Dr. Pyper's room was half-open. Steeling herself, she pushed it open and shone a light on his bed.

It was crimson. Reg lay sprawled across the mattress sideways in a pool of blood, lifeless eyes staring up, the shattered bedside lamp still clutched in his hand.

Kristin backed away, heading for the deck. Then, with her shoulder bag around her neck, she dove in.

When she got to the buoy, Heph was not there. Had she been gone more than twenty minutes? She wasn't sure.

Dear God. Had the assassin found him? She looked toward the wharf and couldn't see a swimmer. If the killer had... There was only one option. She began swimming for the wharf. The moon was out again, silhouetting the wharves with their ship loading gantry cranes, their lighted booms aiming upward every which-way, fingers pointing toward the different constellations in the night sky.

She scanned the water. Still no sign of Heph. The moon dipped behind the clouds again, making it impossible to see whether her son was ahead. Surely her powerful breaststroke should have overtaken him by now. She stopped and called out softly. "Heph! Heph can you hear me?" Nothing—not a sound other than a siren somewhere in the city. Really anxious now, she treaded water, peering into the darkness.

A whisper. "Mom—I'm here."

She turned, felt him touch her shoulder. "Heph!"

"I followed you," he whispered. "I was near the buoy when you swam up, but so was he. He was following us."

"Keep close. We'll swim at right-angles to the shore." Swimming on more slowly so he could keep up, all she could think of was the bloody knife. How could she defend them? What if the moon came out and he could see them? There were breakers now, difficult to swim against. Perhaps they should turn and head in to shore.

She must save her child. If he attacked, so would she. To back off would be fatal. The knife scabbard was on his right side, so he was right-handed. He wasn't a large man but armed with a knife his attack would be—

It was sudden and vicious. Fortunately his first thrust missed, and his knife snagged in the leather bag strapped diagonally across her torso. She turned and kicked at him with all her strength, feeling her heel sink deep into his flesh. Grabbing to drag him under she struggled to grasp his right arm. Where was the knife? As he kicked at her she realized she was now hanging on to his ankle.

Advantage! Twisting and turning, swimming deeper, she kept pulling, rotating his ankle as she imagined him trying to slash at her. Deeper—deeper—his kicking was less violent, and now she'd caught his wrist. She could feel him tense for one last thrust. Air! She needed air! Twist his wrist! Kick him! Drag him down!

Finally the kicking stopped and his body went limp. As she let go and tried to swim upward her arms were like stone. Air! Damn it! Where was the surface?

Lungs bursting, she kicked and pulled. Suddenly she was out. She looked for Heph. Holy Mother! Had he got Heph before he attacked her? "Heph!"

"Right here, Mom. Are you okay? Did you drown him?"

"Thank God." She was amazed to discover her leather carry-bag, its contents secure, was still strapped across her torso. She could feel a deep gash in the leather where the knife went in.

"Okay, Heph—let's swim to shore."

And then what? Exhausted, trying to think clearly, she guided her son through the breakers, toward whatever lay ahead.

… the caldera, the basin-like depression resulting from the collapse at the center of the supervolcano, measured 6.4 kilometers (4 miles) in diameter…

CHAPTER 1

Friday, June 12, early morning

Crouched at the rim of the volcano, Jeff Kingston peered down at the crater's floor. Sunlight glinted off the woman's thermal suit as she looked up over her shoulder and waved. Smiling, he waved back.

The woman returned to her task, edging toward the fiery lake.

Jeff tensed as a shadow loomed behind him, recoiled at the sudden darkness, and woke with a start.

Sitting upright, he swung his legs out of bed and sat on the edge of his mattress. This wasn't the first time he'd dreamed of the woman in the volcano. Even as a child he had watched calmly as she waved to him. But lately, the dream had left him with a sense of dread.

He glanced up at the walls of his dorm room. It was beginning to look like a crime scene investigation; University of Washington pennants had long since been crowded out by his mass of volcano data from around the world—much of it showing an uptick in activity. Hardly surprising a sense of doom had made its way into his dreams.

He glanced at his watch. Time to get up anyway. The guest lecture session would begin at nine, and after that Aunt Dorothy would be by to take him to lunch for his much-heralded twenty-first birthday. Finally, she'd share the big news she'd begun hinting about some time ago—hopefully, something about his parents. Probably not. She and Uncle Ralph had always insisted that they knew nothing about his life before he came to them at the age of nine.

Jeff stretched a bit and began to run through his exercise routine, but was interrupted by a knock at the door. "You up in there?"

"Yeah," he responded. "Come in, Michael."

Michael Lundquist shuffled through the doorway and dropped into a chair.

"You're up early," said Jeff, going back to his pushups. "What gives?"

"Rough night," Michael shrugged. "Happy twenty-first."

"Thanks. Were you up all night again studying your Italian monster?"

"Yeah." Michael glared up at the data on Jeff's walls. "God, it's frustrating! They won't listen, Jeff! I went over it all again. I'm certain Campi Flegrei is going to erupt. And when it does, Italy and half of Europe will be toast! They won't take my calls. They ignore my e-mails. They think I'm just a crackpot student geologist trying to make a name for myself! Here. Look!" He pulled out his phone, highlighted some data and showed it to Jeff. "The area that's about to erupt is four bloody miles wide!"

Standing, Jeff took Michael's phone. "VolcanoWatch, Friday, June 12… the caldera is 6.4 kilometers in diameter…" He glanced at Michael. "I don't use this data source. What's VolcanoWatch?"

"It's an automated direct feed from the monitoring instruments, installed in Naples a few years ago."

"Ah."

"Damn it Jeff, they should listen to me."

Jeff handed back the phone. "How do you pay for all your volcanic data on the Campi Flegrei caldera?" He waved at his data-covered walls. "I can barely pay the user fees for this, and it's a drop in the bucket compared to what you're accessing."

"I hacked into the Naples Volcano Monitoring Center... into their direct feeds. I don't pay for any of it."

"Seriously? Isn't that a bit risky?"

Michael rolled his eyes. "I can hack into the monitoring systems for your volcanoes for you."

Jeff went back to his pushups. "Not my style. Are you going to the visiting lecturer's session this morning?"

"No, I feel lousy—and feeling ticked-off about all this is not helping!"

Jeff looked up at Michael. "Your eyes are still red, and you look like you're losing more weight. We should get you over to the med center."

"I'll be okay with a bit more sleep."

"Well, at least the semester is over; we can enjoy the summer. Fatten you back up."

"Speaking of which..." Michael got up and went to the door. "Coming to the cafeteria?"

"I'll be down in a bit."

Jeff frowned. He and Michael had finished high school together and were now in their third year of the Earth and Space Sciences program at U of W; three years training in the Coast Guard Reserve had welded the bond even closer—in fact Michael was more like a brother.

On a recent field trip in the mountains, the normally energetic Michael had become totally exhausted. His long hours studying on-line data from the monitoring center in Naples weren't helping. Losing sleep analyzing the risks of what he believed to be an imminent volcanic eruption, Michael was a going downhill fast.

In the cafeteria Jeff collected his breakfast and found Michael at a table, toying with a lonely glass of juice.

"No breakfast, huh?"

"I'm going to sit out the lecture and get some sleep." He downed the juice. "I was going to pick Anita up; transit strike's making it hard for her to get around. Can you do it for me?"

"Sure," Jeff said. "Is she still here? I thought she was

leaving for Naples early because she wanted to spend some time in Philadelphia first, with her grandmother."

"She's leaving this afternoon. She couldn't get a flight to Philly until this morning anyway, so she decided to stay for the lecture."

"Yeah, well if it's got anything to do with volcanoes…"

Michael grinned. "We got her hooked, too, poor gal. Lucky her dad's stationed in Naples. She'll get to see my volcanoes before we do." He looked over at Jeff. Your Aunt Dorothy invited Anita to your birthday lunch?"

Jeff shrugged. "Probably."

Michael grinned. "Well, I for one can't wait to hear the big news Aunt Dorothy has been hinting at. Bet you're going to find out you're the long-lost son of a millionaire."

Jeff laughed. "More likely she's going to say I can finally have a beer at the table with her and Uncle Ralph, now that I'm legal."

Michael got up. "I'm going back to my room. How about picking me up when you get back?"

"Will do."

"Make sure you get Anita to the lecture on time."

Jeff watched Michael leave, then cleared the table. Anita would be worried about Michael, too. Since first visiting Mount St. Helens in their teens, the three of them had become friends and had studied everything they could find about volcanoes. Last time they'd spoken, she'd asked Jeff if he'd noticed Michael wasn't well.

He lowered the canvas top on the Jeep to enjoy the brisk June morning air and drove to Anita's place, where she was waiting at the curb. "Hi. I'm your ride. Michael's under the weather."

"Morning, Jeff! Good to see you! Yes, he just called." She swung her tall, athletic body into the Jeep. "What's going on with him, anyway?"

"Beats me," said Jeff. "I wish he'd go to the medical center. Think I'll drag him there after lunch." He waited until she fastened her seatbelt, then eased out into traffic.

"How's your grandma?"

"Out of hospital today, but still not doing too well. I'm flying out tonight so I can spend a few days with her on my way to Naples."

"I'm sorry to hear she's ill. I know the two of you are pretty close."

"She's been very good to me." The wind caught a few strands of Anita's long auburn hair, and she gathered it into a ponytail. "She's taught me a lot about life, too."

"Can I help by driving you to SeaTac tonight? What's your flight time?"

"I'd appreciate that, Jeff. Thanks. It leaves at eight, so plenty of time. And your Aunt Dorothy always insists I come on your birthday." She turned and studied him with dancing blue-green eyes. "I couldn't miss that, especially since it's such a big one. Happy twenty-first!"

He laughed. "Thanks. Another celebratory lunch for the three musty steers, as Aunt Dorothy called us. Remember?"

Back on campus, they headed to the earth sciences building and made their way to a stairway leading to the lecture hall. "Down—down—down into the bowels of the building," said Anita. "A fitting place to hear about volcano creation."

"Just so long as it's about volcano creation and not about religion," Jeff laughed.

"That's always been a mystery to me about you," she said. "An earth sciences student who doesn't believe in God."

He looked at her. She was smart, analytical, and insightful and heavily into science; yet she believed in God. Somehow to him it seemed counterintuitive, yet her intuition told her the opposite.

"You get that summer job in Naples you applied for?" he asked.

"Yup." She grinned. "University of Naples-sponsored student project to study the caldera. I'll be in Naples all summer. Staying with my family at Gricignano, just north of the city. I'm glad Dad's still posted with the NATO base there—worked out beautifully."

"That's great! Good for you!"

"Are Michael's parents still springing for a trip to Naples for you two?" she asked.

Jeff nodded. "Michael is totally concerned about the supervolcano. He's absolutely convinced it's about to erupt, but no volcano experts agree with him. They're brushing him off as a whacko."

Anita frowned and shook her head. "Campi Flegrei is so bloody dangerous. It's like a magnet for us types, isn't it? It's not likely he's right if all the scientists disagree, though. I mean the Bay of Naples is the most heavily monitored volcanic area in the world."

"Yeah, but he's insistent. He keeps on wanting me to study the data with him."

"We'll get together when you get over there," she said. "If you come in early July, I'll be working my project. I've planned to start each day from the Piazza del Plebiscito waterfront restaurant. You can catch me there at breakfast."

Jeff nodded. "Piazza del Plebiscito. Got it."

Their group was directed into the lecture hall, where they found good seats and waited. At exactly 9:00 a.m. a middle-aged blonde woman stepped onto the speaker's dais, shuffled her papers and looked out at them. "I am Dr. Hilda Marsh. I am here to lead you back to when the earth began. You are all geosciences students here, right?"

Silence. She shrugged. "Let us first review what you all should know and then we will get into the tough stuff."

Jeff leaned forward, feeling an involuntary shiver.

"Let us go back a bit," Dr. Marsh continued. "Let us go back to the birth of our planet in our small solar system among the countless galaxies. Let us travel through its turbulent history and to its transformation into the amazing little planet that now supports us all."

Dr. Marsh turned to the enormous screen behind her

and dimmed the lights. "We are about to take a trip back in time—4.6 *billion* years back, in fact." As the theater went dark, everything went dead quiet. Even the air conditioners turned silent.

Slowly, illuminated by a distant sun, colorful swirling gasses filled the enormous screen. In the dim light, coming directly toward them, a huge orange ball of swirling particles churned slowly into view.

Dr. Marsh's words cut the silence. "Earth began nearly 5 billion years ago from a cloud of gasses surrounding the early sun. Like the birth of other planets, particles of dust coalesced and collided to create our embryonic world."

Jeff shuddered again, frowning. Beside him, Anita watched transfixed as light from the young sun picked up highlights from the spinning particles, gradually turning the orange ball into a kaleidoscope of darker colors. He focused his attention on the screen.

"Because the sun was still too young to radiate large amounts of heat and light," Dr. Marsh continued, "our solar system was cold and dark. Now we are going to fast-forward from 4.6 to 4.3 billion years ago."

The huge ball, spinning closer now, was denser at the center. Dr. Marsh turned the room lights up, dimming the image on the screen, and asked a question.

Silence. Jeff forced himself to focus as she repeated her question. "Come come, people. What do you think is happening here?"

Someone spoke behind him. "The earth's interior is compacting because of gravity?"

"That is part of it, yes." Dr. Marsh waited.

Jeff found his voice. "It's radioactivity. The radioactive elements within the earth's interior melted the iron, it being heavier than the surrounding elements. It sank toward the center, forming a liquid iron core. Other elements, such as silicates, created an outer layer, or mantle."

Dr. Marsh held Jeff's gaze for a long moment. "Okay," she said. "What happened next?"

More silence.

Anita spoke up. "The liquid surface spewed out carbon dioxide, nitrogen and steam, radiating from the interior out into space, gradually cooling the surface. This, while it was being bombarded by thousands of meteorites."

"Exactly!" Dr. Marsh nodded, glancing again at Jeff before she turned with a sweeping gesture. "Now, let us fast forward from 4.3 to 3.8 billion years ago." She cut the lights and a new image appeared. The rotating planet slowly darkened as it began to cool, forming a brittle crust that was being blasted by meteorites. The lights came up again. "Okay, so the earth cools and the molten rock congeals, forming a primitive crust. What happens next?" Her eyes settled on Jeff again.

"Where meteorites punctured the brittle crust," he said, "magma surged up on the surface and spread out in vast sheets."

"Right." Dr. Marsh frowned at him, then turned back to the screen. "Now we are fast-forwarding from 3.8 billion years ago to 2.5 billion. Let us watch these next images and you will tell me what is happening."

Continent building would be next. Jeff could almost hear the rush of super-hot air churning over the boiling lava lakes.

The dark, orange-speckled globe rolled toward them and slowly morphed into a more recognizable planet surrounded by a wispy translucent cloud layer. Gradually the cloud layer thickened, obscuring the surface. The image dimmed as Dr. Marsh brought up the lights. "Okay. Now what has happened? Who can summarize it?"

After a moment she looked at Jeff again. "Can you tell us? You with the blue jacket."

Jeff fought off a wave of irritation. "There were gasses billowing out of the planet's hot interior," he said. "They contained water that was sealed in the minerals. These gasses cooled and condensed into a cloud layer."

"Yes? What was happening on the surface?"

Jeff was relieved when Anita responded. "Massive electrical storms," she said. "And lots of rain. They create the early oceans. Lightning from these violent storms helped create the elements in the early atmosphere."

Dr. Marsh nodded at Anita. "Yes? Yes?"

"By now the earth's crust is thick enough to withstand some of the meteorites. The first rivers appear. They erode the volcanic rocks," Anita said.

Someone else cut in. "And they deposit sand and mud to create the first sedimentary layers on the sea floors."

Dr. Marsh nodded, but Jeff had stopped listening. What was this woman's problem? Suddenly he realized she was looking at him again. What was the question? As she continued to stare at him, he guessed at where the dialogue should be and answered, "As the rains fell, they carried molecules that formed the first building blocks of life. Blue-green algae trapped sunlight in the process known as photosynthesis... then volcanoes thrust more magma skyward—" He stopped abruptly. He knew this woman from somewhere, but where?

Dr. Marsh pointed to Anita. "You in the yellow sweater. Can you tell us about oxygen?"

Anita answered calmly. "The algae used energy from photosynthesis to convert carbon dioxide from sea water into carbon for food. Oxygen was expelled as waste from this process."

"Yes, yes, oxygen," Dr. Marsh agreed. "Now we fast forward-from 2.5 billion to 600 million years ago."

"Good work," Jeff whispered.

"Following your lead," she whispered back.

Dr. Marsh dimmed the lights and the earth, now the familiar beautiful blue-green sphere, began to appear.

Over the next few minutes Dr. Marsh led them down through the layers of the atmosphere to the earth's surface, then through the ocean to the ocean crust, down through the mantle into the outer core and then into the inner core of the planet. Finally, she started her main lecture.

As the session wound up Jeff turned to Anita. "Unusual session. I was expecting new science. And she never really focused on volcanoes."

"She didn't," Anita agreed. "She asked us some good questions at the beginning. I thought you and I did well; good thing we don't share a phobia of public speaking, and we both seem to be able to string a sentence together reasonably well under pressure."

Jeff laughed. "I had little choice. I was adopted by an English teacher."

"Your Aunt Dorothy is a gem. It was my father who was the stickler for good diction in our family."

Jeff caught a glimpse of Dr. Hilda Marsh making her way through the students. Taking Anita's elbow, he quickly guided her toward the exit. "Let's get out of here." He looked at his watch. "If we don't hurry, we'll be late for my lunch." He led Anita to his old Jeep and hopped in.

As they exited the parking lot, Anita craned her neck to look behind her. "She sure had lots of questions for you," she said.

Jeff glanced into his mirror and spotted Dr. Marsh, staring at them from the curb. He shuddered again.

"Why the face?" Anita asked.

Jeff realized he was scowling. He shrugged. "That woman gives me the creeps."

"Seriously?" Anita looked at him. "Pretty judgmental, don't you think? You don't even know her."

"I do," said Jeff. "Just can't think where from. I'll have to ask Aunt Dorothy."

Anita put a hand on his arm. "Hey, Jeff, maybe she's from the time you can't remember."

Could she be? Jeff had given up trying to unearth memories from the first nine years of his life. If he had any, they were only vague wisps of things. Which was odd, because he could remember things he learned during those years—the science and the math, the languages, the stuff about volcanoes. All of that seemed fairly clear. But nothing about people, or home, or school; his earliest memories included Aunt Dorothy and Uncle Ralph, who hadn't been part of his early childhood.

Other people assured him that they were filled with personal memories from those years, so why wasn't he? When he asked Aunt Dorothy, her emotional outburst had startled him. "You don't want to know," she'd snapped, tears brimming.

He never asked again.

Later, he looked for answers online. Turned out there were others like him, after all—able to remember facts, but nothing personal. Autobiographical amnesia, they called it.

Jeff turned the Jeep into the lot at Michael's student residence.

"Look!" Anita exclaimed. An ambulance was parked near the entrance. Michael's father's Mercedes was double-parked at the curb. "It's Michael!"

Jeff parked and they hurried to Michael's room.

There, George Lundquist was pacing the hallway. As they rushed up, Lundquist raised a hand. "They're taking him to the University Medical Center. He's very ill. The ambulance attendants are in there with him."

"What's—?"

"We don't know. He phoned his mother saying he was weak, dizzy and in pain. We think he passed out while he was talking to her... Hello, Anita."

Anita looked tearful. "Hello, Mr. Lundquist."

They stepped aside as the ambulance attendants came out with Michael strapped to a gurney. His face was pale and his mouth pinched in pain. "Michael, we're coming with you. Hang in there." As they loaded Michael into the ambulance George Lundquist handed Jeff his car keys. "Bring my car. I'll ride with him."

"He's not been well. I tried to get him to see a doctor."

"Well, he'll see one now."

As the ambulance pulled away with its siren wailing, Jeff called Aunt Dorothy. "Hi. My birthday lunch is off,

I'm sorry to say. Michael's just been taken to the University Medical Center. Anita and I are on the way there now."

"Good heavens," Aunt Dorothy gasped. "What has happened?"

"I don't know," said Jeff, opening the door of George Lundquist's car. "Can you meet us at the hospital?"

"Of course. Where shall I find you?"

"There's a cafeteria on the second floor, facing North East Pacific, I think." He started the engine.

"You get going," said Aunt Dorothy. "I'll find you."

He handed his phone to Anita and swung into the street.

"My God, Jeff," she said, shutting the phone off.

"It's that damned obsession of his," said Jeff. "The guy's totally brilliant in science, mathematics, computer programming and statistical analysis, but he can't seem to think of anything but that Campi Flegrei caldera, and his certainty that it's about to blow."

At the Medical Center they parked the Mercedes and sprinted two blocks to Emergency. "Michael Lundquist," Jeff said to the reception nurse. "Where can I find him?

The nurse consulted her computer. "Are you a relative?"

"He's... like... a brother..."

"He's your brother?" She dipped her head and looked at him over her glasses.

Jeff hesitated. "*Like* a brother,"

Her eyes twinkled and she looked at Anita. "And you are related to him...?"

"He's like a brother. We've known him for years."

"Have a chair over there. I'll check."

Anita sat and Jeff paced until the nurse called them. "Your friend has been taken upstairs. His father is with him and his mother is on her way. Sorry, they're only allowing his parents."

"So we can't..."

"Sorry. Not now. I will send word upstairs if you wish to wait."

"Thanks. We'll wait in the cafeteria. Perhaps someone could tell them we're here? Jeff Kingston and Anita Arneil. Michael's father was expecting us."

The nurse pushed a notepad toward him, and he jotted down their names and his cell number, then passed it back.

"I'll be sure to get this to them," said the nurse.

Jeff gritted his teeth and glanced at his watch. Aunt Dorothy would be here soon; they could wait together.

As they entered the stairwell, Anita paused. "Your phone's buzzing," she said, passing it to him.

He glanced at the display; unknown. Michael's parents?

"Hello?" No response, just a click as the caller hung up. "Probably dropped service in the stairwell," he said.

At the cafeteria, they each ordered a sandwich and tea and took it to a table, where Jeff pushed his aside and looked at the floor. "Michael. Oh, bloody hell!"

"I can't remember when you've used swear words to express yourself." Aunt Dorothy's hand squeezed his shoulder. "It must be serious."

Jeff stood and gave her a hug. "Sorry, Aunt Dorothy. I'm glad you're here."

"Anita, hello."

Anita stood to hug the older woman. "Can I get you something?"

"Just a coffee thanks, dear." Aunt Dorothy settled into a chair. "What have they told you, Jeff?"

"It's serious," he said. "Michael's father knows we're here, and we're hoping he'll be able to let us know something soon."

"Let's hope he's okay," Aunt Dorothy said, a deep frown creasing her brow. "When you boys were over at our house cramming for exams, I could see he wasn't well. I spoke with his mother just the other day, and Joan said she was worried about him, too."

Aunt Dorothy leaned forward and put a hand on Jeff's arm. "I don't want to lose sight of this. It's your birthday today. Your Uncle Ralph and I wish you many more."

"Thank you." Jeff nodded, relieved that she had avoided the term "happy" birthday. He studied her for a moment. The years had been kind; like many women her age she had gained a few pounds and she had crow's feet at the corners of her eyes when she smiled, but she was energetic and she laughed a lot. Her dark hair, now streaked with gray, was tied at the back with a clasp and flowed freely down her back. The only other jewelry she wore was a plain gold band; left un-sized for years, it had cut a furrow into her finger and would not come off.

She was still focused on him "Twenty-one," she said. "Imagine that!"

"Without you and Uncle Ralph, I wouldn't be here." He gave her hand a squeeze. "Thank you."

Anita grinned approvingly. Aunt Dorothy turned to her. "How is your family doing in Naples?"

"They're still loving it," said Anita. "Want to see the latest photos?" She pulled out her phone.

Jeff sat back and watched them. Aunt Dorothy had always enjoyed Anita's company, pointing out often that he and Michael were fortunate to have such a fine young woman for a friend.

He had to agree that from the time he'd met her, she had been an inspiration: always pushing herself to excel at whatever she did, she'd been on a pathway to become a professional tennis player but gave it up to become a geoscientist. Brainy, but warm and caring and always quick to help others. He loved her green eyes and brilliant, impish smile.

For over an hour they killed time chatting, walking the hallways, and worrying about Michael. Eventually George Lundquist arrived.

"Dorothy, thank you for coming," said Lundquist, hugging her before slumping into a chair. "Joan's still in there with him. They're trying to get his pain under control."

"So we have no idea…" Jeff began.

"The doctors seem to know something, but they haven't

told us. Apparently Michael wants to tell us himself, when the pain subsides."

"I'll get you something to eat," Aunt Dorothy suggested.

"No thanks, I must get right back."

Jeff handed Lundquist his car keys. "It's in lot two, row three, on North East Pacific."

"Thanks." He looked at Jeff. "We'll stay with him for the afternoon. You can see him this evening."

"So Michael seems to know what's wrong?"

"He's been keeping something from us." Lundquist ran a hand over his face. "Jeff, all I can say is although he's very ill, the doctors look unconcerned. It's almost as if they expected this. There is something they are not telling us, and it isn't good."

Jeff nodded, swallowing, and turned away.

"Thanks again for coming, Dorothy," said Lundquist. "You and Ralph are well?"

"Yes, we're both well, George," she said, "just very concerned for Michael and for all of you."

Lundquist stood and hugged her, then turned to Jeff. "Take care, Jeff, Anita. I must get back." Squaring his shoulders, he strode down the hall.

Jeff looked at his watch. "So we have to wait until this evening to see him. I should… God, what should I…"

"How about this," Aunt Dorothy cut in. "I'll drive you both back to the students' residence. You can pick up your Jeep and come home for a bit. Ralph wants to see you on your birthday and Anita can come with us… that is, if you're free, Anita…"

Anita looked at her watch. "I'm afraid I really can't now, Mrs. Kingston. I have to finish packing. I'm leaving for Philadelphia this evening to see my grandma—but if you could drop me at my place, after you drop Jeff off…"

"I understand. Sure, I can do that."

Anita turned to Jeff. "Don't worry about driving me to SeaTac tonight. I'll take a taxi. You'll want to visit Michael. Give him my best and explain why I can't be there."

"Thanks. I'll do that."

As they were leaving, Jeff's phone rang. He checked the screen. "Unknown," he said. "Wish I'd thought to ask Mr. Lundquist for his number." He answered. "Hello?" He stopped walking. "Hello?"

No response, just a click as the line went dead. Seized by an involuntary shiver, he frowned. "Aunt Dorothy, have you ever heard of a Dr. Hilda Marsh?"

Aunt Dorothy's brow furrowed. "No, I don't think so," she said, clicking the remote to unlock her car. "Why, dear?"

Jeff opened the driver's door for her. "No particular reason," he said.

Anita settled into the front passenger seat. "She gave a rather odd lecture this morning," she said, launching into a description. In the back seat, Jeff contemplated his phone, then turned it off.

Anita was quiet for a few moments after they pulled away from Michael's student residence. Then she asked, "Do you think Michael is going to be okay?"

Dorothy hesitated. "It's hard to say, dear. Sometimes these things..." She let the sentence hang.

"If anything happens to Michael, it's going to be tough on Jeff."

"Yes." Dorothy slowed for a red light. "Are you worried about him, too?"

"I am. I haven't seen a whole lot of Jeff for the last while. We used to take the same classes but now I've switched into a different class structure, I see much less of him. He looks... well he looks stunned by Michael's illness. Today it was like he..."

"You don't need to worry about Jeff, my dear. He has always been surprisingly strong."

Anita remained silent, hoping Dorothy would continue.

"When Ralph and I adopted Jeff, he was only nine. We

both came to the conclusion that he had been through something very traumatic. It's probably fortunate that he had no real memory of his past. But he was a bright lad and very self-reliant. We never had much money when he was growing up and we moved around a lot. The moving never bothered Jeff; different schools, new friends—he has always been very adaptable. Perhaps *resilient* is the word. We noticed early on that rather than have a lot of casual friends, he preferred one or two very good ones, and to them he was fiercely loyal and supportive."

"I'm privileged to be one of them."

"You are, yes. But, well, there is another side to Jeff. We didn't have the funds to send him to college. He knew that, but was determined to further his education. That's why he joined the U.S. Coast Guard Reserve on graduation from high school, so he could enter their college credit program."

Anita nodded. "Michael told me he was so impressed with what Jeff did that, even though his own family was loaded, he joined the same program and refused any support from his folks, too."

Dorothy smiled. "Jeff is one of those people who leads by example and often others follow."

"Jeff always seemed—driven. You know, highly motivated. He sets a goal and…"

"He's always been that way. When Ralph's back got so bad he had to change jobs, Jeff insisted on moving into a residence so that we could create a basement suite and rent it out to help make ends meet. He says he can make his way on his own. His joining the Coast Guard is just another example of that independent streak."

Anita frowned. "Neither Jeff nor Michael talk to me about the Coast Guard. I'm not sure why."

"Well, Jeff takes it very seriously," said Dorothy. "And he hates to toot his own horn. One of his officers told Ralph that Jeff has numerous achievements, but he keeps all of those achievements to himself. It's just part of that independence, I guess. In fact, there is a really hard bark on our Jeff."

"Sounds like my dad," Anita smiled. The two men were quite similar in looks, too; both tall and muscular, except Jeff had straw-blonde hair and those deep blue eyes. And that smile. And that laugh that always got to her. A hard bark? "Jeff has a soft, compassionate side, too. And a balanced sense of justice."

"Yes, he's kind," agreed Dorothy, stopping at an intersection. "But as one bully learned back when Jeff was only twelve, push him too far and he's likely to retaliate." She studied Anita. "You've known Jeff for a few years. How would you describe him?"

"Oh, I don't know," Anita thought for a moment, trying to push the word "hunk" from her mind. "Jeff is bright, articulate and ambitious. He values brain power, proficiency and knowledge. He wants to accomplish things."

"And?"

"To me he's like being with a constant explosion of ideas. He's intuitive, he loves observing complex things—often others don't understand his thoughts but I do. Why do you ask?"

Dorothy laughed. "Would it surprise you to know he describes you in a very similar way?"

Anita smiled. "In high school, I had a crush on him."

Dorothy pulled up alongside the curb. "I know."

"Thanks for the ride." Anita leaned over for a hug.

"You're very welcome, my dear," said Dorothy. "Give your family my love. And do enjoy Italy."

"I will," promised Anita. She waved as Dorothy drove away, then headed in to pack.

... all active volcanoes are monitored by the International Earthquake and Volcano Prediction Center in Florida...

CHAPTER 2

Friday, June 12, afternoon
Jeff drove the Jeep toward his childhood home, deep in thought. Somehow that woman—that guest lecturer—she was part of his past. The more he thought about her recognizing him, the more he knew it must have been from his life before he was nine. So that meant he had retained features that were recognizable.

He looked at himself in the mirror on the vehicle's sun shade, thinking he looked much different from his boyhood photo when he was ten. But there were thousands if not millions of kids that looked something like his ten-year-old picture. Did he look like his father or his mother as he grew older? Is that how she had recognized him? She couldn't have recognized his name; he had taken the Kingstons' name when they had adopted him.

She must have known him well for her to make the connection. Somehow he sensed it had to do with volcanoes. Perhaps she was connected to the woman down in that volcano, the one he felt must be his mother. But he thought Dr. Marsh looked startled when she recognized him, not happy or excited, but... almost afraid.

He pulled up at the townhouse he once called home,

parking behind Aunt Dorothy's Volkswagen. He went in through the back door. Aunt Dorothy was at the kitchen stove making tea and Uncle Ralph was in his wheel chair at the kitchen table, carving an apple pie. It looked to be fresh from the oven.

"Ah," Jeff said, breathing in with ecstasy, "the wonderful smell of my favorite pie!"

"Come join us, dear." Aunt Dorothy poured boiling water into the teapot.

Uncle Ralph's warm smile was welcoming. "Hullo, Jeff. Sorry to hear about Michael. You okay?"

"Yeah, it's a worry about Michael. I'm fine, Uncle Ralph. How are you?"

"Gettin' by. This kinda dampened your birthday huh? Good you're here. Dorothy and I want to talk with you some. Twenty-one's an important mile marker. One a fella should remember."

Jeff squatted down beside the chair and put an arm around Uncle Ralph. "How is your back today?"

"An honest answer?"

Jeff nodded, serious.

"It's sore, boy. Like every day."

"We'll find a way to get you that operation, Uncle Ralph. They do wonders now. We'll get you out of that chair and back to cabinet-making. How's the accounting practice?"

"I'm a better cabinet maker than an accountant, but it's payin' a few bills."

"He's a great accountant, Jeff. He's studying nights and has several new clients."

Jeff nodded. "How are you doing with…?

"It's going to take a while, Jeff. The operation is expensive and…"

"Enough talk about me," Uncle Ralph cut in. "We have things to tell you, Jeff. I guess I'll let Dorothy tell you what we have to say."

Aunt Dorothy poured tea and cut the pie in generous

pieces. "Yes. We have a few things to tell you, but we had to wait until you were twenty-one."

Jeff pulled up a chair. He accepted his apple pie and cut a chunk of cheese to go with it. "Thanks, Aunt Dorothy!" He took a bite. "Heavenly. So, you have something to tell me?"

"And something to give you." Dorothy produced a key and an envelope, and placed them on the table.

"What's this?"

"Jeff, when we adopted you, we asked that instead of calling us Mom and Dad, you should call us Aunt Dorothy and Uncle Ralph. That's because when you were nine you often woke up asking about your mother. Now you're twenty-one, we must tell you more. We told you what we were told: that your mother was a single woman who died when you were nine. But what we didn't tell you were the circumstances surrounding your adoption."

Aunt Dorothy slid a piece of pie toward Uncle Ralph. "You came to us through a friend of your mother's from Iceland, a Dr. Frida Hansen," she continued. "Dr. Hansen made us promise to change your name but asked that we not register it with the government for a year or so, so no one could trace you. She would send the paperwork. All of this worried us, but we figured it was no big deal so we agreed to it."

"You changed my name?"

"Your Icelandic birth certificate is in the envelope."

Jeff stared at the envelope for a moment, and then looked up at Aunt Dorothy. "Go on," he said softly.

"Dr. Hansen said she couldn't involve herself in your life, and that it would be best if we never tried to contact her in any way. At the time, we lived in New Jersey. Ralph's company had just asked him to accept a transfer to the west, so we drove into New York City, picked you up and drove out to Nevada. After a few months we got a letter in the mail, no return address, with notarized papers that we were to use when we adopted you. Somehow that scared us. We wondered if you were actually Frida's own son. Dr. Hansen seemed a very cold woman, a busy scientist, perhaps about to marry, and maybe you had become an inconvenience to her. We wondered if that was the reason she was secretive about your adoption." Aunt Dorothy swallowed. "Or that maybe something worse..."

Uncle Ralph reached across the table to squeeze her hand, and Aunt Dorothy clasped his gratefully.

"We sometimes wonder if we did the right thing," she continued. "After a year we used the papers and changed your name. But the woman at the courthouse had to do some kind of record check using the papers, so as soon as we could we moved again. Then another letter arrived, this time with the key and a note telling us to give it to you when you turned twenty-one. Dr. Hansen seemed to be tracking us, and we were always a little afraid that she would show up one day and want you back. So we moved around a lot and Ralph changed jobs until we settled in Seattle."

Jeff frowned. "It must have been hard for you, always starting over. And it was because of me."

"Don't you worry about that," said Uncle Ralph. "We wouldn't have had it any other way."

Jeff eyed the envelope. "So my birth certificate has the name I was born with, Hansen?"

"No, not Hansen." Aunt Dorothy smiled. "Go ahead, dear. Open it."

Jeff realized his hands were shaking. He slid out the single piece of paper that could open the door to his past. Did he want that?

He unfolded the paper. "Heph Kristinson," he said. It meant nothing to him.

"We thought Jeff would be an easy name for you to get used to," said Aunt Dorothy.

Whatever had been written in the space for his mother's name had been blacked over; even holding it up to the light, Jeff could make nothing out. His father's name had been listed as unknown.

Jeff folded the birth certificate and returned it to the envelope, noticing a small piece of paper—some kind of tag. "Is this from the key?" He stared at it as if it were a bad omen.

"It's for a safe deposit box in Las Vegas," said Uncle Ralph.

"And you haven't…?"

"No. We have no idea what's in the box."

The tag read *#2274 Wells Fargo Bank, 530 Las Vegas Blvd., Las Vegas, Nevada*. "You must have been curious?"

"Cautious would be a better word," said Aunt Dorothy. "You were happy. We were happy. There was no point in turning over any rocks."

"This is interesting. I attended a lecture with Anita this morning. The lecturer, a woman named Dr. Hilda Marsh, seemed to recognize me. Aunt Dorothy, you didn't seem to know anything about her. Uncle Ralph?"

He shook his head.

"I've learned many things today," Jeff said. "Many things. I have a very sick friend. I'm beginning to think my recurring dream is about my mother. There's a blonde woman professor who scares the B'Jesus out of me. I have an Icelandic history. A woman named Frida Hansen got me to America. You protected my identity for years. There's a safe deposit key that may unlock the first nine years of my life." He sighed and leaned back. "All that in the last few hours."

He looked at the people he'd always considered his parents. "Have you ever wondered why I remember very little personal stuff about my first nine years?"

"Frida Hansen told us you'd suffered a terrible blow to the head only days before we got you. That may be why you can't remember. You barely spoke at first, although we thought that may have been because your first language wasn't English."

"I spoke Icelandic?"

"We think so, but you had no one to speak it with."

"But I retained basic language skills, and all the math, the science, the stuff about volcanoes... it's really only the personal stuff, the memories of my mother that seem so elusive."

"Autobiographical amnesia," Aunt Dorothy said.

"Yeah." Jeff leaned back. They sat in silence until he asked, "Why did you not tell me any of this before?"

"We would have had to tell the whole story. We thought it best to wait until we could give you the key."

He closed his eyes, thinking. "You said my mother died when I was nine. Did Frida Hansen tell you how?"

"We asked, but Dr. Hansen said it would be better if we didn't know."

"And the name Kristinson. Did you research it?"

"A little, when you were asking questions about your past. But we learned in Iceland a son is named after the first name of his mother so we had no way of finding her last name."

"Kristinson... Kristin—son. So my mother's *first* name was Kristin?"

"It seems so, yes. But there were untold numbers of women named Kristin in Iceland, and anyway, we were not even certain it was your real birth certificate. Frida Hansen may have..."

"Yes, to mask the fact that I was her child. But I don't think so, Aunt Dorothy. I think my mother was a volcano researcher and that she died on a volcano. My recurring dream is so real, and my interest in volcanoes runs so deep."

"Makes sense." Uncle Ralph nodded. "But it's still a mystery. Like I said, this'll be a birthday you'll sure enough remember."

Back at his student's residence, Jeff went to his room and grabbed a couple of energy bars. He retrieved his bicycle and took off down NE 45th toward the community food bank, where he usually volunteered Friday evenings from six to eight. He would be a bit late.

Barry, the manager, saw him come in. "Hey, Jeff. I thought it was your birthday," he grinned. "Wasn't expectin' you."

"Hi, Barry. What've you got for me?"

"There's a bread truck at the dock. Several boxes of past-date buns and stuff. Needs to be unloaded and small-bagged. You okay? You look a bit…"

"Yeah, I'm fine."

Jeff started hauling in the boxes. As usual he found the physical work satisfying. It calmed him, seemed to restore his sense of well-being. He often stayed late; it kept him out of the bar scene. But tonight would be different. Tonight he would leave early and visit Michael.

All too soon it was time to go. As he was washing up, Barry came by. "Jeff, I've got something to tell you. We'll be closing this place."

"What's happened?"

"We're four grand behind in our rent. People just don't have the cash to donate. The landlord needs us to pay up; can't say as I blame him. I haven't found another location."

"That's really too bad Barry. Wish I could help."

Frowning, Jeff left and headed for the University Medical Center, not knowing what to expect. On Michael's floor the nurses told him Michael was clear-minded, upbeat and no longer in pain. He found him sitting up in bed.

"So you're feeling better?" Jeff ventured.

"Hi! Decidedly! Hospital drugs rock!"

"What a relief. I'm so glad! Your folks still here?"

"Gone to eat. I talked with the doctor. Out of here tomorrow."

Feeling the euphoria of it, Jeff asked, "So, what is…"

Michael interrupted. "We've built a lot of sandcastles in the air, huh?"

"Yeah, and they're not sandcastles, we'll achieve our dreams."

Michael grinned wistfully. "Do you believe in God?"

"Not in your Catholicism. To me it seems a myth."

"If not Christianity, what do you believe in?"

Jeff frowned; this was not like Michael. "Are you going to be okay? What gives?"

"If you don't believe in God, how did life begin? What you believe in... absolutely?"

"About the beginning of everything?" Jeff thought for a moment. "Well, I know that physicists at the Hadron Collider in Europe discovered the Higgs boson particle. It gives matter its mass. It's a particle so fundamental that without it there would be no atoms in the universe. And therefore there would be no stars and no planets — and no one to wonder about it all."

"Yeah," Michael frowned. "They call it the God particle. They think it's responsible for all matter in the universe. It places us closer to the theory of everything. I know all that."

Jeff rolled his eyes. "And still you hang on to religion?"

"So how did we get here then?"

"I believe the origin of life on earth began about 3.7 billion years ago as primitive cells."

"You believe that, huh? Tell me about it."

"Jeeze, Michael, you know all this! The cells contained molecules that assembled spontaneously," Jeff recited. "They reproduced and evolved, giving rise to all life. The chemical systems included amino acids. They were the building blocks of life. They provided the molecules necessary for self-replication."

"Yeah, but how do we *know* all this? I mean, *really?*"

"Well, there's that 3.5 billion year old formation in Glacier National Park up in Canada that contains these fossilized molecules."

"So you think we evolved from these molecules..."

"Yes, and archaeological evidence and genetic data suggest that modern humans arose about 200,000 years ago in central Africa."

"So you don't believe in life after death?"

"Promises. Repeating the promise of an afterlife is to hold people to their religions." Jeff shook his head. He didn't like were this conversation was going.

"You're wrong about this, Jeff."

"Maybe I am. It all depends on whether or not we have a soul—I'm just not sure."

"You have a soul alright."

Jeff responded quickly. "From a logical perspective I believe in consciousness and not in a soul. There does seem to be something deeper, something unexplainable that I can't put my finger on, but it defies all logic so I ignore it. Maybe I'm wrong—I just don't know."

Michael smiled. "There's still hope for you. But mine has run out."

Jeff sensed this was coming but it was like being hit with a hammer. "But I thought you were getting better." He was afraid to ask what was wrong. He wanted to shut Michael up before he could say more.

"I've always believed that hope was at life's very core," Michael said. "I believed that optimism—hope, confidence in the future or whatever you wished to call it—was the essence of life. I believed that no matter how bad things got, no matter how bleak the future, there would always be hope. It gave my life meaning." His voice trailed off and he lay back on his pillows.

Jeff struggled to find his voice. "Michael," he said, "what are you trying to tell me? I've never heard you talk like this." He swallowed. "Michael, are you dying?"

"I am, Jeff. I've had it. What I've got is terminal."

"Ahh…"

"It's cancer—final stage pancreatic cancer—so I'm afraid none of my organs will even be any good to anyone. But maybe some…"

"Pancreatic cancer?"

"Yeah. It's one of the ones that takes you out fast."

Jeff's eyes filled with tears. "But this so sudden and you are so young."

"The doc told me it's very unusual for pancreatic cancer to strike someone my age. Only two percent of cases are in my age range. Just unlucky, I guess."

"You in pain?"

"Not right now."

"How long?"

"I have a month or so." He tried to smile but only managed a grimace.

"This is—this is just so unbelievable. How can they have not diagnosed this before?"

"I've known for a bit."

"You have?"

"Yeah. I've only now told my parents. I sure screwed up our Italian trip, didn't I?"

Jeff looked at the ground. "You are... like my brother, Michael."

"Yeah, and you're my very best friend." He smiled, reached over and roughed Jeff's hair. "You'll make other good friends after I've gone. And you have the Kingstons. And maybe someday you'll find your birth parents. Who knows, maybe you have a bunch of brothers and sisters down in sunny Florida or—" He stopped short. "What?"

Jeff drew a deep breath. "I just found something out."

Michael's eyes widened. "About your birth family?"

Jeff nodded. "My mother. Her name was Kristin. She was Icelandic. She died when I was nine."

"Do you remember anything about her?"

"No, but that dream I have sometimes, that dream about a woman walking in a crater, into a lava lake—I think that's her."

"And your father?"

"I know nothing of him. I've just learned a couple of other things, stuff about how I came to be with Aunt Dorothy and Uncle Ralph."

"What stuff?"

"The Kingstons were distant relatives of a woman named Dr. Frida Hansen in Iceland. Somehow she got me to America and Aunt Dorothy and Uncle Ralph took me in. Eventually they adopted me." He frowned. "And I think maybe I remember someone else from my past. Today at the lecture, the presenter, Dr. Marsh, she totally creeped me out. She kept staring at me, making me answer her questions. Frankly, she scared the hell out of me. But not as much as this does." Jeff got up, went to the window, gazed out and wiped his eyes. "Ahh, Michael, your illness. Such devastating news."

Michael broke the silence. "You must find out more about your mother, and you need to find your father. Promise me you will."

Jeff walked back and sat by the bed.

"Promise me you'll look for your father."

"I'll give it a try."

"And Jeff?"

"Yeah?"

"Do you have any attachment to Christianity?"

Jeff sighed. "The Ten Commandments, I guess. They are a good code to live by. As for a soul…"

"Jeff, after I've gone, I want you to promise me you'll talk to me."

"Talk to you? After you're—after you're gone? Isn't that bloody weird?"

Michael laughed. "No. If you talk to me, I'll hear you."

"You will *hear*…?"

"Yeah, I will. And maybe if you make this connection with me, you will find your soul."

Jeff tried to grin. "You're so full of it, Michael!" He sat quietly, thinking of their happy times together. It was going to be difficult.

Michael broke the silence. "The doc has promised to discharge me first thing in the morning. Pick me up here. Bring my iPhone, computer and the camping stuff. I want us to go camping up on Mount St. Helens. It's number one on a very short bucket list. And, hey, you got your phone with you?"

"Yeah." Jeff pulled it from his pocket, turned it on and gave it to Michael.

"Let me show you something," Michael said, and after a moment, gave it back to Jeff. "There! Look! I've highlighted it."

Volcanoes around the world are monitored by the International Earthquake and Volcano Prediction Center, (IEVPC) in Florida. Directed by seven scientists in seven countries they communicate with hundreds of other scientists who monitor seismic waves, gas emissions, thermals, hydrology and ground movement in risk areas. Where they sense trouble they collaborate.

Jeff looked up frowning.

"The point is, Jeff, why won't they listen to me?"

"I guess because you are just a student; they are PhDs."

"Yeah. Tomorrow, up on Mount St. Helens I'll show you more."

"Are you sure you are up to the trip?"

"Gotta be. Doc says my strength will wane fast. In two weeks I may not be able to get out of bed."

"Okay. See you tomorrow."

As Jeff headed down the corridor, his eyes filled with tears. He walked blindly to the elevator. Wiping his eyes, he felt a hand on his shoulder.

"Did you find him? Michael wasn't it? Michael... like a brother?" Her voice was caring, concerned and vaguely familiar.

"Ah, from reception."

"Julie," she nodded.

"Jeff,'" he said, extending his hand. "I just visited..."

"How is Michael?"

"It's advanced stage pancreatic cancer. He has only a month or so. And I... I don't know what to..." He swallowed.

"I'm so sorry," she said. The elevator doors opened, and she took his elbow as they exited into the foyer. "If I may share a bit of my experience?"

He nodded.

"While you're with him, Jeff, be upbeat and cheerful. Be happy for the time you have left with him. Do all the things that you want him to remember you by, after he's gone."

Jeff frowned. "Things I want *him* to remember about *me*? After he dies?"

"Yes, of course. Leave him with good memories of you. I'm sure he will do the same for you."

"That just seems…"

She smiled, squeezed his arm. "Do you need a taxi?"

He shook his head, took a breath and squared his shoulders. "I'll be okay to drive."

She nodded, steered him toward the exit and bustled away.

Jeff was suddenly very tired. It had been a dreadfully shocking end to a life-changing twenty-first birthday.

... a Catastrophic Geological Event (CGE) is part of the Monitoring and Warning System, (MWS) and covers stages of a volcano about to erupt...

CHAPTER 3

Saturday, June 13, early morning
After a five mile run, his exercise routine, a few practiced judo moves and a shower, Jeff made arrangements to visit the Mount St. Helens volcano. He collected an iPhone, computer and a travel bag of clothes from Michael's room, loaded their camping gear in his Jeep and phoned Michael's parents.

"Hello George. It's Jeff. I'm so sorry about Michael. I can't believe he has cancer. It's devastating news."

"It is, Jeff. It is. His mom and I are in total shock."

"Yes, me too. It's so... so very sad."

"Michael tells us he wants you to take him camping for the weekend. Joan and I understand. He insisted on the doctor discharging him. We will defer to his wishes."

"I'm glad you're okay with this. We know the area and some of the people at the visitors' center; he'll be okay."

"You take good care of him, Jeff. You hear?"

"Yes, yes of course. I'll have him home with you Sunday evening." Jeff hung up, remembering the nurse. *Do all the things you want him to remember you by after he's gone.* Perhaps for some there was logic in that; to him it seemed rather ridiculous.

He drove to the hospital and found Michael in his room, fully dressed and talking with two young hospital workers. Michael grinned. "You remember Milan from high school?"

A turbaned young Punjabi man wearing a hospital maintenance jacket stopped what he was doing and shook Jeff's hand. "Milan Malholtra," he said. "Freshman year. Mrs. Graham's class."

"Yes! I remember you! How've you been Milan?"

"Fine, Jeff. Good to see you."

"What's going on here?"

Milan grinned. "Mike says I promised years ago—"

"He did," Michael cut in. "He said he'd show me how to tie a turban before I died."

"And they've roped me into it," the nurse said. She was holding the end of a flimsy bed sheet that they had folded into a long narrow strip.

"Nurse Pat," said Michael, "this is my friend Jeff." He turned to Milan. "Okay, my Sikh friend, show us how."

Jeff stood back while Milan showed Michael how to tie a turban. Their first attempt was a pathetic disaster, but on their second try Milan stood back. "Ah, success." He held up a mirror.

"I look rather like a sultan," said Michael. "Your turn, Jeff." He raised his hand regally. "Nurse Pat, another sheet."

"No way," she said. "I have to get back to work."

"Milan, I command you—"

"Me too, Sultan Mike. Next time." He bowed his way out through the doorway.

"Thanks for this, Milan," Michael called after him. Laughing, he removed his turban, set it on the bed, picked up a blue plastic draw-string bag, and turned to Jeff. "Let's blow this pop stand."

As they passed the gift shop, he paused to pick out a flowery card. "Jeff, did you bring my wallet?"

Jeff dug it out of the backpack, eyeing the card. "You fall in love?"

"She's pretty special."

Jeff waited while Michael wrote something in it. "It must be serious. What's her name?"

"Julie."

Jeff's suspicions were confirmed when they dropped the card at the nursing station, where another nurse was counting pills.

"Michael, did they give you any meds to take with us?"

"Holy! You my nurse now?"

"Just wondered."

"Yeah, I've got half the medical center in my plastic bag here." They made their way to the Jeep. "Cleared for takeoff."

"Alright, then. Let's pick up a few supplies and go visit our volcano."

After buying groceries and finding their way to the I-5, they headed south on the freeway to Exit 49 at Castle Rock. There they turned east up the winding Spirit Lake Memorial Highway. It was a warm June day in brilliant sunshine and with the Jeep's soft-top down, the cool mountain air was a refreshing change from the city. Winters were hard on the road surface, and Jeff was on the lookout for rough patches as he told Michael the details of Dr. Marsh's weird behavior and Aunt Dorothy's revelations, about Dr. Frida Hansen in Iceland and about the safe deposit box in Vegas.

"Maybe your mom shared a lab with Dr. Marsh, and she hated having a kid around. Or maybe she's a long lost aunt who scolded you when you were a kid."

Jeff laughed. "Maybe." Glancing in the rearview mirror, he noted that a black SUV had gained on them. The road ahead was relatively straight, so he signaled right and eased toward the shoulder, maneuvering around yet another broken patch of pavement. Behind him, the SUV slowed too. He shrugged. "Not a lot of point being in a hurry on this road," he said.

Michael glanced back over his shoulder then looked at his watch. "We have plenty of time," he said.

Jeff grinned. "Got an appointment?"

"I was going to surprise you. I called Sandy Edwards at the helicopter base. I told him my situation and that we were doing some overnight monitoring of the crater. He said he'd fly us up to the crater today and pick us up tomorrow before the observatory opens and the tourists arrive. He's taking a risk that someone will complain about us being up there overnight but he didn't hesitate."

Jeff looked over at Michael. "You've been busy."

"You know me. Where there is a will…"

"That's fantastic. We'll avoid a two hour climb."

"I couldn't have made the climb. I just don't have the energy."

Jeff pulled into the parking lot at the Johnston Ridge Observatory. The black SUV parked a few spots away, and an attractive young woman climbed out. She glanced toward him on her way to the visitors' center, nodding briefly. Jeff realized he was staring and closed his mouth.

They carried their gear to the Hoffstadt Bluffs helicopter base where Sandy Edwards, a veteran Texan pilot, met them with a wide grin. "Mornin' boys!"

"Hey Sandy!"

He led Jeff and Michael toward the choppers. "We'll take this bird," he said, helping them load their gear. "Where do want me to drop you?"

"How about the top end of Harry's Ridge Trail, just above the crater?"

"You got it." Sandy opened the door. "Mike, you ride up front with me. We'll take the scenic route."

They strapped in. The helicopter lifted and they began climbing toward the top of the strata-volcano's 8,365 foot crater rim. At 8,800 feet Sandy leveled off.

"It's breathtaking up here in brilliant morning sunshine," Michael said. "Look. There's St. Helens' sister volcano, Mount Rainier." He pointed north. "And Mount

Baker." He swiveled to look south. "And way down there, Mount Hood."

Jeff craned his neck downward to see the lava dome in the middle of the crater, about 800 feet below the highest point in the rim. "Relatively quiet down there today," he said. "Only a small plume."

"Yeah," Michael said. "God, it's beautiful up here. You can still see the devastation path of the explosive eruption. What's the tourist spiel, Sandy?"

Sandy grinned. "May 18, 1980... 8:32 a.m. A massive avalanche of rock, triggered by an earthquake, caused an eruption that reduced the height of that mountain by 1,300 feet and replaced it with a mile-wide crater. Left 57 people dead and 250 homes destroyed; over 40 bridges, 15 miles of railway and 180 miles of highway wiped out."

Jeff shook his head in wonder. "And thousands of acres of timber flattened. Amazing."

"Yeah," said Michael. "But when the supervolcano that's lurking under Naples erupts, *millions* will die. The city will be destroyed, and downwind even more people, hundreds of thousands, will suffocate from glass-like shards and a yellow veil of tiny droplets of sulfuric acid in the air."

Jeff nodded. "Someday it'll destroy much of Europe. It's a monster."

"My God!" Sandy exclaimed. "Is it really that bad?"

"Yeah, that bad," Michael replied.

"How many people have volcanic eruptions killed, do you figure?" Sandy asked.

"Well," Michael said, "Lake Toba, about seventy thousand years ago, wiped out pretty much everyone, leaving only about ten thousand humans on earth. And in 1783, Laki in Iceland killed over six million in Europe. Some died from inhaling the killer chemical output, the rest from the famine that happened because the eruption blocked the sunlight for so long."

"Glad they're ancient history," said Sandy.

"Yeah," Jeff said, "but in recent times Huaynaputina in Peru killed over two million. And, let's see… the Santorini eruption in Greece about 1675 BCE began the fall of the Minoan civilization, killing millions outright and causing a devastating famine in China."

"Depressing," said Sandy. "And more than a little scary. So what's this big one you're talking about?"

"Campi Flegrei," said Michael. "When it erupts it could be in that magnitude or worse."

Sandy eased the helicopter down on a wind-swept rocky ridge at the edge of the crater, then helped them unload their gear. "Don't you guys poke anything into that sleeping critter down there!"

Michael laughed. "Thanks for the ride."

Sandy nodded. "See you here tomorrow, eight-thirty."

They watched as the helicopter rose and headed back to base, then hiked down toward the crater. After half a mile they found a sheltered ledge. "It's eleven-fifteen already," said Jeff. "Good a place as any to have our lunch."

"This would be a great place to camp too. It's out of the wind and you can see the continuous monitoring activities on the volcano. It would only be a twenty-minute hike down to the lava dome in the crater."

"What's that up there? Over to the right, a quarter mile off." Pulling out the binoculars, Jeff scanned the mountain. "Ah, it's a global positioning system tripod. And there!" He pointed. "Another one on the ridge."

"Bet there are about fifty GPS stations up here now." Michael unwrapped a sandwich. "They'll be measuring the stratavolcano's ground deformation. Scientists will be monitoring the depth and volume of the magna reservoir and how it is changing. There is precision accuracy in this now as satellites pass over the GPS stations and record each movement. They can measure a fraction of an inch of lateral movement at the surface."

"It's amazing how subtle changes on the surface show what's happening deep below."

They watched as a helicopter approached the lava dome a half-mile below. "What the heck are they doing down there?" Jeff wondered.

"Give me the glasses." Michael took the binoculars and watched a helicopter hover near the dome. "There's a black box hanging under the chopper. And they've dropped a technician on the ground with a camera. That's for their camera-gas sampling procedure."

"So they have some volcanic gas emissions today."

"Probably. See the tilt-leg spider on the dome?"

"I see a tripod with instruments."

"It's not a tripod, dummy. It has six legs. They're measuring something on the dome, close to the vent."

"Give the glasses back."

"They drop those tilt-leg spiders from a helicopter on the more dangerous and inaccessible areas to measure the amount of tilt on the dome face. That's what they are doing alright. The readout data from those sampling stations are measured from satellites passing overhead."

Jeff watched. "I see they're still using those old square solar panels on the sampling stations to keep their batteries charged. I wonder where the cameras are."

"They'll be back a bit. We better behave ourselves. There will be a network of ground-based cameras focused on the mountain from a distance, measuring time-series images of the terrain and how it is changing."

As they munched sandwiches and rested, Michael pulled his computer from his backpack and fiddled with it. "Look at this." He pointed to a complex graph. "By reading the secondary gasses in addition to carbon dioxide and sulfur dioxide, they get minute changes on the infrared spectrum. Using infrared, in addition to CO_2 and SO_2 they get readings on hydrochloric acid gas, carbon monoxide and water vapor. They also get hydrogen sulfide. The rest is developing statistical probabilities until they get a pattern."

"Hydrogen sulfide is deadly," said Jeff. "You don't want anyone to get a whiff of that stuff."

"Sulfur dioxide is more important; the greater the amount of SO_2, the greater the chance of volcanic activity. And Campi Flegrei in Italy is going off the charts on SO_2. In fact all the indicators, even the seismic data is positive for an eruption. You know how all the Campi data is fed into the automated VolcanoWatch system which is shared with scientists around the world? The Campi Flegrei data predicts a current stage 5 on the CGE scale, and still not a peep of warning coming from the scientists."

"But stage 5 is…"

"Within weeks. *A catastrophic geological event is called a CGE,*" Michael read aloud from the screen. "*The Monitoring and Warning System, or CMWS, covers the warning stages of a volcano that may be about to erupt. Stage 1 predicts it may erupt within ten years; stage 2, within 3 years; stage 3, within 2 years; stage 4 within months; stage 5 within weeks; stage 6 within days; stage 7 within a day; stage 8 is within hours; stage 9 is within minutes and stage 10 is the actual eruption. The difficult objective is to predict the CGE in time to warn nearby populations.*"

"Holy," said Jeff, "within weeks!" He leaned over to look at the screen. "You can access this direct data feed from the volcano on your laptop?"

"Yup." He pulled a memory stick from his pocket. "I've downloaded everything I've tracked to this jump-stick, along with the address of the VolcanoWatch direct feed into the Naples Monitoring Center." He scowled. "Unfortunately no one seems to agree with me. Here." He gave the flash drive to Jeff. "You can access the data feeds each day and study my stuff later."

Jeff put it in his pocket. "I'll do that."

"My figures say the eruption will be about June 29th. It's sound prediction science, Jeff. By my calculations there will be a pre-eruption event a few days before the 29th, then the mega-eruption on June 29th that will wipe out half of Europe. It will kill millions and impact global weather patterns for decades—that's only sixteen days from now—and nobody's warning anyone, and no one believes me! It's incredible!"

Jeff grinned. "Easy there! The Naples area is the most densely monitored volcanic site on the planet. The scientists have seen this, and they're not raising an alarm." He patted Michael on the shoulder. "You've been watching too many disaster movies."

Michael grunted. "This is no movie plot, Jeff! And with this damned cancer, I may not be around on the 29th to say I told you so!"

"Hey! You'll be around a lot longer than that!" He frowned. "Michael, who in the scientific world have you been trying to convince?"

"The International Earthquake and Volcano Prediction Center in Florida."

"Well if anyone would know, they would. What did they say?"

"That the data I am viewing is a hoax—that the same thing has been tried at other volcanic hot zones with people claiming to have inside information only to find it is bogus data. They tell me there is no truth in the data I'm viewing. They ask me to get off the phone and quit bothering them. It's clear they view me as a trouble maker."

"Well it seems like your data must be wrong. Have you considered that? After all, you said you did *hack* into their system—or what you *thought* was their system. But maybe it's not."

"But the direct feed data agrees with all the rest of my... oh, shit! Forget it."

Jeff remained silent while he finished setting up their camp. The whole thing seemed far-fetched. Still, Michael was a brain. He glanced at his friend, who was scowling over his computer.

Michael caught his look. "Damn it Jeff! If there's no way I can convince you now, at least follow VolcanoWatch from the Naples Monitoring Center! And study my notes, goddammit!"

"Okay, settle down! I promise I will do that."

"You bloody well better!"

After a strained silence Michael said, "While I'm on the internet, I'm going to start looking for your mother."

Jeff settled next to him. "Good luck with the Icelandic spelling," he said. "I couldn't find anything last night."

"What about that dream of yours?" asked Michael. "The lava lake?"

Jeff grimaced. "Lately that dream's been turning into a nightmare—the kind where you wake up with your heart pounding."

"So maybe that's not your mom down there," suggested Michael. "Maybe it's the creepy lecturer, Dr. Marsh."

Jeff shrugged. "Where is there a volcano with a deep crater that has an open lava lake? I was looking down on the woman, and she was walking toward it across a crater floor."

"Well, in the Philippines, there's... oh, it could be Nyiragongo in the African Congo. I've seen pictures of the boiling lava lake, deep down in the center of the crater."

Jeff peered at the screen. "Okay. Maybe news for Nyiragongo, from about twelve years ago when I had just turned nine."

Michael typed it in. After a few minutes Jeff exclaimed, "Look! Look!"

Two Gisenyi mercenaries reported the death of scientist Dr. Kristin Stefsdotir in the Nyiragongo crater above the African city of Goma two days ago. The death occurred just hours prior to the large fissure eruption on the volcano that resulted in a lava flow which decimated part of the city. While 40,000 have been safely evacuated from the area, the eruption has killed 147 people.

Two other scientists, Dr. Hilda Marsh—Jeff sucked in his breath—*and Dr. Antonio Camponolo, were brought down from the mountain in a daring rescue by local officials. They had been alerted to the presence of the scientists by their guide, who had made his way into a nearby village with an injured child.*

The boy, identified as Dr. Stefsdotir's young son, routinely accompanied his mother on field trips around the world. The guide claims to have found the boy near the rim of the volcano, where he was suffering from a serious head injury.

Unfortunately, the boy did not survive. The guide was unable to provide further information, and the injured scientists are being sought by this paper to shed more light on Dr. Stefsdotir and her son's deaths.

Tragedy struck the same team only a month earlier when a colleague of Dr. Stefsdotir, scientist Dr. Reginald Pyper, was murdered aboard his yacht in Naples. That case has not yet been solved.

Jeff looked at Michael for a long moment. "I must have seen my mother die down near Nyiragongo's lava lake. If I did, that's the only memory I have of her."

"And that's where you knew that lecturer from, that Dr. Hilda Marsh. She creeps you out. I'll bet she had something to do with your mother's death. Maybe she even killed her. Maybe your mom had figured out that Marsh had already killed the other scientist, the one on the boat."

"Pyper." Jeff pointed to the screen. He frowned. "I guess this would account for Frida Hansen declaring me dead and then smuggling me to America. She was trying to protect me." He paused. "No wonder Dr. Marsh was acting so weird during the lecture. She thought she knew me. I wonder if she recognized me."

"Probably just thought you seemed familiar," said Michael. "Let's see if there's anything else on here about your mom, now that we have her name."

They had no luck, but a search for Dr. Antonio Camponolo yielded results. "He's a professor at the Università degli Studi di Napoli Federico II," said Michael. "That's the University of Naples, in Italy, right?"

Jeff nodded. "Let's look for Dr. Hilda Marsh at UCLA."

"Weird," said Michael. "There's nothing except a brief bio. No picture. Something's showing in the cached results, but whatever was on the site has been purged."

Jeff leaned back against the rocks. Off in the distance,

overhead and to the west, a small group of hikers appeared near the rim of the volcano. Taking turns, they posed for photographs. Further along the rim, a single figure stood silhouetted against the sky. Female, he thought, recalling the woman from the SUV. He picked up his binoculars, and Michael followed his gaze.

"Think it's the babe from the parking lot?"

Jeff grinned. "One can only hope," he said. "Yep. Looks like her."

"Time for my power nap. Wake me up if she starts heading our way."

While Michael dozed, Jeff tried a few more searches for Dr. Hilda Marsh, but found nothing of interest. Searching for news about her colleague Dr. Camponolo again, he was startled to see results that included organized crime—but not, he realized, for Antonio.

Jeff re-focused the glasses on the hiker. Picking her way slowly down from the rim, she stopped regularly to take pictures. Too bad for Michael; if anything, her route was taking her further away from their camp. He set the glasses down and began studying Michael's reams of data on Campi Flegrei. When he realized he'd been staring at the same graph for the past few minutes, he closed the laptop, lay back, pulled his hat down and closed his eyes.

Jeff was making supper when Michael woke. "Smells good," said Michael, stretching, "So, did she come for me?"

Jeff looked at him. "Did who come for you?"

"SUV babe." Michael scanned the crater. "She was checking me out in the parking lot."

Jeff laughed. "She was taking photos, last I saw."

Michael opened his laptop. Jeff could see he was back at the Campi Flegrei site. It was proving to be quite the obsession: the two of them were up close and personal with a real live volcano, but Michael couldn't just relax and enjoy it.

"Grub's about ready," he said.

As they ate, Michael raised his spoon and waved it at him. "You've got to go to Naples, Jeff. You've got to warn them to evacuate the city."

Jeff nodded. "Right."

"Hey! Don't humor me." He chewed for a moment. "While you're there, we can keep in touch by texting."

"Michael," said Jeff gently. "You are too ill to go and we can't expect your father to pay for my trip."

They ate in silence until Michael said, "Thank you for bringing me up here, Jeff. Let's just relax a while and enjoy the evening."

Jeff breathed a sigh of relief.

He woke in the near-dark, scratching, and realized Michael was doing the same. "Ants?"

"Way up here?" Michael was pulling of his shirt and giving it a shake. "I wouldn't have believed it, this soon after the blast."

"Must have come in on somebody's firewood," said Jeff. "You'd think the little buggers would have made themselves known in the daylight." The faint glow in the sky beyond the rim was in the west. He sighed, pulling on his boots. "Guess we better move. Bloody hell, wish I'd thought to bring a flashlight."

"Let's just move the bedrolls," suggested Michael, standing to give his a good shake. "We can get the rest in the morning."

Picking their way carefully along the slope, they found another ledge and settled in.

Michael's breathing was soon steady, but Jeff sat deep in thought as darkness closed in on the blast-shattered mountain.

There was movement above them on the rim. Suddenly alert, he focused on it. In the dim light a slim figure was briefly silhouetted against the pale sky. She crouched. Jeff saw a spark of light. Was she lighting a cigarette? Then he heard a muffled *bang,* and seconds later a massive tumble of rocks came roaring down the slope, directly onto the ledge where they'd first set up camp. Above, the woman stood, hands on her hips, watching.

Michael sat up, and Jeff quickly reached over to place a hand on his mouth. "Shh," he whispered, watching the woman. After a few long seconds, she trained a flashlight over the slide area. The light caught something gleaming in the pile of rubble: their overturned cooler. After a few more seconds the woman focused her search on the area near her feet. Crouching, she collected a few items from the ground. After casting her light slowly over the rock pile once more, she turned to make her way back down the mountain.

Jeff leaned close to Michael. "Wait here." He picked his way carefully up the slope. Eventually the terrain leveled out. Bobbing down the other side was a single beam of light. He watched until it disappeared from sight, then he crept back down toward Michael. In the dark, he was sure he'd gone too far. "Michael?" he called softly.

"Over here." Jeff made his way back up and east. "You were right," he said. "She *was* checking you out. Maybe you have stumbled on something with your research. Looks to me like somebody wants to shut you up."

Sunday, June 14, night
Jeff sat in his room at the U of W student residence with his door locked. He and Michael had stopped on their way back from the mountain to replace Michael's laptop. Fortunately, Sandy hadn't seemed to notice that their cooler was dented, or that they were packing out less than they'd brought in; he'd been concerned that the monitoring equipment had picked up a rockslide during the night, and more than a little relieved to find them in one piece.

While Jeff drove Michael to his parents, Michael had loaded his new laptop with the contents of the memory stick. "So," he'd said, watching the data transfer, "you think this was worth an attempt on my life? I've been making a stink about this for weeks." He frowned. "You're pretty sure that it was the babe from the parking lot?"

"You said she was checking you out."

Michael handed the memory stick to Jeff. "Here, put this back in your pocket. And yeah, I know I said she was checking me out. Actually, Jeff, she was looking at you." He closed his laptop. "Much as I want you to look at my Naples data, first thing you'd better do is find out what's in that safe deposit box."

Jeff had spent the rest of the day relaxing with Michael's family, and they'd insisted he stay for supper.

Now, Jeff opened his desk drawer and pulled out the key Aunt Dorothy had given him. He set it on his desk, alongside Michael's memory stick. Was a massive eruption really only fifteen days away?

Michael seemed pretty convinced that it was, yet he still thought it was more important for Jeff to find out what had happened to his birth mother than to review his research. How could his family history be more important than saving the lives of millions?

And why did Hilda Marsh make him feel so afraid?

A noise in the hall made him jump, and he laughed at himself. Then, remembering the rockslide, he sobered.

Who was the target?

There was heavy security at the university residence, so he felt reasonably safe for the moment. No point in going to the police. He would need much more evidence before he could do that.

Using his iPad, he checked the airlines. He could get a seat the following day. The round trip from Seattle to Las Vegas would take two and a half hours each way. A city bus would get him from the airport to the Wells Fargo branch on Las Vegas Boulevard. He could collect the contents of the safe deposit box and be back in Seattle the same day.

He checked his finances. He could manage it without going too far outside his carefully followed budget.

Taking a deep breath, he booked the flight.

... the National Institute of Physics and Volcanology in Naples reports the Campi Flegrei caldera unchanged...

Chapter 4

Monday, June 15, morning
After his exercise routine and a few practiced judo moves, Jeff had his breakfast and hurried down to his Jeep. Alternating between high anticipation and a sense of dread, he drove to SeaTac airport.

The Delta flight was crowded but uneventful. Midmorning, Las Vegas was hot and dry. The bus from the airport to the Wells Fargo Bank on Las Vegas Boulevard took only minutes. Inside, he found a teller.

"Safe deposit boxes, please."

"This way sir." The woman led him to a vault room with an array of numbered steel doors.

"Two-two-seven-four, please."

"Sign here." She watched him sign, counter-signed the sheet herself, and led him to his box. She had him insert his key and turn it. Then, inserting her own key, she opened the door and waited while he pulled out the tray. "You can use one of those cubicles, sir," she said. "Please replace the tray when you're done, and re-lock your box."

Alone, he took the covered tray to a cubicle, sat, and looked at it. Lifting the lid, he found a note addressed to him from Dr. Frida Hansen, along with a book of blank Wells Fargo bank drafts. Attached was an I.D. card with a personal identification number. Beneath that was a bundle of letters tied with string, and a stack of notebooks.

The note from Frida Hansen read:

Dear Jeff,

I promised your mother that if something happened to her I would deliver these letters, papers and funds to you when you reached the age of 21. You may not yet know this, but your mother died while studying the Nyiragongo volcano in Africa. You were with her and you were in danger.

You were nine at the time. The local guide was loyal to your mother. He helped me get you safely out of Africa and into the United States.

Your mother wanted me to tell you that your father is Doctor Curtis Munson, a geologist from Ottawa, Canada. He is not aware that you exist. He is a fine man and while she loved him dearly, their careers were divergent and he never learned about you. She instructed me not to bring you to him. Her previous connection to him may have caused the wrong people to make note of your sudden appearance, endangering both of you. I can only assume from her death and your own terrible injury that her fears were not unfounded.

I have opened and read the first letter of the bundle I am enclosing. You should read it. The rest are sealed and are marked confidential to your father. There was also an unfinished one that I have sealed. Of course, it is up to you to decide what to do with them. I recommend you deliver them to your father. I am certain he will share some of them with you after he has read them.

You should withdraw the funds from the bank as needed. These were all the funds left in your mother's bank account. The account I have opened is in your adopted name, Jeff Kingston. I was pleased that the Kingstons have moved so often, making it more difficult for even me to keep track of you. I will continue to follow your progress if I can.

A word of advice: If you are happy with your life, you should probably burn the letters and your mother's journals. If, on the other hand, you decide to find your father I am certain it will be a positive experience for you.

Should you decide to contact me, use your adopted name and call me at the university where I work.
Sincerely,
Dr. Frida Hansen, PhD. Geophysics, Professor
Department of Geophysics and Geology
University of Iceland

Jeff's hand shook as he retrieved the bundle of letters and undid the string. These were actual letters from his mother! It was as if time slipped backward.

About a dozen letters fell from the package. They were addressed in a woman's handwriting—her handwriting! The return address read Kristin Stefsdotir, 1231 Stokksnes, Reykjavik, Iceland.

The first envelope was addressed to Munson, c/o Galaxy-21, Box 1341, Nome, Alaska.

Across the back of the envelope was written *Personal and Confidential*. The envelope had been opened. He took the letter out and studied the date: eight months and two weeks before he was born. He considered; she would not have known she was pregnant when she wrote it.

Her handwriting was small and well formed. In an optimistic fashion, it sloped slightly upward on the page.

My Dear Munson:

When you phoned me tonight, I was cruel in the way I ended our relationship. I hope this letter will soften the blow.

My flight back has been uneventful but it has given me time to think about what our lives would be like together—or should I say, what our lives would be like apart. My work takes me worldwide constantly. While I live on international aircraft and on volcanoes, you explore the high Arctic for petroleum on the very outer edge of human existence, keeping you away from civilization for months at a time. Your field exploration team is a great group, but being with you up there is like being cut off from the rest of the world. You live in tents and on bush planes, comfortable being loners in the high Arctic. I could never live like that, Munson. And you could not accept my way of life.

You did not enjoy being dragged up onto Katla's lava beds

when you came to see me in Iceland, yet being out on an active volcano is my life. You see what I am trying to say, my dearest? It simply won't work for us.

We had a wonderful time together on the Hawaiian Islands. The climb up Kilauea was especially memorable. And our camp out... our long summer night... our tent near Kilauea's crater rim overlooking the moonlit Pacific... well, let me just say it was the most unforgettable night of my life.

But this is the end of our story, dear man. I don't know how else to say it. I have deep feelings for you but I know that our lives will never intertwine like that again... at least not in this world. Take care of yourself. I will never forget you. Please don't try to keep in touch. It would be too painful for both of us.

Goodbye and God bless,
Kristin

Jeff slowly placed the two pages back into the faded envelope. Had he been conceived on a volcano? As Frida Hansen had explained, his father would not have known about him. Even if he had read the news clippings about Kristin's death, and had realized that he may have fathered her son, the same news would have told him that this son had died. But why had she never sent the letter? Or, for that matter, any of these letters?

He thumbed through the sealed envelopes; the rest of them had Munson's name on them, but were unaddressed. The last envelope had nothing written on it, and it wasn't sealed. In it were two newspaper clippings and a picture of a man and woman in mountaineering garb with backpacks. Scrawled across the back was written *Kristin and her friend Munson. Iceland's Katla Volcano.*

Jeff drew in a breath. The image of his mother brought back a vague memory. So this was her! And that was his father!

The photo showed a handsome, athletic couple gazing out across the black lava beds of Katla. His parents looked tanned and fit. His mother had an attractive, pleasant face. He looked closely and realized that he'd grown up tall and sandy haired with eyes like his father's, but his facial features had come from his mother.

He set the photo back into the envelope and took out the clippings. The first was small and yellowed.

DECEASED SCIENTIST'S SON
DIES OF INJURIES

Following a small fissure eruption on the southern slope of Nyiragongo on July 16th, two Gisenyi mercenaries reported the death of scientist Dr. Kristin Stefsdotir. Stefsdotir's nine-year-old son has also died of injuries suffered on the volcano that day. Their local guide is being sought by this reporter to shed light on the deaths of Dr. Stefsdotir and her son.

Two other scientists, Dr. Hilda Marsh and Dr. Antonio Camponolo were brought down the mountain with minor injuries and have left the country.

The second clipping was too faded to read.

Jeff replaced the clippings. The guide must have believed little Heph's life had been in danger, probably from the same person responsible for his mother's death. Had she and her colleague been murdered by Dr. Marsh, or by Dr. Camponolo—who may have a family Mafia connection? Or were both Camponolo and Marsh involved?

If Marsh *was* involved, and she *had* recognized him at the lecture—perhaps Michael was right in thinking that Jeff was the rockslide's target.

The lecture. Jeff sucked in his breath. Anita had been with him. If Dr. Marsh *was* after him, would she use Anita to get to him? Dr. Marsh couldn't have known that Jeff had no memory of the events on Nyiragongo—she could easily assume that Jeff had told Anita everything. If Dr. Marsh was his mother's killer—

Did Dr. Frida Hansen know who had killed his mother? Did the guide know? And who *was* the guide?

Jeff quickly repackaged the letters and tied the string around them, tucked them and the journals into his travel bag and returned the empty safe deposit box to its slot. Going to a teller's cage, he presented the I.D. card and asked for his account balance.

"My goodness," the teller said, "We haven't used these I.D. cards for years!"

"It's the first time I've used the account," said Jeff. "It was waiting for me to turn twenty-one. I have a PIN code."

"Happy birthday," she said. "I'm afraid I'll have to get this authorized." She left for a moment and returned with another woman.

"Hello, Mr. Kingston. I'm an accounts manager. May we have your address, phone number and two additional pieces of I.D. please?"

Reciting his phone number, he handed her his driver's license and Coast Guard Reserve I.D. She looked them over, then passed the driver's license to the teller. "Just enter this," she said, pointing. She waited, then she returned both cards. "Now Mr. Kingston, you can go ahead and enter your PIN."

Jeff entered the number, and the teller gave him a read-out. The bank balance was $446,543.08.

"It appears to have been gathering compound interest for a long time," said the accounts manager. "We don't offer these high interest savings accounts anymore."

"Thank you." Trying to mask his excitement, Jeff made a quick decision. "I would like to withdraw $30,000 please, in hundreds, and I would like a certified cashier's check for $150,000, made out to this name." He wrote it on the back of the read-out and slid it across the counter to her.

"Certainly Mr. Kingston. Come over to that office for privacy. We'll count the cash and cut you a cashier's check. We'll also provide you with a debit card for this account."

He waited in the office, heart racing, until the teller returned with thirty packages of crisp $100 bills. "We will count each package of ten bills, Mr. Kingston." It took only moments. "Okay, I'll get you to sign the slip. And here is your cashier's check. Finally, please enter a code for your card. We recommend only four digits if you plan to use it in other countries."

Jeff typed in a code. "Thank you," he said, placing the card in his wallet. Stuffing the cash and the cashier's check into his travel bag, Jeff left the bank walking on air. "To hell with the bus," he laughed aloud. "For once, I'll travel in style!"

Hailing a taxi he grinned at the driver. "Airport please! An extra $20 if you hurry!" He would be careful with the money his mother left him, but this once, it felt good.

He looked at the cashier's check. This would get Uncle Ralph the corrective surgery he needed to get out of the wheel chair. Perhaps, if there was some left over, he and Aunt Dorothy could put it against their mortgage.

At the Las Vegas McCarran Airport he found a payphone. It was 11:40 a.m. local time. In Iceland it would be late in the afternoon and Frida Hansen may still be at the university. It took some time to make the connection.

"Ja?"

"Dr. Hansen?"

"Ja, Ja?"

"Hi, I am Jeff Kingston, but you would remember me as…"

"Oh, yes, you are the student from the States that would like to meet with me."

"No, I'm Jeff Kingston, I…"

"I understand. I have been expecting your call on this day. My personal email is fridaland at fint dot i-c-l. Please make an appointment to talk to me in private here in Iceland." She hung up.

Jeff scribbled the email address down, hoping he remembered it correctly. Judging from her abrupt reaction, calling had probably been a mistake. Did she expect him to travel all the way to Iceland? Evidently, if he wanted to talk to her, that's what he'd have to do.

He still had time to kill before his return flight so he found a table in a corner and ordered a sandwich and a beer. He searched the internet and read about his father, Dr. Curtis Munson. It was fascinating. Then, digging in his bag, he retrieved one of his mother's journals and began to read. Each entry had been neatly written in Icelandic on the left half of the page, and translated to English—the international language of science—on the right. It was a format he'd seen before in other journals.

Her carefully formed writing was small and neat. In these thin volumes unfolded a myriad of her observations of volcanoes around the world. He focused on a typical passage and tried first to read the Icelandic, then the English:

Koltvisỳringur er mikilvægur til skjár puí paò koma frá bergkvika djú pur í the eldfjall. Carbon dioxide is important to monitor as it comes from magma deep in the volcano.

Giving up on the Icelandic, he picked another passage.

All active volcanoes have a muffled ultra-low frequency sound which signals that magma is present. Although it is well below the range of the normal human ear it is a growl in the .05Hz to 7Hz range. These sounds, we believe, is magma creating bubbles in the rock of the earth's crust and converting it into a sponge-like stone. The sound increase in pitch when a volcano is active and about to erupt and when it reaches 7Hz it will erupt.

We are installing our VolcanoWatch monitoring system in major volcanic danger areas including on the supervolcano that lays half beneath the City of Naples and half beneath the Bay of Pozzuoli. It has been our current focus, for soon we expect this massive volcano will signal an eruption that will threaten the lives of millions.

He switched over to Michael's data and read:

The National Institute of Physics and Volcanology in Naples monitors the Campi Flegrei Caldera with 350 leveling benchmarks, 13 continuous GPS stations, 8 tilt-meter stations and 28 gravity stations.

"It's extensively monitored," Jeff muttered, frowning. "If it's about to erupt, why are the experts not concerned?"

Jeff suddenly realized he'd been reading for well over an hour. Gulping down the beer and wrapping the sandwich in a napkin, he paid his bill and jogged toward his gate. At security, he placed his bag on the belt and watched it go through check-in without a hitch. Once through the scanner he grinned to himself. If they only knew how close they were to his thirty grand. He thought about that. Perhaps it wasn't that uncommon, after all this was Vegas.

At the gate he checked in and again buried himself in the journals.

"Paging Mr. Kingston."

Jeff got up and went to the flight desk half expecting to be wait-listed. Not everything on this day could be expected to continue flawlessly.

"Good news, Mr. Kingston. We're upgrading you to first class this morning. Let us exchange your boarding pass."

Perhaps they had noticed the money in his bag. Jeff found his seat up front beside a four-thousand-dollar suit who gave him a disdainful you-must-be-economy-class stare. He grinned back.

After the flight took off he placed the sandwich on his tray and continued reading.

"I've been a flight attendant for thirteen years and this is a first!" He looked up into the dancing blue eyes of a young man. "Would you like a glass of ice water with your sandwich, sir?"

Jeff eyed the tray, realized his sandwich looked a little ridiculous in first class, and burst out laughing.

"I can replace that with something far more appetizing."

"I'll stick with the sandwich, but a cold beer would be..."

"You got it!" The flight attendant hurried away.

The suit seated next to him squirmed sideways and looked down his nose.

Jeff picked up the partially eaten sandwich and put the journal down. His seat mate squirmed even further away.

Jeff raised his eyebrows at him. "You have no idea what you're missing." Grinning, he devoured the rest of the sandwich and then continued reading.

According to the notes in her final journal, his mother had been studying the seismically active area between the African and European plates in the Mediterranean. It included the volcanic-tectonic activity near the Sicilian island of Pantelleria in the Strait of Sicily. The nine mile long island had been the site of a submarine eruption in the 1890s. Her notes told of studies by others that showed the African plate in the earth's mantle pushing northwards into Europe. And it was creating a collision zone under the sea and the surrounding landmass.

Further, a number of micro-plates formed subduction and fault zones under the Mediterranean as the continental plates were in collision.

He considered. That could create a huge volcanic danger area. He pulled out his iPad and checked the internet date. In 1500 BCE the both Vesuvius and the Thera volcano in Greece erupted suddenly and wiped out most of the region's population. He returned to Kristin's notes. From her study of long term seismic readings in the Naples area, she had uncovered evidence that Campi Flegrei and the Vesuvius volcano may have a common magma chamber. Further, Vesuvius was on a fault running north-south and Campi Flegrei was on an east-west fault line.

Those observations were intriguing. She had drawn a chart showing Campi Flegrei could erupt soon, probably within the next two decades. And there were notes about a prediction protocol she and Dr. Pyper had developed. Included were details of the data-feed system they installed to automatically monitor volcanic instruments in the area.

Could she and Dr. Pyper have been murdered to quash their scientific paper?

What if Michael was right about Campi? His mother seemed to have come to the same conclusion Michael had. Scientists had been successfully predicting eruptions for years now. Could Michael have stumbled onto—but no, the experts had told him his stuff was a hoax.

Jeff searched for the number of the IEVPC in Florida, then took out his cell phone. He'd missed two calls in the past couple of hours, both from unknown numbers.

He dialed.

"International Earthquake and Volcano Prediction Center. Good afternoon."

"Good afternoon. My name is Jeffrey Kingston. I'm a third year Earth and Space Science Student at the University of Washington. I would like…"

"Just a moment please." There was a pause. "What is your request, sir?"

"I would like to speak to one of the volcanologists about a volcano…"

"Which volcano do you require information on, sir?"

"I'm concerned about the Campi Flegrei caldera. I think it's about to erupt."

"I'm sorry, sir. The Campi Flegrei caldera is very dangerous but it is stable. We screen our calls. I have been instructed not to put any calls through about that caldera from undergrads at your university. I'm told you have been the victims of a hoax."

Jeff hesitated. Okay, so Michael had poisoned the well. "Then could I just speak to someone in charge? My mother was a leading volcanologist and she believed that…"

"You will have to give me the name of the person you wish to speak to, sir. And a good technical reason for your call. I will have to clear your call first. If it is legitimate, I will make an appointment for a call at some future date. Our people are very busy."

"Thank you." He cut the call. "Bloody hell!"

As Michael had explained, apparently none of the data the IEVPC was collecting showed an imminent Campi Flegrei eruption. There had been no CGE Stage classification issued. There were no warnings in place. He shook his head. This was a troubling inconsistency.

He would study Michael's data further; he had it all in his iPad. At some point soon he would have to make a decision about going to Naples. But how could he convince anyone when he himself wasn't convinced?

There were other mysteries to solve, and these were more personal, more certain. He had to find out who the woman was on Mount St. Helens, and if she was working for the person who had killed his mother. And he had to talk to Frida Hansen in Iceland. Judging by her reception to his phone call, something was amiss.

And the guide. He should find him, too.

And then there was the nagging worry about Anita's safety, real or imagined.

Also, but less urgent, he must find his father and deliver Kristin's letters.

And, of course, there was Michael. He should not be away during his friend's final weeks but perhaps it couldn't be helped. There was much to do and more questions than answers, but there was a silver lining. Thanks to Frida and his mother's savings, he was now financially capable of doing whatever it would take.

This had all started on his birthday, Friday, he mused as they approaching Seattle. What an amazing four days.

Preparing to disembark, Jeff turned to the man in the suit. "Have a great day!" Grinning, he gathered his things. After deplaning, he took a bus from SeaTac into the city. At his student's residence, he was shocked to see his door was temporarily secured with a hasp and padlock. Clearly someone had kicked the door in. A note tacked to the door read *Please see Security*.

He checked with at the security office, and the guard accompanied him back to the room. "I should warn you," he said, "your place has been trashed. Any idea who?"

"No." Jeff replied. "Did you get it on surveillance?"

"We think so. Big man with a lot of hair and a cookie-ring beard came in to the building about noon and left ten minutes later, but we have no idea where he went in the building. Lots of people coming and going, with the end of semester."

"What's a cookie-ring beard?"

With a finger, the security guard drew a circle around his mouth. "You know, everything shaved off except around his mouth and chin." He flipped through his clipboard and handed Jeff a photo. "Here, it's a print from the entry door camera. Ever seen the guy?"

Jeff looked at it carefully. "No. It's pretty fuzzy, but... no."

"The cops have the film. You can report any theft to them."

The guard removed the padlock and Jeff walked into a room in complete shambles. Everything had been pulled out of drawers and cupboards and strewn about the floor.

Jeff waved the security guard out. "Thanks, I'll let you know if anything is missing."

Once alone, he phoned Aunt Dorothy. "Are you and Uncle Ralph okay?"

"We're fine. We just got back from visiting Michael and his family."

Breathing sigh of relief, he told them about the break-in. "I'm not sure what's going on," he said. "Please be careful over the next few days."

Aunt Dorothy was quiet for a moment. "Did you... did you find what you'd hoped to find in the safe deposit box?"

"That and more. I'll be sending you a little something to contribute to Uncle Ralph's surgery."

"Oh, Jeff, you don't need—"

"I know, but I want to. And trust me, I can afford it. I'm going to replace my cell phone. I'll call you later with the new number."

"Why not come for supper?"

Jeff considered for a moment. "Thanks, but I think I'd better clean this place up."

Surveying the mess, he picked up a chair and heaved it

across the room. "Bloody hell!" He was certain now; he had been identified by that woman, Dr. Hilda Marsh. After twelve years, he had again become a target. Maybe all the people he cared about were targets now, too.

His cell phone vibrated. Unknown number, again. He answered. "Hello?"

He was certain he could hear breathing before the line went dead.

The hairs on the back of his neck stood up.

Suddenly his priorities were clear: he must get out of here. He would fly to Iceland, meet with Dr. Frida Hansen and find what was going on. On his way, he would stop over in Ottawa, find his father and deliver Kristin's letters. Somehow he would contact Anita. But what if they were monitoring her phone to see if she was involved in all this? A phone call may put her more at risk. He would have to think of a way. She would likely be in the air right now, on her way from Philadelphia to Naples.

He packed a bag of clothes along with the cash, letters and journals, and his iPad, then drove to a mall. There, he bought a throw-away cell phone on a prepaid plan, two envelopes, and a stamp. He stuffed one envelope with five thousand dollars, sealed it and tucked it into his backpack, then made his way to the mall's food court. Pulling out his notebook, he settled at an empty table and penned a letter.

Hi, Aunt Dorothy,

This is a part of an account in the Las Vegas bank that was bequeathed to me twelve years ago by my birthmother. Now is a chance for a bit of payback to the two of you for all your love and care for me. Get Uncle Ralph scheduled for surgery. It's time he got out of that chair so he and I can do a little fishing and hunting and he can get back to his cabinet making. He's not getting enough exercise in that chair!

Love to you both, Jeff

Addressing the second envelope to Aunt Dorothy and Uncle Ralph, he tucked in the note and the cashier's check, applied the stamp, and dropped it in the mail on his way out to his Jeep. Swinging by the food bank, he stopped to slide the envelope of cash through the office's mail slot.

Back in the Jeep, he drove to a nearby playground, pulled into the parking lot, and made a call. "I'm looking for a listing in Ottawa, Canada. A Dr. Curtis Munson. I don't have an address."

"We have a Dr. Curtis Munson on Beacon Hill."

"That's it." He waited, heart racing, as she placed the call. This was his father!

"Dr. Munson's residence." A woman's voice.

"Dr. Munson please," the operator said.

"I'm sorry, he's not here."

"Do you have a number where he can be reached?" asked the operator.

"Wait a minute, please... Dr. Munson is at the Hyatt Regency Hotel in Vancouver. In British Columbia. Sorry, I do not have a number."

"Thank you," the operator said, "Sir, do you want me to connect you with the hotel?"

"Yes. Person to person, please."

After a few moments she completed the connection.

"Yes?"

"Dr. Munson?"

"Who is this?"

"My name is Jeff Kingston. Dr. Munson, do you remember an Icelandic woman named Kristin Stefsdotir?"

A sharp intake of breath, then silence. Jeff could feel his heart beating in his chest. Time seemed to stand still. He swallowed hard, waiting...

"Yes. Yes, of course."

"Was it about twenty-two years ago that you knew her?"

More hesitation. Was he going to hang up? "Yes, I suppose it was about twenty-two years ago. I met Kristin while she teaching at the University of Iceland. That would have been..." he paused. "But why do you ask?"

"She was my mother."

"Well I'll be...! I read about your mother's death about

ten or eleven years ago. I was deeply saddened. I also read that she had lost her young son. I hadn't realized she had married and started a family. I'm sorry for your loss."

"She never married. Are you married, Dr. Munson?"

"No, I'm a bachelor. But why do you ask?"

"I'm twenty-one, Dr. Munson. Please don't hang up. I believe that you are my father." He waited, his mouth dry.

Finally Munson spoke, "What... what leads you to that conclusion?"

"This week I received several of her unsent letters, letters she had written to you."

More silence. "Unsent letters. To me? From Kristin?"

"Yes. I only read one of them." Jeff was struggling to speak around the huge lump in his throat. "The rest are unopened. I have them for you."

"Where are you calling from?"

"Seattle. I attend university here."

"What did you say your name was?"

"My adopted name is Jeff Kingston but my name at birth was Heph Kristinson."

"Heff? How do you spell that?"

"It was H-e-p-h on my birth certificate."

"I'll be damned!" Munson chuckled. "Well you are Kristin's son alright. Kristin loved Greek philosophy. Did you know that your mother named you after Hephaestus, the Greek God of Fire and the Underworld?"

Jeff clutched the steering wheel. "No. I didn't."

"The Icelandic Government controls Icelandic names. She must have ignored them... What's your birth date?"

"I turned twenty-one three days ago."

After a brief silence, Munson said, "I was in love with her. I don't... I suppose it's possible, but... Kristin's son died at the volcano. Was that your brother?"

"She only had one son. I was badly injured, but I survived. I have a letter from a Dr. Frida Hansen explaining that she feared for my safety and brought me to America."

More silence. Then, "That sounds so... unlikely."

"This must be a shock to you," said Jeff. "I've recently read about you. Looked you up on the internet. And I've seen your picture. I am tall with sandy hair, blue eyes, strong jaw line liked you, but with some of the facial features of my mother."

"When did you discover all this?"

"Just today. I learned you lived in Ottawa, and chased you down."

"Let's see what you look like. Send me a photo of yourself with your phone."

"Okay." Jeff turned the phone around, took a picture. "Here's one."

"Hmm, you're a good looking young man, Jeff. So! What now?"

"I want to meet you, if you're willing. I want to give you my mother's letters." And on a whim he added, "And I need your advice."

"You do, huh?" There was more hesitation. "You're twenty-one. What are you studying?"

"Earth and space sciences."

"I could have guessed! Let me check my schedule." The line went quiet. Jeff could hear Munson shuffling papers and muttering to himself. "Caesar's ghost! If this don't beat all! Heph, she named him! Let's see..." He came back on. "I could come down to Seattle to see you tomorrow afternoon."

"What if I drove up there? It's not far. I'm planning to fly to Iceland. I could do that from Vancouver."

"Iceland? Okay. If you drive up tomorrow morning, come by at noon. I'm at the Hyatt Regency. It's on Georgia Street. Downtown Vancouver. And don't make reservations to Iceland yet. I'll fly you as far as Ottawa tomorrow afternoon in our business jet. You can leave your car at the airport and pick it up on your return."

"I'll take you up on that. See you tomorrow." Still holding the phone to his ear, he heard Munson mutter, "I'll be darned... a son... she never told me..."

Jeff scanned the playground and the parking lot; no one appeared to have followed him. He sat for a moment.

His new-found father was obviously a man of action. He liked that. There was no sense hanging around Seattle where he was in danger and had no place to sleep.

He phoned Aunt Dorothy, explained what he was doing and gave her Munson's home phone number as an emergency contact.

Starting the Jeep, he headed to the Interstate. Once on the I-5, he turned north toward Canada. He had a growing sense of urgency about all this. After all, if Michael was right about his volcano…

... Campi Flegrei semi-annual GPS leveling benchmarks are showing ground uplifts averaging 78 centimeters...

CHAPTER 5

Tuesday, June 16, late morning
Jeff drove into the city of Vancouver. A strange sense of apprehension gripped him. What was Munson like?

What would his father think of him? He wasn't exactly spit and polish, having slept in the Jeep. Well, at least he was clean and well dressed. That accounted for something.

He arrived early at the hotel on Georgia Street. In the rotunda, he found a leather chair behind a potted fern with a view of the registration desk and settled down to wait.

He recognized the voice first. "Good morning, miss," Munson greeted the clerk. Although dressed like a businessman he had a windblown look. Tall and sandy-haired with a close-trimmed graying beard and piercing blue eyes, the same as Jeff's, he wore a brown suede leather sports jacket, sharply creased tan trousers and a turtleneck sweater. His shoes looked expensive, as did the watch on his left wrist. "Is there someone here waiting for Curtis Munson?" Placing a card on the desk he looked about the rotunda.

"No one has asked for you, sir," the clerk said.

"A young man will ask for me. Send him up to 1526."

Jeff's heart skipped a beat, watching as Munson walked to the elevators. He waited a couple of minutes, then picked up the house phone and called 1526. "This is Jeff. Should I come up?"

"Sure, come on up."

Conscious of his heartbeat, he walked to the elevator and punched 15. Checking that his mother's letters were in his pocket, he felt conflicted, pulled back into the past by his mother and into the future by his father. He would not tell Munson about the assassin who had been stalking him, the break-in or the man with the cookie-ring beard. He didn't want his father to be involved in the danger it posed. Besides, it was his problem; he would deal with it.

The doors opened on 15. Munson was standing there, waiting. Jeff tensed as he stepped forward. "Hi."

"Hello, Jeff." Arms outstretched, Munson nodded encouragingly. "It's okay to hug your father. I've checked you out. I'm convinced you are my son. I had no idea that you even existed."

As Munson stepped forward and hugged him, Jeff felt stiff and uncertain. Munson was a bit shorter, his suede jacket smelled faintly of leather but while the material was soft, the man under it was hard and muscular.

Jeff stepped back.

Munson's eyes twinkled. "You were here early. I saw you waiting for me behind the potted plants down stairs."

"You did?"

Munson nodded. "It's something I would have done."

As they laughed together, Jeff wiped a tear away. The tension was gone.

"Come," Munson said, leading the way to his room. "We'll raid the bar-fridge and talk."

They opened cans of soda, went to the balcony and settled into chairs overlooking the busy city. Jeff gave the pack of letters to Munson. "The first one was opened by the woman in Iceland, Dr. Frida Hansen, who mailed them to a safe deposit box in Vegas years ago. I was given the key on my twenty-first birthday. I've read the first one. The others have not been opened. I figured they were personal."

"Is this why you're going to Iceland?"

"I want to know what really happened to my mother."

Munson stared at the letters. "I'll get my laptop," he said, went back into the room, returned with it and inserted a memory stick. "I lost all my possessions in a recent house fire. Luckily all my computer stuff was at my office." He handed Jeff the laptop. "While I read the letters, you can look at these photos. They were taken during the time I knew your mother."

Jeff looked at the screen. "Wow." The first photo was taken from the rail of a ship. Stretching for miles in either direction was the face of a huge glacier, perhaps a thousand feet high. At the ship's rail stood his mother and father, much younger, wearing parkas, watching the ice that seemed to be calving off the glacier's face into a bay.

"That first one is of the Humboldt Glacier on the north west tip of Greenland," Munson said. "The glacier front where it meets the sea is ninety miles long. It's the largest glacier in the northern hemisphere. We were visiting one of my company's exploration ships at the time."

As Munson began reading the letters, Jeff scrolled through the photos. In them, the couple looked to be very much in love.

"Ah," Munson sighed, "Why? My God, why did she not send these to me?" He got up and took the letters inside while Jeff sat quietly, glad that he hadn't read them.

After a bit Munson returned, looking shaken. "Your mother was the most wonderful, most fantastic woman." He smiled wistfully and sat for a minute. "Some advice. If you find your perfect mate, don't let anything keep you apart."

"You were in love with her, weren't you? I could see from the pictures."

Munson nodded sadly.

"And in all the twenty-odd years that followed, you never fell in love again?"

Munson shook his head. "I came close once, but..."

Jeff pointed to a photo. "Tell me about her."

Munson took a breath, smiled. "Kristin was a very logical, rational person. Intuitive and observant, she viewed the world as full of possibilities. She loved gathering information and generating ideas from it. Your mother valued intelligence. She was insightful and quick to understand new ideas." He paused. "She loved adventure. She had a reckless streak. She loved danger... living on the edge. She was strong, athletic and kept herself very fit. She..."

"Yes?" Jeff prompted.

"She was not particularly good at explaining her ideas to others but I never had difficulty following her train of thought. She was a leader... a strategist... quick to make judgments..."

Jeff got up and stood at the deck railing. "I think I got a few her traits."

Munson laughed. "No doubt you did, and some of mine too. Let's go to lunch. Then we'll go to the airport. I'd like to be wheels up about three, local time."

As they walked to the restaurant, Munson put a hand on Jeff's shoulder. "What have you learned about me so far?"

"I know some stuff from the internet," Jeff said. "You had a twin sister, Emily, who died a tragic death. You've been in the news lately. You uncovered the Saudi oil shortfall and discovered platinum in the Arctic. And you're involved with a new hydrogen power system."

Munson nodded. "This past year has been chaotic. I've survived air disasters, lost my twin sister and my father... your grandfather. You would have liked him." His eyes widened. "I guess I'll have to introduce you to your grandmother!" He frowned again. "I've also been pursued by assassins who were intent on destroying an energy discovery entrusted to me. I've found a new business partner and started a mining operation. Along the way, I got in the middle of a resource war. Things come at you so fast sometimes there's no time to think."

"And now I've shown up."

Munson's expression brightened. "Yes. Tell me about yourself."

The waiter appeared and they placed their order. "Let's see," said Jeff. He began with his first recollections from when he was nine, and worked forward.

"So you remember nothing before you were nine?" Munson shook his head. "That's a big chunk of your life missing. When you phoned you said you needed my help. What is the problem?"

Jeff rubbed his chin. "It's complicated."

As the waiter came with their lunch Jeff studied his father. "It's not so much that I need your advice as I need your judgment. You are a geologist with years of experience. I'm a novice. Yet I'm struggling with something that, if I handle it wrong, may cost millions of lives."

"You've got my full attention."

"I have a friend named Michael, third year earth and space sciences at U of W, like me, who has made a prediction. Thousands may die if he's right." He paused. "You don't know Michael, and you've only known me for a couple of hours. Hopefully you think that I am rational?"

Munson nodded.

"I suspect have you checked my background, my school marks, my sports accomplishments, my math tutoring job, maybe even talked to my teachers?"

Munson laughed. "I have, yes. I've checked you out. I've even learned your hobby is yachting and you have an ICC certificate to operate a power craft up to twenty meters. Things like that."

Jeff grinned. "Michael's father has a small yacht, and Michael and I are both in the reserve Coast Guard. But do you think I'm a normal, intelligent, practical person?"

"So far."

"Well my friend Michael is a solid thinker, just like me. The difference is that he will be dead of cancer within weeks." Jeff swallowed. "Over the past two years, Michael has developed an obsession. And out of it grew this... this prediction of his. He's got some science behind it. Strangely enough, Michael's science ties in with my mother's work, the VolcanoWatch technology."

Munson listened intently to Jeff's story, then sat thinking for a bit. "So your friend really believes Campi Flegrei will erupt soon," he mused. "Yet the experts say his data is a hoax." He shook his head. "They should know, Jeff. Perhaps you're beating a dead horse here."

"Yes, but what if the data Michael's tracking isn't a hoax? What if the scientists haven't investigated the validity of their own data? Michael's been studying Campi Flegrei for months. Any peripheral data I can find seems to support Michael's theory. The ongoing tiny changes in land deformation far out from the crater center—all the other factors he's been tracking—they could be signaling rising lava in the supervolcano's magma chamber."

"Yes." Munson nodded. "But you are students; they are experienced scientists, experts. And you have no time to intervene. Only thirteen days if your eruption date is right."

"Yes. And they won't talk to me."

"You seem determined. You feel you simply must warn people?"

"I feel responsible. If this is not a hoax—all those people will die, and I haven't warned them, their deaths will be on my conscience. Then there's Anita and her family."

"Anita?"

"Anita Arneil. She will be on the NATO base near Naples this summer, with her sisters and her parents. Her father is in the military. She has a student job to help scientists study the caldera. She's a fantastic person—a good friend, not a girlfriend—and she and her family are right in the middle of this."

Munson was quiet for a moment. "My sense is you may be over-reacting to your friend Michael, but I understand your concern."

Jeff took his iPad from his backpack, brought up a section, highlighted it and showed it to Munson. "As an example, look at part of today's VolcanoWatch data feed summary."

"*Campi Flegrei semi-annual GPS leveling benchmarks are now showing ground uplifts averaging 78 centimeters,*" Munson read aloud. He nodded, but then his expression slowly changed. He looked out into space, a deep frown creasing his brow.

"You look troubled."

"It's about your driving need to tell the Italians to evacuate. An imminent eruption must be proven first. What you're proposing is damned dangerous." He stared at Jeff. "Do you know what the European authorities and business leaders will do to crackpot earth sciences students who are preaching a European Armageddon? The multi-billion dollar tourism industry alone would burn you at the stake for keeping tourists away from their sandy beaches. Michael's lucky he didn't get anywhere with this. Gain any credibility, and you'll become a marked man. The Cosa Nostra, Camorra and the new international mafia, the C-2, they all have their fingers deep in the economic pie, and they have considerable experience in making people disappear. They have their people among those you want to convince — the movers and shakers in the government, the city administration — they will become your biggest enemies. Get anyone important to start listening, and these people will shut you up. If they can't silence you through ridicule, they won't hesitate to kill you. I have some experience with being pursued by assassins. It's not pretty."

Jeff thought about the rock slide, his trashed residence. Were they after Michael, or after him — or both of them?

Munson rose from the table. "Finish your lunch, Jeff. I'll check out of my room and be down in a minute."

Jeff looked at the floor. Criminal organizations using assassins to maintain the status-quo… a difficult task had just become all but impossible.

If he tried to publicize Michael's data, every organization in Europe would be aligned against him. They would brand him a crazy American activist. The incomes of the rich and powerful would be at stake—hundreds of billions of euros.

Disappointment engulfed him.

Get hold of yourself, he thought anxiously; you haven't even fully committed to this mission.

Setting his napkin on the table, he met Munson at the check-out desk. "What's wrong?" Munson asked.

"This is hopeless, isn't it? No one will believe me. There is no one I can depend on to…"

"There's at least one I can think of." He put a hand on Jeff's shoulder. "Come over here, sit for a minute. I want to show you something." He led Jeff to chairs in the rotunda. "Do you remember anything about your mother?"

"Very little. A dream of her walking near a lava lake."

Munson reached into his jacket and took out Kristin's letters. Opening one, he gave it to Jeff. "Here, read this."

My Dearest Munson,

It has been almost ten years since I chose my volcano research over a life with the man of my dreams. I have written you several letters during these years, but of course I never mailed them.

Munson, this will come as a shock to you but we have a son, a wonderful boy. Heph (recognize the Greek Mythology?) is nine now, a fine lad. From the time he was a toddler I carried him with me in a backpack up onto Katla's lava fields. There he soaked up everything I've taught him about predicting volcanic eruptions. I did not realize it until he was seven or eight, but he has extraordinary natural ability to understand a volcano. For a lad of nine his level of understanding is unheard of. He reads my notes and, for the most part, he understands them.

I wasn't going to tell you about him, but he and I were recently the target of an assassin. We may still be in grave danger and I'm worried. My partner (who was recently murdered) and I have developed an automated volcanic monitoring system and implemented it at several active volcanic sites including Campi Flegrei. It is called VolcanoWatch. I think this new software is bringing danger down upon us, yet I do not know why.

I love my son dearly and if anything happens to me, it will be traumatic for him and he will need his father to protect him.

Jeff looked up, eyebrows raised.

"Yes, it's unfinished," Munson said. "Three things from this letter. First, it looks like Kristin was murdered because of the VolcanoWatch system she helped develop. Second, if it is the new international Mafia, the C-2, and if they now know where to find you—even though it was years ago, you're still in danger. And third, after reading this it's evident from an early age, you have had exceptional volcano savvy." Munson put a hand on Jeff's arm. "I think you should be able to recover the knowledge about your mother. No doubt something traumatic happened to you up on Nyiragongo. I have a good friend in Ottawa, Theresa Creighton, a practicing psychiatrist, who can show you how to begin unlocking that knowledge."

Jeff hesitated. Should he tell his father about the assassin and the break-in? No, he'd already decided not to. But perhaps seeing a psychiatrist would help. "Maybe on my way through Ottawa, I could see her."

"I'll call her and see if she can see you tomorrow."

"What advice do you have for me?"

Munson thought a moment. "You have very little time. I'm not convinced about this. But if you must proceed, find out who killed your mother and her partner. If you are at risk from them, find a way to protect yourself—perhaps you can expose them, so there's no longer a reason for them to pursue you. Then, once you are free to act, check the validity of your friend Michael's hacked data-feed. If it's real, find a way to convince authorities to warn the whole of Europe."

He stood. "Jeff, if what you and Michael suspect is true, it will be like Armageddon. Call me when you need my help. I'll be there for you."

... a significant seismic and inflation crisis and a spherical deflation has occurred, showing the large magma source...

CHAPTER 6

Tuesday, June 16, afternoon

Instead of taking a taxi to the Vancouver International Airport, Munson rode in the Jeep with Jeff. "We're across the main runways in a commercial area on the south side of the airport," Munson explained. "They used to call it Hudson General."

They drove around to the business terminal, parked, and went to security area.

After passing through the metal detectors Jeff turned his attention to the plane, a sleek white Learjet 8000. He estimated it was about a hundred feet long and had a wingspan of just about the same.

"She's a beaut," he said. "What's her range?"

"She'll fly over 14,600 kilometers at mach point-eight-five with maximum fuel."

Jeff did an instant calculation. "Almost 7,900 nautical miles."

"You're quick. Can you convert that to surface miles?"

Jeff grinned. "That would be, let's see, rounded that's 9,100."

Munson shook his head. "When I checked you out, I learned that in high school you were in the gifted math program."

"I still tutor math students."

Munson nodded. "Well, I'm impressed."

"About ten passengers?" Jeff asked, looking at the sleek machine.

"Eight, plus a crew of two or four. Come." He led the way up the steps to the cabin. "Come into the next chapter of your life, Jeff."

In the plush cabin, Munson introduced him to the other passengers. "This is my son, Jeff," he announced. "He's studying geology at the University of Washington."

Jeff shook hands with them: two mining engineers, two contractors and two employees of Munson's company, Seafire Platinum.

At the front of the cabin, Jeff sank into a large soft-leather chair across the aisle from his father, put on his seatbelt and relaxed back into astounding comfort. The plane's cabin was quite obviously a high performance workplace yet he was surrounded by outrageous luxury; it was quiet during take-off and its thrust was amazing. "What kind of engines?" he asked as the plane cleared the runway.

"GE second generation jets with sixteen thousand pounds of thrust," Munson grinned.

After they attained cruising altitude, Munson leaned over. "Should we research Campi Flegrei?"

Jeff nodded. "Sure."

Munson maneuvered the screen on the bulkhead so they both could see it, and then swung a computer into position. "Let's bring up the latest scientific studies and see what they say about your Mediterranean monster."

A web page filled the screen.

Campi Flegrei is a supervolcano. Although there is no volcanic cone, hidden beneath the seemingly placid landscape and ocean bay is a volcano of immense power. An eruption here, worst case scenario, could see it obliterating much of Europe.

In this eventuality the earth's surface would swell and crack and a series of eruptions would cause the four mile wide caldera to collapse into the larger magna reservoir that would in turn blast magma to the surface with massive force. The last time the ground gave way like this was 39,000 years ago when the caldera was formed. It created the cliffs on which the postcard town of Sorrento stands now, volcanic deposits over 300 feet deep. If the same kind of eruption happened today, this part of Italy would cease to exist, and the ash clouds would blot out the sun and lower the earth's temperature. Life as we know it would end. We would lose our livestock, crops and three quarters of our plant species, plunging us into a new dark age of rioting, starvation and continuous winter.

Now an international team is drilling down inside the caldera to better understand exactly why part of it has risen continuously since 1969. The area at the epicenter of the swelling has seen whole streets and houses crumble and collapse. The threat is imminent. The last time the ground rose like this (between 1430 and 1538) there was an eruption that created a new volcano with a disastrous loss of life.

They read on about how a public outcry stopped the international team of volcanologists from drilling further into the volcano, for fear it would cause an eruption and destroy the city. Meanwhile, the U.S. Navy had moved off the coast, twenty miles inland to escape their earthquake damaged base; green meadows had been transformed into atrophic scars of sponge-like rock, out of which gurgled pools of hot muddy water that was devoid of all life.

Now, intense earthquake swarms were rattling the city. A few suggested that for the first time in 450 years an eruption, this time perhaps a huge one, may be imminent. But no one listened; people had been predicting doom for centuries and life in the city continued on as it had for untold generations. Evacuation plans were presumably in place, but even they were not taken seriously by most city dwellers. If it ever happened, there may be no warning, no time to escape anyway, so why bother with evacuation plans? Besides, the article stated, local authorities were confident that the danger index should not be elevated.

Munson looked at Jeff. "I see now why you asked for my thoughts," he smiled. "You didn't pick a small problem to tackle, did you? But if your friend is right, this one may be a planet-changer and over time millions, perhaps billions, will die anyway and whatever you accomplish won't matter."

"But I have to try. I mean, the force of the eruption may not be a worst case scenario. It may only destroy the city."

"First you have to prove your ability to predict the eruption date or no one will listen. And if you are able to get people listening, politicians, industrialists, business and the European financial world would try to silence you. They want status-quo; no change. They want no interruption to their economy. They want the euros to keep rolling in."

Jeff nodded.

"If you decide to pursue this, tell me first. Okay? You mustn't try to do this on your own. It's too dangerous."

Jeff didn't answer.

"So you are going to Iceland. Then you're coming back home, right?"

"That's the plan."

"What will you do for the rest of the summer?"

"I'm in the Coast Guard. I've been training every summer since I turned seventeen. I've taken all the training now. It keeps me fit."

"So you are proficient with weapons?"

"Side arms, rifles, 400-rpm deck guns."

"You any good with them?"

"Pretty good." Jeff didn't want to say he'd made top marksman in basic training; it felt like bragging. "I've been at it for over three years."

Munson smiled. "I have some work to do, you will have to excuse me." He pulled out some files and began to read.

Jeff settled back, closed his eyes and surrendered to the soft drone of the engines and comfort of the cabin.

His thoughts turned to Anita. He would contact her

after checking things out with Dr. Frida Hansen in Iceland. Yes, Anita... during high school he had always enjoyed being around her. He'd found himself reddening while he was telling Munson about her. What was that all about? They had always had fun together, but he had never even gone out with her. He had always paired off with others; Karen until she moved away in grade 12, then Sylvia, and then... well, besides, up until recently, Anita had been involved with Brad, a mutual friend. Jeff had been surprised when they'd broken it off.

Anita was damned attractive—soft Nordic features and long auburn hair. There was something about her eyes; something mischievous in them. And that hot body...

When he awoke, the cabin was in darkness. It was quiet except for the restful hum of the jets; the passengers were asleep, except his father who was working on his laptop. Leaning toward the aisle, Jeff looked forward into the cockpit. The plane's liquid-crystal avionics glowed softly in the dim light. The pilots were talking quietly. Outside his window, a patchwork of lights shone in the darkness far below; small towns stretched out across Canada's vast prairies as far as the eye could see.

Soon they would be landing at the Macdonald-Cartier Airport in Ottawa. He moved his watch three hours ahead; it would now be 12:10 a.m., Wednesday, June 17th... twelve days to a Campi Flegrei eruption?

The cabin lights turned up and the sound system chimed on. "Good morning, people. We'll be landing in Ottawa in twenty minutes."

As they left the airport in Munson's Ford King Ranch pickup, Jeff asked, "Where do you live?"

"I used to live on Argyle Street, near the Rideau Canal. I had a duplex townhouse. The other side belonged to my sister. But in the midst of an oil resource struggle, my adversaries torched it. I lost everything of personal value."

"That's tough. And I'm sorry about your sister, too."

"Yes. You would have liked Emily. She was a wonderful person." They drove into the underground parking below a new concrete and glass apartment building. "I'm renting here, temporarily."

"Looks like it does the job. Dad, if you can get me in with your shrink today, fine, but tonight, if I can get a flight to Toronto, I'm moving on."

Munson's place was modern and more like a hotel suite than a home. There was a spare bedroom that looked like it had never been used. Jeff phoned the airlines and made a reservation to Toronto with connections on a flight to Iceland leaving Ottawa late that evening. Maybe he shouldn't be booking flights in his own name. But how else? They'd need to see his passport. He frowned, wondering if the man with the cookie-ring beard had already figured out where he'd gone. If not, he hoped Aunt Dorothy and Uncle Ralph weren't in harm's way; if so, he didn't want to be bringing anything down on Munson.

Best to move on as soon as possible.

He climbed into bed and was soon asleep.

Wednesday, June 17, noon
Jeff was awakened by Munson shaking his shoulder. "Hey, I got you an appointment with Dr. Theresa Creighton. As a favor she'll see you at two."

"Okay." Jeff bounced up, looking at his watch. "Wow, it's noon already!"

"There's a café down the street. Let's get a bite to eat before you meet with her."

"Good. I'll take a shower and meet you there in a few minutes." He was a bit nervous about seeing a psychiatrist, but if it unlocked memories and solved the mystery of his mother's death, it would be worth it.

At the café Jeff told Munson about his travel plans, then pulled out the old clippings from the material Frida

Hansen left him and passed them to his father. As Munson examined the second clipping, the faded one that Jeff couldn't read, he held it up to the light. "Let's see... *Mr. Maurice Labouef will move back to France next...* Hm, can't make that out. *It is believed... he will settle near his... home in Fabron on the outskirts of Nice. Mr. Labouef is... known in... Goma area for... guided trips to the Nyiragongo summit...* It fades out. And I can't read the date."

"That must be him! The guide!" Jeff took the clipping and held it up to the light, squinting. "You have good eyes." After Iceland, he could fly on to Nice and look for Maurice Labouef.

There was no point in creating more worry for his father. "Thanks, Dad, that's a good lead."

Munson was silent a moment. "I pay for the storage of a small yacht at a port town near Nice. An acquaintance owned it but he passed away recently. It's berthed at Saint Tropez. It may come in handy if we decide to visit your Naples volcano."

Jeff remained quiet. The yacht may come in handy but he wasn't planning to drag his dad into his troubles. Munson didn't deserve to have a murderer on his trail.

"You can use it, if you like," said Munson, pulling a notebook out of his pocket and scribbling on it. "It's in the Master's Boat Club, slip 139. The key is taped inside the bell." Munson tore the sheet from the pad and handed it to Jeff. "I'll meet you at the airport for dinner tonight before your fight takes off. I'm flying to Winnipeg this evening—Air Canada this time. My flight staff needs a break."

"Thanks, Dad. I'll wait at the Air Canada lounge. See you there."

In the taxi, he took out his phone and emailed Dr. Frida Hansen. *Arriving Reykjavik Airport 7:30 Thursday morning, June 18th. Only a 90 minute layover. Please have breakfast with me at the airport? Please confirm. Jeff.*

Dr. Theresa Creighton waved him to a chair. In her fifties with long grey hair piled in a neat bun and secured with a colorful comb, she had a pleasant face, understanding eyes and a calm that put him instantly at ease.

"It must have been exciting to find your father."

"Very."

"He's a fine man. Brilliant. A bit of a loner. I've known him for years."

Jeff nodded, looking around at the framed credentials on the walls. "Thanks for fitting me in, Dr. Creighton."

"Call me Theresa. Tell me about yourself, Jeff."

Jeff gave her an outline of his past starting when he was nine and ending with the details about his mother gleaned from the letters and journals.

"So other than that, you have no memory of your mother?"

"Only the dream."

"Lean back, close your eyes and tell me about your dream."

"It's always the same." He closed his eyes and told her about it. When he opened them, he searched the doctor's face. She had her eyes closed, too, as if concentrating with him. "Tell me more," she said. "What happens next?"

"That's just it. I don't know."

She smiled. "I may be able to help you remember. Have you ever been hypnotized?"

"No."

"Do you want to try to access your memories using hypnosis?"

"Sure. If these are memories, I'd like to unlock them."

Dr. Creighton's voice was low and calm. "If I put you under hypnosis, I can assure you that you cannot be made to say anything you don't want to."

"Okay."

"Are you okay with me recording our session, so that you can watch it when I've brought you back?"

Jeff hesitated. "Will you keep a copy?"

She smiled. "Never. I can make a copy for you if you like, or simply delete the file once you've heard it."

Jeff nodded. "Okay, then."

"Lean back and relax," she said, dimming the lights. "I want you to let yourself go… relax. Just look at this and let you mind go blank…"

In the faint light, he watched her twirl a shiny pendant above him on a chain. As it picked up lights and reflected them, her voice became muffled. "I want you to relax each part of your body… relax your legs…" He was unable to keep his eyes open. "Relax your hips… your waist… relax your back… your neck…"

Jeff's tension disappeared. "You are relaxing in the summer's warmth… lying quietly in the shade on a grassy meadow beside a gurgling stream. You are safe, warm… you are relaxed…"

He opened his eyes, stared at the twirling pendant and closed them again. "You are safe, you are peaceful."

He felt calm; he was without any care.

"Every word you hear is putting you further into a deeper more peaceful state. Sinking down… down…"

At the snap of her fingers, Jeff opened his eyes. He felt relaxed and rested. He sat up and grinned. "Was I a good subject?"

"You were. How are you feeling?"

"Fine. Did we learn anything?"

"I think so." Dr. Creighton passed him her recorder. "Go ahead and listen."

Jeff pressed the play button.

"Tell me about your eighth birthday. Where are you?"

"We are on the Kamchatka Peninsula."

"Where is that?"

"It's part of the Russian Federation on the far east of Russia. The peninsula stretches down along Russia's east coast."

"Who are you with?"

"My mother and Dom-Dom."

"What's special about the place? Why are you there?"

"It's the most active volcanic area in the world. It has twenty active volcanoes. We are forecasting their eruptions."

"Who is Dom-Dom?"

"Dr. Dmitry Ivanov."

"What's he like?"

"He is very tall and thin, and he is kind to me."

"Now you are with your mother. It is your ninth birthday. Where are you?"

"I'm on Uncle Reg's yacht. There's danger. I'm swimming away with my mother. A man has hurt Uncle Reg. We have to get away. The man is fighting with my mother, under the water. We have to get away..."

"You are safe now."

"Yes."

"Tell me about your dream."

"I... I am on Nyiragongo with my mother."

"What are you doing?"

"Climbing up the volcano toward the crater rim."

"You are on the crater rim. You are looking down toward your mother on the crater floor."

"She is walking toward a lava lake..."

"What happens?"

"She waves at me."

"And then?"

"I wave back."

"Then what?"

"Mom starts walking again and..."

"And what?"

"I don't remember."

"Are you alone?"

"I don't remember."

"Do you go back to camp?"

"I don't remember."

"Do you see your mother again?"

"I don't remember."

"When I snap my fingers, you will wake up from a sound sleep. You will feel calm and refreshed."

"Was I a good subject?"

"You were. How are you feeling?"

Dr. Creighton gestured to the recorder. "If you don't need a copy, go ahead and delete it."

Jeff pressed the erase button, then selected *yes* to confirm. The tiny screen read *erasing* then *done,* and the file counter on the recorder indicated zero.

He passed the recorder to Dr. Creighton.

"You have vivid enough memories of your childhood," she said, "but you were unable to remember anything substantive about your experience on Nyiragongo, beyond what you know from your dream. Near the point your memory fails, you may have experienced a serious trauma. Do you suffer headaches?"

"Not any more. I did learn recently that I had a blow to the head when I was nine."

"Hmmm. Now we've prodded some of those shadowy recollections, you may gradually begin to recapture them."

"What do I owe you?"

"It's on the house; your father is a friend. But you should come back. Little can be done in one session."

"Thank you, Dr. Creighton. Perhaps I will."

Jeff shouldered his backpack, left the doctor's office and took a cab to the airport where he would meet Munson for dinner. On the way he checked his email and found a reply from Dr. Frida Hansen: *Looking forward to it. Frida.*

"Well that seems more receptive," he muttered.

His flight to Toronto would take off at six to connect with a late evening flight to Iceland. A strange sense of determination gripped him. His mind was made up.

Regardless of anything he learned in Iceland, he was going to Naples to warn the city.

Munson was waiting when he got to the Ottawa airport. As they entered a restaurant Munson insisted on a table close to an exit with a good view of the entrances. At their table, he slid a photo over to Jeff. "Recognize him?"

Jeff picked it up. He recognized Munson's Ford in the

apartment building's underground garage. The stocky man standing near a cement pillar seemed to be taking note of the truck's license plate.

He had a cookie-ring beard.

"Security guy thought he was behaving a bit strangely," said Munson. "He seemed interested in my truck."

Jeff kept his face neutral. If he told Munson that this man had already broken into his student residence, his father would probably want him to stay in Ottawa while they got to the bottom of it. The sooner he left, the sooner, he'd draw the danger away. He'd already drawn it away from Michael.

"I don't know him, Dad," he said. "That's a nice truck you have; maybe he was just admiring it."

Munson raised his eyebrows, then shrugged. "Maybe."

At dinner Jeff avoided explaining his decision, instead agreeing to call his father before leaving Iceland. He kept the discussion centered on his session with Dr. Creighton and on his father's business affairs, waiting to broach the subject of the volcano until it was time to leave. "Dad, you realize I can't afford to be wrong about Campi Flegrei."

"I know. But don't try to do this on your own. You'll call me, won't you?"

"I'll call you from Iceland. I don't want you to worry."

"I can't help worrying. I sense you've made up your mind to take on the volcano."

"Perhaps I have." Jeff shook his father's hand, and then gave him a hug. "Bye Dad, and thanks."

"Be careful."

"You can bet on it."

Jeff scanned the rest of the waiting passengers; no sign of the man with the cookie-ring beard. Yet. On the aircraft, he felt thrust into a new world of total self-reliance. It was six days since all this started. Pulling out his iPad, he searched the internet, found Icelandic phrases and tried to sort out the pronunciation, memorizing a few of them while the plane taxied to the runway.

He checked the latest feeds from the Naples Monitoring Center. *A significant seismic and inflation crisis and a spherical deflation has occurred, showing a large magma source is centered at a depth of 4.8 to 4.2 km beneath the Bay of Pozzuoli and the City of Naples.*

Of one thing he was now certain: he could not take a chance that Michael was wrong. He was determined to warn the city.

The jet was on the runway, engines revving.

He was pushed back in his seat by the jet's thousands of pounds of thrust as the plane cleared the runway, catapulting him headlong into his mission. "Here we go, Michael," he muttered. "Damn it, you better be right about this!"

... current earthquake swarms are compatible with the intense seismic swarms that occurred during 1985...

CHAPTER 7

Wednesday, June 17, evening
As Jeff's flight climbed out over Ottawa, he gazed down at the capital city's parliament buildings, a massive stone complex dominated by the Peace Tower, housing both Canada's parliament and senate. He settled back. The flight to Toronto would take twenty-seven minutes; plenty of time to craft a letter to Michael.

He planned how to write it. Michael told him he had lost all hope. Hearing him say that had been devastating. How could a person give a dying man hope? Then it came to him. Of course! The nurse had given him the answer.

He pulled out his iPad and began to pen the letter.
Dear Michael (also known as Vulcan, Greek god of lava and smoke),

It's amazing what a guy will do for a friend... even if that friend is more like a brother than a friend, and maybe more like a twin than a brother...

Okay. It's been two days, and already you're anxious to hear what's going on with me. I'm checking your direct Volcano-Watch data feeds from the Naples Monitoring Center each day...

It took him twenty minutes to sketch out most of what happened in the past three days and when he had covered everything, he wanted to end of the letter in a way that would give Michael back his sense of hope. Finally he wrote:

So you met a nurse at the hospital… Julie wasn't it? Well I met her, too, and she recognized the pain I was in as I left your room Friday. She left me with a comforting thought: "Do all the things you want Michael to remember you by after he's gone." (Re-read that.) Neat huh?

Anyway, I'm agreeing with your request to warn the people of Naples. I'll be unable to phone much but I'll get word to you how it's going. Don't try to contact me, friend, brother, twin, fellow Greek god and Volcano doctor, because I have a hunch that using electronic communications is a bad idea. Whether that rock slide was meant for me or for you or for both of us, I think they're tracking me. Hopefully they'll leave you alone. But I'm on your mission. We'll see how it goes…

Jeff (also known as Heph—for Hephaestus, Greek God of Fire and the Underworld)

He clicked send as the plane taxied to a stop in Toronto. Gathering his belongings he readied to disembark and make his connection.

Thursday, June 18, early morning
He woke as they were losing altitude. Iceland was dead ahead. Formed eons ago as the North Atlantic's mid-oceanic ridge buckled up above the ocean's surface, the island was being gradually torn apart by eruptive fissures and monstrous volcanoes. The first, now directly below the plane, was on the tiny island of Heimaey just off the south Icelandic coast—Eldfel, the mountain of fire. Ahead, dwarfing Eldfel, was the enormous Eyjafjallajökull volcano on the mainland coast, and the dangerous Katla, with its twenty-five-mile-long eruptive fissures and craters, lay beyond. Reykjavik, the nation's capital, lay just ahead on the southern coast. It was a good-sized city at over three hundred thousand.

As he watched the scene unfold, excitement gripped

him. Below, nestled among the volcanoes, was the city where he had lived with his mother until he was nine.

He shivered.

As the plane landed, he joined the departing passengers, passed through customs and at the currency exchange bought some króna. From there he went to the main restaurant to meet Dr. Frida Hansen. The place was deserted; apparently they had only just opened.

"*Goðn daginn,*" Jeff attempted. "*Morgunmatur?*"

The server laughed. "Very good sir... yes, good morning. Breakfast it is!"

"How many languages do you speak?"

"Hopefully a sufficient number to serve everyone breakfast," the server grinned.

"How about ham, eggs over easy, hash browns and coffee?"

"Ah, a man who is hungry! Your order will please the kitchen."

"I will wait to place that order, please. I'm meeting someone here. Just coffee for now."

"Very good sir." He left the menu and hurried off.

Jeff took out his cell phone and considered for a moment. Although there was no sign he was being followed, he wouldn't be surprised if someone was still on his tail. He phoned the Reykjavik Radisson Blu Saga Hotel and used his credit card to make a reservation under his own name.

Should he risk contacting Anita? This might be his best opportunity for a while, since he'd be leaving the area within a couple of hours. He looked at his watch; it would be 9:00 a.m. in Naples. Unless her grandmother had taken a turn for the worse, Anita should be home with her family by now. He looked up the NATO Base at Gricignano and made the long distance call.

"*Buongiorno.* North Atlantic Treaty Organization. *Può oi aiuto?*"

"I'm trying to reach Colonel Arneil's family."

"Just a moment."

"Hello?"

"Hello, Mrs. Arneil. This is Jeff Kingston. How are you all doing over there?"

"We are just fine, thank you Jeff. Are you looking for Anita? She's out at the moment. I'm expecting her back in a few minutes."

"Yes, please tell her that I will call back in an hour."

"Fine. I'll tell her. Take care, Jeff."

As he drank his coffee and watched for Dr. Hansen, he checked his air reservations. On his way to Naples he would stop off in Nice and find the Nyiragongo guide, Maurice Labouef. If Dr. Frida Hansen had nothing to tell him about the way his mother had died and who was responsible, he would surely get answers from the guide.

He checked the latest VolcanoWatch. *Current earthquake swarms are compatible with the intense seismic swarms that occurred during 1985. It indicates rock under the Bay of Naples is fracturing to a depth of several kilometers.*

He looked up into smiling eyes.

He rose quickly. She was a striking figure with long silver hair tied back with a clasp. She wore a stylish grey leather jacket with an orange blouse and grey slacks. She looked vaguely familiar. Did he remember this woman? He held out his hand. "Dr. Hansen? Dr. Frida Hansen?"

She spoke softly, "Ah, Heph. But now we call you Jeff, don't we?"

"Yes. It is Jeff Kingston now."

"Yes, it is, yes." She looked at him carefully. "You've grown into a big handsome fellow. Your hair is darker now; you were very blonde as a boy... but your face... your face I remember... even with the little beard. You have your mother's nose and high cheekbones. You are Kristin's son! Shall we sit?"

After she was settled, he said, "Thank you for everything in the safety deposit box. They were a welcome surprise, particularly the letters my mother left you. I found my father..."

Frida Hansen looked nervously around at the people beginning to arrive. "Not so loud..." She leaned forward and said in a low voice, "We have to minimize contact with each other. You see, you are in great danger. There are people... if they find you, they will kill you. Squash you like a gnat! I have a new personal email address. They don't know about it yet."

A shiver went up Jeff's back.

"If they have learned of your existence, they will resume watching me. Look. I will explain everything quickly and then I must go."

"No breakfast?"

"No. You go ahead and order."

"I'll wait. Coffee?"

"No."

Jeff hunched over, rested his elbows on the table, cupped his chin in his hands and attempted a smile. "You have my complete attention."

Frida remained grim. "Twelve years ago, Dr. Reginald Pyper, a leading British volcanologist, was assassinated in Naples. Pyper and your mother were outspoken scientists who had implemented an automated monitoring system for the Naples volcanoes. They were predicting a massive eruption of the Campi Flegrei caldera within fifteen years and were about to announce a breakthrough in volcanic eruption prediction."

The waiter came with the coffee pot. Dr. Hansen shook her head and said a few words in Icelandic.

"Thanks," said Jeff. "I'll order in a few minutes."

"You and your mother were with Dr. Pyper on his yacht when he was murdered. The two of you escaped. Your mother did not tell me how. The assassins were never found. A month following the murder, you, your mother and her colleague Dr. Hilda Marsh flew on to central Africa on a mission to study the Nyiragongo volcano which was threatening the city of Goma. You were joined there by another scientist named Dr. Antonio Camponolo."

"I have no real memories of this."

"There may be a reason you have no memories. Days before the two of you left for Africa, your mother gave me the things you found in your safety deposit box, and her instructions. If anything happened to her, I was to spirit you away to America. She toyed with the idea of taking you to your father, but realized that because Dr. Munson was part of your past, anyone looking for you might watch him. So a new identity would be required. When you were age twenty-one, I was to deliver those items to you along with the balance in her bank account.

"Kristin died on Nyiragongo. She must have taken her guide, a Frenchman named Maurice Labouef, into her confidence. When he found you unconscious on the rim of the crater, he carried you down the mountain and contacted me immediately."

"You must have suspicions about my mother's death on Nyiragongo?"

"One of your mother's team on there was Dr. Antonio Camponolo, an Italian scientist. He had a younger brother, Manuel, who was one of the contract managers for the City of Naples. Manuel was killed recently. Rumor had it that he was involved with the Italian Mafia, possibly a leader. That rumor seems to have been true."

"Dr. Camponolo had a Mafia leader for a brother?"

"Yes. I asked my lawyer to suggest this connection to the police, and he was told that it would be fatal for me to pursue it. My lawyer believed that the police had heard whispers that Manuel Camponolo may have had Dr. Pyper murdered. One of Manuel's known associates washed up on shore a few days after the murder. Of course, their evidence was not enough to indict him. Manuel probably was involved—people with money invested in the Naples economy would want the opportunity to divest themselves before the general public could deflate stock values." She scowled, leaning forward. "But my feeling is that Antonio Camponolo was directly responsible for the death of your mother. He was with her on Nyiragongo's crater floor that day." She sat back, watching him.

Jeff nodded. "The crater floor—I have a dream about that..." He shook his head and re-focused. "And all this was to end their involvement with monitoring Campi Flegrei?"

"Yes." Frida Hansen leaned closer. "Your mother had told me that they didn't want her or Dr. Pyper around as consultants for their VolcanoWatch system. Perhaps they feared he and your mother were about to predict a Campi Flegrei eruption in the near future. They had considerable credibility, and everything would have changed. Change threatens financial empires, and criminal ones too."

"Yes. My mother's journals say they foresaw an eruption sometime in the next two decades. Their monitoring equipment would have helped them pinpoint the timeline."

"You mother told me that the Campi Flegrei caldera's magma chamber was almost fully loaded years ago. Now I fear the supervolcano is primed and ready."

Jeff nodded. "But the tourism industry doesn't want to hear that."

"Neither do any of the other movers-and-shakers in Europe."

"I have a good friend whose current research agrees with my mother's findings. I'm planning to go to Naples. I'll tell them his research shows the caldera will erupt on the 29th of June."

"Holy Mother..."

"Yes..."

"Jeff, they will kill you."

"I know the risks," he said. "I'm determined to try to warn the city."

Frida looked at the floor. "You are like your mother. I am glad you lived to do this, but it may be the end of you. You said you found your father. Do you like him?"

"He's amazing, Dr. Hansen."

"Call me Frida. Did he ever marry?"

"No."

"Your mother was a fine person, dedicated to her work but a lot of fun and with a great sense of humor. She was fiercely loyal to her friends. When I knew her, she only had three loves in her life: you, her work and your father, in that order. She followed his career after they broke up." Dr. Hansen gazed wistfully out the window. "She never got over him."

"But then, why would she not…?"

"She took you to see him when you were four. She decided you needed to meet your father and that he should meet you. I went with her to Montreal for moral support. I remember the day. It was to be a total surprise. She hadn't seen or spoken to him for five years. He had no idea that we were at the same restaurant, sitting at a nearby table. Your mother got up, and holding you by the hand, began walking toward his table. But just then two men came in and called out to him. Your mother stopped and watched as they went over and sat at his table. Then she turned and walked out of the restaurant with you. It was just not meant to be, I guess." She smiled reassuringly. "If your mother had lived, she would eventually have reconnected with Munson. I feel certain of that.

"Your mother was a brilliant volcanologist. In addition to the work she did with Dr. Pyper, she spent her last seven years developing knowledge to precisely predict volcanic eruptions by measuring many things like gas emissions and sound waves."

"Sound waves…"

"Yes. She explained that volcanoes emit low frequency sound. It is caused by magma and gas interaction within the magma pool. Most volcanoes emit frequencies between, as I recall, 0.5 and 2 hertz. And just before eruption that frequency increases to a wider range between 0.5 and 7 hertz. Volcanic whispers, she told me. Warnings from the gods." She smiled.

"Your mother was a spiritual person. She had an odd ritual each night when she put you to bed. She always wore a small Icelandic Trinity cross on a gold chain. She would take it off and put it around your neck at night and say, 'God keep you safe this night.' Did you know you were baptized? At the Hallgrímskirkja, a Lutheran Church near the center of the city. Just a little way north of where you lived. Do you believe in God, Jeff?"

"I believe in Christian principles. I've had no religious exposure that I recall."

She looked at Jeff sympathetically. "You have, you know. Such a pity that you do not remember. Did you read the letters?"

"The first. The rest I gave to Munson unopened. The first letter led me to him. Then he let me read another, so I've read two."

"It is interesting that you call your father 'Munson,' as your mother did." Frida sighed. "So. You will go to Naples."

"Yes."

"She named you Heph, after the Greek god of fire and the underworld, you know. But be careful, Hephaestus, pursuing this could be very dangerous. Tourism is a multi-billion dollar golden goose. Those who benefit from this goose will stop at nothing to prevent even a feather being plucked from their precious bird. Do not end up as your mother did."

"I think there is more to it than the tourism angle," Jeff said. "I think it has something to do with their Volcano-Watch system."

"Perhaps. Do you remember being on the Kamchatka Peninsula, on Russia's east coast?"

He decided not to mention the hypnosis revelation. "I have only vague recollections… but I know that it is the most active volcanic area in the world."

"That is where your mother and Dr. Pyper developed their automated data feed from volcano monitoring instruments. She spent a year there with you. She worked with an elderly Russian colleague named Dr. Ivanov. You called him Dom-Dom. Do you remember this?"

"Vaguely, maybe." Jeff shook his head.

Frida nodded. "I loved your mother, Jeff. And I care about you." She got up. "Come. Give this old woman a hug. I must go. And good luck to you."

Jeff rose and gave Frida a hug. "Thank you for saving my life. For everything."

He watched her leave, wishing he could stay and get to know her. He signaled the waiter, who nodded and ducked into the kitchen, then glanced at his watch. It was almost time to call Anita.

... deformation field geometry confirms faster uplift and the caldera is emitting sound between 0.5 Hz and 4.5Hz...

Chapter 8

Thursday, June 18, morning

Jeff ate quickly. Patrons now occupied several tables, and although there were no familiar faces he found a place in the airport where he was unlikely to be overheard before placing his call.

"Jeff? What a surprise!"

"Hello Anita. Look, are you alone? Able to talk without being overheard?"

"Yes. What's—"

"I'm calling from Iceland. Listen, because we were sitting together in that lecture last week you may be in danger."

"Danger? Well, something is sure as heck going on. The University of Naples cancelled my Campi study. I've got an appointment with a Dr. Camponolo tomorrow to see—"

"Camponolo? Holy crap! Whatever you do, don't go to see Camponolo! He's the guy who put some kind of Mafia hit out on me."

"Jeff! Mafia hit? You're scaring the hell out of me."

"Listen. You know that my mother died when I was nine and I was adopted. Last Friday, when I turned twenty-one, Aunt Dorothy gave me a key to a safe deposit box... You still there?"

"I'm listening."

"From the papers in it, I learned my birth mother was a volcanologist. When I was nine, she and I were near a murder that was probably a Mafia assassination. Shortly after, my mother died on the Nyiragongo volcano. That was probably murder, too. Her friend got me into hiding in America."

"Wait a minute. Your mother was murdered?"

"Yes... and that speaker at the lecture we attended? That Dr. Hilda Marsh? She was on Nyiragongo with us when my mother died. She may have been involved in her murder... and I'm certain she recognized me. She saw us together. The next night, when Michael and I were camping on Mount St. Helens, someone started a rock slide above our camp."

"My god! How—"

"We'd moved after dark. If we hadn't... I thought maybe Michael's research was stirring up a hornet's nest, but now I'm sure it's me they're after. Someone trashed my room at the university, and the same guy followed me to Ottawa."

"Ottawa?"

"Long story. But that creepy Dr. Marsh has something to do with this. I'm sure of it."

"Do you think you might have seen Dr. Marsh kill your mother?"

"She and Dr. Antonio Camponolo were there. I think Camponolo was with her when she died."

"Holy! And this Dr. Camponolo is the professor who just cancelled my study grant. Too coincidental!"

"And he wants to meet with you! Dr. Marsh saw us together. They want to know what you know—about me, and about Michael's research. They won't want you anywhere near Campi Flegrei. Anita, Camponolo's brother was connected to the Mafia. Don't go near him."

"My God! Scary! But your mother's murder was twelve years ago. I don't see how—"

"I don't understand the details yet. Evidently the reason they assassinated my mother's colleague, Dr. Pyper, was to prevent them from continuing a consulting contract they had monitoring Campi Flegrei. Interestingly, Camponolo's brother was employed with the city before he died."

"Do you think the people at city hall are involved?" Anita asked.

"I don't know for sure. I'm making a lot of assumptions here. But they seem to think I can expose whatever it is they were doing, or that I can identify my mother's murderer. I think they'll destroy anyone who has the potential of exposing them or what they are up to. They may assume I've confided in you and that's why you've gone to Naples, or they could be afraid that you're there to pursue Michael's research. They've made it so no one will listen to him, but if you're right there stirring the pot..."

"So you have... or rather, *we* have inadvertently kicked over the mob's ant hill."

"Yes. And it gets worse. Michael made a prediction that Campi will erupt."

"Yes."

"Now he says it will be on June 29th."

"Whoa! That is only... let's see... eleven days from now! Do you really think he's right? Is there any science backing his prediction? I mean, there are no warnings here, and..."

"That's the point! Michael believes he has hacked into direct feed from the Naples Monitoring Center. He's given me access to that feed. Everything on his data feed suggests Campi Flegrei will erupt, yet the experts disagree. I've tried to contact the IEVPC in Florida to find out why the experts haven't acted to classify it as a CGE and warn the city. They won't talk to me. They think that, like Michael, I'm a pain in the ass publicity seeker."

"A catastrophic geological event? That's the IEVPC classification for stage 5, eruption within days," she said. "But don't you find it troubling that International Earthquake and Volcano Prediction Center volcanologists wouldn't be all over this? I mean, Jeff, really! It can't be going to erupt if they—"

"I don't have an answer to that. But I've read Michael's notes. You know how one of the keys to predicting is measuring vapors? Changes in concentrations of CO_2, SO_2 and other gasses provide some of the data for an accurate prediction; others are ground deformation and seismic data and actual low frequency sound from the volcano? Well, Michael used studies by USGS teams who successfully predicted eruptions in recent years and compared them with the Campi data. He's a genius at this stuff. I have great trust in his work. It's hard to explain all this…"

"Campi does seem poised," said Anita. "My family says there have been multiple deep earthquake swarms and a strong smell of sulfur on the coastlines. If Michael's right, we may lose a city and millions beyond it."

"In the meantime Anita, we are both in danger."

"So what do you suggest?"

"Steer clear of me. Get out of Naples, go back to the States and make yourself scarce. And get your family to leave, too."

"I don't think that will work. And how come you're in Iceland?"

"Turns out my mother was Icelandic. On the way to Naples I'm following leads on her murder. I'm on my way to Nice this evening to look for a possible witness. Then I'm going to Naples to try to warn city officials."

"But how will you get through Naples customs? If what you say is right, the Mafia will have their people watching for you."

"I'll think of a way. Please, tell your family to leave Naples. The volcano…"

"I'll do that. Look Jeff, I have a lot of questions. I'll hop a flight to Nice. I've pulled the airlines up on my computer and there's a flight that gets in about seven. Where can I meet you?"

"Anita—"

"I'll be careful. I'd best get out of here while I figure out what to do. So! In Nice, where can I meet you?"

"I'll check the incoming flights from Naples and meet you at the main Hertz rental kiosk at the airport. But I don't think—"

"Okay. See you this evening." She hung up.

Jeff shook his head, frowning. Thank the lucky stars he phoned her before she went to Camponolo! This was one hell of a turn of events. How could he get her out of this?

Anita finished booking her flight, then sat for a moment. She shared Jeff's opinion of Dr. Hilda Marsh. She, too, had picked up bad vibes from the woman during the lecture as she singled them out with all those directed questions.

She'd made a very quick decision to join Jeff in Nice. Had it been a good evaluation of her options? Her first impulse had been to help a friend in trouble, but sometimes her first response wasn't the best one. She always seemed to jump in where angels feared to tread.

Still, if she was in danger she shouldn't make her family part of the target. Although she might be safer on a military base. Jeff had military and martial arts training and would be a good partner if things got rough. But what excuse could she give for blowing off her appointment with Dr. Antonio Camponolo? She shivered. He evidently had her targeted for some kind of who-knows-what.

She needed time and space to figure out what to do.

Of course there was the option of doing nothing. If Jeff was wrong about Camponolo, she may be clear of all this and could leave Jeff to fight his own battles. But that was a non-starter because if Michael and Jeff were right about the threat from Campi Flegrei, Jeff had to find a way to prove it and warn the city.

And there was a good chance Michael was right. Let's face it, Michael was a brain and Jeff was no slouch either.

Yes, it had been a spur-of-the-moment decision. But it was a good one.

Her first order of business would be to pack; the second, to find out all she could about this Antonio Camponolo. The more she and Jeff knew out about their adversary the better. Lastly, she must warn her family about the catastrophic threat from below. Her heart was beating a little faster. Perhaps this was her chance to make a difference. If the big caldera beneath them exploded without warning it would be game over for several million people. It was also likely to start the next ice age.

Told that his flight would be delayed for four hours, Jeff rented a car and headed for the nearby Hallgrímskirkja Lutheran church, hoping it would stir some memories.

The church's spire was like a spaceship with swept-back wings pointing straight upward. It dominated the skyline and could be seen for miles against the pale waters of the North Atlantic.

To the south, a street wound between the buildings. Drawn by memories, he followed it, and—there! Yes. There was the building where he and his mother lived. A woman sat on the porch, and he was about to introduce himself when he realized it would be best to remain nameless. He drove back and parked, then crossed the massive stone promenade to one of the benches.

There, he phoned Munson as promised. "Hey Dad. Guess what! I'm looking up at a two hundred foot church spire."

"Hello Jeff, I'm glad you called. I…"

"You'll be interested to know I've learned a bit more about Kristin's death on Nyiragongo. I promised to call you before I left Iceland. From here, I'm going on to Nice, to see our Nyiragongo guide. I'm hoping he can shed more light on it."

"Jeff…"

"Yes?"

"Jeff, I've just received some bad news. I heard from your Aunt Dorothy. Your friend Michael passed away about an hour ago. It was very sudden. He went for a run. Uphill, no less. His heart stopped. He didn't suffer."

"Oh, no..." Jeff closed his eyes.

"I'm sorry, Jeff. You told me you two were close." Munson paused, and Jeff tried to gather his thoughts. "Are you okay?"

"Yeah."

"Your Aunt Dorothy gave me a message. It's a note he left for you. I wrote it down."

"Okay."

"It reads: 'Jeff. Keep going. Warn the city. And talk to me. Now, I will hear you.'"

Jeff bowed his head.

Munson remained silent.

"Dad?"

"Yes?"

"Please call Aunt Dorothy back and ask her to convey my sorrow to Michael's parents. We all knew this was coming. It is just so sudden."

"Yes."

"Thanks for this. I'll call you from Nice."

He tucked the phone away.

An Arctic tern landed on the church, ruffling its feathers and looking down at him. A huge statue of the Icelandic 11th century hero-explorer Leif Erikson stood in the courtyard. Several puffins sat nearby, watching Jeff, their colorful beaks almost seeming to smile.

"Okay, guys," he told the birds. "I'll see if the doors are open." He entered though the large double doors. Inside, the massive concrete structure it seemed more like a huge man-made cavern than a church. Graceful white pillars soared upward toward the towering roof like stalagmites. The church had little ornamentation except for a beautiful golden pipe organ built into an end wall. Simple bench pews of dark wood lined each side of the wide aisle. He sat, realizing he had been here often with his mother. The words of the Lord's Prayer came back to him, and he bowed. Our Father, who art in heaven…

Michael had taken the "hill climb" route for his last run. They had challenged it many times together and Michael had known exactly what he was doing.

"Well, I promised I'd talk to you, my ghostly pal. I suppose in spirit you're here with me. You better give me a nudge now and then!"

Leaving the church, Jeff waved to the puffins and shrugged out of his backpack. Taking out his iPad, he checked the latest VolcanoWatch from Campi Flegrei. *Uplift unrest exceeds previous modeling. The deformation field geometry confirms a faster uplift. The caldera is emitting sound between 0.5 Hz and 4.5Hz.*

He frowned. The low frequency sound was increasing toward the 7 hertz threshold that volcanoes make before they erupt. He shook his head, got back into the car and headed for the airport. He had better hurry or he would miss his flight. As he drove through the old neighborhood, he felt re-invigorated. It had been a good experience recalling old childhood memories. He focused forward.

Michael was gone. But he had entrusted his work to Jeff, and it was time to move on.

At the airport, he returned the car and checked in. Another flight had just arrived from somewhere in Canada and the disembarked passengers were walking toward the baggage claim area. He stopped by a pillar and watched them, shrinking back as a large man with a cookie-ring beard passed by.

He did a quick appraisal. His adversary was perhaps six foot four, about 230 pounds, his heavily muscled arms and neck covered with grotesque tattoos. Built like a fireplug, he may be difficult to fight, hand-to-hand. Two ugly scars ran diagonally down one cheek as if he'd been cut with a beer bottle. His long reddish hair was pulled back in a ponytail—there was one advantage. Another was the pair of eyeglasses perched on his adversary's nose.

Cookie-Ring held his arms out at his sides as he walked, limping slightly on the right. He and carried a satchel with the strap over his head and right shoulder; probably left handed.

Jeff glanced at his watch and headed for his departure gate, nodding grimly. At least now he'd had a good look at the man.

Jeff settled back, thinking about Michael as the plane gained altitude out over the North Atlantic. When the fasten-seatbelt sign came off, he rose and went to a washroom. The mirror seemed to reflect a sadness in his eyes he hadn't seen before.

He washed up, studying himself for a moment. For years he'd looked at that image wondering who he was, who his parents were, and if they had loved him. Now as he looked at his image in the mirror he knew the answers to all those questions.

He felt torn.

Despite his deep sadness over Michael's death, something positive had happened. Without Michael's urging he might not have gone to Vegas; he still wouldn't know who his parents were. "I wish you were here, my friend..."

He felt a surge of resolve. Today was June 18th. If Michael was right, there were only eleven days to go until Campi Flegrei erupted. He frowned at the mirror. He must get on with it.

Returning to his seat, he turned on his iPad and inserted the memory stick containing Michael's notes. He looked at the data covering changes in CO_2, SO_2, hydrochloric acid gas, carbon monoxide and water vapor that came from deep in the fiery lair of Campi Flegrei. It seemed to him that some of the notes were a bit easier to understand when read for the second time. Then, lost in a sea of equations, he stopped reading.

The low frequency sound being emitted from Campi Flegrei had already moved toward the danger zone. It seemed increasingly possible that Michael was right about the Mediterranean monster.

... caldera is growing a resurgent dome at triple the historical rate and deep earthquake swarms continue...

CHAPTER 9

Thursday June 18, afternoon
Outside the aircraft window, dark clouds brought a premature dusk. The flight pulled up to the gate at the Nice Côte d'Azur International Airport under heavy rain. As the "fasten seatbelts" sign switched off, a flight attendant arrived at Jeff's seat.

"Sir," she said, "we have you listed for priority deplaning. Come with me and I'll ensure that you are the very first off the aircraft."

Jeff winked at his seat mate, a young American, and turned back to the flight attendant. "This is the gentleman who is in a hurry," he said, rising to let the man out.

"Ah... okay... yes." The young man stood to collect his carry-on. Following the flight attendant up the aisle, he looked back and mouthed a "thank you."

Jeff grabbed his gear and followed. Loitering a few seats back, near the aircraft's exit door, he donned his shades, rumpled his hair, pulled his shirt tail out, and slung his jacket over his shoulder to partly hide his face.

As the door was opened, he followed a group of passengers and, squeezing by the commotion of his seat-mate being detained by security police, hurried on down the concourse.

How were they tracking him? His passport? Having cleared French customs in Paris before his connecting flight to Nice, he no longer had customs to worry about. He'd topped up his cash supply in Paris, too, in case they were using his bank activity to trace his movements.

He headed out to the taxi stand and caught a cab to the city center. Using his iPad, he scanned a map of the downtown area until he'd spotted a Punjabi clothing store in close proximity to a Jokers Masquerade store and a department store. He asked the driver to drop him at a nearby hotel, where he hailed another taxi and asked that driver to drop him near the shops.

The department store wasn't particularly busy, so he took his purchases into one of the handicap restrooms, got out the hair dye and the beard trimmer, and set to work.

Twenty minutes later he hailed another taxi and asked the driver to take him to the nearest car rental agency. There, he rented a BMW SUV and asked for maps and detailed directions for following the coastal highway to Genoa, Italy. He was assured he could leave the rental at his destination for only a small drop-off charge.

Anita's flight from Naples was due in a half hour. It would take another half-hour for her to clear customs and arrive at the airport Hertz kiosk, so he drove back to the airport and parked in their lot. Then he trotted through the rain to the airport entry.

Standing behind a pillar across the street from the main doors, he looked for signs of trouble.

He didn't have long to wait. A grey Mercedes pulled in behind the waiting taxis at the curb and a tall, slim man emerged from the passenger side. He was joined by a heavyset man at the curb. They exchanged a few words, then the man on the curb swatted the slim man. He called to the driver, *"Chi?"*

"Arneil," the driver called out. "Anita Arneil!" The man at the curb turned and ran toward the terminal.

Jeff stood for a moment, undecided. The driver would

see Anita coming out of the terminal and if he had a description or a picture... Should he try to take out the driver? He could give him a quick chop to the neck and take his weapon. But no, it would blow their cover. He had to think of an alternative.

From the baggage claim near the airport entry, Anita stared out the large windows onto the street. Passengers hurried about in the heavy rain, some catching taxis, some running for the car park and others just arriving. She caught a glimpse of Jeff standing by a pillar across the street, just as a large man on the curb stepped into her line of vision.

Or *was* it Jeff?

The large man moved aside. The guy by the pillar had Jeff's stature, but his hair was too dark. And a beard—had there been enough time for Jeff to grow one? She squinted through the rain. He was watching as a large grey car pulled up right in front of the window. The man on the curb stepped forward as a tall, thin man got out of the car. They exchanged words with the driver, then hurried to the entry doors. The large one had an ugly, pockmarked face and a partial beard; the tall one had a dark, angry face.

Anita retreated behind a pillar and shivered as they scanned the crowd, making their way further into the building. She turned her attention back to the window and a quick movement caught her eye. Jeff—it was him, after all—dashed across the street to talk to a policeman. He pointed to the grey car.

The policeman went over to the car, exchanged a few words with the driver, and waved for him to move the car forward. The driver argued and then reluctantly drove off. Jeff had ducked back across the street and into the shadows.

Anita scanned the crowd leaving the airport. A group of girls at the baggage claim, a team of some kind, had collected their gear and were heading for the exit. Adjusting her backpack, she joined them and, tugging her scarf over her head, followed them out through the downpour and into the parking lot.

As they neared the Hertz kiosk, she broke away and trotted inside.

"Hello there!" Jeff's grin was disarming.

"I almost didn't recognize you," she said quietly, hugging him. "What's with the black hair and the beard?"

"It's a partial disguise."

"Those men—were you sure they were after me?"

"The driver used your name. They didn't see you. I've already rented a car. Ready?"

They ran to the BMW. She threw her backpack into the back seat, then climbed into the front. "Good to see you, Jeff."

He nodded. "I wish it was under better circumstances. I'm sorry to have brought all this down on you. You're in danger here. The three in the grey Mercedes… you can't stay."

She laughed and wrung the water from her scarf. "I'm staying. Camponolo was after me in Naples, and I'm pretty sure others were after me as I tried to leave. I'm safer with you."

Jeff pulled up alongside the kiosk to pay the parking fee. "Look, I'm probably facing the C-2."

The gate rose, and he pulled forward.

She put a hand on his arm. "If Michael is right about his Campi prediction, there are millions at risk. I want to help. I'm staying. End of discussion."

Jeff had pulled into traffic, and he waited for an opportunity to look at her. "I have sad news," he said, reaching for her hand. "Michael is gone. He went jogging. His heart gave out."

"Oh, God." She crossed herself. *Jogging? What was he thinking, in his…?*

"He knew it would do him in, Anita."

"That is… That was just like him… death on his terms. I'm sorry. At least he didn't suffer." She squeezed his hand.

"We are going to miss him," Jeff said. He glanced at the mirror. "Watch for the grey Mercedes behind us. They're armed. I think they mean to kill us. I just wish you hadn't been dragged into this."

"No one dragged me. And there's no sign of the car. And, Jeff, I've got news. I can't wait to tell you what I've learned about our Dr. Camponolo."

Jeff squinted, trying to see through the rain drenched windshield. Visibility was poor. He held the car just above the speed limit, watching in the late evening light for signs of a tail. As he pulled out onto the freeway heading east toward the city, he relaxed a little.

"So, what have you learned about Camponolo?"

She loosened her seatbelt and sat forward so she could look behind. "I found out that he is a very powerful man in Italy. He's the chair of... Hold it! We're being followed!"

"Yeah, I see them. Same car, the grey Mercedes. I hope we can outrun it." Jeff tramped on the accelerator, and tugged the wheel as the SUV slid a little. "Rain's made this oily pavement pretty slick."

"I have a suggestion."

Jeff glanced over. "What?" There was an explosion of sound and the left mirror shattered. "Get down! They're shooting at us! What's your idea?"

"We've got three lanes. Take the middle lane. Lure him over to the fast lane on our left as we round this curve. Keep him behind you."

"Stay down," Jeff urged.

"There's an off-ramp to the right. As soon as you get around that big rig up ahead, cross in front of him and make for the ramp. Now! Cut in front of him! There's the off-ramp!"

Jeff cranked the wheel hard. The rig's horn blared as their BMW screeched across the right lane, skidded sideways and barreled down the off-ramp. "Where is he?

"He's blown by the exit, but he's braking," she said.

They were on a side street now and Jeff turned right, then left, then right again.

"I think we lost them," said Anita.

"Hope so." Jeff grinned. "You were great back there!"

"Teamwork." Her grin looked more like a grimace. "I've never been shot at. Have you?"

"Yes, military training with live ammunition whizzing over my head as I crawled in the mud. These guys are well connected; they knew the moment we left the parking lot."

"I wish we were armed. You don't have a weapon, do you?"

"No."

They drove on for a bit in silence. Finally Jeff asked, "So tell me about Dr. Camponolo. You say he's powerful."

"He is. It's confirmed that he's tied in with the international Italian Mafia, not the Cosa Nostra or the Camorra. The Cosa Nostra is headquartered in Sicily and the Camorra is in Naples, but he's tied to the new international Mafia that INTERPOL refers to as the C-2. Camponolo also heads a group of influential scientists. They sit on a Naples seismological committee and a city emergency planning committee. He's well connected with big city brass and has friends in the Italian government. Word is, he acts for the tourist industry to keep the lid on things. On top of that, the guy is loaded."

"That's bad; it means that his influence comes from his intimidation of the population by violent criminal acts as well as from his scientific expertise." Jeff glanced in the rear view mirror. Still no sign of a pursuit.

"Right," Anita said. "And apparently Camponolo is the voice of caution when it comes to emergency planning. Like trying not to panic the population, reminding folks that seismic events cannot be accurately predicted, and so on. The last emergency planning simulation in Naples a year ago was done over the objection of Camponolo and his group. He's Doctor Darkness, Jeff."

Jeff nodded. "It fits. Lulling the population into complacency to protect their interests. I'm told everything the Mafia does is based on money. What did they use to transport people out of the city during that emergency simulation?"

"Busses, trucks, cars, everything."

"How long did they figure it would take to clear the entire city?"

"I'm not sure. Twenty-four hours, I think. But many may refuse to leave their homes."

"Yeah, that will be a problem. You've gathered some valuable information. It looks like we've lost out pursuers. Enough of this looping around. We need to find a town called Annot, where a guide named Maurice Labouef may be able to explain how my mother died."

"Who's he?"

As they drove, he filled her in. "Labouef used to have a shop in Fabron, but I called there for directions and the recording said he's moved to Annot."

The rain had stopped and it was dark by the time they found Moe's place. The little mountain climbing equipment store was located in a ramshackle building on a side street in a bad part of town. The store was closed but there was a light in the window and they could see movement inside. Jeff knocked on the shop door and called out Moe's name. A small man peered out the window at them and looked at their car. He opened the door and, after looking them over carefully, removed the chain and he motioned them in.

Jeff smiled. "Thank you for seeing us."

"Ah, *monsieur*. It is late. My shop is closed but always open if you have money and wish to buy."

"Are you Maurice Labouef?"

"Who is asking, please?"

"Jeff Kristinson. My mother was Dr. Kristin Stefsdotir."

Moe scratched his head. *"Ah, oui…* this is a name I have not heard for many years." He studied Jeff for a moment. "I am thinking you will come to see me someday. You are how old now?"

"Twenty-one. My mother died twelve years ago. This is my friend Anita."

"Mademoiselle." He took her hand for a moment and turned back to Jeff. "Time, it does go by. And how can I be of help?"

"It's about my mother…"

"Ah," he nodded sympathetically. *"Oui.* It is about your mother's death?"

"Yes. I have little knowledge of how she died, Mr. Labouef. I was hoping…"

"Moe. Please, you come back here." He retreated to the back of the shop. On the walls were maps of hiking trails on volcanoes and one of Nyiragongo showing trails up the mountain. Around the shop was an assortment of camping gear including tents, pack-boards, bedrolls, climbing ropes and mountaineering gear. Jeff smiled. This was certainly a very specialized store.

In the back, Moe was fussing over a small electric hot plate. Above a desk hung a sheepskin attesting to the fact that Maurice Labouef had once received a degree in Agriculture and Environmental Science from the University of South Africa in Pretoria.

"Who are your customers?" Jeff asked.

"Internet," Moe replied. "You are very tall, young Heph. Your hair was much lighter, as I recall."

"I guess I'm a tad bigger than when you last saw me. I go by Jeff now."

"Yes, yes. Have a chair, Anita. Tell me about your life, Jeff. What has happened since the friend of your mother, Miss Jane Smith whose real name I was not to know, took you to be safe?"

While the coffee was brewing, Jeff explained how Aunt Dorothy and Uncle Ralph had adopted him and how they had crisscrossed their way across the country over the years, finally settling in Seattle. He explained how his interest in science and math had led to studying earth and space sciences, including how Michael shared his strong interest in geology and volcanoes. "Through the years, the only memory I had of my mother was a recurring dream of her in a crater, walking toward a fiery lava lake. I think that was when she died."

Moe's brow furrowed. "Marsh and Camponolo." He was matter-of-fact. "These two were responsible for your mother's death. They planned it. They killed her." He paused and dropped sugar cubes into two cups and filled them with coffee. Handing the cups to them, he leaned against the counter and poured another for himself. The little man looked to be about seventy, although Jeff found it difficult to judge the age of Africans, and Moe seemed in excellent physical condition.

"Camponolo and Marsh." He scowled. "They allowed—no, encouraged—your mother to walk into danger. They did not try to stop her." He sipped his coffee, looking at Jeff over the rim of his cup. "I will take you up there someday. I will show you. I cannot prove this, but I know it was hydrogen sulfide gas. Camponolo was monitoring the gas warning instruments that day, and he did not tell your mother the truth."

Moe watched Jeff, waiting.

"Maybe we can fly down there someday to see where it happened," agreed Jeff. "But Moe, why didn't you tell anyone you suspected they murdered my mother?"

"There was no law there. No court. If I had told the authorities what happened, Camponolo would have killed me. He and Marsh told me Kristin had been careless, that you had seen her die and that you had stumbled, running to her, that you had fallen and hit your head. They thought you were dead. I could see that you were alive, but I said nothing. I volunteered to take your little body down to the village. Your mother had been fearful for your safety after

Naples, and she did not know who to trust. She had made arrangements in case of trouble. I called your mother's friend in Iceland. She came to get you from the hospital."

"Dr. Fr—"

"Tut tut tut!" Moe held up a hand. "Please, even today it is safer not to know."

"Miss Jane Smith, then. I wouldn't be here if it wasn't for the two of you." Jeff put his cup down and gave the little man a hug. "Thank you for saving my life, Maurice Labouef!"

"Non, non!" Moe protested weakly. He turned to one of the many posters on his wall, a map of the Nyiragongo area. "You can read a volcano, you know," he said. "As a small boy you predicted a fissure eruption that day. You seem to have a gift. This may be in your mother's journal."

"You've read her journal?"

"Only enough to see what it was, whether or not it was important to keep. I brought it down the mountain that day."

"You've got it?" Jeff was incredulous.

Moe disappeared into the back room and came back with a dusty leather carrying case. "This belonged to your mother. It is her journal, her notes. She told us you could understand volcanoes by reading her instruments."

Jeff shook his head. That was highly unlikely; perhaps Kristin liked to brag about him. Still, Moe's belief that he could do this may help convince the Italians.

As Moe placed the case on the counter, Jeff reached out and ran his hand over its dusty leather surface. "I remember this case!" He opened it and stared at the journal, the notes. They had found their way to him. He recalled the words of a Christian hymn… *through earthquake, wind and fire…* On the inside cover of the case was pasted a brief handwritten note in his mother's neat writing, its English translation alongside:

Serengeti
Thirty million years ago the African continent was torn

apart by a fiery inferno below. It created the Great Continental Rift, a long valley that stretches 6,000 kilometers from the Jordan Sea in the north and down into the wilds of the interior. It formed a basin that has been a haven for life and the cradle of mankind. The volcanic soil of its high plateaus is a refuge for antelope, for elephants, for cheetahs, for birds — for many living things. Serengeti, it is called, which means boundless land. I love this land and its volcanoes. Life began here. Life will end here.

Kristin Stefsdotir

He swallowed. Did his mother have a premonition of her death? He turned to Moe. "There is big trouble ahead and I may need your help. I must tell you about it."

Eyeing the journal thoughtfully, the little man nodded. "Will it take long?" he asked. "I am making my supper. You will tell me over a little meal?"

Jeff glanced at Anita. "Thanks, but we have little time. We must hurry on to Naples."

"We should accept Moe's hospitality," Anita said.

"You will tell me over a bowl of *potage*." Waving Jeff to a chair, he brought the covered pot from the hot plate. "I have made enough for three. It is a coarse soup. Made with a purée of vegetables. Now, we will eat."

"That will be fine," Jeff said, "Thank you."

"And now young Kristinson, ah... I mean Kingston, I am, as they say, all ears," Moe grinned. "Tell me. About your big trouble."

Jeff explained everything, right up to their problem of warning the city.

Maurice Labouef listened while they ate.

As Jeff finished, he got his computer, brought up the latest VolcanoWatch summary, highlighted it and showed it to Moe. *The caldera is growing a resurgent dome at triple the historical rate and intense deep earthquake swarms continue.*

Moe nodded, concerned.

"So that's the story, Moe. Very soon, I may want you to come to Naples. I was hoping you could attest to my ability to read volcanoes..."

Moe looked at the floor. "You will both be doomed to die first," he said.

"Doomed to die?"

"*Oui.* I must warn you. They will not listen to you. It is dangerous. People in lofty places, they will stop you. This is what got your mother murdered." He shook his head slowly, his mouth down at the corners.

Jeff rubbed his stubble-covered chin. "I know about the danger, but I must do this. And I need them to believe me. Will you come and testify to my background if I call?"

Moe was silent.

Jeff stood. "We must go now," he said. "Thank you for the supper, Moe. And I do hope that someday you can take me back up on Nyiragongo again."

"If you live through this." Moe closed Kristin's case and handed it to Jeff. "Be warned. They will not listen in Italy. You will be a target." He turned to Anita. "Miss Anita, you must understand—there is much danger in this."

"Thank you, Moe." Anita shook his hand. "But we have to find a way to warn the city."

Moe nodded sadly. "You are both brave. I will come to help if you call me."

The skies had opened up again. Jeff drove the SUV along the twisting highway toward Castellane, switching his headlights from high to low. Between the shining rain and the black pavement, visibility was terrible. He passed a sign for a campground and considered pulling in to wait out the storm, but decided instead to keep going, hoping the rain would cease.

It didn't. When another campground sign appeared, he eased off the highway and parked.

"Might as well get some sleep," he said. Reaching over the seat for their packs, he passed Anita hers and rummaged through his own for some extra clothing. "I'll take first watch."

... this interferogram from SAR orbit images shows 3.5 meters of displacement in the 4 kilometer wide deflated area...

CHAPTER 10

Friday, June 19, early morning
Jeff woke at five o'clock, refreshed. He started the SUV and headed south toward the port town of Saint Tropez.

"You didn't wake me," said Anita, yawning.

"I fell asleep myself," said Jeff, sheepish.

"Good thing they didn't find us." Anita leaned forward to return her seat to its upright position. "I thought we were heading for Naples. Shouldn't we be going east?"

"My dad has a yacht in Saint Tropez," said Jeff. "It would give us a place to stay, safer transportation, and maybe an opportunity to hide in plain sight."

"If those guys in the Mercedes find this SUV in Saint Tropez, won't that be a clear give-away?"

"You're right," said Jeff. "Maybe we'd better stash it somewhere along the way. Too early in the morning to swap it out, though."

"Moe was an interesting man. I liked him."

"I did too. We may need him to bolster my credibility."

"Hmm. I've learned some interesting stuff about the Campi since I saw you. Have you read about Lake Toba in Indonesia?" she asked.

"I know it was a mega-caldera volcano like Campi. It erupted eons ago and caused a mini ice-age."

"Right. A Campi Flegrei eruption would be similar to the Lake Toba event that occurred 75,000 years ago, according to the scientists."

"How did they figure out when it erupted?" Jeff asked.

"The Greenland ice probes have provided an accurate history of the earth's atmosphere. Scientists bored down into a mile and a half of Greenland ice, bringing up ice cores. The ice was formed by 200,000 years of falling snow. The cores are a record of the earth's atmosphere. They examined the cores and found that 75,000 years ago there was a cataclysmic event that has been traced back to Lake Toba."

"Cool." Keeping his eye on the rear view mirror, he swung back to the fast lane.

"Yeah, well Lake Toba was formed when an underground mega-volcano blew up. It caused a terrifying global disaster that they figure wiped out sixty percent of all life on earth. Billions of tons of ash, rock, gas and pyroclastic material rose for tens of miles into the atmosphere. An enormous ash cloud of sulfur dioxide spread across the globe." She paused. "Do you know what happens when sulfur dioxide mixes with water?"

"Yes. It forms sulfuric acid; it's deadly."

"Right, well it formed billions of tiny droplets of sulfuric acid, which formed a yellow veil around the earth. Yellow death. The earth cooled causing snow to fall. The snow reflected the sun's heat back into space. Vegetation died, glaciers advanced, and fertile soil disappeared. A mini ice age began."

Jeff was quiet. No one was following them as they approached Sainte-Maxime. "What did they have to say about the actual eruption? What would have happened to the animals and to the people?"

"You don't want to know."

"Tell me."

"Those who had been far enough away to survive the initial blast—if they breathed in the ash they would have died a painful death. Breathing in the ash would be like breathing in millions of tiny glass needles. As your lungs fill with fluid you die a horrible death."

Jeff looked at her, realizing with surprise how far she was into earth science. "I'm impressed with your understanding of all this."

"Thanks. If Michael was right about this, everything will shut down. Vehicle engines and jet engines will clog with ash, planes won't fly, cars won't run, trains won't run, electrical generators—everything will stop."

He nodded grimly. "I'm beginning to believe Michael was right about this. Have you told your family?"

"Yes. Dad says I shouldn't listen to you. There's no way Michael could know."

"And your mom?"

"Because she knows about you and Michael and me and volcanoes, she listened. She promised to talk to Dad and to arrange a flight out of Naples for the whole family, but I'm not sure she will."

"Don't worry. We'll make sure they do. I've been thinking," he said, as his stomach rumbled. "We need supplies, so watch for a grocery store."

"There's a café that's just opening," said Anita. "I need a washroom, and some breakfast."

They ordered food they could eat in the car. While they waited for it, Jeff got out his iPad. VolcanoWatch had updated its information, and the site had added a satellite interferogram photograph covering the area of the caldera. *This interferogram is obtained from the SAR images from orbit numbers 8560 and 4286 respectively. The inset area on the image shows 3.5 meters of total displacement in the 4 kilometer wide deflated area.*

Jeff studied the interferogram photograph. The surface was continuing to bulge upward. He frowned and shut down the iPad.

Anita returned from the washroom. "How far is it to Saint Tropez?"

"Half an hour, at most," said Jeff, picking up their breakfast and heading to the SUV.

When she'd finished her bagel and coffee, Anita leaned into the back and rummaged in her pack. "I'll start a list of stuff we'll need."

"We'll buy supplies for two weeks," said Jeff, crumpling his napkin into his empty cup. "There'll be a freezer on board. Maybe we should ditch the SUV in town and get a cab to the marina. Do you need a notebook?"

"No, I found—oh my God, look!" Anita pointed.

On a side street bearing down on them was the grey Mercedes. Jeff floor-boarded the BMW. He could see that the driver was a huge man with a cookie-ring beard and then the Mercedes was piling into them, T-boning them, the heavier car pushing the SUV sideways and almost off the road. Regaining control, he urged the SUV onward.

Shots rang out. Jeff swung off down a side street toward the ocean. The steering wheel was like lead, difficult to turn. There were few houses on the street, and patches of heavy undergrowth between.

"Steering's gone," said Jeff. "Our best chance is into that bush. Hang on!" As he reefed hard on the wheel, the car careened off the road and down a hillside, crashing over rocks and through dense brush, finally ramming up against a stump as the airbags deployed.

"You okay?"

"Yeah."

"Get out, quick! Follow me!" Squeezing out from behind the bags, he helped her out the driver's side. They ran down the steep hillside into a dense brush thicket. There they crouched down, listening. It was nearly impossible to see through the thick foliage. Trying to breathe quietly, they waited. Seconds ticked by.

Branches snapped to their left. To their right someone cursed. Scraping sounds came from directly above them. Jeff looked at Anita. He placed a finger over his lips, picked up a rock and waited.

More breaking branches to their left. Through the thick brush, they could see one of the men. He was grasping a weapon and pointing it downward, coming downhill toward them, a hundred feet away.

Jeff threw the rock toward their left. As the rock hit the bushes, the man above them whirled and fired a volley of automatic fire in the direction of the noise.

A groan, then silence.

Further to their left, through the brush, they caught a glimpse of the huge man with the cookie-ring beard.

"Elles descendre, Jean?" The first man called out.

"À côté gauche," Jeff replied quickly, throwing a second rock in the direction of the man with the cookie-ring beard. As it hit the ground, the Frenchman fired a second volley in the direction of the bearded man, who immediately returned fire.

"Son of a bitch," the bearded man hollered. "I'm hit!"

Jeff and Anita waited, and then crept toward the first Frenchman. He lay on his back, not moving, his rifle nearby. "This one's dead," Jeff mouthed, picking up the weapon. "You stay here, I'll check on his partner."

He moved cautiously toward the second man, rifle raised. The man lay gasping for breath, blood gushing from a low chest wound. Jeff moved cautiously forward, ready to bring the rifle-butt down if he made a move. Instead he gasped and stopped breathing, staring at the sky.

Jeff crept back to Anita, held up two fingers, then ran his hand across his throat.

"Let's go," mouthed Anita.

They crept uphill, Jeff holding the rifle ready. He sensed movement from behind them and whirled too late. A shot rang out, and pain seared Jeff's arm. He dropped to his knees and grasped his wounded arm. The man with the cookie-ring beard toppled toward them, gurgling. Then silence. Anita picked up the rifle and trained it on the prone man while Jeff rolled him onto his back. He lay still, his face ashen white and contorted. Suddenly Jeff was in the ocean, hugging his mother while a man bobbed nearby on the surface, his face white, his eyes bulging.

"You okay?" asked Anita.

Jeff shuddered. He looked at the scene around them, angry for foolishly allowing her to be involved in this hideous affair. "We've got to get out of here."

She nodded. "But shouldn't we check their pockets to see who they're working for?"

She'd already bent and fished a wallet and a phone from Cookie-Ring's pocket. "Adofo Vizzini," she read from the wallet. "No listed address. Lots of cash. Payoff for killing us, no doubt."

Opening Vizzini's phone, Jeff memorized the number of the last call made and dropped the phone on the man's chest. "Wipe it all down and put it back," he said. Awkwardly working with one hand, he wiped the rifle they'd handled, then backtracked the few steps to leave it near the first dead man. Sirens were wailing in the distance, and voices from below were drawing nearer. Scurrying uphill they cautiously approached the wreck, which was crumpled against the tree trunk with its front doors open. Anita shouldered her backpack, then helped Jeff's pull his jacket over his bloody arm. "Can you carry your bag?"

"I'll have to. We need to look natural."

The sirens grew closer. Jeff and Anita angled alongside the road, through the bushes, watching for an opportunity to step onto the road while there was no traffic.

A driveway cut across the bush.

"Look," said Anita.

Jeff turned to see what she was pointing at. A pick-up truck and three bicycles were parked in the driveway; beyond the truck, a path wound down the hill toward a house.

"Check their tires," said Jeff. Using the truck for cover, Anita ducked her way over.

She squeezed both front and back tires on all three bikes, then nodded.

Jeff crept over, fumbling hopelessly in his jacket pocket. "Anita, help me get this."

She put in her hand and pulled out the roll of bills, eyes widening. He peeled off several bills. "Is the truck unlocked?"

"Window's open," she said.

"Stuff these through," he said. As she did, he struggled to mount one of the bikes. She hopped on another.

They pedaled out onto the highway, and coasted down the hill. Another emergency vehicle screamed past, and they slowed and turned to watch, playing the curious onlookers, before pedaling toward town.

After a few miles, Anita pulled up alongside Jeff. "We need to deal with that arm," she said. "I can see the blood dripping from it."

Jeff nodded. "How about there?" A dirt lane led to a small rest area, deserted at this hour. Stashing the bikes in the bushes, they ducked into the restroom.

She pulled up his bloody shirt sleeve and examined the wound above his elbow. "Hurt much?"

"I can't really feel it. It's numb."

"It's a flesh wound, high up on the outside of your arm. It's gone clear through. Hold still while I fix this." She tore off a piece of his shirt, and began bandaging his arm. "What was it that you yelled out in French?"

"Beside, to the left."

"Well, it was brilliant. I had no idea you could speak French."

"Aunt Dorothy's mother was French," said Jeff. "I only picked up a little." Watching Anita's deft fingers bandaging his arm, he was conscious of her standing very close. She was almost as tall as him, and her green eyes were still teary from the shock of their violent encounter, her auburn hair tousled from running through the underbrush. But her movements were controlled, her shakiness almost gone. Calm head but a taste for danger—the perfect partner in a struggle to save a city.

"We're lucky to be alive," she said. "It happened so fast—did you get a shot off?"

He shook his head.

Anita was suddenly very serious. "We were lucky, weren't we? I mean, we should both be lying dead up there…"

"No. After they started shooting at each, other we had the advantage."

Anita looked dubious. "It was three against…"

"Don't think about it," said Jeff. "It's over."

Anita dug in his pack for a clean shirt and spotted the rest of his cash. She looked at him, wide-eyed. "Where'd all this cash come from?"

"Oh, that," said Jeff. "Along with her journals, my mother left me some money. It was invested for the past twelve years at a tidy rate of interest."

"Jeez, Jeff." Anita shook her head.

Retrieving their bikes, they pedaled back to the autoroute and then on down into Saint Tropez. There, they blended into the morning activities.

After buying supplies, they cycled to the marina and found the *Cannelle* berthed among dozens of vessels. It was a sleek, modern 55-foot motor yacht, its hatches secured, its rigging stored and its forward-leaning shape hinting of speed and seaworthiness.

Jeff shook his head in admiration. "She's a beaut, isn't she?"

"She's that alright."

They carried the bicycles on board and found the keys where Munson had promised. The cabin door swung open to a luxurious salon, dining area, galley and pilothouse. Below, they looked at the master stateroom. Jeff inspected the engine room with its twin 735-horsepower diesels.

Satisfied all was in order, he returned to the captain's chair and studied the controls. It had a hydraulic tilt steering system, mechanical push-pull controls, boat thrusters, stabilizers, sonar system, auto pilot, a GPS and a computerized navigation system. On the console was a hand-held remote control that could be carried out on deck, allowing the yacht to be controlled from there. The fuel tanks were full, the batteries showed charge. "I think I've got most of it figured out," he said. "Know anything about yachts?"

"Some. I'm comfortable on the water. I was a member of a sailing club, and—ah. I see our taxi has arrived."

They carried their supplies on board and Jeff warmed up the diesels. After few preparatory tasks they were ready to cast off.

"How will the voyage take?" Anita asked.

Jeff scratched his head. "Let's look at the charts. Her cruising speed is about 30 knots and 1 knot is 1.151 miles per hour. Let's lay out our course to Naples. It looks like it's about 420 miles, so 420 times 1.151 equals... 483 nautical miles. Now, the yacht cruising speed is about 30 knots so 30 times 1.151 is 34.530 miles per hour. And 483 divided by 34.53 is 13.98. So there you have it. It'll take us about 14 hours to reach Naples."

Anita raised her eyebrows. "Now I understand why you tutored math students. So we'll arrive just after midnight Saturday morning."

Jeff grinned. Anita was properly dressed for the voyage in jeans, runners and a rain-proof jacket. She had braided her auburn hair into a ponytail and threaded it through the back straps of a pale green baseball cap.

"The green brings out the green in your eyes." Damn. He turned to the controls. "I'll set up our course on the computer for the auto-pilot after we get under way. You can cast off. I'll back her out."

"Do you think anyone will be watching for us?"

Jeff nodded. "Maybe. You know what? I screwed up. I think having the taxi bring our groceries was a big mistake."

"Ok, then," she said grimly. "I'll cast off. Let's get out of this bloody damned marina and out to sea."

He grinned. "That's the first time I've heard you swear."

"How come you never do?"

He laughed. "Because with you I'm on my best bloody damned behavior."

... the surface is beginning to crack and swell, threatening a series of small eruptions...

CHAPTER 11

Friday, June 19, mid afternoon
They had been at sea for several hours, on a bearing east-southeast. The course plotted by the GPS navigation-assist was taking them around Cape Corse and past Capra Island into the Tyrrhenian Sea. Anita had prepared sandwiches in the galley and brought them to the pilothouse, but the brilliant Mediterranean sunshine seemed to have done little to lift her spirits.

"It's weird isn't it?" she said. "I feel almost guilty for their deaths."

"They were trying to kill us, Anita."

"I know. But experiencing something like that is traumatic. It's sobering—hard to let go of. I don't know if I'll ever get over it."

Jeff was silent for a bit. Then he spoke slowly and deliberately. "Screw them. They killed each other. We didn't fire the shots that killed them." He left the captain's chair and faced her. "Listen, Anita. We have the right to protect ourselves."

"I know, but—"

"I've got to concentrate on the big picture. I have a mission, and if I don't make it, hundreds of thousands may die. How would you like to be responsible for untold thousands swept out to sea or buried under tons of pyroclastic flow and killer fallout?"

"I wouldn't!" She jumped up, suddenly angry. "And damn it, Jeff, it's no longer *your* mission. It's *our* mission. I'm not running away from this. I'm part of it! That's why I'm here. But you better be right about all of this!"

She gathered up the remains of their lunch and began to leave the pilothouse. "I'm sorry," he called after her. "Anita, we should talk about this." She kept going.

He should never have dragged Anita into this. Maybe it would have been better to take her back to the NATO base and help her convince her father to get their family to safety. This mission to save millions could fail—probably *would* fail, he admitted. At least one family could be saved.

He snorted. As if Anita would have stood for that. She was here because she believed in Michael and in him, even though she wasn't completely convinced. Michael was totally convinced. Jeff suddenly realized he was in this in part for his mother. How much was he letting his own need for closure color his thinking? Not just closure, he conceded; he needed vindication. Vindication for his mother and for her work. And for Michael's work, too.

If his mother and Michael were the driving force that kept him going, what kept Anita going?

Courage, he decided. She was smart enough to know what they were up against, and brave enough to try. She'd succeed or go down fighting. And he'd better not get in her way.

What they really needed was some kind of proof that the data Michael had uncovered, the data that supported Kristin's theories, was being ignored or intentionally suppressed. If the scientific community *was* actually looking at the real data, Anita would be relieved to go home. And Jeff could enlist Munson's help in getting to the bottom of Kristin's death.

Jeff switched the yacht to autopilot, picked up the binoculars and walked out on deck. On the horizon to the rear, he could see a yacht following them about three nautical miles back. It looked like the same one that had been trailing them about an hour out of Saint Tropez. The craft was slowly gaining on them. He frowned, wondering if it had originated from Saint Tropez. Toward the forward horizon the ocean was clear, calm and bathed in sunshine, but clouds signaled rain squalls.

He lowered the binoculars. They were alone with their unknown follower.

Returning to the helm, he used his iPad to do more research into the C-2. According to reports, the Mafia was responsible for murdering an estimated 25,000 people in the past thirty years. The C-2 was new and even more deadly. He shook his head in disbelief, hoping the mystery yacht back there had no connection. Still, it seemed unusual that they would be following in the exact same course.

Of course they, too, could simply be going to Naples.

Naples. Once he and Anita arrived, they ought to visit the National Institute of Geophysics and Volcanology. Did they provide public tours or education sessions? He searched for their website.

Anita returned on deck, seemingly over her anger.

"I apologize for my self-centered comments," he said. "And this has become our mission. Are we cool?"

She grinned and nodded. "Thank you. Now, we are very cool." She paused. "Jeff, I've been thinking. To help confirm or allay your fears about Campi Flegrei, why not call the International Earthquake and Volcano Prediction Center in Orlando again?"

"I don't know if I can get through to them," said Jeff. "Maybe if I don't tell them I'm from U of W. But I will try again."

Anita nodded.

He handed her the glasses and pointed aft. "See that yacht? She's gaining on us. If she's after us, she's probably got the firepower to blow us out of the water. Should we take cover? That's Capra Island off our port bow."

She studied the craft and considered for a moment. "Let's look at the charts. About an hour ahead is Montecristo Island, right?"

"Yes, and it looks like rain squalls ahead."

She looked at him with raised eyebrows. "What's your gut tell you?"

He frowned, trying to get on her wavelength. "We could go full throttle for a bit. If we keep him a couple miles behind us we have options at Montecristo. If it's a really heavy rain squall he may lose sight of us and pass."

Anita grinned. "Then follow your gut." She put a hand on his wrist. "How's the wing?"

"It's sore, but okay if I don't use the arm much."

"I'll be in the galley storing our supplies if you need me."

He watched her leave. Then, turning back to the task at hand, he checked the *Cannelle's* instrument panel; the yacht was handling like a thoroughbred. He advanced the speed to full, settled back in the captain's chair and thought about Naples and their volcano sensors. It was time to begin planning what he would tell the Italian scientists. Unable to concentrate on that, he watched the mystery yacht, realizing suddenly that he might have a way to find out who was behind all this: Cookie-Ring Vizzini had been involved since Seattle, and Jeff had memorized the last number dialed from Vizzini's phone.

He took out his cell and called the number.

After the fourth ring a woman answered. *"Buongiorno, la casa di Dr. Antonio Camponolo."*

Nodding grimly, he cut the connection. Anger rose in his chest. Camponolo! The same man suspected of killing his mother!

Keeping a keen eye on their follower, he noted that the mystery yacht continued to gain on them. He adjusted his course slightly and watched. Within minutes, the yacht adjusted her course and followed.

Jeff grabbed the intercom. "Anita! I need you on deck!" He sat at the wheel feeling the yacht surging forward. It was now at top speed, cutting cleanly through the choppy waters of the Ligurian Sea. Just ahead, a heavy rain squall fell like a dark blanket from the sky.

Anita arrived in the pilothouse.

"I changed course; so did they," he said. Off their port bow, the faint outline of Montecristo was visible at the leading edge of the rain storm. Aft, the other yacht was less than half a nautical mile back and gaining. The storm was coming straight toward them, looking ominous.

Jeff went in and checked the charts. Unless another vessel appeared, there were no obstacles between them and the island. Undecided, he waited as the storm drew nearer and the wind picked up. Finally, with choppy seas, heavy wind and the rain beginning to pelt down, he made a decision. "We'll head in to the island," he said, turning the diagonally into the storm. "Watch for a sheltered bay."

They quickly lost sight of both the island and their pursuer. "They may not have seen us turn," Anita said. "What's the betting they'll sail straight by?"

"Let's hope they do. But keep a sharp eye out."

As the island loomed dead ahead, Jeff throttled back and followed the coastline until they saw a sheltered bay filled with yachts at anchor. There they stopped, waiting for the rain to abate, relieved that there was no sign of their follower.

"You look tired," Jeff said. "Think you could sleep?"

She nodded. "If I lay down, I'd be asleep in minutes."

"Get some rest," he suggested. "Soon as this clears a bit, I'll get us under way again. I'll wake you in two or three hours. Then you can take the helm."

"Okay. I'll be in the salon on the divan if you need me."

Jeff went below, checked the engine room and returned to the pilothouse. There, he made notes for his discussions with the Naples volcanologists. Then he went online and pulled up a map of the Naples area, looking for an appropriate place to berth. To the east of the city, superimposed on the map, was drawn a circle, perhaps a mile and a half in diameter, encircling the Vesuvius volcano. To the south, including part of the city, was a very much larger circle, perhaps four miles in diameter, showing the size of the Campi Flegrei caldera. It took in the entire Bay of Pozzuoli and much of the city. He zoomed in. There was a wharf in the village of Pozzuoli, at the exact center of the larger circle that was drawn on the map.

Zooming back out, he glanced at the article the map was attached to. An international team had been poking at the caldera with drilling rods expecting to reach a depth of three kilometers, or 4.8 miles.

His eye skipped down a few lines.

... a volcanic blast of billions of cubic feet of superheated rock, hot gas and ash 200 times worse than that of the Icelandic volcano Eyjafjallajökull which brought chaos to Europe in 2009 could incinerate and suffocate millions...

Millions. He ran a hand over his eyes, feeling anxious to get going.

Then out of the downpour emerged the yacht that had been following them, easily recognizable from its unique flying bridge. Jeff reached for the intercom and was about to warn the sleeping Anita below when he did a double-take. An old man and woman appeared on the other yacht's bridge, dressed in colorful raingear. In the yacht's wheelhouse another elderly man was drinking a beer while an older woman was at the helm.

Two old couples on a pleasure trip.

The vessel slipped past and disappeared into the mist. The name on the yacht was covered by a fallen canvass, but he could make out the words *Carmel Calif.* and an American flag on the stern.

Jeff exhaled a long breath. "Imagine that!"

A few minutes went by. The rain was slowing now, the clouds gradually giving way to sunshine and calming seas.

A helicopter flew low overhead, then out to sea in the same direction they were headed—a good sign the storm had passed. Jeff fired up the diesels and began to edge the yacht out of the bay. Easing the *Cannelle* back on course, he checked his watch. They had lost a little more than an hour. Not bad, considering.

Forty minutes passed. In the distance, a helicopter was heading back toward Montecristo Island. Was it the same helicopter he'd seen earlier? He could see smoke on the horizon dead ahead. In open water, that could only mean one thing. Had the helicopter been on a rescue mission?

He pushed the throttle forward and approached the burning ship at top speed. As he got nearer, he recognized the yacht from Carmel. "Oh my God," he said, picking up the intercom to call Anita.

The yacht was completely consumed in fire, sinking by the bow. With the glasses he could make out some of the printing on the stern. Carmel. One hand on the helm, he grasped his forehead and closed his eyes. "Oh, holy Jesus." The sudden appearance of the smoke, the helicopter — that was no rescue mission.

Anita appeared at his side. "What's happened?"

"The yacht that was following us. It passed while we were waiting out the storm — just two elderly couples." He scanned the waters desperately looking for survivors but only floating rubble surrounded them.

"How awful!" Anita shuddered.

"A helicopter left Saint Tropez as soon as the storm cleared," he said. "It just flew back."

Anita's eyes widened. "You think—"

"Those poor people," said Jeff, nodding. "They died because of us."

Anita picked up Jeff's iPad. "Jeff, is this how they've been able to track us?"

"Oh, my God." Jeff reached over and disabled the iPad's Wi-Fi connection. "This is all — my God."

Anita put her hand on his arm. With the engines at dead slow, they searched on. There was no sign of life anywhere. They circled the area several times with no success.

"They must have used rocket propelled grenades," Jeff said. "Those people didn't stand a chance."

"C-2?" Anita wondered.

"Dr. Camponolo *is* after us. That number on Vizzini's phone? I called it. Camponolo's residence."

"Bastard!"

They stood looking at the floating rubble, feeling the horror of it. Although Jeff didn't believe in God, he thought perhaps they did, so he crossed himself. "God be with you," he said. "I'm so sorry. They were after us, not you. You didn't deserve to die."

Anita took his arm. They stood on the deck in silence, then returned to the pilothouse to put the *Cannelle* back on course. Camponolo would now believe that they were dead, so they were safe for the moment. There would be no immediate search for them.

Scanning the ocean, Jeff realized this could be their best opportunity to change identity. He went below deck and returned with a box of tissues and the bags from the stores in Nice. He handed the tissues to Anita, who blew her nose.

"What's all this?"

Jeff set the bags in a deck chair. "I figured we'd have to mask our identity so we can reconnoiter the city and study Campi. We'll need to observe what's going on here, talk to local volcanologists, and reach a conclusion about Michael's prediction before we get everyone excited about an eruption, right?"

"Yes."

"So we have to travel the city incognito. There will be surveillance cameras everywhere. Your auburn hair. Our height and coloring. We would be picked up immediately, especially if we're showing interest in Campi Flegrei. I've got this bag of stuff I bought. Look, I'll show you and tell you my plan."

She blew her nose again and settled into a chair.

"I figured a turban could be helpful. You can cover

your head with this long shawl. And we both have these trousers. Should be pretty comfortable—loose at the top and tight at the ankle, kind of like pajamas. These tunics are pretty loose-fitting, too; nice in the heat. And each outfit has this colored sash. I have a skin darkener cream that will add to our 'young Sikh American couple' identity. It's the perfect disguise."

"So I have to learn Hindi?" She was trying to smile. "Isn't this a little extreme?"

He shook his head. "Punjabi... we're Sikhs. But no, we are second generation Sikh Americans. We speak very good English."

"How did you come up with this?"

"Something I was told about Sikhs wishing to pass unnoticed... they believe they have nothing to show to the world, so they usually wear simple, colorless, formless garb. Incognito."

"What about your blue eyes? My green eyes and auburn hair?"

"Brown contact lenses."

She made a face. "So we're in one of the most beautiful places in the world, and we'll be seeing it through brown colored glasses?"

He smiled. "They're clear to look through but change your eye color. And I didn't think you'd want to dye your hair, although I did buy a couple of bottles of it for you just in case that's what you wanted. I got you this great black wig. I figure with it already done in kind of a bun thing, it would look right under the shawl."

"You are quite the planner." She held up a pair of trousers. "And you're right, these do look really comfortable."

"They have to allow for good freedom of movement." He hesitated. "How far did you get in your judo classes?"

"Nowhere near your brown belt," she said. "I'll have to rely on the element of surprise. Am I draping this shawl properly?"

"Looks right. Your name will be Anjeela Kaur Gill." He

spelled it out. "I'm Jeet Singh Atwal. Got all that?"

"I think so. I should write it down; that'll help. What's the rest of this for?"

"That's the stuff we need right now. While I was shopping for our new identities, I bought this large stick-on sign lettering to change the name of the yacht. The letters spell *Mastveer*. And these small letters are for *Florida, USA*. If anyone bothers to check, there actually is a yacht registered under that name. And for our main mast, I have this American flag. And to fly aft, there's this smaller flag of India. With Camponolo and his gang thinking we've been sunk, we should be able to sail anywhere around here without raising suspicion."

She cast a glance at the ocean, closed her eyes for a moment, and turned back to Jeff. "American Sikhs. Do you know how to tie a turban?"

"Believe it or not, an old school friend of ours taught me. Do you remember Milan Malholtra? That's who gave me the idea."

"I remember him. What about riding our bikes—won't the cops get you for no helmet?"

"I checked that on the internet. Devout Sikhs can ride bikes and motorcycles without helmets in Italy."

"Okay, Jeet, my friend, looks like you've got everything covered." She blew her nose again and squared her shoulders. "What now?"

He scanned the ocean again. All clear. "Keep a watch out," he said, getting a rope ladder and stringing it from the rail. "I'll need some window cleaner and towels for starters. If nobody shows up, I'll redo the lettering while you switch the flags."

Anita took the helm and Jeff went below to try to sleep. He tossed and turned, thinking about the horror that befell the old people. If he hadn't been using his iPad to search the internet, to access the VolcanoWatch site…

He thought of the last VolcanoWatch summary. *The surface is beginning to crack and swell, threatening a series of small eruptions. If this continues the caldera floor will collapse into the larger magna reservoir and cause a four mile wide explosion of magma to atmosphere.*

He frowned, retrieved his mother's notes and began reading. Some about the Naples volcanic area drew his attention again. From her study of long-term seismic readings, she believed the Campi Flegrei caldera and the Vesuvius volcano may have a common magmatic chamber, a huge cavity of liquid magma pressing upward under the entire city. While other scientists disputed it, she believed it was four miles wide and stretched from deep below up to within 4.8 miles from the sea floor under the caldera, with a common magma pipe extending up within a half mile from the top of the Vesuvius cone.

He thought about that. The center of the massive Mount Vesuvius cone beside Naples was about five miles distant from the center of the Campi Flegrei caldera which lay under the bay in front of the city. If his mother was correct, this may be very important.

"This is significant, Michael," he muttered. "The lair of our monster may be a hell of a lot larger scientist think, and it may hold the answer to how we deal with it." Fully awake again, he figured he may as well let Anita get some sleep.

Just after midnight, Jeff anchored off Preocida Island. They were now on the outer edge of the submarine part of the Campi Flegrei caldera.

After setting the anchor, he cut the diesels and entered the salon. The lights were still on. Anita lay sleeping on the divan, her computer in her lap. He gently lifted it, saved what she had been writing, turned it off and doused the lights. Laying back in one of the leather chairs, he raised the footrest and drifted off.

... the inner caldera contains several explosive eruptive vents that are slowly becoming active...

CHAPTER 12

Saturday, June 20, early morning
"Hey, Rumplestiltskin!"

Jeff awakened to the aroma of coffee and bacon. Sunshine filled the salon, and Anita stood over him. "Breakfast is served on the quarterdeck."

"Rumplestiltskin?"

"Maybe it was Rip van Winkle."

"You mean the man who slept for a hundred years?" Jeff stretched. "That *was* Rip van Winkle."

"Speaking of, you're growing quite a beard there. How long since you've shaved? There's a razor in the—"

"I'm leaving the beard on," he said. "It's a key part of my disguise."

She rubbed her own chin thoughtfully. "Guess that's why I get a shawl instead of a turban."

Jeff cleaned up and joined her on the quarterdeck where she laid out their breakfast. It was barely six o'clock and the day was gorgeous. They lay at anchor a half nautical mile off the island. There, the dazzling white buildings of the village of Terra Murata were overshadowed by a high-walled earthwork of a great fortress that overlooked the bay. Jeff wondered if the brilliant sunshine reflecting off the water masked an imminent disaster lurking below.

"I've been thinking," Anita said as she poured the coffee. "Let's assume we've determined Michael is right. And let's assume we've been unable to convince the scientists and politicians in Naples that Campi is about to erupt. Okay?"

"I'm tracking."

"We'll need a contingency plan, and we'll have very little time to implement it."

Jeff nodded. "An entirely likely scenario."

"To warn the people of the city and of south-eastern Europe, I started working on a desperate idea last night."

"I saw you were writing something."

"In that scenario, why not use the social media?"

"It would put us at immediate risk, but those channels would certainly drive the story."

"What I'm proposing is that I begin writing your story. It will chronicle your mission to alert the European people of the danger from the imminent Campi Flegrei eruption. In summarized form, of course."

"And you'll post it on the social media…"

"Yes. In addition, we can send a more detailed version to all leading newspapers. Here, look at this." She showed him a list of news organizations: *La Stampa, La Republica, Il Matino, L'Expresso, Il Giornale, Kijk, Wetenschap Techneik, Bild der Wissenschaft, Die Zeit, BBC World News, BBC Radio, New York Times, Associated Press, Napoli Notte, Il Tempo, La Torre, Osservatore Romano, Scienza e Vita, The European, Metropolis, Newsweek, L'Unita.*

"You got these online?"

She shook her head. "Not from here. I already had them. I'd hoped to publish what I learned in my summer studies—the list was part of my now-defunct project."

"You're a good writer," said Jeff. "You would have provided them with some interesting copy."

"Thanks." She tapped the list. "I can capture people's interest, get them to pay attention. I'll seed in the backstory with your unusual volcanic family history, and with Michael. And I'll tell of the assassins, too."

Jeff frowned. "If we tell all, we'll probably be putting ourselves in even more danger. But it may be the only way."

"If we decide to use this, we'll release a summary of the story over several days. If we keep moving, they may not catch us. We'll hold it until we're desperate. What do you say?"

Jeff thought about it. Newspapers relied on reporters and syndicated columnists for this type of story. The media experts would have to investigate it all for themselves and there wasn't much time. Using social media would avoid this. "Sounds like it will probably work."

"I can weave it all together so that it will attract a reader following each day," she added. "We can have a countdown to day zero. By then, hopefully, everyone is out of the city."

"Okay. How can I help?"

"Allow me to interview you about your life and the past week for the back-story. Be my proofreader and give me the time to write."

"You got it. My life is an open book… but it has really become *our* story."

"Then I'll make it our story."

"That will expose you even more to the Mafia."

She smiled. "We've already decided we're a geological team of two. Hopefully we can add a few team members along the way. The Mafia has my number already and we're going to need some heavy-hitters on our side."

"You know the danger." He shrugged. "What will we call the story? Something catchy."

"Well, you've referred to a volcano's magma chamber as a monster's lair. How about Lair of a Monster?"

Jeff grinned. "That's catchy."

While they were cleaning up the breakfast dishes, the bell on the dryer chimed. "I've washed the new clothing," Anita said, heading for the laundry. "I figured we'd better assume our new identities." Below deck, she pulled the trousers, tunics and shawls into a laundry basket and brought them to the table. "So," she said. "Our ship is now the Mastveer, registered in Florida?"

"Yup. Anyone checking the yacht registry will find our yacht is owned by an American named Jeet Singh Atwal with family roots in India."

"And you found this out…"

"On the internet, in Nice; I wanted a yacht owned by American Sikhs, so I just checked the registry."

"Sometimes you scare me." Anita thought a moment. "But how did you know he was a Sikh?"

"He's probably Sikh," said Jeff. "I did a search with his name to make sure I wasn't borrowing trouble, and came across a website that explained some of the naming patterns—Singh for men, Kaur for women. Apparently I'm a lion and you're a princess."

"Seriously?" Naming patterns, customs, dress codes—how was she going to keep all of this straight?

"Chin up, Anjeela. It's time to transform ourselves. Then we'll haul anchor and sail to Pozzuoli to check out our submarine monster."

"So who am I supposed to be? Your girlfriend?"

"We are ourselves," said Jeff. "We're colleagues—third year university students studying the volcanic area here for the summer. We're studying at U of W, Seattle. We've borrowed the yacht for a few days from my father, Jeet Singh Atwal senior, who is from Orlando and is currently touring Europe. Hell no, you don't have to pose as my girlfriend."

"Hell no?" Anita tried to sound indignant. "Hell no to me being your girlfriend? Well you're not such a damned fine catch yourself!"

Jeff laughed. "That's what all the auburn-haired ones tell me."

They went below deck. Anita was surprised to find that her outfit fit perfectly; the loose trousers narrowed gracefully just above the ankle and the attractive tunic seemed made for her. She chose a pale blue sash, then piled her hair under the net that came with the wig and settled the wig itself into place. Then she arranged the shawl to partly mask her face. On the street, except for her green eyes, no one would have given her a second glance.

Jeff knocked on the door.

"C'mon in," she said.

"You look great. What do you think?"

"I'm amazed," she said. "It fits perfectly. I like it."

Jeff was similarly dressed, except his sash was black. He held up a white cloth. "Help me with this," he asked, handing her two corners of the thin fabric. He stepped back and stretched it out so they held it by the four corners. The strip was about three feet wide and fifteen feet long. They folded it in half lengthwise six times so that it was a few inches wide and still fifteen feet long. Then he rolled it up. "I hope I can remember how to do this."

Anita watched his reflection while he placed one end across his chest, gripped the cloth with his teeth and began carefully unrolling it, winding it around his head, first slanted slightly to the left. Three times he went around, partly covering his ear and half of his forehead, slightly higher with each turn. Then he wound it three times slanted slightly to the right to cover the other ear, creating a flat inverted V at the center of his forehead. He tucked the back end up and under, against his head, and then tucked in the front the same way.

"That's how Milan taught me," he said, turning to model his new look. "What do you think?"

Anita studied him critically. "Very neat. Overall, your beard should be longer but… it's good except for the blue eyes." The wig was enough to get used to; she wasn't looking forward to trying the contact lenses.

"Dark glasses should do for now," said Jeff. "What do you think about our skin?"

"We're both already pretty tanned," she said. "The

pale fabric makes us look even darker. I think it'll pass without darkening. And that's good, because makeup rubbing off on the fabric will cause us grief."

"Good point." Jeff turned to the mirror and shook his head quickly back and forth, up and down. "Seems secure enough. Okay, then; let's sail in and anchor off the coast of Pozzuoli. Then I'll figure out a way to begin our work."

With Anita at the helm, Jeff went back to reading his mother's notes. In them, she had listed some of her colleagues, people she had worked closely with. There were several in the Mediterranean area, but Dr. Giovanni DaRosa, a scientist from the National Institute of Geophysics and Geology in Naples caught his eye. The name seemed familiar. Had he been a friend? Jeff researched Giovanni and found the scientist currently worked at the Naples volcano monitoring station. It was a great place to start. He didn't want to use the cell phone, and the internet was out of the question. He'd have to find out when the scientist was on duty and visit the center in person.

They approached the city from the south. Jeff took the helm so Anita could get her story online; hopefully, their internet access would go unnoticed, a needle in a haystack. Anchored near Santa Lucia, the coastal center of Naples, were dozens of yachts and mid-sized vessels. Just to the east, two enormous cruise ships lay berthed at the city center wharves. Of the forty million tourists visiting Italy each year, most came through Naples on dozens of cruise ships—floating cities of wealthy tourists flush with cash and eager to party. Naples invited them with open arms, and had built the new cruise ship terminal walking distance from the city center. Any disruption, even a short one, to the Naples tourist industry would be unthinkable.

Slowing the yacht to a crawl, Jeff watched for a good place to anchor. Surveying the shoreline, he recognized the village of Pozzuoli. He had been here before!

Dropping anchor, he drew a long breath. His mother's teachings about the Mediterranean were flooding back—a story she told of continents in violent collision... the earth's mantle folded, thrust upward into the Himalayas like so much modeling clay... seas pulled down into the earth's crust by subduction over millions of years... seawater trapped below the surface... and the forming of a common magma chamber for both Vesuvius and Campi Flegrei. Deep below, an enormous plume of superheated rock would meet that sea water and explode upward...

"Memories," Jeff murmured, walking to the rail. "Right here, directly beneath us, Anita! Moving upward through the earth's mantle at this very moment, a huge plume of superheated rock is rising from the earth's core, coming straight at us."

Anita stood beside him.

"My mother and I were here when I was a boy," he said, staring at the water as if tempting the giant. He turned to her. "Notice anything on the social media yet?"

"There's a buzz, alright. It's starting. I'm trying not to spend any time online. I did look at VolcanoWatch while I was on." She pulled a piece of notepaper from her pocket. "The most recent comment was *the inner Caldera contains several explosive eruptive vents that are slowly becoming active.* That was posted just half an hour ago. So what's next?"

"We need to hurry this," said Jeff. "First I'm going to take a carefully crafted letter I've written to the deputy mayor of Naples, then—"

"Why not the mayor?"

"According to the radio news, he's away on vacation."

"Ah."

"Then I'll find my way to the volcano monitoring station and find out when one of my mother's colleagues, Giovanni DaRosa, is working. I'm hoping to meet him and build his trust. I'll take the motor launch and my bicycle."

"I'll stay and write," she said, looking out at the bay. "Any chance it may erupt early?"

"Who knows? But today is Saturday June 20th; counting today, we should have nine days left."

"Let's hope so."

Jeff loaded a bicycle into the yacht's speedboat and took off to the wharf at Pozzuoli. As he shut down and coasted in, the stench of sulfur burned his throat. Hopping on the bike, he rode the short distance from the wharf along the Via Diocleziano into the city. Cycling to the main post office, he paid for a post office box and stopped in a nearby office supply shop to buy a city map and a new laptop computer, which he loaded with Michael's data and stashed in his backpack. Then, riding to the monitoring station and wheeling the bike into the building, he stopped at the security desk.

The guard sized him up. *"Posso domanderLe?"*

"Atwal a vede Dr. Giovanni DaRosa."

The man frowned and looked Jeff over. "Giovanni DaRosa, eh? You from the Punjab?"

"America." While the security guard called up to the monitoring center, Jeff stood on one foot and then the other.

"Atwal di vede Giovanni," the guard said into the phone. He waited, looking at Jeff quizzically. *"Sì,"* he said finally, pointing to the elevators. He held up three fingers. "Floor three. Go left."

Jeff leaned the bicycle against a wall, then took the elevator to the third floor.

As the elevator door opened into the hallway, a small wiry man with long bushy grey hair, a ruddy complexion and dark friendly eyes peered at him over half-spectacles. Giovanni frowned. *"Buondì. Parli italiano?"*

"No, io non capisco molto bene l'italiano."

"Then you will suffer my poor English, Mr. Atwal. How can I help you?"

"Please forgive my intrusion." Jeff lowered his voice. "I'm trying to visit you without anyone knowing. I am Jeff Kingston. I was born Heph Kristinson. My mother was Kristin Stefsdotir."

Giovanni looked skeptical, but he led Jeff to a small office and waved him to a chair.

"Kristin Stefsdotir. Yes, she had a son. He died."

"That was what they said," Jeff nodded. "They were trying to protect me."

"Protect you?" Giovanni narrowed his eyes. "There were rumors. How old are you?"

"I'm twenty-one."

Giovanni lowered his glasses and peered thoughtfully at Jeff. "Kristin had a very clever little boy. He knew many things about volcanoes. Tell me, what is the basic principle of the inertial seismometer?"

Jeff thought a moment. "They have a weight that can move within a motionless frame. A system inside holds it firm to the frame. If there is no motion it does not move. If there is motion it moves within the frame."

Giovanni nodded. "And this weight is what?"

Jeff guessed. "Internal mass?"

Giovanni threw his arms up. "Is that all? Explain."

Jeff winged it. "In some seismometers the mass is held almost motionless to the frame. I think it's by an electronic feedback that sets up a magnetic or electrostatic circuit. I believe the motion of the mass... relative to the stationary frame is measured by the force expended. As I recall, it's measured by the voltage needed to generate this force."

"Close enough." Giovanni smiled. "And now, name three other types of these instruments."

"Well..." Think Jeff! Think! "Teleseismometers, accelerographs and... geophones."

Giovanni extended his hand. "Okay. I will talk with you, Mr. Kristinson. You recall all of this from when you were young?"

"I'm not sure. I only recently found out who I really am. But I have always been fascinated by volcanoes, and now I am an earth sciences student."

Giovanni shook his grizzled head. "Why do you wear this disguise?"

"I'll explain, but first we must talk about the volcano."

"And I suppose you are now going to tell me that Campi Flegrei is about to erupt. I am hearing these—how do you say—rumors."

Jeff nodded and used a phrase he had practiced for the meeting. *"Lo so che è vero."*

"Ah, so you know it is true. And you know this how?"

Jeff started from the beginning with Michael's hack and how his findings had dovetailed with Jeff's mother's predictions. By the time he had finished, he could read the Italian's concern.

"Much has happened since your mother's work was so tragically ended," said Giovanni. "The volcano science has developed a great deal in the past ten years." He seemed to be trying to make up his mind about something, and finally looked at his watch. "Come! I am on duty in the control room for the next four hours. We will have our standard tour for visiting students of earth sciences. I will show you our modern computerized volcano monitoring system. This is what we depend upon."

He led Jeff down the corridor. "This is the Naples control room. National Institute of Geophysics and Volcanology." They entered a large, well lit room. Giovanni nodded to a technician who passed him a clipboard, said a few words in Italian, and left.

Completely surrounding them on all four walls were built-in desks. On each were computer keyboards and banks of large LCD screens, dozens of them. Down the center of the room, more banks of computers and screens reminded him of mission control at Cape Canaveral. All were live and transmitting data.

"Sixty screens display a feed from fixed sensors around Campi Flegrei, Vesuvius and beyond," Giovanni explained. "In *Golfo di Pozzuoli* we have tidal gauges to measure sea-bed levels. And here are the quake monitors."

"Impressive," Jeff said, slightly overwhelmed.

"These instruments monitor our densely populated

Neapolitan volcanic area, about one-and-one-half millions of peoples," Giovanni continued. "However, in the danger zone, over three millions of peoples must be evacuated. This is why monitoring eruption precursors is become very important. We take this very seriously. If Vesuvius is to erupt it will affect over three millions of people, you see?" He hesitated. "Of course if Campi Flegrei is to erupt it can kill a hundred times this number. Eventually maybe hundreds of millions of peoples."

He showed Jeff along a bank of LCD screens monitoring thirty kinematic stations across a vast area, which was shown on a map of the Naples and surrounding district. Other screens showed GPS and leveling networks across the same area. Realizing he'd never remember it all, Jeff started using his cell phone to record Giovanni's explanation. Giovanni pointed out another bank of colorful screens which showed three-dimensional satellite views of Campi Flegrei and Vesuvius, computer color-coded to show any change as it occurred.

"These monitor horizontal and vertical displacements in the deformation area," Giovanni said. "If a serious seismic event seems imminent, the scientists in our Com Unit will then advise the Italian Ministry of the Interior." He spread his arms. "And they will then issue orders to evacuate the city and twenty-six surrounding towns."

"What is the Com Unit?"

"It is Communications Unit," Giovanni explained. "All data is fed through VolcanoWatch to the Com Unit. They interpret this data."

Giovanni worked his way through the various recording instruments, patiently answering Jeff's questions. Then he leaned against one of the desks. "This caldera, it is 35,000 years old," he said. "It rose in 1538 creating the cinder cone of Monte Nuovo. The magmatic chamber of Campi Flegrei is at depth about 8.2 kilometers, or as you Americans would say it is at about 5 miles. There have been two main uplifts of this ground. One from 1969 to 1972, another in

1982 to 1984. Both had moderate seismic activity. These did not result in eruption, but they were the cause of much damage to buildings."

He pointed to another screen. "We are again in a period of land uplift at the center of our caldera. We are again now having numerous earthquake swarms, and we see moderate evidence of eruptive activity."

"My mother believed Campi Flegrei and Vesuvius shared a common magmatic chamber," said Jeff. "What do your people think?"

Giovanni frowned. "I would disagree, as would many scientists. We would also disagree with your assessment of an imminent eruption."

Jeff shook his head, frustrated. "Why?"

Giovanni shrugged his shoulders. "You see?" He swept his arm in a big arc around the room, encompassing the myriad of instruments. "These changes, no matter how small, are interpreted by scientists and shared with many colleagues around the world. We watch this very closely."

"But look!" Jeff produced his computer and brought up the VolcanoWatch summary. "Look at this data! This shows Campi Flegrei is about to erupt!"

Giovanni peered at the screen. Then he pointed. "Look at this query search address," he said. He got a pad, read the address from Jeff's computer, jotted down the address, then went to one of the computers in the center and fed the address in. "I have seen this before," he said, pointing to the screen. "Yes. This is rogue VolcanoWatch address. You are victim of a hoax. It is a fraudulent address."

"But..."

"Ah, I am sorry, young man. As you Americans would say—you have been had."

"You are certain this is not the correct VolcanoWatch address? Can you give me the right one?"

Giovanni laughed. "I am absolutely certain. And no, I am not permitted to provide the VolcanoWatch address. It is for scientific use only—classified—protected."

Jeff thought a moment. "Is your family in Naples now?"

"My wife is here. My children are now on vacation in America. That is where you should be. Go home, young Kristinson!"

"So you are worried. You sent your children away."

The Italian made a dour face. "You are—how do you say?—paranoid my friend. This site you are monitoring is bogus. We have had this happen before. Someone is getting their satisfaction deceiving people. They know that even with intensive monitoring, Campi Flegrei is unpredictable. They prey on people and generate fear. This is sad."

"But you are concerned."

Giovanni looked at Jeff for a long moment before glancing upward. "Always I am concerned. That is why we are here."

Jeff changed the subject. "So where is the readout for the Campi Flegrei drill probe? The one where international scientists were drilling into the—"

"This is not operational yet," said Giovanni. "No data."

Jeff frowned. During their tour he noticed an active LCD readout for *"Vesuvius Firmo Leggo Sistema."* If Campi Flegrei erupted from beneath the sea, it could wipe out all life in Europe. So why was an international team of scientists poking at it with drilling rods? Could this be another deep probe? Not into the caldera, but into Mount Vesuvius?

He walked back to the screen and memorized the address on its corner. He turned to Giovanni. "I must have misunderstood," he said. "What is this readout?"

"Do not be concerned about this," Giovanni said, putting an arm around his shoulder and moving him toward the door. "Vesuvius is a baby compared to Campi Flegrei. To evacuate people who live under Vesuvius we have a 48-hour evacuation plan. We will in this time get the citizens of all towns to safety from a 12-mile radius. An eruption of Vesuvius could be very serious but nothing compared to Campi Flegrei. And now, young man, I have shown you everything." He inclined his head up and to the left, and Jeff realized there was a security camera mounted in the corner of the room.

"Thank you for the tour," he said. "Most interesting. Can you walk me to the elevators?"

"Sì."

Once out in the hallway, Jeff lowered his voice and asked, "Do you interact much with a volcanology professor at the university named Dr. Antonio Camponolo?"

Giovanni frowned. "You know him how?"

"He was with my mother when she died."

"Ah." Giovanni nodded walking toward the elevator. "You must go now. They must not find you here."

"So, you do work with Dr. Camponolo?"

"Sì."

Obviously out of options, Jeff gave up being cautious. "If you tell Camponolo I was here, they will kill me."

"They?"

"The C-2. Evidently my mother and I witnessed the murder of her colleague, Dr. Reginald Pyper, twelve years ago. That murder may have had something to do with the VolcanoWatch system they implemented here and their ongoing contract to monitor the volcanoes. Or it may have been to prevent them from implementing their prediction protocol. I'm not sure. I believe Dr. Camponolo and a volcanologist named Dr. Hilda Marsh murdered my mother on Nyiragongo a month later, for the same reason. Now, Camponolo has assassins after me."

Giovanni stopped mid-stride and stared at Jeff. "Go now. Leave the building. I will erase the surveillance tapes in our control room, in the elevator and on main entry cameras. You were never here. If Camponolo finds out you have been here, we are both dead! It is lucky for us, he is gone away to London until Thursday."

He took Jeff's arm and led him toward the elevator. "You should not have come here, young Kristinson. You have never met me. I did not show you anything!"

"I was never here." Jeff pressed a card into Giovanni's hand. On it he had written Jeet Singh Atwal, Naples Main P.O. Box 3865. "I will check daily," he said. "We must warn the city."

Giovanni pressed the button to summon the elevator. "*Arrivederci.*"

"Thank you." Jeff took Giovanni's offered hand. "Nine or ten days."

Giovanni nodded. As the elevator doors closed, Jeff could see him already scurrying down the hallway.

The good news was, Camponolo was out of the country for a few days and likely thought he and Anita were at the bottom of the Ligurian Sea. But Giovanni's evasiveness about the Vesuvius monitor was prompting Jeff to dig deeper. He was almost certain that the LCD screen that he'd asked about was a drilling probe down into the Mount Vesuvius core, similar to the one into Campi Flegrei. He got out the city map and looked for the address that he'd seen on the corner of that screen. It was in an industrial area, on the eastern outskirts of the city.

He cycled there, determined to check it out.

It was a large low building sitting back from the street, surrounded by a high wire fence with an open gate. A large fork lift and several trucks sat in its yard and a sign on the gate read *Vietato l'ingresso.*

No admittance, probably.

The logos on the trucks belonged to the Ministry of the Interior. The main door to the building was open, so he left the bike near the gate and walked into the yard, skirting past the trucks to peek inside the cavernous warehouse. Long rows of florescent lights hung from a high ceiling, illuminating row upon row of narrow waist-high industrial tables that stretched from one end of the building to the other. Jeff stepped in for a closer look. On each of the long tables were eight rows of long narrow boxes. In each box was a long cylindrical reddish colored rock core. The cores were about six inches in diameter and were marked at about three foot intervals with tags. One of the tags read *Campi Flegrei–1002*; the next read *Campi Flegrei–1003*.

So! These were not Vesuvius cores; they were from the Campi Flegrei supervolcano. Drilling cores, likely drilled diagonally, down thousands of feet into the submarine supervolcano. He was alarmed to note that they were igneous pumice and igneous basalt, both very porous rock that would be capable of trapping water, making any future eruption highly explosive.

He walked along the tables, checking the type of rock in the rest of the cores. It appeared to be rock strata starting at the surface and reaching down 1,560 meters; 4,700 feet. He walked back to the first cores taken near the surface and followed them downward again.

Just beyond, another group of low tables contained similar looking cores. He examined them. These *were* from Vesuvius. At the deep end they contained cooled lava, most likely from the plug currently blocking the volcano's magma chamber.

Turning to leave, Jeff saw a man in coveralls watching him and making a phone call.

Jeff walked back out to the street.

"Un momento!"

He wasted no time hopping on the bike and taking off. Once out of sight, he cycled hard for three blocks, then ducked into an alley. Soon a police car whizzed past, headed toward the storage building, its siren silent.

He pedaled casually toward the city center. The mayor of Naples had temporarily halted the Campi drilling in reaction to a public outcry from citizens who seemed to think the drilling itself could actually cause an eruption. That could account for the secrecy around the Vesuvius drilling project; perhaps the Italian public was not aware that their government had drilled into both volcanoes.

He rode down Via Ammiraglio Fernando to the Maschio Angioino, passed the beautiful landmark castle that dominated the Naples waterfront, and turned right into the Piazza del Municipio. The mayor's offices were next to the historic Baron's Hall. With no other way to make an appointment, he took the risk of speaking with the secretary at the reception desk, where he left his carefully crafted letter asking for a meeting with the deputy mayor. To confirm the appointment, he'd provided the number of his throw-away cell.

Back on the bike he turned and pedaled toward Pozzuoli. It was time to get back to the *Cannelle* and talk with Anita. It had been an interesting day.

... hydrothermal fluids appear to be lubricating existing faults in basement rock...

Chapter 13

Saturday, June 20, late afternoon
At the Pozzuoli wharf, Jeff loaded his bike into the boat and headed back to the camouflaged *Cannelle,* anchored in the bay. The danger from Camponolo may have temporarily decreased but there was little doubt in his mind the danger from the caldera was still escalating.

Anita was waiting for him on the quarter deck. "How did it go?"

"Not bad," he said climbing aboard and taking off the turban. "Giovanni didn't buy it, although he is worried. He claims our VolcanoWatch data feed is a hoax. He says we have a fraudulent address and are victims of a deception."

"Well, that's a relief."

"I'm not so sure," he said. "I think maybe *they* have the fraudulent address. And there's a connection between Camponolo and Giovanni. However I think we can trust Giovanni." He followed her to the salon. "But I have other news."

"I've got coffee on, and made sandwiches. Tell me."

As they ate, he brought her up to date, including the worrying discovery of highly soft, porous rock beneath the bay and the good news that Camponolo was on his way to London.

"You still think the monster is going to erupt?"

"Yes."

"So you don't believe Giovanni…"

"I don't think Giovanni's job is to evaluate the data, just to monitor the equipment that produces it and passes it on to others who evaluate it. He called them the Com, or Communications, Unit." Jeff reached for another sandwich. "I don't think we should be swayed by this. Even if the VolcanoWatch data is a hoax, something's going on."

"Okay. I'd better warn my family," Anita said. "But my dad was to be away in Germany until tomorrow. I'll wait until he gets back. I want you to come with me."

"Then we'll go tomorrow morning." Jeff rose and reached for his computer. "I'll feed this new Campi data into Michael's processes. While Giovanni was giving me the tour, I managed to film the read-outs on the Campi monitors. I'll enter that in, along with the porous rock strata samples, and we'll see if his statistical brain would have predicted anything different."

"You can do that?"

"I think so. Want to help?"

"Better you work this carefully by yourself." As she left him to his task, she looked back. "If Camponolo is out of the country, can we suspend the Sikh identities for the next few days? I'd like to put on some shorts."

He nodded absently, already engrossed in Michael's complicated process. Three hours passed as he worked and reworked the prediction mathematics. When it came to statistics, Jeff was not at his best. In the end however, he was convinced. Looking up, he saw Anita sitting, waiting. A half smile crossed her face. "Well?"

"No change. The new data along with figuring in porous rock strata… which will be saturated with sea water to a depth of perhaps a mile… when liquid magma hits the…"

She frowned. "… it will cause a cataclysmic explosive eruption lifting the entire mile-deep layer of saturated rock, the sea floor and sea above it, miles into the air…"

He nodded slowly. "You have the picture."

Her eyes were unwavering. "When?"

He held her gaze for a long moment. "With all the current data from the monitors, just as Michael predicted, it will erupt on June 29th or in the early hours of the 30th. We have nine days, maybe ten."

"So in your mind, you've confirmed it."

"Yes. To be precise, using EVPC and Michael's Campi protocol, if I've fed the new data in correctly and adjusted the overburden resistance accurately, it will explode exactly nine days and three hours from now." He held up his cell phone. "The monitoring center instruments are also monitoring a site of a magma pipe in the Lake Fusaro area. One screen read *E minus 4*. Michael was on to this, too. His notes predict a pre-main-eruption event there along with earthquakes about four days before the main eruption."

"What did he base the time difference on?"

"I'm not sure, but it agreed with the note I saw on the screen. I didn't realize what it meant until I was back here, so I didn't get to ask Giovanni about it."

She thought a moment. "If there is a pre-eruption event, perhaps it will help us gain credibility to have the city and surrounding area evacuated before the big one."

"Good thinking."

Jeff stood and moved away from the chair. "I want you to come and look at this. Go over everything I've done, and see if you can confirm it."

Anita stared at the mass of calculations. Her first impulse was to tell Jeff that she would just accept his conclusion. But this was an opportunity to help confirm the validity of their mission. Besides, she really wanted to understand Michael's certainty about the eruption.

"Sure," she said, huddling with him over his computer. "Walk me through it."

As Jeff explained Michael's process, she checked Jeff's

math and process logic. Time slipped by as they studied and queried each other, heads together. While she focused on the task, she was also acutely aware of being so close to Jeff, how energizing it was to work with him so intensely.

"Well?" Jeff asked as they wrapped it up, and was surprised to realize she was disappointed that they were finished. "What is your conclusion?"

"I agree," she said. "This baby is going to erupt, and there could be a pre-eruption event. We're not far from Lake Fusaro. Tomorrow, let's go check for any indicators at the surface."

"You got it. How are you doing with the publicity plan?"

"Look at this," Anita said. "In addition to getting our story in the social media, I finished our introductory print media release. See what you think."

She had done a brief and powerful introduction to two American geology students' mission to warn the city. The article ended with the countdown; its headline screamed EIGHT DAYS TO THE ERUPTION. As he read it she watched his expression, confident that she had done well. She had another initiative to tell him about and had left the best for last, interested to see how he would react.

"Impressive," he said as he finished. "You've used our real names. That's important."

"Yes. It will alert Camponolo, though."

He nodded. "Can't be helped."

"Now I have a surprise for you. There's a syndicated columnist on her way to see us. Her name is Catrina Rossi. She does a daily column in more than twenty of the mainstream European media. She's coming to visit us on the yacht this evening."

"So she's from Naples? How did you…"

"I looked her up on the internet. In the summer, she lives on a sailboat, Firefly, anchored over there," Anita pointed. "I found it with the field glasses and took the dingy over. We had coffee. Turns out she's been worried about the Campi Flegrei for years."

"And she'll print our story?"

"I'll give her this write-up as background. She wants to interview you. She'll do the rest."

"That's fantastic!" Jeff squeezed her arm. "We've got so little time to whip up public awareness. To find a columnist who'll work with us without direct electronic communications? You're amazing!"

Anita was pleased that he'd seen the benefits of inviting Catrina Rossi to help them. "If Camponolo is away, maybe we could use our phones."

"Don't even think about it! We are already at risk. I had to leave my cell number at the deputy mayor's office to get confirmation of a meeting."

She nodded, smiling inwardly. They were at risk alright. They were sitting atop an active, ready-to-erupt supervolcano, and he was worried about a cell phone call?

Catrina Rossi, a graying woman of sixty, had the lined face of a smoker, piercing brown eyes and the lithe build of a person charged with energy. Jade earrings and a narrow orange headband drew attention to her long braided hair, and her red leather briefcase clashed with her bright green jacket and orange sash.

As she climbed aboard, she extended a hand flashing with numerous gold rings. "So you are Hephaestus, the young god of fire and the underworld!"

"Better known as Jeff." He took her hand. "I see someone had been telling you about my mother's passion for Greek mythology."

"Yes, yes!" She turned to Anita. "Hello dear."

"Good evening! Welcome aboard!"

Catrina turned back to Jeff. "You have a champion who is very persuasive. It is not often I have been so captivated by a short visit."

"I'm privileged to have Anita on my team."

"Mm, yes and you have others on your team too!"

Jeff grinned, thinking about his father, and the others along the way. "I do," he said. "And we are hoping you'll join us. I only have one request. For security, no photos."

"Okay. And I have already joined you, young man. Shall we find a place to work?"

They sat quietly in the salon for a few minutes, allowing Catrina time to skim through Anita's document. Finally she looked up and said, "Well written! Of course my column will be from this interview and in my own words."

"Are you concerned for your own safety if you take this on?" Jeff asked.

Catrina grinned. "You mean the C-2? I am too high-profile. There would be hell to pay if they did me in. My publicity brings in millions of tourists every year. Besides, if you are wrong about this it will only affect tourism for a couple of weeks. And of course if you are right, it will no longer matter."

Jeff decided to push a bit further. "Do you know Dr. Antonio Camponolo?"

"Everyone in Naples knows who he is. He is not a man to be messed with. I would suggest you steer clear of that one. Now, let us get back to your mission."

Jeff nodded slowly. "Do the publications you write for cover the downwind countries like Yugoslavia, Albania, Greece and Turkey?"

"All but Turkey and beyond. I will look after that."

"How about cruise ships?"

"They will be covered too."

"And all of the city of Naples and surrounding area?"

"Of course," Catrina said. "But you know what the city hall response is going to be. They will scoff at us." She deepened her voice. "'This city has been here for three thousand years, and you are trying to convince us it will cease to exist thirty days from now? Hogwash,' they will say! It is highly unlikely the city administration will encourage the residents to listen to us. Now, let us get on with the interview. Tell me about the eruption."

"It's in nine days," Jeff said. "And we now believe it will be preceded by a lesser event in perhaps four days." He showed her the Campi Flegrei VolcanoWatch for the previous week. "See the newest summary? *Hydrothermal fluids appear to be lubricating existing faults in basement rock.* Every summary comment we see ramps up the reality of there being an eruption."

Catrina spent two hours with them. When she left, there was little that either she or Anita didn't know about him and Michael. He had opened up their lives far beyond what was comfortable.

But it was necessary, he told himself. How else was he to instill the trust needed for people to believe his warning?

After Catrina Rossi left, he looked approvingly at Anita. "You found a gem there."

"She's a gem alright. You can also thank your father."

Jeff's eyebrows shot up. "My father?"

"She called him while I was on her sailboat to confirm what I was telling her about you. He added to what I was telling her. She knew his reputation. She once did a story on him when his people uncovered the Saudi oil shortfall. Your father's opinion went a long way toward bringing her on side. Also, she told him about us trying to make an appointment with the deputy mayor. Your father said he would call and pave the way for us. Turns out Curtis Munson is known and respected in the Mediterranean."

Jeff nodded slowly. *A comrade in arms...* "Cool," he grinned. "So you talked to Munson?"

"On Catrina's phone. I did. He sounds very supportive, but he's worried about us. He was concerned I understood the danger we are in. I told him you tried unsuccessfully to scare me off, but that I'm sticking to you and he's not to worry about us." Anita put a hand on his arm. "We should check your bandage, and then I'm going to turn in."

"It's okay," said Jeff. "I retied it."

"Good night, then." She went below.

Jeff leaned on the rail. Along the bay, wharves and the

hulks of ships were silhouetted black against the shoreline; the water reflected an angry sunset.

The air smelled slightly of sulfur.

Sunday, June 21, morning
As Jeff prepared breakfast, Anita appeared dressed in jeans and a short sleeved shirt. "Tell me how your family is doing in Italy," he said.

"So far, it's Dad's favorite posting with the UN Special Forces," said Anita, pouring herself a coffee. "I think Mom likes Italy, too; of course it's always easy for her to find work, and that helps with the transitions."

"Good thing she's a nurse and not something less in demand," he said. "How about your sisters—they're what, twelve or so? Must be tough for them to adapt to school in a foreign language."

Anita shook her head. "Not an issue. They go to school with the base's other American kids. Cheryl's thirteen and Janet's eleven. Naturally they're both pains in the butt."

"From a guy who spent his life as an only child, let me tell you how lucky you are to have siblings."

She cocked her head sideways, thoughtful. "I suppose."

After breakfast they loaded lunch, the new laptop and the bikes into the motor launch. Pulling away from the yacht, they turned west.

Later, after securing the launch to the wharf at Castel dell'Ovo, they cycled across the causeway to the mainland and headed west on the Via Riviera di Chiaia. The city's European architecture bore testament to the Italian culture handed down through the ages. Buildings of light colored stone reflected the dazzling sunlight, and along the busy sidewalks people in brightly colored attire waved and smiled at them as they passed. In the park, children played soccer and young people pushed strollers and wheelchairs with older people, oblivious to a pending disaster.

Further on, they passed through crowds of happy

shoppers and waited for a religious procession to wind its way across an intersection. They turned onto the Via Milliscola. Through the open spaces between buildings, areas of lush rolling countryside were visible. "this is a wonderful place," said Anita. "The people are so warm and friendly... and the children... they're all so happy..."

"It's a beautiful city," agreed Jeff, "filled with good folk who deserve a future. So tell me, when we get through this, are you still planning to transfer to the University of Pennsylvania and take up oceanography?"

She nodded.

They were turning onto the Via Cuma, not far from Lake Fusaro. "We have a good oceanography program at the U of W too," said Jeff.

Anita looked at him. "Yes, I've researched it. They're both good programs. I'm torn. I'd like to be closer to my grandmother."

"When do you have to decide?"

"Pretty soon," she said. "If we make it out of here."

"We will," he insisted.

They cycled to the eastern shore of Lake Fusaro. The lake wasn't large, and no houses dotted its bleak shoreline. Its surface was calm, although bubbles rose to the surface near its center. As the wind shifted, a strong smell of sulfur drifted their way.

"The maps show a large fissure dead center in the middle of the lake," said Jeff. "See the bubbles?"

"Yeah," said Anita. "Spooky."

They parked the bikes, had lunch and planned their next move. They wanted to find Lake Avernus, a nearby volcanic crater lake. Jeff had seen it on the wall map at the Naples monitoring center. It was on the northern volcanic boundary of the Campi Flegrei caldera and may offer a further clue to what was happening below.

On a satellite map, they found the lake located two and a half miles from the center of the Campi Flegrei caldera, northwest of Pozzuoli.

It was mid-afternoon when they found the lake. Roughly circular and about a mile wide, it nestled in a depression left by the volcanic crater. Steam and bubbles rose from its surface, carrying a strong odor of sulfur. The surrounding area was devoid of growth.

Anita whistled. "This must be the northern edge of the caldera. My God, Campi is massive! When it blows, it'll blast a crater six miles across! It'll take out the whole of Southern Italy… and, downwind, most of Europe and Central Asia! Jeff, this really is a doomsday volcano!"

"Yeah," Jeff said. "And we are not more than seven miles from your folks at Gricignano di Aversa."

"Too close! Good thing Dad's back tomorrow. We've got to get them out of there."

... using 24-hour span data from satellite orbits the GPS antenna are measuring 24 millimeters horizontally, and 13 centimeters vertically...

CHAPTER 14

Monday, June 22, early morning
Jeff and Anita took the motor launch to the wharf at Pozzuoli and cycled north across the city and toward Gricignano di Aversa. The military residences compound was near the NATO base. A guard greeted them with, "Hello, Miss Arneil, your father has been asking about you. Your pass card, please."

"So Dad is back."

"He is. And you, sir, are?"

"Jeff Kingston. U.S. Coast Guard."

"I'll need your military I.D."

Jeff provided his U.S Coast Guard identification.

"Proceed," the guard said, returning their documents.

"We live in one of those apartment complexes." Anita pointed to a neat cluster of buildings on their left. As they cycled toward them, Jeff had a flashback. A brick apartment building... a Russian flag, a huge mountain... a man he called Dom Dom... a nice man...

"Jeff?" She was looking back over her shoulder at him.

He realized he'd slowed to a crawl. "Sorry," he said, catching up. "I haven't seen your folks for a while. Anything new I should know about?"

"Don't pet the Siamese cat until he gets to know you."

"What's his name?"

"Ripper, after Jack-the-Ripper. His claws are talons. He's been known to attack people he doesn't like.'"

"Thanks for that. I'm feeling better already."

At the third complex, Anita led the way in, punching the security codes and leading him to the elevator and then up to a top floor apartment. At the door, she used her key card to let them in. "It's me!"

"Anita!" Sandra Arneil was an attractive, dark haired woman with Anita's beautiful green eyes. "So you're home. We've been worried. And the girls tell me you're on Facebook—Hello Jeff. My, what is it with the dyed hair? And the black beard…" Jeff extended a hand. Her grip was firm and she held it for a moment. "Have you been keeping my Anita safe?"

"We've been keeping each other safe, Mrs. Arneil."

"Mmm. Come, Keith is in the kitchen."

Jeff flashed Anita a look. In the kitchen, a tall athletic man with a brush-cut and piercing blue eyes stood at the counter, shirt sleeves rolled up, punching a large ball of dough. "So you're both okay," he said. "We were concerned when we couldn't reach you."

"Hi, Dad. No need to worry." Anita gave her father a hug. "You remember Jeff Kingston."

"Hello, Colonel. It's been a while."

Keith Arneil showed his doughy hands. "I'd shake but…" He grinned. "Last time I saw you, you were in a Coast Guard uniform. You still in?"

"Yes, sir. I've been a member for three years now."

"You are in our home; cut the 'sir.' Anita told us you are trying to warn the city."

"Yes. Trying to figure out *how* to warn a city, Colonel."

The colonel raised his eyebrows. "You really believe an eruption is imminent? The experts don't agree."

Jeff nodded. "But there's going to be hell-to-pay a week from now. There will be earthquakes and a serious pre-eruption just south of here. Unless something changes, one week from now the entire city is going to be blown off the map by Campi Flegrei."

Colonel Arneil frowned, brushed the flour off his arms and studied Jeff. "Anita tells us you are a bright, competent young budding geologist. On a scale of one to ten, how certain are you of this?'

Jeff didn't hesitate. "Nine point nine."

The cat came over and rubbed against his leg.

"The hell you say!" The colonel began washing his hands. He turned to Anita. "Where do you come in on this scale?"

"I'm a nine, Dad. You and Mom need to hear this."

"Okay. Put the coffee on, Sandy. We better hear their story." He turned back to Jeff. "First, give me the short version."

"We have seven or eight days until the major eruption. But two or three days from now a large earthquake and pre-main-eruption event will occur under Lake Fusaro. It will send a shock wave across the city and spew magma and hot, choking ash thousands of feet in the air. Within minutes it will be difficult, if not impossible, to breathe. All the way from the eastern coast and down through the city center—"

"Whoa, back up. I want to know how you came to this conclusion."

"There is no short version for that, Colonel. I'd need to start from the beginning."

"Our base is in touch with the National Volcano Institute daily. There is no evidence for any of this."

"It will start with earth—" Jeff paused, listening. "Hold on," he said. "There's one coming now..."

The rumble came from the south. Quiet at first, it soon sounded like a freight train was bearing down on them. Suddenly, their building seemed struck by the train. The ground shook. Dishes rattled their way out of the cabinets and crashed to the floor.

"The girls!" cried Sandra. Anita and her mother ran from the room.

When the shaking stopped, Jeff looked at Colonel Arneil. "That was early," he said. "There will be more."

The colonel was silent for a long moment. "That was the largest one we've felt here. I do want to hear the rest of what you have to say. But first, come with me. I want to check for damage on the base."

As the colonel led Jeff down to his Humvee, he asked, "What happened in Saint Tropez? French police report a car you rented was found near a shooting."

"We were followed from the airport," said Jeff. "We thought we'd lost them, but they caught up. When they ran us off the road, we were lucky there was enough cover."

"Did you kill any of them? Did…" Arneil swallowed and thrust out his chin. "Did Anita?"

"No sir," said Jeff. "I would have, if I'd had to. They weren't the brightest bunch, and we were lucky we weren't caught in their crossfire. One of them, a guy called Vizzini, had trashed my room back in Seattle. I called the last number on his cell phone. Dr. Antonio Camponolo."

"Camponolo. That's bad news. Sandy told someone at work that Anita would be meeting with him, and she got an earful." The colonel shook his head. "The French police told me the three dead men they found near your rental car all had bad reputations. Their ballistics reports match what you've told me. I haven't yet told Anita's mother any of this, but she should know." He climbed into the Humvee and motioned Jeff in. "Were you armed? Did you fire your weapon?"

"I was not armed, Colonel. I picked up one of their rifles but never fired it."

"I hope you wiped it."

"Yes, sir, and I left it where I found it."

"How did they find you?"

"They were watching for Anita at the airport. We really thought we'd shaken them."

"So why?"

"Why are they after us? They want to shut us up."

Arneil pulled to a stop at the base gate. "What the hell have you gotten my daughter into?"

Jeff squared his shoulders. "Look, Colonel, within a couple of days Lake Fusaro on the eastern edge of the Campi Flegrei caldera will explode. It's a precursor of what's to come."

Arneil held up his hand. "That can wait."

At the base the Colonel arranged a temporary pass for Jeff, checked out his helicopters, and then drove to a long, low building at the far end of the base, surrounded by high mounds of earth and a tall chain link fence, its top festooned with barbed wire. "Wait here," said Arneil, climbing from the Humvee. After talking to a guard, he removed the padlock and entered the building.

A few moments later he emerged, re-locking the gate.

"Ammo okay?" Jeff asked.

"Yeah. We've been storing some of the United Nation's unused high explosives, left over from the destruction of Middle East poison gas supplies. We'll be glad to get it out of here. It's like Centex but far more powerful. Disintegrates everything when it blows. Scary stuff, difficult to handle. Only good thing about it is it needs an electrical charge to set it off."

"You got a lot of it?"

"Enough to flatten the base and the whole goddamned city with it. Should have been out of here by now, but you know how bureaucracy works."

"Can high heat set it off?"

"Not unless it's over 900 degrees. It's intended to be used with an electrical charge."

Anita's family was still in the kitchen, cleaning up broken china that had fallen from their cupboards during the quake. Cheryl and Janet stared at him.

"Everything alright?" asked Sandra, tying the trash bag.

The colonel nodded, putting his arm around his wife's

shoulder. "The rest of this can wait," he said. "Time for us to listen."

"We've got coffee," said Anita. "I think we have enough mugs left for everyone. Sit, Jeff."

Jeff settled at the table, and the cat jumped into his lap.

"You've made a pal," Sandy observed. "He usually dislikes strangers."

"I like animals…"

Arneil took the seat directly across from Jeff. "Pull up a chair, girls," he said. "You should hear this too."

Cheryl continued to stare at Jeff. "You look funny. You have a black beard but your eyebrows are, like, blonde."

"Thanks," Jeff grinned. "I'll have to fix that."

Half an hour later, the girls buzzed with questions and ideas. How could they help to warn the city? Where would they go to escape an eruption? What would they do with their cat? Would the planes fly? How big would the first eruption be?

The colonel remained quiet. Finally he turned to Jeff. "What do you plan to do now?"

"The mayor is away, so I'm trying to set up a meeting with the deputy mayor."

Arneil raised his eyebrows.

Jeff shook his head. "I haven't convinced you, have I?"

"No. You may think you can predict these things, but there are dozens of scientists watching this area, monitoring it, measuring every little bit of movement. They send the data to the Volcano Prediction Center in Orlando, where scientists from around the world monitor and interpret the data. They would have seen something." He shrugged. "The earthquake timing was a coincidence. We often get them around here."

"What if someone is intercepting the data," said Anita, "manipulating it for their own purposes?"

Her father turned to her. "Why wouldn't someone else have noticed? You think you kids are the only ones paying any attention? If you're wrong, you've panicked a whole lot of people for absolutely no reason. You're creating a situation where they'll be less likely to listen to the authorities when there really is a reason to evacuate."

Jeff looked at the floor. What the colonel said was true. "Colonel Arneil, when there is an earthquake, does the disaster response plan include using your helicopters to help rescue people in the city?"

"Of course. Why?"

"An earthquake could be the prelude to the eruption. If you are in the air when the eruption occurs, it will explode ash and pyroclastic material over a vast area in the matter of seconds. A helicopter would be a death trap."

The colonel looked at Jeff with a pained expression.

Jeff ran a hand over his face. "Of course, you already know that. I just…" Damn it, this was hopeless. Jeff stood up and pushed his chair toward the table. "Well, thanks for listening."

Cheryl tugged his sleeve. "But I have more questions…"

Her father shook his head. "That's enough, girls!"

Anita stood. "Mom, you must take the girls and leave Italy." She moved to Jeff's side. "I have to go with Jeff."

The colonel was about to respond when Jeff held up his hand. "Wait! Can you give Anita and me a minute alone please?"

She followed him to the hallway.

"Anita, you have to stay with your family, convince your mother and sisters to leave here at once. It's their only hope. If you don't do this and they don't survive, you'll never forgive yourself."

She held his gaze for a moment. "You're right. I'll convince them. Then I'll rejoin you."

"Take your mother and sisters away. Perhaps back to the States."

"No. I'll convince them. I'll get them on a flight out of here. You have to go to the city council. You can't do this alone."

"Well, you may be right."

"I'll meet you at the wharf at... let's see... I'll be there by 10:00 p.m."

"I'll wait for you there." He turned and left.

Outside of the apartment complex, a military escort swung in beside him. At the NATO base, a convoy of trucks was returning from the city. Pedaling slowly past, Jeff thought about the long, low building surrounded by earthworks, wondering just how much explosive was stored inside.

Jeff stopped at city hall. A young woman stood at the counter. He was relieved to see several small signs in different languages, one of which read *Yes, we speak English*. "I'm Jeff Kingston. I asked for a meeting with the deputy mayor. I left a letter?"

"One moment please." She checked her computer. "I can confirm a meeting for you tomorrow at 3.00 p.m. in council chambers. The full city council is meeting. You will have ten minutes."

"Thank you. I will be there."

He grinned. The full council! He cycled to the main post office and checked his box. There was a note from Giovanni.

Mr. Kingston.

I have received an angry call from Dr. Camponolo. He found out you visited the control room. I do not know how. Camponolo returns from London tomorrow. June 23. Morning flight. I thought you should know of this. Giovanni.

Damn! Camponolo would be at the council meeting.

As he cycled toward Mount Vesuvius, his sense of foreboding grew. Preparing himself for the meeting with the deputy mayor, he had come to realize there was something else... something even more enormous than a Campi Flegrei eruption. His mother's studies of seismically active areas between the African and European plates in the Mediterranean subduction zone—what if his mother and her murdered colleague were predicting a cataclysmic event similar to the ones that occurred in 1750 and before? In those, huge earthquakes and tidal waves ninety feet high killed hundreds of thousands of people and decimated Mediterranean cities.

There had been numerous recent level 6 and 7 earthquakes in the Mediterranean. What if—?

That kind of prediction would surely cause economic devastation. Would Mediterranean business interests kill to prevent them from becoming public? Jeff stopped, got off the bike and gazed up at Vesuvius towering over the city, thinking.

When he arrived at Herculaneum's Ercolano Scavi station, it was nearly noon. He bought a sandwich and pushed his bicycle toward the taxi kiosks. Eating his sandwich, he read the Mount Vesuvius tourist brochure and listened to the taxi drivers talk among themselves. One of them, a tall young man, approached him. "You want to visit the volcano?"

Jeff nodded. "Your English is excellent," he said. "Know anything about the volcano?"

"I'll soon have a degree in earth science from McGill University in Canada." He smiled. "That's why they hired me to take tourists up the mountain."

"Great." Jeff had finished his sandwich, and he tucked the brochure into his backpack. "Can you get my bike up to the car park near the summit? I want to do some of the trails and get back down before dark."

"There's lots of trails up there." The driver looked at his bike. "Looks a bit light for them, though."

"It'll do fine." They loaded the bike onto the taxi's carrier rack and headed up the mountain.

... 4.1 earthquake and 3.8 aftershock on the cross-axis fault, running north and south and creating volcanic uncertainty...

CHAPTER 15

Monday, June 22, early afternoon
Jeff settled into the back seat of the taxi as the driver coaxed the vehicle up the steep, winding road toward the Vesuvius crater. "So tell me about the volcano," he said.

"It began on August 24, 79 AD. The day after the annual celebration they called *Volcanalia*, the festival for the Vulcan god of fire. A dense cloud of pumice and boiling ash shot from the central cone as if from a cannon and turned day into night. The city of Pompeii, just six miles below, was covered in pumice and several inches of ash within an hour."

"I was kind of hoping for the technical stuff, not the tourist—"

"We'll come to that. Herculaneum was closer than Pompeii but, being upwind, it was only covered with a light coat of ash. Then, about midnight, the central column in the volcano collapsed and a deluge of boiling hot gasses, rock and pumice flowed down over Herculaneum, covering it in 65 feet of volcanic rock and magma. It sealed the town in minutes."

Jeff nodded, groaning inwardly.

"The following morning, Pompeii and its inhabitants were buried under twelve feet of pumice and ash." The driver geared down to navigate a small trestle-like bridge. The road was growing steeper as they wound their way upward. He glanced at Jeff. "Some of the people buried in the city were turned to pumice and dug out for you tourists to see. Grotesque forms captured as they were, in their horrible moment of death. But as the tourists walk by each day, gawking at the sad forms, they say nothing until they come to the form of a small dog. Then, these same tourists who have nothing to say about the people who died such a horrible death, they stop and 'Oh' and Ah' about the poor little dog."

Bet that's not part of the usual spiel, thought Jeff. "You may be misreading them," he said, "The human forms may be far too sad and shocking to them, and the tourists may feel speechless as they walk by. Only when they see the dog do they feel free to comment."

"Perhaps." The driver sounded doubtful. He returned to his script. "Vesuvius eruptions occurred every hundred years until 1037. There was calm for six hundred years; then in 1631 a massive eruption destroyed the towns that had grown up around the volcano. Over the next six hundred years there were twenty-three eruptions, all smaller, the last in 1944 when Allied forces were attacking Italy."

Jeff frowned. "So the volcano may be about due for an eruption now."

"Most observers think that because there has been a major eruption every hundred years for centuries, and now there hasn't been a major eruption for six hundred years, it is building for a big one." He shrugged. "Who knows?"

Jeff nodded, looking down at the city below as the taxi climbed the switch-backs up the north side of the mountain. He sat up straighter. He had been on Vesuvius before, and looked down at the city from here.

Yes! He and his mother had been up here and looked down on the beautiful, vibrant city with centuries of human history on display. His mother had told him it would be her responsibility to make sure... He shuddered.

"The volcano has experienced eight major eruptions in the past 17,000 years," the driver continued. "The mountain is about sixty percent silica, meaning the volcano creates andesite lava, the most explosive and dangerous type."

"You must have studied this at McGill."

"Yup," the driver grinned. "The Campi Flegrei and the Mount Vesuvius calderas are both located on the Africa plate subduction zone." He glanced at Jeff. "You know anything about plate tectonics?"

Jeff nodded.

"It's part of the Campanian volcanic arc. It's a line of volcanoes that formed over a subduction zone. It's the convergence of the Eurasian and the African plates. This subduction zone stretches across Italy on an east-west axis, and has formed Mount Aetna, the Phlegraean Fields and Stromboli."

"By the Phlegraean Fields you mean Campi Flegrei."

"Yup. The lower part of the slab has torn and shattered apart. It has formed what is called a slab window. It makes the rocks chemically different from the other Campanian volcanoes."

"Have you heard anything about a scientific project to drill down into the volcano? Poke at it with drilling rods?"

"Nothing about that," said the driver, pulling into the car park. "Where'd you hear it?"

Jeff got out and stretched his legs. "Probably just speculation," he said, counting out the euros.

The area was buzzing with activity. A tour bus had just disgorged a noisy group of tourists. The driver helped him unload the bicycle, and they agreed on a time for pick-up. Jeff secured the bike to a post near several others, then joined the rest of the tourists for the 2,500-foot climb up to the crater rim.

Most of the boisterous group from the bus was ahead of him on the roped-off path, so he stepped aside to wait for the rest of them to pass. Below, in the car park, his taxi driver was engaged in an animated cell phone conversation, gesturing up to the ascending crowd and then nodding vigorously. Still waiting for the crowd to pass, Jeff watched with dismay as the driver went over to his bicycle and jabbed at the tire. What the hell? Jeff ducked around the last few stragglers from the bus, but the taxi driver was already in his cab, heading back down the mountain.

The climb to the crater could wait. He returned to the bicycle and crouched down, examining the tire.

"Flat?"

A trim older man in riding gear, maple leaf sewn onto the sleeve, was unlocking one of the bikes.

Jeff stood, nodding.

"Sorry, I don't speak Italian," said the man.

"I'm American," said Jeff.

"Canadian," the man grinned, nodding toward the tire. "Can it be repaired?"

"Looks like it," said Jeff, "but it never occurred to me to bring a repair kit."

The Canadian leaned over his saddlebag. "Here." He tossed Jeff a small kit. "They sell these all over the place. Better get a couple. Terrain here is pretty hard on tires."

"Thanks," said Jeff. "What do I owe you?"

"Just pay it forward," said the Canadian, waving over his shoulder as he pedaled away.

Jeff repaired the tire. Then he studied the sign that showed the trail locations, selecting one that looked promising; leading around the mountain, it appeared wide enough to accommodate a large vehicle.

Signs on the path, written in several languages, read *Stay on the trail. No straying off the path.* Changing gears, he bore down recklessly, speeding along the rough trail cut into the volcano's steep slope. Eventually he came to an intersection where a branch road switched-backed downward. The road signs warned *Chiuso. Vietato l'ingresso. Strada Private*, repeating it in English for good measure: *Closed. No Admittance. Private Road.*

A metal fence bisected the road; the sign on its locked

gate read *Stazione 16*. He smiled. Station 16 had been one of the headings on the Vesuvius LCD screen at the monitoring center.

Ahead, he could the hear voices of cyclists. He stashed the bicycle and his backpack behind some rocks and climbed the fence. As he jumped down on the other side, pain shot down his injured arm. Wincing, he ran down the road, around a bend and out of sight of the people on the bicycle trail.

Soon he was at a widened area at the end of the road that was fenced off around a large metal building. Signage on the door read *Osservatorio Vesuviano-INGV, Napoli.* Two dish antennas projected from the roof. On the down-slope, fine rubble from a drilling operation was clearly evident. He scrambled up and over the fence with a grin, ignoring his sore arm, certain of what was inside.

Then he groaned.

The big double doors of the building sported a large hasp with a padlock.

Now what.

"Maybe…" he reached out and gave the padlock a tug, suppressing a whoop of glee when it pulled open. Lifting it from the hasp, he opened the door and peered inside.

An eight-inch diameter pipe protruded at a slight angle from the concrete floor. From inside the pipe's cap, a cable ran to a bank of instruments. A gas powered electrical generator sat in the corner, bolted to the floor, its exhaust line leading outside. "Well now, Vesuvius," Jeff breathed, "they have been poking at you with a drill pipe, haven't they?"

He examined the instruments but could discern nothing. Above the pipe in the floor was a heavily-built steel frame holding a large motorized spool of half-inch cable, with a mechanical system to keep the cable constantly over the pipe. "They've been lowering instruments down into your depths, huh?"

The log book diagram showed the probe projected 1,200 meters down beside the cooled lava plug that blocked the magma chamber. Nothing was rising in that chamber; Vesuvius was clearly not about to erupt.

Jeff looked up, listening, and recognized the whine of an approaching motorcycle. It sounded like the machine had stopped on the main trail, at the outer fence and gate. He slipped outside, closed the door, hooked in the padlock and considered his escape. Was there enough time for him to climb the inner fence and hide behind those nearby boulders, or should he run behind the building?

A volley of shots and pinging metal rang out. What the hell? The rider must be blasting the lock off the outer gate. Jeff was almost over the inner fence when the motorcycle and its helmeted rider skidded around the corner.

Jumping to the ground, he ran headlong for the boulders. More shots—the rider was firing from the motorcycle. Heart pounding, diving behind the boulders, Jeff tried to catch his breath. Now the rider was on foot, still firing, keeping him pinned down. Jeff couldn't stay where he was; not enough cover. He dove down the mountainside toward some larger rocks.

"Perché tanta fretta?" The gunman laughed and fired another burst, sending a down a shower of rock chips. Jeff squirmed further down the slope and fell over a six foot bank, relieved to land on his feet. Above, he could hear his assailant. Pressing his back against the bank, he waited, under the slight overhang of sod and grass, watching.

All was quiet; then another short burst of gunfire. The assassin had dropped to one knee almost directly overhead, slightly to Jeff's right. He could see the man's left ankle. Reaching in one quick motion, he grabbed the ankle and heaved, throwing all his weight forward. Shots rang, spraying wildly as the man tumbled over Jeff's shoulder and swung crashing down, his head thunking against a rock.

Jeff scrambled downhill for the assault rifle. Keeping it trained on the prone gunman, he made his way cautiously back to where the man lay motionless. He bent down and checked for a pulse; it was strong and the man was breathing. Jeff aimed the rifle at the back of the man's right knee and fired. His leg jerked as the knee shattered, and Jeff spotted a bulge near the ankle. He bent to uncover a holster. Removing the Beretta, he tucked it into his own waistband, then used the man's sweatshirt to wipe his prints from the rifle before tossing it down the bank.

The outline of a wallet formed an outline in the man's pocket. Keeping the Beretta against his assailant's spine, Jeff fished out the wallet and checked its meager contents: a driver's license in the name of Luigi Marini, a few euros and little else. His front pocket held only a cell phone.

Jeff stashed the cell phone in his jacket and began climbing back up toward the trail, tucking the Beretta back into his waistband as he approached the motorcycle, a big Honda hybrid gas/electric super-sport touring bike, keys dangling from the ignition. He grinned.

The assassin's helmet lay on the ground nearby, and he strapped it on, fired up the motorcycle and headed back up to the main trail. Closing the gate, he hung the broken padlock on the hasp. Hurrying to where he had hidden his bicycle, he retrieved his backpack, stowed the cell phone and the Beretta, and made his way back to the car park.

Only a couple of cars remained, and the busses were gone. By the time he was heading down the main road, it was already dusk. Below, the city lights twinkled for miles, contrasting with the dark waters of the bay.

He crossed the short trestle bridge, then swung the big bike around and parked. Getting off, he climbed down the bank in the dim light and looked under it. Built of timbers, it spanned a steep ravine. "This'll do nicely," he muttered.

Crawling back up onto the road, he heard a car coming up the mountain. It had already rounded the bend and Jeff ducked down. Taxi, the same company that brought him up the mountain earlier. It slowed as it passed the parked motorcycle, then rumbled over the bridge on its way up the mountain.

The rest of the ride down the mountain was uneventful, and Jeff thought about the drill pipe. He needed specialized knowledge—an understanding of things only a military specialist or a terrorist would know. The information was probably on the internet but he'd need yet another laptop; even still, he'd probably be leaving a cyber-trail that led straight back to him.

Maybe use the assassin's phone! At a bicycle path, he pulled off the road and out of sight, then fished the phone out of his backpack. He skimmed the phone's archives; hundreds of entries, all in Italian. He found the internet and began a search, pulling up a few promising sites, squinting at them. He scanned a couple of them quickly and realized he'd have to look further when he had time.

Jeff jockeyed the Honda through the city and along the ocean dock to the Dream Line Cruise center kiosk. He glanced at his watch; Anita would be here in ten minutes, if she wasn't already. After maneuvering the bike past dozens of people, he recognized her tall figure, her long auburn hair blowing in the breeze. As he pulled near her she clutched her backpack and stepped back, wary.

He stopped and removed his helmet, and she flashed him a relieved smile. "Nice bike."

"Donated by our usual friendly welcoming committee. How did you make out?"

"Mom will take the girls to London tomorrow. She'll stay there until we see what happens."

"Great!"

"Dad relented a bit, although he's not convinced."

"Good for you! *Che donna!* Did I say that right?"

"What a woman?"

He grinned, digging in his jacket pocket. "There's another helmet in that saddle bag. Here's the spare key."

She found the helmet and adjusted the straps. "You sure you know how to ride this?"

"I'll be careful."

"Maybe you should let me."

"I suppose you're an expert at riding motorcycles, too." Jeff grinned. "That's good. Hang onto that key, then; you'll need it if anything happens to me."

They took the Via Ammiraglio Fernando westward until they found a corner café that was still open. He pulled into the alleyway behind the building and parked. While transferring the Berretta from the bike's saddlebag to his pocket, he drew a nod of approval from Anita.

"I took it from the guy who owned the bike." He grinned, following her inside where they found a table at the back near the rear exit.

"I did some shopping," she told him as they settled at their table. "Picked up some electronic gizmos to record your meeting with the deputy mayor."

"About that. We're meeting with the full council, not just the deputy mayor," said Jeff. "Gizmos, you say… so if our meeting is unsuccessful, you can mail a recording to the local press?"

"You got it."

"Good. When we leave here we'll go back to the yacht and get some rest. First thing tomorrow morning, we'll need to plan our strategy."

"Order me a latte," Anita said. "I'm going to find a washroom."

He pointed over her shoulder. "Down the hallway near the back door."

The waiter approached their table. *"Cosa ti piacerebbe?"*

"Tè con latte," Jeff said. Two men had entered the café and were scanning the occupants. *""Con dolci, biscotti?"*

The waiter nodded. *"Biscotti, sì, sì,"* and pointing at the empty chair, asked. *"Signora?"*

"Caffelatte." Below the tabletop, Jeff slid the Berretta from his pocket and slipped off the safety.

"Sì." The waiter disappeared into the kitchen.

One of the men locked eyes with Jeff, and he tilted his

head at his partner. They approached Jeff's table, reaching inside their jackets.

Jeff looked over the men's shoulders and hollered at the top of his lungs, "Anita, run!"

Startled, the men glanced back.

Jeff rose and leveled the Beretta at them. *"Fermata!* Stop!" They froze, their weapons half-drawn. Jeff held the Berretta on them with both arms extended, and began backing down the hallway toward the rear exit. One of the café patrons screamed. A waiter emerged from the kitchen, between Jeff and the men, and dropped his tray with a crash. Other patrons began to scream and duck.

"Anita!" No answer. The men raised their weapons as Jeff ducked through the rear door and into the alley.

To his relief, Anita was already on the motorcycle, revving the engine. He jumped on behind her, pulling on his helmet. "Go, go, go!"

They took off down the curving alley and were nearly out of sight by the time the gunmen resumed fire.

"My God, Jeff!"

"Keep going! Turn onto the freeway and head for the wharf. We'll hide the bike and take the Zodiac to the yacht." Still wound up from the confrontation, he was gripping Anita's shoulders tightly for balance. Now he loosened his grip and relaxed. She sat tall and strong on the bike; her lithe body molded to the machine.

"Who's after us?"

"Two rough-looking characters," he said.

"How did they—"

"Probably my fault." Reaching into his jacket pocket, Jeff pulled out the assassin's cell phone and removed its battery, hoping there was no homing device on the motorcycle. "Good thing you were in the can."

It was just after midnight by the time they secured the Zodiac on the aft deck of the *Cannelle*. "Hopefully we'll be safe on board the yacht tonight," said Jeff. "I'll take the first watch. We'll move further out in the morning."

"Okay. I'm beat. Wake me in three hours, or when you figure you can no longer stay awake."

After watching her disappear down the stairway to the staterooms, he went to the galley and made a batch of strong coffee. He was over-tired and staying awake would be difficult. With a mug of the strong stuff, he went out on deck and relaxed in a chair. It had been a hell of a day.

He should have made Anita stay with her parents. They needed to be ready for anything. Some kind of grab-and-go kit. Maybe he should leave half the money on board, keep half with him. He'd find a safe place to stow it in the morning. He repacked his small leather backpack, thinking Anita should have some cash on her at all times, too.

He checked VolcanoWatch, skimming the summary quickly. *The 4.1 earthquake and 3.8 aftershock occurred on the cross-axis fault, running north and south, its epicenter at 40.8450° N, 14.2583° E creating volcanic uncertainty for both the Campi Flegrei and Vesuvius volcanoes.*

Tight lipped, Jeff returned to planning for the next day's meeting with the city and went over the key points of his message. His eyes were heavy now; almost falling asleep, he got up and refilled the coffee mug.

Settling down again, he closed his eyes.

Tuesday, June 23, early morning
"Good morning."

Snapped awake, Jeff sat up in the chair. It was daylight. "Guess I fell asleep. What time is it?" She was standing over him.

"It's 6:10 a.m. I've made breakfast."

Getting to his feet, he rubbed his eyes and looked around. "What day is it?"

"It's Tuesday, June 23rd."

"Shit! Six days, maybe seven!" They were still at anchor on the edge of dozens of small yachts moored closer inland to the east. Everything was quiet.

He felt lousy. "I'll be back up in a minute."

"You can take a shower later. I've got everything ready."

He used the toilet, then splashed water on his face. When he joined her in the salon, she was placing a bowl of fresh fruit on the table along with heated cinnamon rolls. She eyed him carefully. "There's fresh orange juice in the pitcher. You'll feel better after you've eaten."

"I hope so."

"When was the last time you ate?"

He sat and downed a glass of juice. "I don't remember." He scooped some fruit into a bowl and started on a cinnamon roll. "I keep thinking about the eruption and its aftermath. It will be like another Permian extinction. All living things, doomed."

"Then we have to stop it from erupting."

"Yeah." His laugh was without humor. "I've been working on that. It's really not—"

"I was joking," said Anita. "Of course that's impossible."

"How it the publicity going?" he asked.

"It's going great! There's a buzz in the city. People are beginning to pay attention. Catrina's stuff is out, and it's already causing quite a stir."

"Good. Anita, where's your passport?"

"Right here." She slid it from the hip pocket of her shorts. "Figured we'd need it in a hurry. Why?"

"Just thinking." He nudged the backpack with his foot. "I should make sure you have some cash with you all the time. If we'd gotten separated yesterday…"

She bent and picked up the pack. "Heavy. What's in it?"

"Take a look."

She unzipped it and peered inside. "Money, your passport, the gun—"

"Just a sec," said Jeff. He got up and went out on deck. He could hear a whup-whup-whup coming from the east. After the disaster at Montecristo, helicopters made him nervous. He watched it for a few moments as it hovered over one yacht, then another, positioning itself so it could read each craft's name before going on to the next. "Holy shit! Anita! It's them!"

"Oh my God!"

"He's seen us!" He grabbed the pack, then Anita's hand. "Out the door! Over the side! Go, go!"

They burst out across the passageway and dove headlong over the rail in unison, hitting the water as the yacht exploded in an enormous fireball.

The water was cool. Anita was beside him. He grabbed her arm, keeping her under as debris began shooting past them into the depths. Finally, they surfaced, gasping for air, only to dive under again as wreckage rained down and fire spread out from the burning hulk.

Above, the surface seemed on fire as they swam away under the water. Surfacing again and again to gasp for air, he struggled to get the strap of his pack over his shoulder. They kept swimming toward the shore.

Finally they stopped swimming and looked back. What was left of the *Cannelle* was a smoking hulk, blasted away and burning almost down to the water line. Through the smoke came the chopper.

"He'll see us!" They began swimming again, underwater toward the distant docks, popping up for air as the helicopter, searching for them, circled overhead. When they reached the wharf they clung to the posts, watching and waiting, utterly exhausted.

"That was close, Jeff."

"Yeah." He looked at her and tried to grin. "Well at least now I don't need a shower."

She shook her head. "Thank God you grabbed me and pulled me with you overboard."

"We saw what they did to that other yacht—"

They worked their way under the wharf to the shore. "Your dad's boat... was it insured?"

Jeff shrugged his shoulders. "After the eruption, it won't matter."

Anita looked at him, her jaw set. "What's next?"

"Maybe we should rethink this," said Jeff as his feet found bottom. "It's going to get us both killed..."

"Whoa there! You going to let these bastards win?"

Reading the defiance in her eyes, he grinned. They worked their way along the shore, feigning casual interest as the emergency vehicles arrived, grateful that in all the excitement no one seemed to notice their dripping clothes. Jeff checked the contents of his go-kit; a little water had gotten in through the zipper, but not much. When one of the beach shops opened, he went in and bought them each a pair of canvas shoes, a T-shirt, swimming trunks and a beach towel. Anita's hair finally stopped dripping.

"Let's see if our transportation is still here."

The motorcycle was where they had hidden it, safe and sound. Jeff did a daylight inspection for tracking devices; again, he found nothing. They got their helmets out of the saddlebags and rode up to the freeway.

It was going to be a beautiful morning, and it was exhilarating to be alive.

… Geodetic benchmarks show rapidly increasing deformation at the center of the caldera…

CHAPTER 16

Tuesday, June 23, early afternoon
Several hours after the *Cannelle* sunk in the harbor, Jeff and Anita were back in downtown Naples on the motorcycle. With only a day or two until the pre-eruption event and six days to the main eruption, Jeff was feeling anxious.

Turning north into the Piazza del Municipio they were surrounded by happy crowd of tourists, street vendors and the warm-hearted people of Naples. Music from street musicians and a colorful group of dancers added to the air of revelry.

"Keep a sharp eye out," Jeff warned.

"There is such a sense of history here," Anita commented as they parked the bike. "It's difficult to understand how these wonderful Italian people can have such evil people in their midst."

"All societies have them, but I know what you mean," Jeff agreed. "Here, among these open and friendly people, they don't seem to fit at all."

Studying the tourist map to find the right building, they were directed to Baron's Hall where the deputy mayor was in a meeting of the city council. They climbed the long flight of stairs from the Castel Nuovo courtyard to Baron's Hall.

Only fifteen minutes until their appointment.

"Nervous?" Anita asked.

"No. Just worried. I wish we had Frida Hansen or Moe Labouef here to support us."

At the entrance to the hall they were stopped by two security police. *"Anita Arneil e Jeff Kingston per vedere Erico Benvenuti,"* Anita explained smoothly.

They produced their identification, and one of the guards pointed to the right, down a high-ceilinged hallway.

"Maybe we should wait," suggested Anita. "We're a bit early." They stood by high windows overlooking the courtyard, partly obscured from the hallway by large potted ferns, watching people come and go. Three people were walking toward Baron's Hall, and Jeff sucked in his breath. One was the volcano control center scientist, Giovanni DaRosa; with him were Dr. Hilda Marsh and a tall, good looking man, who smoothed his wavy black hair with the palm of his hand as the trio walked by.

"That tall guy is Dr. Antonio Camponolo," Anita said.

"Oh, shit!"

The group stopped to talk to a young woman who sat at a desk in front of the main council room doors, then went on through. "What did she say?" Jeff asked.

"She said to go right in and join the council; they are currently taking a break."

"This is going to be a bloody disaster, Anita! The other guy was Giovanni from the Naples monitoring station."

They approached the reception desk. "I'm Jeff Kingston." He smiled. "And this is my colleague Anita Arneil. We are here to see the deputy mayor and council."

"You can wait in the reception area," she replied in perfect English. "The regular city council meeting has ended. Your meeting starts at 3:00 p.m."

"Thank you. Perhaps you could—" Glancing back toward Anita, he stopped abruptly. "Look! They're all here!" He pointed to the tall sandy-haired man with the close-cut beard who was coming down the hallway with three others—Moe Labouef, Dr. Frida Hansen and a tall elderly man who looked vaguely familiar.

"Hello, Jeff." Munson gave him a hug. "We've brought your friends for support. And you must be Anita." He beamed, grasping her hand.

"Hello, Dr. Munson," she said.

"Everyone calls me Munson."

Moe Labouef shook hands with Jeff and Anita. *"Ça va?"* he grinned.

"We are very glad you're here, Moe."

The tall, elderly man stepped forward.

"Dom!" Jeff exclaimed. "Dom-Dom! It's you isn't it?"

The elderly Russian grasped Jeff's hand and grinned with pleasure. "Hello, Jeff!"

"A few days ago Dr. Hansen got me thinking about you. You were once like a grandpa to me!"

Dr. Frida Hansen grinned, offering her hand, which Jeff took in both of his.

"Thank you for coming! This is Anita Arneil. Anita this is Dr. Frida Hansen and Dr. Dmitry…" He hesitated, trying to recall his Dmitry's last name. "Dmitry Ivanov. Both are world renowned volcanologists!"

As Anita stepped forward to exchange hellos, Munson pulled Jeff aside, concerned. "How are you holding up? You look…"

Jeff hesitated. "Sometimes real life becomes so bizarre, it feels like fiction."

Munson nodded. "Brief me," he said. "I hope we can help."

"I'm glad you could come, Dad, but if any of you testify, I'm very concerned for your safety. The two volcanologists who engineered Kristin's death, Hilda Marsh and Antonio Camponolo, are going to be in that meeting today. We've been pursued by assassins since Nice—"

"That's why I didn't even try to give you a heads-up we were coming. I couldn't risk the phone call. Don't worry about our security. Your friends know that being here on your behalf puts them at risk of being jailed. It seems likely that some in the city administration are involved in keeping the public in the dark. We've agreed to leave here and fly out immediately after the meeting."

Jeff looked into Munson's piercing blue eyes. He had only known his dad for a few days, yet it seemed like a lifetime. "I'm lucky to have you as a father! But I've got more bad news. Dad, I'm sorry—they sunk the *Cannelle* this morning. Blew it out of the water. Damned near killed both Anita and me. We were on board just before they struck."

Frowning, Munson stroked his beard. "My God, Jeff, what have you two gotten yourselves into? We haven't got much time before the meeting starts. The deputy mayor is unfriendly. Let's decide how we are going to do this."

The door to the council chamber opened. A man poked his head out. *"Venga per questa strada,"* he said. "This way."

"We'll have to wing it, Dad. Let's go in."

As they entered the cavernous Baron's Hall, Jeff halted in amazement and stared upward. Similar to the Pantheon in Rome, the oculus ceiling dominated the huge chamber. Its heavy masonry arches stretched up from the tops of towering pillars to meet high above at a tiny skylight at the center of the room. The drab, unadorned walls hinted of long-since-removed tapestries that may have once provided a softer ambiance to the now bleak surroundings.

At the center of the great hall, reminiscent of the circular furniture arrangement of the United Nations, curved desks formed a large circle. The desktops bristled with electronics, microphones and computers, all of which looked totally out of place in the ancient chamber. A clerk, bustling through a narrow break in the circle of desks, delivered documents to several seated people on the far side. Some of them wore earphones, and some were studying their computer screens.

Near the center of the group, one of the silver name plates read *Erico Benvenuti: Vice Sindaco, Napoli*. Behind it, the deputy mayor sat reading a document. He didn't look up as they entered. Several city council members were gathered around Camponolo and Marsh, chatting and laughing. Giovanni was seated separately from the others.

Their guide explained the translation ear pieces and microphones and motioned them to be seated. Behind the city council, three translation booths were vacant and two were occupied with the lights on. One read *Itaniano-Inglese* the other *Inglese-Italiano*.

As the group continued to chat with Camponolo, Jeff whispered to Anita. "What are those councilors talking to Camponolo and Hilda Marsh about?"

"Apparently they're thanking Camponolo for inviting them to a party he hosted at his villa."

"Holy crap!" So they were all pals. "Okay, Anita, you sit on one side of me. Frida, you sit on the other, and seat Dad and Dmitry beside you." As Jeff settled into his chair, the group broke up and Dr. Hilda Marsh and Dr. Antonio Camponolo took seats around to their left.

"Still nervous?" Anita whispered.

"Yes." He adjusted the translation head-set. "Giovanni looks worried."

"He does." Anita squeezed his arm. "Be your articulate self. Let it flow!"

The deputy mayor finally looked up. Glaring at them, he scowled as he spoke. The translator's voice came through the earphones in a monotone. "This is a special session. Take your seats."

After everyone was seated, he said to Jeff, "So you've brought a delegation, have you? You have created quite a sensation in the last two days. All of Italy's television and radio stations are talking about you two. It appears Catrina Rossi started this with an exclusive on your crazy predictions." He leaned back and folded his arms behind his head and looked down his nose at them. "Twenty minutes. No longer."

Jeff made a quick judgment. Twenty minutes, not ten.

That was a bonus. He wouldn't speak of the Armageddon-like disaster facing the Mediterranean when Campi erupted. There wasn't time and it was too complicated. Nor would he mention that it was originally Michael's prediction. That would be distracting. Or VolcanoWatch. They would argue it, and he had no defense to their argument.

He would focus on the city.

Placing his wristwatch face-up on the desk, he turned on his microphone. "Mr. Deputy Mayor and Councilors," he began, "thank you for making time today. My mother was Dr. Kristin Stefsdotir, an Icelandic volcanologist whose research was in predicting volcanic eruptions. She taught me many things about volcanoes before she died. The scientists with me have travelled from around the world to support my prediction that the Campi Flegrei supervolcano is about to undergo a violent eruption six or seven days from now. The city will be destroyed."

A burst of laughter began with Camponolo and riffled around the circle. Giovanni looked uncomfortable. Jeff paused. "Can you afford to be wrong about this?"

Nodding toward Giovanni, he said, "I have already explained in detail what is about to happen to your Dr. DaRosa here. I have with me, among others, volcanologists Dr. Dmitry Ivanov from Russia; Dr. Frida Hansen from Iceland; and Maurice Labouef, a volcano guide from the Congo, to add weight to this. Please listen carefully, for within two days there will be a forerunner earthquake and a small eruption of the Campi Flegrei supervolcano that will inundate the downtown area. It will be followed four or five days later, on or about June 29th, with a massive eruption that will destroy the entire city and possibly much of the eastern Mediterranean." He paused for a moment, appraising the skepticism in the faces around the circle, but remained confident of his opening.

Dr. Camponolo jumped in. "We have the best volcanic monitoring systems in world. There will be plenty of warning if we ever—"

"I have given him twenty minutes," the deputy mayor interrupted in a bored tone. "Let him speak."

"To your point about a warning, Dr. Camponolo. In 2002 the Nyiragongo volcano erupted suddenly. Because of an early warning, 400,000 people were successfully evacuated from the city Goma below. Only 147 died, and untold numbers were saved.

"As you all know, below us is a much bigger monster. Within the next couple of days, it will hiccup. This will be but a warning of a cataclysmic eruption that will follow on about June 29th.

"How do I know this? All active volcanoes have a muffled ultra-low frequency sound which signals that magma is present. Although it is well below the range of the normal human ear it is a growl in the range of about 0.5 to 7 hertz. This sound, scientists believe, is magma creating bubbles in the rock of the earth's crust and converting it into a sponge-like stone."

He described his mother's findings. "Interestingly, Dr. Camponolo and Dr. Marsh—" he waved a hand toward them "—once worked with my mother." He turned to look at them. "In fact, they were with her when she died." Dr. Camponolo smirked; Marsh refused to meet his eyes. He turned back to the deputy mayor.

"I have applied her formula to the current Campi Flegrei data, which I observed on a recent visit to your data center. The results of these calculations are clear. You have less than two days to evacuate the southern part of the city and surrounding oceans for the pre-eruption event. You must do it now or many will die. The rest of the city and surrounding down-wind populations as far away as Greece must be evacuated within six days." Jeff looked at his watch. "I believe I have about nine minutes left. I will call on my colleagues." He turned to them. "You each have three minutes to convince these city leaders they can save hundreds of thousands of people if they act now."

Dmitry Ivanov rose and introduced himself. "The

Kamchatka volcanic belt is a museum of active volcanoes. Ten years ago, this young man's mother and I worked to perfect the reading of volcanoes. We correctly predicted the eruptions of two of the Kliuchevskoi volcanic group. We then successfully predicted the Vskovsky eruption in November that year. I lost track of Jeff after his mother died, but I can attest to his knowledge of this subject at the time. He is working from his mother's journals. I would suggest you not ignore his prediction."

Dmitry sat down abruptly and Frida Hansen rose and introduced herself. "As a colleague of Dr. Kristin Stefsdotir, I was aware of her son's unusual understanding of volcanoes from the time he was a young boy." She provided examples, and finished with, "I can assure you, this presentation is not a hoax; it is a reality."

As Frida Hansen sat down Moe Labouef rose, but before he could speak, Camponolo intervened. "Their time is up—"

"Let them finish," the deputy mayor said tiredly. "You took some of their time."

"I was with Dr. Stefsdotir when she died. So were Dr. Camponolo and Dr. Marsh. I heard Jeff warn of the Nyiragongo eruption. Nyiragongo erupted the next day. Best that you all listen!" He sat.

"That's about it," Jeff said. "On June 29th Campi Flegrei will experience a mega eruption that will shut down all transportation in the northern hemisphere and likely threaten the climate of the entire planet. *Lo so che è vero.* I know it is true."

"Now I believe that your time is up," Deputy Mayor Benvenuti interrupted through the translator. "Do the councilors have questions?" He glanced around. "Hearing none, I will say this. I agreed to hear you because of all the adverse publicity. What you are doing is most destructive. You must stop frightening the public. As for the city: we are responsible, not you. I ask that you and your delegation leave now. I also ask that Dr. Camponolo and Dr. Hilda Marsh along with Dr. Giovanni DaRosa remain for a few minutes so we can discuss your presentation. I understand that your delegation has booked rooms at the Hotel Miramare. Kindly return there and wait for our response to your presentation. We will call you within the hour."

Anita rose from her chair. "Mister Deputy Mayor, allow us to stay to hear the discussion," she objected. "It is only fair. Surely you don't want us to tell the Italian press that you are meeting in secret. This involves every resident of the city."

Benvenuti turned red. "And who are you?"

"I'm Anita Arneil, the team's media communications specialist."

Benvenuti covered his microphone. *"Ah, molto giovanile Americano ragazza,"* he chortled, and Camponolo laughed. He uncovered the mike. "We have no time for you. Go."

"Perhaps to you I may be a very young American girl, *Sindaco,*" Anita responded, "but I was not too young to transmit a live video and every word that has been said here to a local television station so it can be aired shortly." She held up an electronic device. "This has been recording, filming and transmitting this meeting."

"You cannot do that!"

"No one instructed us not to film the meeting. It has already been streamed live to a local TV station."

Benvenuti's mouth opened, closed, and opened again. *"Non Mi piace molto!"*

Camponolo stood. "Let them film this. It will do no harm." His words seemed less condescending in the translator's monotone.

"What?" The deputy mayor seemed uncertain, but he shrugged his shoulders. "If this is televised, I suppose the citizens should hear both sides."

"Exactly." Camponolo threw up his arms. "The young man's rambling statement was outrageous, an amateurish intrusion into highly specialized science. This man is an immature activist with a concealed agenda that could cost the Mediterranean billions."

Benvenuti pursed his lips. "What do you mean?"

"Our volcano monitoring expertise is second to none. It shows no sign of a pending eruption. None of the scientists around the world who get the data believe it is going to erupt." He turned to Giovanni. "Isn't that right?"

Giovanni leaned forward. "There is nothing to—"

"There! You see?" Camponolo smiled. "It is a publicity stunt. All of us around this table understand monitoring these volcanoes is a precise science, and that it is of critical importance. Commerce in the Mediterranean depends on it. We simply cannot allow alarmists like young Kingston here to incite panic among our citizens and visitors."

One of the councilors stroked his chin. "So you are suggesting?"

"International tourism is a highly competitive business," Camponolo continued via the translator. "Other areas of the globe would be pleased to entertain the hundred million visitors who come to the Mediterranean each year. An eruption panic would draw millions of them away from us for months, perhaps years. No doubt this young man is on their payroll. He is likely being paid to start a panic."

"A hundred million?" Benvenuti sounded skeptical.

"Last year there were one hundred and seven million visitors to Mediterranean. Can you imagine the wealth they leave among us?"

Another councilor spoke up. "So you believe this is a conspiracy to siphon our visitors to other regions."

"Yes! Yes! Of course it is." Camponolo smiled. "We must not be fooled by these tactics. These old retired scientists who just spoke to us are almost certainly also on the payrolls of our competitors."

"Thank you, Dr. Camponolo," the mayor cut in. "Dr. Giovanni DaRosa, do you have confidence in your instruments? Are there any signs, any indication of a Campi Flegrei eruption?"

"Well, your worship, I am a technician, not an expert in detecting all the elements needed to predict if it will erupt.

Others do that. But there was the earthquake this week and there have been several small undersea earthquake swarms, some minor bradyseism and some episodes of ground lift on the edges of the caldera. However there is nothing I see to indicate an imminent eruption. The magma overpressure is largely unchanged although it is increasing. Mr. Mayor, I would add that this volcanic area is active. It is not possible to guarantee that there will not be an event. Our science, while state-of-the-art, is not perfect."

"We understand," the mayor said.

"I would suggest you place the city on high alert over the next week to be on the safe side," Giovanni continued. "The young man seems to have an unusual—"

Camponolo snorted. "For the love of God," intoned the translator. "Hilda Marsh and I have known him since he was nine years old. There is nothing unusual about the… rotten little… mutt except for his ability to rabble-rouse."

The deputy mayor frowned. "No need for offensive language, Dr. Camponolo. Giovanni recommends the city should be on high alert." He turned to Hilda. "Dr. Marsh, you know Mr. Kingston? What do you think of him?"

She shook her head vehemently and pointed a finger at Jeff. "He is a trouble-maker. He should be jailed until you decide what to do with him. Look at the panic he has been stirring up. He should not be left free to roam your city."

Camponolo nodded. "Police should hold all of them for a week, until these dates they have predicted are past. Then let them free. Everyone will laugh at them."

The deputy mayor raised his eyebrows and cast a glance around to all of his councilors. A few shook their heads.

Frowning, Benvenuti turned to Jeff. "Your group will leave the chamber and wait at your hotel. We will call you within the hour."

As Jeff rose from his seat, he glared at Camponolo and turned to the mayor. "I am not an activist representing a rival tourist industry. The only people I represent are your citizens who, unless you evacuate them, will die in your city next week!"

"Enough!" Benvenuti commanded. "Out!"

Leaving the council chambers quickly, Munson spoke to Jeff as they hurried down to the Piazza Municipio. "We need to move quickly," Munson said. "They may try to detain us."

"Right! But Anita and I have to stay. Anita wants to be certain her family gets out. I have an important plan to implement."

"I understand. How did you live-stream that meeting to a TV station?"

"I'm not sure we did." Jeff turned to Anita. "You were great in there! Did you…?"

She grinned. "Sometimes bullshit baffles brains."

Munson shook his head as he flagged down a taxi. "You have quite a partner there."

"I know. What do you think? About the meeting I mean?"

"Benvenuti made up his mind before we got there. He's angry about the concern from the publicity you're getting. Maybe he's involved with Camponolo and Marsh, and those two scientists are damned dangerous; psychopathic, I'd say. I don't know about Giovanni. As for the council, you did well, but you were speaking to deaf ears."

"It's beyond disappointing," said Jeff. "It's bloody demoralizing."

As the taxi pulled up and the four bundled in, Jeff thanked them for coming. "The general aviation center," Munson told the cabbie. "You speak English?"

"Sì, yes."

"Twenty euros extra if you take every shortcut. We're in a hurry!" As the taxi began to leave, Jeff heard Munson on the phone to the pilots. "Take-off in less than ten minutes," he was saying as he waved goodbye.

Anita grabbed Jeff's arm. "Let's follow on the bike, make certain they make it."

"We need to change into our new Punjabi clothing," said Jeff. "We need to hide our identities, especially now."

"We can do that after." She was already running for the motorcycle.

"No, I really think…" By the time he caught up, she was already on the bike and starting it. "Anita—"

"Get on. Sometimes you have to live dangerously."

"Damn it!" He gritted his teeth and got on behind her. "You really get off on this danger stuff, don't you?"

"You sound like my father."

They followed the taxi to the nearby commercial airport center, parked the bike and hurried inside. Munson was already herding Frida, Moe and Dmitry through customs.

"Thank you all for coming!" Jeff called.

"I hate leaving you both here," Munson called back as he passed through the gate. "Good luck!"

As the group hurried off toward the planes shouting their goodbyes, Jeff and Anita ran outside to watch through the fence. Soon the stairway was up and the plane moved off toward a runway.

"Thank goodness, they're away safely," Anita said. "Wait while I mail the meeting video to the media from that kiosk in the airport. Then we'll go."

"Mail it later. We should get out of here…"

"It'll only take a minute."

"Jesus, Anita!"

She'd only been gone a minute or two when he heard the sirens. He was on his way in to get her when she emerged. "Let's go!"

They were too late. Two police cars arrived and cops began running into the terminal; several more police cars, their sirens wailing, drove past the terminal, toward the tarmac.

Anita frowned. "They think we are all on board the plane. They're going to try to stop the jet from taking off."

She lingered as he tugged at her, watching as the plane lifted off. "Okay, back to the bike."

They turned, and found themselves face-to-face with two policemen.

"Oh shit!" Jeff breathed softly.

"Mi faccia i suoi documenti," one of the officers demanded.

"They want to see our papers," Anita, said, searching for and finding her birth certificate.

The officer looked at it. *"La figlia Colonel Arneil, NATO. Tu vada! Vada!"*

Anita hesitated. "He knows my father. I can go."

"Then go," Jeff said, "Go! Go!"

She gave him an "I'm sorry" look, mouthed the words, and walked away.

"Come si chiama?" the cop asked Jeff.

"Jeff Kingston."

"Lei è americano?"

"Sì." He waited.

"Jeff Kingston, *venga!"* They pulled his arms behind him and slipped handcuffs on.

They held him for a moment, conversing in Italian. Then he was led to their police car and locked in the back seat. Jeff twisted around. There was no sign of Anita, but the motorcycle was still parked where they left it. Where had she gone?

He listened as the policemen talked, picking up a few words here and there. They were taking him to an old jail in Baiae, just off the Via Fusaro. He shook his head and looked at the floor. The Baiae area was exactly where the first eruption was about to occur. If they locked him up there, it would be game over. "Damn-damn-damn!" he breathed.

After about a half hour in the car, they hustled him into an old stone prison building, blindfolded him and led him down what seemed like a series of long corridors. There was a faint odor of urine and human feces. When they took the blindfold off, he realized he was at the end of a long, dimly lit hallway. They took everything out of his pockets, threw him into a cell and slammed the iron-barred door.

He looked around in the half light. A bare bulb shone from above. The windowless walls were covered with graffiti. Against one sat an iron bed with relatively clean blankets, and at the end of it sat a toilet. Three walls were some kind of irregular cinderblock; the fourth was open to the hallway, blocked by rusty iron bars.

He sat on the cot worrying about what had happened to Anita. There had been a lot of police around. Had one of the others arrested her?

A long way off, he could hear footsteps. Finally an old jailer hobbled up and peered through the bars.

"What am I charged with?" Jeff stood. "Do I get a phone call?"

"No phone. Nobody find you here. *Tra due settimane…* we set you free in two weeks."

"You can't do this!"

"*Tra due settimane*. We set you free," the jailer repeated. "We feed you until then. You be okay."

"Listen. I have an urgent warning to—"

"No warning. They tell me about you and this warning." After checking the locks he started to leave.

"Hey, wait. I want to talk to my lawyer."

"Lawyer? No," said the old man, shuffling off. "Jail closed long, long time. Just me here. And you. You and me. Everything gonna be okay. Two weeks. You see." He was gone.

"Bloody hell," Jeff murmured as he looked around his cell. "Damn it to bloody hell!"

... the emission of low frequency sound at 5.2Hz is now within 1.8Hz of an eruption level reading...

CHAPTER 17

Wednesday, June 24, morning
Jeff awakened lying on the prison cot, trying to ignore the lumpy mattress. It had been a long night. The cell was musty and the faint odor of urine troublesome, but the blanket seemed clean. He was hungry, thirsty and worried but he tried to stay positive. What were the most positive things in his life? His pursuit of an earth sciences degree. His long friendship with Michael. Aunt Dorothy and Uncle Ralph. His new father. Anita.

He got up and began his morning exercise routine. He hoped Anita had gotten away. She must have! Perhaps she would find him in time. But somehow he just knew they had arrested her.

He stopped exercising when he realized it was making him thirstier. There was no sink in the cell and no water except for the old toilet. He flushed it and opened the lid on the toilet tank to see it he could get clean water from the intake. The inside of the tank was green with slime, but the water from the tiny copper feeder pipe seemed to flow clear. He cupped his hand, directed water into his palm and tasted it. It might be unfit to drink, but he would chance it.

He drank, then lay down on the cot and considered his

plight. "What would you do Michael?" He closed his eyes and tried to relax.

He must have dozed off. Alerted by voices speaking loudly in Italian coming from down the hallway, he rose and peered down the dimly lit passageway. Someone, it sounded like the old jailer, was crying out in pain.

"No! No!"

"Il ragazzo!"

"No!" Two gunshots and then silence.

Jeff waited, listening. The sound of heavy footsteps coming toward his cell sent him searching in the dim light for a weapon. Nothing! But maybe... Grasping the heavy toilet tank lid he raised it above his head and flattened himself against the cell wall near the bars.

The man was huge with a mop of black wavy hair. His pock-marked face broke into a crooked grin as he saw Jeff. *"Ah, buon giorno ragazzo!* Caught you sleeping, eh?" Shaken by a coughing fit, he hawked up some phlegm and spat it on the floor. "I'm here to put you to sleep permanent, *ragazzo!"* He aimed a wicked looking short-barreled military rifle at Jeff through the bars. "You know who sent me, boy?" He was enjoying himself.

"Camponolo," said Jeff.

The man laughed again, then doubled over in another fit of coughing.

Seizing the moment, Jeff brought the tank lid crashing down onto the gun barrel. Unfazed, the gunman pulled the rifle back. *"Esatto!* So you know your enemy."

"Camponolo, with the help of the C-2," Jeff said, heaving the tank lid edgewise out the bars at the man, who sidestepped it easily. "You're C-2," Jeff added in frustration.

"Ah, *ragazzo,* but that is where you are wrong. As you are about to die, I'll let you in on a secret. Everything gets blamed on the C-2. But while we work with them, we are not the C-2. We are much worse that the C-2. We have no scruples whatsoever. We kill for the sake of killing, sometimes just to keep us proficient at our art."

"So your boss Camponolo is a psychopath."

"The very best kind, *ragazzo!*"

The point of the rifle barrel was through the bars again, so Jeff dove at it, knocking it sideways as an explosion of semi-automatic rifle fire began ricocheting off the cell walls.

Landing on the floor, Jeff rolled as the gunman pulled the rifle back to stop the bars from impeding his aim.

The gunman paused, pleased with himself. "So you know who signed your death warrant. But did you know they got your *ragazza amica* locked up too? After I kill you, I go visit her."

They had Anita! Jeff lunged at the bars, hoping to grab the rifle barrel and yank it.

Two loud explosions rocked the prison walls. The big man's head seemed to disappear in a mass of bloody foam, plastering it into a gory mass against the end wall as his body crumpled to the floor.

Stunned, Jeff strained against the bars to peer down the hallway. The old jailer, covered in blood was staggering forward, a double-barreled shotgun clutched in his hands. "*Stupido,*" the jailer gasped. "*Cagnaccio...*" He toppled, face forward, arms outstretched, shotgun clattering to the floor.

As Jeff watched, the jailer squirmed in a growing pool of blood. He had taken something from his pocket and thrown it forward toward Jeff's cell. "*Americani...* no one... ever find you..." the jailer whispered and lay still.

Lying on the floor in front of him, far out of Jeff's reach, was a bloodied ring of keys.

He stared at them. He had to find a way to... Anita was here, too, locked away somewhere.

"Anita!" He waited a moment, hollered again. Anita!" No answer. The assassin's huge body lay against the far wall of the hallway, his rifle under him; there was nothing within reach there either.

Jeff tore the mattress off the bed: the frame was made of heavy metal and bolted to the floor. The mattress had no coils of springs, nothing useful, no wire, nothing to reach out with.

The lone light bulb hung from the ceiling by a flimsy electrical cord. Maybe if he could reach it, he could pull the cord out further. He stood on the bed and reached over, grabbed the live cord and yanked. The wire pulled out of the plastered ceiling and broke off. It was only two feet long. Now the cell was in darkness, lit only by the dim hallway lights. The short piece of wire seemed useless, but still it may help in some way.

He tried to examine the lock on the cell door. It was on the outside, protected by a steel plate. He couldn't reach it. He couldn't even see it. Finally, he sat on the bed, head in his hands. There were no windows to scream from. "It simply can't get any worse," he muttered.

The lights in the hallway began to flicker. A *pop* in the ceiling above told its own dreadful tale. The loose wire end had shorted out the hallway lighting system. The windowless prison wing was now in complete darkness. How stupid he had been!

He sat down on the bed and closed his eyes. Think!

Finally he reached down and felt the blanket. He could braid it into a rope. Working with great difficulty in the darkness, he tore three narrow one-inch strips off, the full length of the blanket, and braided them together. When finished he had a braid six feet long. He repeated the process four times, braiding the ends together until he had a rope over twenty feet long. "That should be long enough." He dunked the rope in the toilet water to give it some weight, then tied a loop about two feet in diameter and threaded the piece of electrical wire into the loop to keep it open.

Now to snag those keys! Tying one end to his wrist, he coiled the rope and, feeling his way to the bars in the darkness, he threw it down the hallway and pulled it back. Nothing. He repeated the process over and over, but the rope loop refused to snag the keys. After continuing to try for what seemed like hours, he finally stopped in defeat.

He woke with a start. How many hours had passed? The cell smelled of death; the bodies in the hallway were beginning to decompose. What woke him was the rumble, starting low and then growing. He made his way to the bars and hung on.

Just as before, the earthquake sounded like a freight train coming. It hit with enormous force, lifting the floor upward, buckling the walls and cracking open the ceiling in a cloud of choking dust and debris. As sunlight flooded in from the caved-in roof he yelled at the top of his voice, "Bring it on, Campi! Bring it on!"

The noise of ripping, grinding rock was all consuming. "Set me free, you son of a bitch! Set me free!"

It shook for about fifteen seconds and then stopped as abruptly as it had started. As the dust began to clear, light from a hole in the ceiling illuminated the area. Coughing and choking, still standing with his arms anchored around the iron bars, he began rattling the cell door. It was still firmly locked. He looked up. The hole in the ceiling was too small to crawl through. He assessed the rest of his cell. Its walls were solid.

The toilet tank no longer had water flowing into it.

"Bloody hell!"

He staggered around, trying to regain his equilibrium, and sank onto the debris-covered bed. Fighting off a rush of disappointment, he lay down, covered with dust, feeling utterly defeated.

Time ticked by. The pre-main-eruption event was getting closer. It was directly below him. He got up and peered down the hallway. The corpses were covered with dust. The keys were still on the floor, but now even further out of reach, well beyond where his makeshift lasso could net them.

"Yeah, of course," he muttered. For them to have jiggled toward him would have been too much to ask.

And, he wondered, what had happened to Anita?

"Anita!" he yelled. "Anita!" No answer. He returned to the bed sat down and closed his eyes. The smell of sulfur and decaying flesh was burning his throat. His hunger had left but his thirst was overwhelming. He stood on his bed, as close as he could to the hole in the ceiling, and yelled for help. It was useless. He might as well face it; he was going to die in here.

Time seemed to stop. The sky outside was darkening. A storm, or night time? He settled back. For him, and worse, for Anita and the whole city, it was over.

All over.

The voice floated in like a dream. "Jeff? Jeff? Is that you in there?"

He was hallucinating, hearing the voice of an angel.

"Jeff? Are you okay?"

He jumped up. "Anita!" He reached out through the bars in the darkness and touched her. She was real.

"I heard you calling," she said. "I tripped over a body. The stench here is unbelievable. But how am I going to get you out of there?"

"There's a key ring on the floor about fifteen feet back. The body you tripped over was the jailer. There's another body behind you on the floor against the hallway wall."

She got the keys, unlocked the door and they got it open a few inches, then a few more. He squeezed out and, holding her hand, led her down the passageway to better air. "I'm so glad you're okay. I was worried about you," said Jeff. "You are okay, aren't you? They didn't…?"

"I'm okay. Dehydrated. Need water."

"Me too. We've got to get out of here. What day is it?"

"Wednesday, I think."

"Shit!" They hurried along the hallway. "How did you get free?"

"I was locked in another wing. My door was damaged during the quake. It took a while, but I jimmied it open. I knew you were in here somewhere."

"So after the police took me away, they arrested you?"

"Another cop stopped me. This one didn't know my father. I'm very sorry! I should have listened to you. Next time, I will." They turned down a narrow hallway in the dim light past more empty cells.

"I was blindfolded when they brought me in. Can we get out this way?"

"Maybe. I think it leads to the front of the prison." They reached a well-used area where the lights were brighter. "Look, I think that's the jailer's room."

She hurried forward. "Here! Bottled water!" They guzzled the life-saving liquid.

Jeff rifled through the desk drawer. "Our stuff!" He grabbed the envelopes. They were moving on to find a building exit when Jeff heard the rumble start again. "Another earthquake's coming! Get to the wall and stand against it. The roof may come down!" He held her against the barred wall.

She looked at him, startled. "Are you certain—?"

It hit with enormous force, buckling the floor and bringing the roof crashing down ahead of them. Behind them the walls collapsed inward, blocking the hallway and sending up a cloud of choking dust that rolled toward them, filling the blocked hallway.

They ducked into the cell and groped around in the darkness, choking and coughing. "The... the hallway," gasped Anita. "I think... I think it's blocked both ways... we're trapped again!"

They surveyed their confined space, trying to breathe in the dusty, sulfur-laden air. Anita collapsed onto the dusty mattress of the cell's narrow bed and broke into tears. "Oh my God, Jeff! This time we really are going to die!" Then she shook herself, dropped to her knees, crossed herself and closed her eyes.

Jeff watched, marveling at the look of complete trust on her face as she prayed. She believes, he thought—why can't you? She rose to her feet and paced another circuit around the room and back out into the blocked hallway, where she stopped.

His voice was a hoarse whisper. "Well, what now?"

"There may be a doorway down there. Some light is coming through." They struggled down the debris-strewn darkened hallway and suddenly they were out into the open.

"My God," Anita gasped, "we're out!"

Every bone in Jeff's body ached, and he was dehydrated and weak as a kitten, but elated. "Yes! We're out!" He put an arm around her in a victory hug. "You okay?"

"I hurt all over, but I've never been better!" She raised her arms to the sky. "Oh my God, the pain of being alive feels good! I feel like that bird up there."

"Yeah, well we'll be up there with that bird if we don't get the hell out of here. This whole place is going up. Hurry!"

They jogged northward toward the NATO base at Gricignano di Aversa. The earthquake had caused street damage and destroyed buildings, some of which were on fire. Toxic gas escaping from cracks in the pavement and the smell of sulfur hinted of what was to come. People struggling from buildings were all heading north. Police and fire crews, intent on their work, paid no attention to them as they hurried along.

A motorcycle roared past with two riders, its driver pushing the machine along at high speed. Soon a fire truck screamed past. Heavy smoke filled the air. They rounded a turn in the street; a large apartment building was on fire. The motorcycle that had just gone past had been left at the curb. It was an old bike, with its key in the ignition and two helmets on its seat. Jeff looked at Anita. "Do you think they're coming back?"

"Look!" A couple dressed in riding gear was helping two old people into the back seat of a car. They got into the front seat and the car began backing out of the driveway.

Anita called out to them. "Can we use... *Usare lo?*"

The young man rolled down the window and called out, *"Sì, salva voi stessi!"*

"He said to save ourselves. Get on." Anita was already on the seat of the machine, throwing him a helmet.

Jeff put on the helmet and got aboard behind Anita.

"We'll head for the airport," yelled Anita. "We'll get the big bike and see if our stuff is still in the saddlebags."

"And then we'll go to the NATO base!"

"Yes!" Slowing for an intersection, she yelled, "Which way?"

He pointed, and she swerved eastward.

"I need my phone. I want to call Dad."

"Won't he be at the base?"

"Maybe."

They stopped at the airport, found the big Honda Supersport exactly as they left it. Locked in the saddlebag were Jeff's computer and the rest of the equipment they'd bought to replace what they'd lost on the yacht. Anita phoned her father and listened to a message. He had been called out on a helicopter rescue mission in the city. She checked the local news channels. "Your predictions are all over the news. Some are leaving the city."

Jeff nodded. "Wait a few hours and then maybe they'll all believe." Anita motioned to him to take over the bike. She hopped on behind and they headed back toward the freeway, now aware of increased traffic flow going north. Within minutes they were slowed to a crawl. Vehicles filled with people clogged the streets and as they entered the freeway the congestion was even worse.

"This is encouraging," Jeff shouted as they swung over onto the shoulder and maneuvered past the slow-moving cars. "I wonder if they've announced an evacuation."

After picking their way through traffic, listening to ambulance and police sirens from several directions, they turned west toward the NATO base at Gricignano di Aversa. The roadway was clogged with people on foot as well as in cars and on bicycles. Eventually they arrived at the NATO residences gate. The guard recognized Anita, checked their I.D. and motioned them in.

When they entered the Arneil's apartment the land-line was ringing. Anita ran to it. "Yes, Dad, it's me. I'm home. Jeff's with me. We're okay." There was a long pause. "She is? Oh, my God, they didn't leave…? No, they're not here. Where could they…?" She listened for a minute and clicked the receiver. "He's just taking off. They're flying people injured in the earthquake to hospital. Mom and the girls never left… they are still around here somewhere… maybe with her friend up the valley." She dialed a number, pulled a glass from the cupboard and turned on the tap, tilting her head at Jeff, who got himself a glass.

"Sherri, this is Anita, are you okay? … Good. Are Mom and the girls there? … Okay. Can you put her on?" She took a gulp of water. "Mom, listen. The earthquake is just the beginning. There's going to be an eruption. Not the big one. The smaller one. Stay there and keep the girls there with you. … No, Mom! Nothing here is worth risking your lives over. You are three miles further north and much safer where you are… Yes. We're just grabbing a bite to eat and then we're leaving. I'll call again in a few minutes."

She shook her head at Jeff. "She still doesn't get it. Use the bath in my parents' room for your shower. I'll use the shower in my sister's room. It's down the hall here. Oh, and let me dig out some of my dad's clothes for you—here, you can wear a set of his khakis; he won't mind."

The master bedroom was large, with a small alcove which housed a desk; above it were photos of the girls and a large schematic of the NATO base. Jeff set his backpack in the desk chair and unzipped it. He still had the Beretta, his cell phone and its battery, and a decent amount of cash. He plugged in the computer to charge its battery, turned it on and checked VolcanoWatch. The end of the summary read *…the emission of low frequency sound at 5.2Hz is now within 1.8Hz of an eruption level reading.* No question: Campi was going to erupt. As he closed the computer, he heard a small thud and looked down at his feet.

A wristwatch. He bent to retrieve it, placing it on the

desktop. Past suppertime already. When was the last time he'd eaten?

In the bathroom he turned on the shower, shed his filthy clothes and stepped in. Enjoying the cascade of warm water he also felt a surge of adrenalin. With Colonel Arneil's khakis, he could... but would it work? Adjusting the water until it was as hot as he could stand it, allowing the heat to ease his aching muscles, he soaped away the grime of the jail and thought things through.

He toweled off. As he dressed, he studied the schematic of the NATO base.

The colonel was almost as tall as Jeff so everything fit... almost. The pants were a bit short, but looked okay with the high-top army boots. Surveying himself in the mirror, he made a face. "What do you think, Michael? In this outfit I'll blend in around here. And with what I've got planned, I bloody well better!"

After another good look at the NATO schematic, he walked down the hallway and listened. Anita was still in the shower. He knocked on the bathroom door. "Anita? Think your dad will mind if I borrow a watch?"

"No, go ahead," she called back.

"Okay. I'm going out to see if anyone needs help. I'll be back shortly. I'm starved. Maybe you could make us something to eat?"

"I'll have something ready when you get back."

He paused to borrow a pair of the colonel's gloves, then hurried down the stairway. At the NATO compound he showed his pass. Soldiers were scurrying about, looking after displaced civilians. No one paid any attention to him. The motor pool area was jammed with trucks, Humvees, Jeeps and armored vehicles all parked in neat rows.

He decided on a Humvee for its larger size and carrying capacity and jumped in, thankful for his familiarity with military vehicles. He ran the motor for a minute and made sure its fuel tank was full, then drove to the long, low building surrounded by high earth berms at the far corner of the base, where the explosives had been stored. With any luck, they'd still be here.

Happily, the guard was gone. Although unguarded, the building was encircled by a high wire fence with rolls of razor-wire along the top. The padlocked gate sported a sign that read *Authorized Personnel Only*. Jeff drove back to the building marked *Maintenance and Supplies*. Inside, he approached the wicket.

"I'm with Colonel Arneil's outfit," he told the soldier. "I need a self-contained breathing apparatus and a pair of bolt cutters."

The soldier nodded, turned on his heel and strode down the aisles of supplies, returning with an air-pack, an extra canister and a set of bolt cutters. "Sign here."

Jeff scrawled something illegible, stashed the equipment in the Humvee, and drove back to the apartment.

Anita was in her mother's kitchen. "Just in time," she said. "I hope you like pasta with tomato sauce and chicken nuggets."

"Sounds great!"

He sat on a stool at the counter and waited while she served. "The base doesn't look like it suffered any damage. They're busy with the injured folks in the quake's aftermath."

"Very many injured?"

"It doesn't look too bad, yet." He wolfed down some pasta and bit into another chicken nugget. "Sure wish your mom had gone further away."

"I'm sick about this," said Anita around a mouthful of pasta. "I don't think Mom's been well; she's not making good decisions. I'm afraid she's going to come back here."

"Anita, you must go to your mother and get them all the hell out of here." Jeff took a handful of euros from his wallet and gave them to her. "After we eat, it's time for you to go."

"And what are you going to do?"

"I'll meet you back in…" He hesitated. "Oh shit! Brace yourself! I think we're about to—"

The massive shockwave knocked them off their stools as windows blew in. "Oh my God!" Anita yelled from the floor, covering her head. She pulled herself into a crouch.

Jeff tried to stand. "Are you cut from the flying glass?"

"No, I don't think so." She got unsteadily to her feet, and they stared out through the empty window frame. To the south, a cloud of ash was exploding skyward, spreading out at its base and boiling up like an atom bomb.

Seconds passed. Then, with a distant thunderous roar, everything on the horizon was obscured by dust and debris.

"Dear God," said Anita. "Dad was in a helicopter…"

"Let's hope he was on the ground. The wind is from the north. It'll take the ash cloud southward and out over the sea." He put a hand on Anita's arm. "Does your mom have a vehicle with her?"

"They usually take the bus to Sherri's." Anita pulled open a drawer. "Keys are here. Good, she won't be able to drive back down. Do you think the busses will be running?"

"Probably not in this direction. But what if she borrows a car, talks someone into driving her back here?" Jeff held her arms, looked into her eyes. "Anita, your family comes first. You have to go and get them to safety."

She nodded. "Yes. I'll drive them up to Rome and fly them to Spain. That's upwind from an eruption and—"

"Fly? Out of Rome? Camponolo will have the airports watched. They'll be on to you in minutes!"

She pulled free of his grasp and went to the window. "He'll be too busy with everything else that's going on. If we can get a flight from Rome, it's the quickest way to get them out of Italy."

"I don't like it," said Jeff, running a hand through his hair. "You'll be safer going through France on the highways."

"We'll figure it out, Jeff. Dad will stay with his outfit. We'll never convince him to leave, but Jeff, you've got to come too."

"I can't."

"Look. We've saved many in the city. They understand

our media messages. They've been warned. Now for sure they'll leave the city. You can't do any more."

"I've got to try. And I'm going after Camponolo. I want a confession about my mother's murder."

"Jeff, surely it's not worth…" She followed him back to her parents' bedroom and watched him re-pack his bag, wincing at the Beretta. "You've got something bigger in mind, haven't you?"

"Yes."

Closing her eyes she said, "Oh damn it, Jeff… somehow I knew it would come to this."

"You must get your mother and sisters out of here." He picked up Colonel Arneil's watch. "You're sure borrowing this is okay?"

She nodded, reaching over to strap it on his wrist.

"I'll put the battery in my cell every so often to check messages." He zipped his backpack. "Please, Anita, drive to Paris and then fly home to the States. You'll have a better chance of staying undetected on the highways and getting out of Italy before you use an airport."

"We'll be okay."

"Do that. Be safe." He took her arms again. "I have to leave now."

She tried to smile. "Damn it, Jeffrey Kingston! I've begun to… to really care for you!"

He placed a finger under her chin and lifted it. "The feeling is mutual. You've been a phenomenal partner."

Tight lipped, she nodded. "I'll never see you again, will I?"

He gave her a long look. "We have been an awesome team, Anita. We'll get through this, too. I'll see you back in the States." Suppressing an almost overpowering urge to hug her, to hold her close and tell her he loved her, he turned and hurried out the door.

... in addition to the current eruption, earthquake swarms, a smell of sulfur and increases in hydrochloric acid gas and carbon monoxide...

CHAPTER 18

Wednesday, June 24, evening
Pandemonium had gripped the NATO base. Although it was barely dusk the skies were dark; falling ash cast eerie, shifting half-shadows under the emergency lights. Soldiers ran in all directions, some shouting orders, readying a medical relief convoy to the city.

The explosives storage area was still deserted. At the gate he cut the padlock and drove into the compound, closing the gate behind him. Then he cut the padlock on the double doors of the storage unit, drove inside and closed the doors.

Turning on the lights in the windowless building, he hurried down the long center aisle until he found a carefully stored stack of crates with warning signs that read *Danger! Explosives!* He pried one open an examined the contents. It looked and felt like Silly Putty.

Jeff counted the crates. "Unbelievable," he muttered. "There's enough here to destroy half a city!"

He loaded several crates of the stuff into the back of the covered vehicle. Searching the adjoining storage bay he grabbed several electrical probes, timers, and detonators. Then he shut off the building lights, opened the doors and backed out. The whole exercise had taken eleven minutes. Not bad!

He drove toward the main gate and joined a line of military vehicles, a medical relief convoy, in the process of leaving for the city.

The moving line of vehicles stopped at the gate. He held his breath. At the front of the column, guards were questioning each driver as, slowly, the trucks began moving forward. Then the guards stepped back, and the line began to move faster. When he, too, was waved through, he sighed with relief.

As the motor convoy rumbled forward, he struggled to keep the big Humvee the proper distance from the vehicle ahead. They turned south. When a traffic jam sent the NATO vehicles scrambling from the line, each apparently seeking its own way around., he seized the opportunity to leave the convoy and turned east.

Once he left the convoy, the wide military Humvee drew puzzled stares. Too damned conspicuous. Probably had a GPS which could be tracked, too. When he passed a large building marked *Posta Centrale*, he wheeled down the next side street and took the alley back.

Dozens of postal delivery trucks sat in rows in the yard. Most of them were small, but one was a Mercedes van. Parking beside it, he smashed a side window to get in; the spare keys were stashed behind the sun visor, saving him the trouble of hot wiring it.

After transferring everything to the van, he stashed the Humvee behind the dumpsters. Then, easing the van out into the street, he headed south toward San Sebastiano al Vesuvio, tuning the vehicle's radio to a local station.

In a taped message, Deputy Mayor Erico Benvenuti was urging calm, assuring people that there was no need to evacuate. The small eruption had simmered down, he said, impacting only a small portion of the city outskirts. Their volcano expert Dr. Antonio Camponolo was quite confident there was no indication of a further eruption.

Shaking his head, Jeff yelled, "Damn you Camponolo! Damn you! Damn you!"

Pulling over, he unzipped his backpack, jammed the battery into his cell phone and called the Arneil's number. Anita picked up on the first ring.

"Have you had the radio on?" he asked.

Anita was sobbing.

"Anita, what is it?"

"He's dead, Jeff," she said, her voice shaking. "His helicopter went down over the city during the eruption. The military says there were no survivors."

"Oh, Anita! I'm so sorry!"

"I'm still in shock." She blew her nose. "There are hundreds of dead in the city, Jeff. They told Mom. Of course she's devastated and not thinking clearly. I'm already on my way to pick them up and get them out of here. It's terrible, Jeff."

"I can imagine. I'm so sorry about your dad. I wish I could be with you."

"Be careful, keep safe. You will, won't you…" She ended the call.

He waited a moment, listening to the dead air.

"Just keep on driving, Anita."

Night had already fallen by the time he began climbing Vesuvius's flank. As he wound his way up the switchbacks, he wondered about his plan. It was such a long shot, but there was no time to think of anything else.

He wished he could have bounced it off Anita, but she would never have let him do it. Worse, she might have insisted on coming with him. He wondered what Michael would think.

Michael.

God, the past two weeks seemed like a lifetime.

At the bridge across the ravine, he stopped, took four packages of explosives, installed the charges under the bridge and set timers rigged to be detonated by a cell phone. Returning to the van, he continued to climb the deserted road to the volcano.

The car park near the summit of Mount Vesuvius was dark and empty. Getting out, he stretched his legs and climbed the walking trail to the volcano's crater rim. Light volcanic ash was falling from the mini-eruption but it was not yet enough to cause breathing problems. He sat and studied the lights of the city to the west. In the darkness he could see that area of the eruption near the far coastline where the street lights were out. Only the glow of fires from burning buildings illuminated that part of the city. Across the night sky a dark cloud of ash was rising from the area and blowing out to sea, its long shadow blotting out the stars. Soon it would be Thursday June 25th... and four days to volcanic doomsday.

He held up his hands, formed a circle with his fingers and thumbs and looked though them, tracing the massive six mile wide outer circle of the Campi Flegrei caldera that lay below. "Unbelievable," he breathed.

A flashback! He had done this before! He and his mother.

He lay down, imagining he could hear the faint growl of Vesuvius below and asked aloud, "Were you right? Kristin, my mother? Do the Vesuvius volcano and the Campi Flegrei caldera have a common magma chamber?"

As he looked up into the night, a shooting star flashed across the sky. "Let's hope that's a good sign," he muttered. Rising wearily to his feet, he returned down the trail.

Back at the van, he turned off the road and onto the path, easing along the narrow trail cut into the volcano's steep eastern slope. Hugging the inside bank, he came to the intersection where the branch road switch-backed down to the monitoring shed.

He retrieved his stashed bicycle, then used the bolt cutters to open both gates and the large double doors of the building. He drove the van inside and closed the doors.

After starting the electrical generator, he turned on the interior lights and re-examined the eight-inch-diameter pipe that protruded from the concrete floor. At some point in the past, a drill bit had cut a path deep down into the volcano's magma chamber. The steel frame above the pipe held a motorized spool of cable, ideal for what he planned. Its mechanical system would keep the cable over the center of the pipe as he fed it down into the shaft. He smiled. "Today, we are going to lower more than just instruments down into your depths, Mr. Volcano!"

Jeff counted the number of coils of cable on the big spool, measured the cable diameter and depth to the axle and the outside and inside circumference and quickly estimated the length of the fine-wire cable: close to three thousand feet, almost enough to reach down near the bottom of the probe.

"Okay, Vesuvius," he continued. "They've poked a drill pipe way down beside the hardened plug that's blocking your magma chamber, haven't they? Now we're going to see if we can loosen that plug. Hopefully, if you share the same magma source with Campi Flegrei and if we can get you to erupt, maybe you can reduce the upward pressure on the caldera and maybe… just maybe, we can prevent the big guy from erupting." He paused a moment. "One chance in a hundred, Michael? One chance in a thousand?"

With his ear to the drill pipe, he listened for the volcano's growl. Nothing. *"Have* you built up pressure under there, my fractious friend? Let's bloody hope so!"

He returned to the van and carefully unloaded the crates of explosives. Reopening the first crate, he counted the separate charges on the first layer, figured the depth of each layer and calculated the number of charges in a single crate. Then, counting the crates, he nodded with satisfaction. The log book on the dusty desk implied that the probe projected over 3,000 feet down the cooled rock plug.

"What do you think? Will one thousand, one hundred

and fifty eight sticks of high explosives, poked down the volcano's throat, be enough to loosen that plug?"

Jeff shut down the monitoring instruments and, with the pulley system, began pulling the lead wires and instruments out of the hole. An hour later everything was out and the pipe was clear. He wiped his brow, hoping everyone at the monitoring station would be too busy to figure out what was going on.

He lowered a few feet of the cable from the motorized spool into the hole and then began carefully molding each charge of explosives around to the cable, connecting each with electrical probes and lowering them as they were attached, down a few inches at a time until all were fixed to the lowered cable.

Hours later, he was finished.

Now, the tricky part. Inserting the final electrical contacts into the last charge and attaching the long detonating wire, he slowly lowered the cable as far as it would go.

Attaching the lead to the detonator, he connected it to a second cell phone-activated detonator, hoping the microwave towers on Vesuvius's slopes wouldn't be affected by the earthquakes.

He shook his head. If the temperature in the drilled core topped 900 degrees, it could set off the explosives prematurely. *Might be joining you sooner than I'd thought, Michael.*

He was done. Arneil's watch showed 7:15 a.m.

What was it like outside? Poking his head out the door, he found it unusually dark with almost six inches of ash on the ground and heavy ash still falling.

Shit. The wind had changed. He'd be lucky to get off the mountain.

He went back and checked everything. The phone detonator would have power for six days, so within that time, if he called the number—and if the cell towers still worked—his call would ignite the explosives and, hopefully, set off a Vesuvius eruption.

He sat down for a moment and considered. Then he inserted the battery into his cell phone and called the Naples Monitoring Station.

"Sì."

"Giovanni?"

"Sì."

"E parlo... confidenza?"

"Sì. Uno momento!"

There was silence, then, "I have made the telephone secure. Is that young Kristinson? Er... Kingston?"

"Yes. Have you noticed the Vesuvius monitor is off?"

"Yes. We lost Vesuvius monitors... ah. You are up there now."

"Giovanni, I correctly predicted the current pre-eruption event. Do you believe me now?"

"Yes."

"Have you implemented a city evacuation order?"

"Yes. A mandatory evacuation. The deputy mayor has finally agreed."

"How long to clear the entire danger area?"

"Forty eight hours, minimum."

"Have you phoned other scientists around the world?"

"I am not allowed to give out scientific information. No one at the monitoring center here has that authority. They rely on data feeds from our instruments."

"Are you alone at the station?"

"Yes. I have sent everyone away."

"I'm coming to see you. I have to talk to you."

"How long will you be?"

"About an hour. Maybe more."

"So you are up on Vesuvius..."

Jeff cut the connection and pulled the battery. He moved the air-pack onto the van's passenger seat and put the spare compressed air cylinder in his backpack. Pausing to drink from his water flask, he opened the building doors and backed out onto the ash covered road.

After making certain the air conditioning was off and

no outside air could enter the system, he was ready. Turning the vehicle, he headed down the trail with a cloud of ash rising from the rear, wondering how long the motor could hold out.

The van operated normally for the first mile, but as he neared where the bicycle trail intersected with the road, the engine began to overheat. As he turned onto the road and headed downward toward the switchbacks, the van began skidding sideways in the ash, its motor gasping as it started to seize. So with the transmission in neutral, he allowed it to gather speed.

He barely negotiated the first switchback without touching the brakes. Gathering more speed into the next turn, he hit the brakes lightly, just enough to get around the turn. "Easy there," he breathed, braking gently as his speed increased again. He could smell the burning brake discs and released them; the next time when he touched the pedal there was nothing. "Holy, holy, holy…" The van hit sixty approaching the next set of switchbacks. "Well, no hope of making this turn, so here goes…" Gripping the wheel, he cranked it and sent the van off the road and straight down the mountain.

Hurtling downward at a steep angle, the van was like a bucking bronco. Bouncing over rocks, it gained speed until it flew over the embankment of the next switchback. It landed on the road, creating a huge cloud of ash, and bounced off again. Careening on, it plunged down a shale slope, finally crashing against a boulder where it stopped with its engine smoking.

Shaken and bruised, Jeff collected his wits. Heavy ash was falling and smoke billowed around the van, so he put on the breathing apparatus. As he turned on the compressed air, he paused, listening carefully. Yes! He nodded with a half grin; Giovanni had activated the sirens.

He forced the van door open and jumped out, struggled around to the back, and pulled out the bicycle and his backpack.

Then he hurried down the shale slope carrying the bike and trying to breathe in the full face mask, finally arriving at the road below. The ash fall was lighter now, and he swung onto the bicycle and allowed it to gather speed.

Ten minutes later he was on Via Vesuvio. Now the ash fall was very light. The bicycle was running fast, but not too fast the make the gentler corners at the base of the mountain. He glanced at his watch. It had been thirty-eight minutes since he'd left the top. Checking his compressed air, he found he still had eight minutes in the first canister. There was a possibility the falling ash from the small pre-eruption may still be too thick to breathe without searing his lungs. It was all downhill—virtually no effort if he just let the bicycle run.

Continuing on, he was struck by the folly of what he had done. If it did work, it would almost certainly cause the volcano to fire its molten rock and pyroclastic flow outward toward the southeast and away from the city. But even then, would the eruption be enough to stop the rising Campi Flegrei?

At the Autostrada Napoli-Salerno, his air-pack ran out of compressed air. He pulled the spare canister from his pack, installed it, and turned west toward the Naples city center. The ash was much lighter down here; the wind from the storm was sweeping the ash off the streets. It was still all downhill but gentle now, and his brakes were shot so he continued to let the bike coast.

People were heading north, away from the danger. Some were in cars, some walking northward, breathing through clothing or scarves wrapped around their necks. They stared at him as he went past; an apparition with his air canister and mask, going against the flow.

He rode toward the monitoring station in downtown Naples. The streets were jammed with evacuees.

He thought about Anita. Hopefully she and her family were far north by now.

Traffic was gridlocked. He rode on the shoulder to get

past stalled vehicles, ignoring the mass of panicky humanity and the wailing evacuation sirens. Finally he was at the volcano monitoring center. The compressed air had run out so he dumped the breathing apparatus and, carrying his bike, went inside past the deserted security desk and up the stairway to the monitoring room.

Giovanni was sitting on a high stool in front of a bank of monitors when he burst in. The little Italian turned to face him, sucked in a breath and squinted at Jeff over half-spectacles. *"Per amor di Dio!* We have no security? You walk right in!"

Jeff grinned and brushed ash off his shirt. Phones were ringing everywhere but Giovanni ignoried them.

"Why have you dressed in military?"

"Borrowed clothes."

"I have talked the deputy mayor into this. He has allowed me to activate the sirens."

"Everyone is leaving now. It was the right thing to do."

"Come! Look at this!"

Jeff looked over the little scientist's shoulder as he flashed through several computer read-outs on the screen:

Significant changes in CO_2, SO_2 concentrations. Ground deformation at outer edges falling; at center rising. Seismic data shows increased volatility. Sound data recording shows Campi Flegrei emitting frequencies between 0.5 and 6.6 hertz.

"That's the range volcanoes make before they erupt."

"Yes. Yes." Giovanni nodded quickly. "Just before."

"It looks like Campi is poised to blow, alright."

"And see, in addition to the current eruption, earthquake swarms and a strong smell of sulfur along the coastlines."

"What are the secondary gas readings?"

"There are increases at all sampling sites and an increase in hydrochloric acid gas, carbon monoxide."

"And water vapor?"

Giovanni pulled up another screen. "Increasing."

"Why did you send all your staff away?"

Giovanni smiled sadly. "Look!"

He walked over to a large screen showing the entire area from space. An uneven red circle with a radius showing 5,400 meters from its center surrounded the city of Naples and the Bay of Pozzuoli. "The caldera's active area is now 11,000 meters wide and it grows every hour."

Jeff nodded. "Roughly six miles wide at its narrowest point but maybe more like seven miles long. It truly is a monster."

"But that is not all. There is much activity along the east-west fault lines."

"What do you mean? And Giovanni, should you not answer the phones?"

"Screw the phones! I activated our remote out-feeds on all monitors. Scientists everywhere have access now to all of our monitors and they are watching this. They can see what is going on here from their laptops. Look at this!"

He led Jeff to a screen showing the entire Mediterranean all the way to Greece, the Aegean Sea and Turkey. "This is the seismically active area between African and European plates in the Mediterranean." He traced a finger across the screen. "It includes volcanic and tectonic activity near the Sicilian island of Pantelleria in Strait of Sicily, here." He pointed to the island. "The long island, nine miles long… it had a submarine eruption in the 1890s." He pointed to the screen again. "Now see this rough east-west line along the Mediterranean sea floor?"

"Yes."

"This is where the African plate in earth's mantle pushes north into Europe. It creates a collision zone under the sea and surrounding land."

"Yes," Jeff said. "That was in my mother's notes. A number of micro-plates form subduction and fault zones under the Mediterranean as the continental plates are in collision."

Giovanni nodded. "The sea is sinking into the mantle along crack in this crust through Spain, Italy, Greece, and Turkey."

"A volcanic danger area."

"Yes. You recall in 1500 BCE both the Thera volcano in Greece and Vesuvius erupt, destroying the whole area and wiping out much of population." Giovanni paused. "Now take a guess, Kingston. What do you think we learned this day that caused the city to activate the sirens?"

"Thera is coming to life?"

"Thera became active this morning. This is not all. The submarine volcano in the Straight of Sicily also stirs, and Sicily's Aetna shows unusual activity."

"Scary."

The phones continued to ring. In frustration, Jeff picked one up. "Yes?"

"This is Francis Demming with CNN International in Atlanta Florida. Do you speak English?"

"Yes," Jeff replied.

"We are reporting on the projected eruption on Campi Flegrei and would like a direct data link to your volcano monitors so our experts here in the United States can comment on the evolving threat…"

"Just a minute…" He gave the phone to Giovanni, and waited until he dealt with it. "Did you give CNN a direct data link?"

Giovanni nodded. "I gave them a direct feed to VolcanoWatch. This is our automated data feed that goes only to scientists. I will lose my job for this, but soon all of this will be gone. So what the hell?"

"This is far worse than BCE 1500," said Jeff, reaching over the desk to disconnect the phone lines. "It is not Vesuvius erupting together with Thera, it is Campi, the supervolcano."

Giovanni nodded. "Volcanic doomsday."

... indicates rock under the Bay of Naples is fracturing to a depth of several kilometers...

CHAPTER 19

Thursday, June 25, morning
Jeff considered Giovanni for a moment. "This may be Armageddon," he said, "but there's a chance... You explained that the Mediterranean is where African plate in earth's mantle pushes north into Europe, creating a collision zone under the sea and surrounding land."

"It does, yes," Giovanni nodded. The little man seemed beside himself with anxiety.

"This was also in my mother's notes," Jeff said. "She wrote that a number of micro-plates form subduction and fault zones under the Mediterranean as the continental plates are in collision. And the sea is sinking into the earth's mantle along a crack in its crust. The fault line runs east and west through Spain, Italy, Greece, and Turkey."

"Yes. Yes it does. It forms a volcanic danger zone. Your point?"

"My mother's notes read that Vesuvius is not on that east-west fault. She noted that Vesuvius is on a fault line that runs north and south, from Sicily, up through Italy. Her belief was that when both the Vesuvius and Thera volcanoes erupted in BCE 1500 the two events were completely unrelated."

"Perhaps, but I do not see..."

"The point is, Giovanni, Campi Flegrei is on that east-west fault. It runs diagonally down the Tyrrhenian Sea, through the Bay of Pozzuoli, across the outer part of Bay of Naples and through Italy's landmass into the southern Adriatic. The Campi Flegrei Caldera is directly over that east-west fault line."

"But I do not understand your point. When Campi Flegrei erupts it will set off the Thera volcano in Greece and…"

"Yes," Jeff said. "But if Vesuvius were to erupt and relieve the pressure on the Campi Flegrei caldera, the rest of the Mediterranean volcanic danger zone would not be affected."

Giovanni stared at him.

"Think of it, Giovanni. In 1945 when Vesuvius last erupted, it did not set off a chain reaction. Thera did not erupt."

"Well, no, it did not. But Vesuvius is not about to erupt." Giovanni shook his head. "And even if it did, it would not relieve pressure on the caldera. There is no way it would prevent the supervolcano from erupting."

Jeff grinned. "But my mother believed Vesuvius and Campi Flegrei had a common magna chamber. If that's true and Vesuvius were to erupt, it could relieve enough of the upward pressure in the magma chamber to tame this monster."

"I have heard this theory of a common magma chamber, but there is no proof!" Giovanni frowned. "Most scientists discount the theory."

"But what if my mother was right?"

"Even if she was right, Vesuvius is not about to erupt."

"Ah, but I'm hoping it will."

Giovanni squinted at Jeff. "Is that why our Vesuvius monitor is not working? Have you been up there interfering with our deep probe?"

Jeff grinned. "I admit nothing. Can we see the data from the Thera volcano? What does it show?"

Giovanni picked up a laptop and handed it to Jeff. "Take this. It is set up with all the data feeds from this monitoring center and you can get the various other data collection feeds as well. No need for anyone to remain here. I hope to see my children grow up. You come with me."

"Thank you." Jeff put the lap top in his backpack, wheeled his bike out and waited while Giovanni locked the monitoring room's doors. Hurrying down the hallway, Giovanni asked, "Did they not arrest you? Take you and your friends to jail?"

"Just my friend Anita and me. We broke out of jail. The others had already left Naples."

"Ah. You made big waves, sending the tape of the council meeting to radio news. Then we begin to get death threats here at the monitoring station. People in the city want the heads of the deputy mayor and all of us, too, especially Camponolo."

"They won't be after you, Giovanni; you did try to warn the council. It was Deputy Mayor Benvenuti going along with Dr. Camponolo and Dr. Hilda Marsh—they are the ones who did the damage."

Giovanni shrugged. "Camponolo had our deputy mayor in his... how do you say this? ... in his pocket." He led Jeff down a flight of stairs.

"I need to talk to Camponolo about my mother's death. Any idea where I can find him?"

"He works at the *università* and lives in a villa on the coast. If he is not there, he keeps a yacht, *La Signora Luisa*, at Gaeta. This is a small coastal town ninety kilometers north of the city."

He opened a door to the basement. "You come with me. I have an electric scooter down there. We will use the passageways to move under the city."

"Underground? Wouldn't the earthquakes have blocked it off?"

"Perhaps. But falling ash kills. It is chaos above. The streets are clog, and roaming bands of thugs will soon take over. It is safer to stay underground if we can." The scientist opened a locked compound and disconnected his electric motor scooter from its power source. "Get on in back of me."

"I'll need the bike. I'll follow you."

"You will not keep up. You have no light on this bicycle. You will get lost in the tunnels."

"I'll keep up."

"Io ho fretta. I must hurry. I do not think you can do it."

"It's okay. I'll keep up. You go. I'll follow. Don't wait for me, though."

Giovanni strapped on his helmet. "Thank you for warning the city. You and Miss Arneil saved many Italian lives and turned several cruise ships away that could have been caught here." He opened a door that led outward from the basement and took off, his tail light shining brightly in the dark.

Following, Jeff bore down on the pedals, realizing that it would take everything he had to keep up with the scooter. Riding headlong into the dark, with only the scooter's tail light to follow, he geared upward, throwing caution to the winds.

Dimly aware of a maze of tunnels heading off in all directions, he realized that Giovanni was right; he could get lost and die down here. Now the wound in his arm was really hurting.

Around blind corners they sped, down stairways, up inclines and down long dark corridors. They finally broke out into a wide, well-lit passageway. After a quick glance back, Giovanni kept going, pulling away a bit as Jeff strained to keep up. Finally, at a steep stairway, Giovanni stopped, got off and began lugging the heavy scooter up the stairway to the passageway above.

Jeff arrived at the stairs, shouldered the bicycle and hurried upward, gaining the top with Giovanni. "Another kilometer," the little man panted. "When I signal, you must turn to the right. You will connect with Autostrada del Sole near the airport. Good luck."

"Thank you, Giovanni. Good luck to you too."

An aftershock rocked the area, sending clouds of dust and debris down all around them. Speeding on and still struggling to keep up, Jeff kept following the disappearing tail light until Giovanni stopped at a lit intersection. Waving toward the right, Giovanni glanced back at him; Jeff waved acknowledgement, and farewell.

To the right, the tunnel opened out into a brightly lit but deserted underground mall. Ahead a steep stairway sign read *Autostrada del Sole*. He was making his way toward it when the lighting failed, and he stopped to dismount, making his way the last few yards to the stairs in complete darkness. Feeling his way, he lugged the bicycle upward. At the top he could see daylight in the distance, so he rode slowly forward until he broke out onto the surface.

Suddenly he was near the crowded freeway, heading out of the city.

Exhausted, he sat on the side of the road, watching the people struggling north. He had considered getting out his cell phone to ignite the Vesuvius explosives, but he'd obviously have to wait, allow more time for all these people to evacuate. In the meantime he would deliver his own form of justice on Camponolo. His interference had put their lives at risk, and goddamn him, he was going to pay for this.

Thirsty and tired, he got back on the bike and headed north with the others. The trip north to Gaeta was grueling; traffic was barely moving and pedestrians shared the freeway. He tried a few side routes but soon realized they were just as bad, although on one loop he was able to get a bite to eat.

The meal left him even more tired. After struggling a few more miles he gave in to his exhaustion, leaving the road again to sleep under an overpass.

He finally arrived in Gaeta, a beautiful community on the western sea coast. Doubling as a tourist town and a place where the Naples wealthy kept their yachts, it was surrounded by vineyards and exclusive estate wineries. A few people were arriving from the Naples evacuation but most were bypassing it on the main vehicle routes.

Jeff found a shop that was open and bought new clothes, then checked into a small hotel, registering as Fred Jones. He started shaving, checking first to make sure the skin under his beard wasn't pale enough to attract unwanted attention. After a long hot shower, he dressed and visited the hotel's colorful restaurant.

The waiter came over to his table with the menu. *"Buonasera. Che cosa desidera?"*

Jeff tried his Italian. *"Bistecca con patate fritte. Insalata verde con pomodori."*

"Caffè?"

"Per favore."

"Are you American?" The waiter asked in perfect English. "Your Italian is good."

"I'm just learning. And yes, I'm American."

"Ah! I know who you are! Your picture has been on the television. The people call you *Volcano Ragazzo*… Volcano Boy. And your young woman friend they call *Volcano Ragazza*, Volcano Girl."

Jeff frowned. How did they get his picture? Was it from surveillance in the council chambers?

"But this is a happy thing," the waiter insisted. "The people of Italy, they love you! Everyone reads the Catrina Rossi news story each day."

"Ahhh…" Jeff relaxed a bit.

"Did you just come from Naples? I hear it is hell down there. They have ordered a full evacuation. Imagine! Is Campi Flegrei about to erupt, as you say?"

"It's looking that way." Jeff sighed, then smiled at the waiter. "Please, just get my order and I will add to your tip if you don't mention you've seen me here."

The waiter nodded. "Okay, but you will be recognized. You and your friend have become a very big news story."

Jeff considered this while waiting for his meal. Maybe he shouldn't have shaved; he could have gone back to his original disguise. The public profile was going to make it tougher to get to Camponolo and force him into confessing. He had to get enough evidence for the police to charge him with murder. Should he give it up?

No. Many Naples residents had just perished because of this man, and Hilda Marsh. If Camponolo would not admit the murder, perhaps Jeff would just kill him and be done with it.

And Dr. Marsh?

The waiter arrived with his meal. "I understand Naples celebrities keep their yachts at the marina," said Jeff. "Have you seen any of them lately?"

The waiter thought for a moment. *"Sì.* Luigi Marco was here early this morning. Antonio Camponolo—you know him!—he was just here. And also Angelo Marini, he was here a few hours ago. They are all taking their yachts out to sea to keep them safe."

"Why wouldn't they be safe here?"

The waiter shrugged. "It seems to me they would be okay. You see them right down there in the marina."

"Ah, it must be nice to have money."

The waiter grinned. *"Ah, deniro, deniro."*

Jeff finished his supper and was leaving a tip when six men entered the restaurant. Similarly dressed in black field gear, at first glance they could have passed for a S.W.A.T. team or emergency response unit, except they carried no visible weapons and their boots were all different. They took a table, called out to the waiter for coffee and, with their heads together, began an intense conversation.

Jeff could overhear a few words including *el sindaco* and *non si sorprenda* which he thought would translate to "the mayor" and "it's not surprising."Could it be that the mayor of Naples was coming here? As he left his table and walked toward the hotel lobby, one of the men called out, "Hey, *Americano Ragazzo!"*

Damn! Ignoring the man and not looking back, he continued on and took the elevator up to his room. There, he checked the Beretta's ammunition clip, snapped it into place and slipped the weapon into his right jacket pocket, the cell phone and its battery in the inner pocket.

It was dusk when he left the hotel by a side exit and headed for the nearby marina. The *Signora Luisa* was moored at the far end of a long row of luxury yachts. It wasn't large, about the size of the *Cannelle.* The cabin lights were on and people moved about inside its main deck salon. Jeff ducked behind a shed at the end of the boat slip and watched as a man arrived wearing a trench coat, collar up, and carrying a briefcase. As he boarded the yacht, the salon door opened, revealing Dr. Antonio Camponolo.

"*Buonasera, Erico! Vendi la tua casa?*" Camponolo asked.

"*Sí. Appena in tempo!*" Benvenuti waved the briefcase.

"*Buona, buona!*" Awkwardly embracing his visitor, Camponolo turned, looking back into the salon. "*Andiamo!* Hilda, tell them to start the engines!"

Bloody hell! What now? Both Camponolo and Hilda Marsh were right here within his grasp, but what could he do? And the sleazy deputy mayor was with them.

Deciding the opportunity was too good to pass up, he sprinted across the wharf, up the walkway and onto the stern. The *Signora Luisa* shifted ever so slightly. The deck lights came on and Camponolo called, "*Chi c'è?*"

Jeff froze against the bulwark, not daring to breathe.

"Who's there?" Hilda cried out. "Is someone there?"

Another man's voice. "*Che cos'è?*"

"*Niente, nessuno,*" Camponolo said. "Hilda, it is no one. Just calm down."

Jeff entered the lower deck. With pistol drawn, he made his way along the unlit passageway until he found an unlocked door marked *Privata*. He pushed it open. It was dark inside. Weapon ready, he slipped inside.

Something crashed down on his forearm, sending the pistol flying. Another arm encircled him from behind and a hand clamped over his mouth. Cold steel pressed against his throat, and a gruff voice whispered, "You not move, *ragazzo!* You not move a muscle!"

In the darkness, Jeff stood perfectly still, the edge of a sharp blade pressing against his jugular. As the cabin lights came on, he recognized the men from the hotel restaurant. They studied him until one nodded silently. They took his weapon, pushed him down onto the bed and placed slipties on his wrists and ankles. The leader looked down at Jeff, tucking the Berretta into his coat.

"*Un momento*," Jeff objected quietly. "*Che... che cosa significa... questo?* Does anyone speak English?"

Grunting, one of the men stuffed a rag in Jeff's mouth and covered it with tape. The men waited silently as the yacht's diesels started up and the craft nosed out of the marina.

Their leader was short and stocky with the swarthy look of a hard working Italian farmer, but he had a take-charge attitude, a military erectness and walked on the balls of his feet like and athlete.

Looking around the cabin, Jeff saw five concrete blocks with eye hooks; the kind that when tied together could be used to moor small watercraft off-shore—not something you'd usually see in a sleeping cabin. Twenty minutes passed. They would be well out to sea now. Finally the leader spoke. "*È ora di farlo*," he said, turning off the lights. They left silently, closing the door behind them.

There was a sudden commotion above; shots rang out and the sound of shrill voices. Thuds. Someone yelled, "*Abbastanza! Abbastanza! Perchè? Non, perchè? Non!*"

More commotion—shots, a scream and a loud splash.

Silence. As the minutes ticked by, Jeff's mind raced. Someone had gone overboard. Was he next? He struggled with his bonds. Rolling to the edge of the mattress, he only managed to fall face first to the floor.

Shit. Now his nose was bleeding, making it tough to breathe. Best to just relax before he suffocated.

The throb of the diesels and the sway and roll of the ship was somehow comforting, reminding him of the ill-fated *Cannelle.* An hour passed and no one came. Had they forgotten him? Had Camponolo somehow overpowered them? Exhausted, Jeff fell asleep.

Friday, June 26, early morning
Jeff woke with a start. Light streamed through the porthole. Footsteps. The door opened. Three of his captors came in; each picked up a concrete block and left with it, this time leaving the door open.

Two concrete blocks remained. His heart beat faster. Hell of a way to die, and crap timing—before knowing about Campi... before activating the Vesuvius explosives.

The cell phone! Where the hell was the cell? They hadn't taken it. He couldn't feel it in his pocket, but maybe it was there. With his hands tied behind his back there was no way... He should concentrate on something positive and calm himself. Camponolo and Marsh looked to be about to get theirs...

Scraping noises from above, a scuffle. Minutes passed. More footsteps; two of the men came in. Cutting his ankle ties, they pulled him erect and led him up a stairway to the next deck. Still struggling to breathe, Jeff could see a trail of blood and bloody footprints leading from the salon door across the deck toward the outer deck rail. The railing was also smeared with blood. Whoever had gone overboard had been shot first, then thrown.

Jeff was pushed along the aisle toward the after-deck. There, a grisly scene was unfolding. Deputy Mayor Erico Benvenuti sat against the aft cabin wall, his head bloodied, his mouth taped, his hands tied behind his back, his legs chained to a concrete block. Beyond, three of the captors stood guard over Antonio Camponolo and Hilda Marsh.

They sat awkwardly on the deck with their hands tied behind their backs and their feet chained together. Two concrete blocks sat near them but had not been attached. Camponolo was groaning. His mouth was puffy and bleeding.

Jeff was thrown onto the deck. They retied his ankles and attached them to one of the concrete blocks. Heart pounding, he watched as the men did the same to Camponolo, who cursed them loudly in Italian.

"*Mi porti un'altra,*" the leader ordered.

"*Sì, Riccardo.*" The leader waited while one of his men brought another concrete block from the lower deck. As they attached it Hilda Marsh's feet, she cried silently. Then Riccardo and his men climbed the stairway to the pilothouse, leaving them alone in their misery.

Jeff twisted around, looked at Camponolo, and scrunched his eyes in a smile. Camponolo muttered an oath. "You dumb little shit. You should have died with your mother."

Dr. Marsh raised her head. "I told you. We should have been out of Italy long ago. But no. You and your—"

"Shut up, Hilda."

Jeff lay quietly, anger boiling in him. At least they would die with him today. He wondered what it would be like to drown. How long would he hold his breath?

The men came back down the stairway, ignoring a string of Italian oaths from Camponolo. Riccardo walked over to Jeff and ripped the tape from his face. To Jeff's relief, the rag came partway out with the tape, and he was able to spit out the rest.

Riccardo looked down at him. "So you no speak Italiano," he said. "So, who are you? Why are you here?"

"My name is Jeff Kingston."

The leader nodded and glanced at his men. "So, Jeff Kingson, why are you here?"

"Do not believe a word he says," Camponolo interjected. "The boy is a liar! *Per amor di Dio! È serve—*"

Riccardo kicked Camponolo in the gut. He turned back to Jeff. "Why are you here?"

Jeff hesitated. "It's personal," he said. "Twelve years ago these people murdered my mother. Then, to stop me from predicting the eruption a few days ago, Camponolo sent assassins to murder me and my colleague, Anita Arneil. He fire-bombed the wrong yacht, killing innocent people, then blew up our yacht while my colleague and I were on board. He and Marsh have worked together to deceive the people of Naples, causing untold deaths. When we tried to warn the city, Camponolo had us thrown in jail and tried to kill us there. I came on board to force Camponolo to confess to the murder of my mother. I planned to record it on my cell phone as evidence to give the authorities." He jutted his chin toward Camponolo and Marsh. "They should both be in prison."

"If they refuse to confess, you would shoot them?"

"I—" Jeff spat out dried blood. "I didn't really have a plan for that."

"How did you arrange to meet with this crook, the deputy mayor?"

"I didn't know Benvenuti *was* a crook." Jeff snorted. "I thought he'd listen, help evacuate the city. I still don't know why—"

Riccardo leaned down, felt through Jeff's coat, retrieved the cell phone and its battery, and looked at them for a moment. He fit the battery to the phone, then placed it in his own pocket. He cut Jeff's bonds. "We know how they sink your yacht," he said. "You have nothing to fear from us. Get up." Riccardo took a sheaf of papers from his coat. "We enter Camponolo's villa yesterday. In his wall safe we find much money, records, bank accounts. And we find this. It is draft scientific report written ten years ago. It is written in English."

He gave Jeff the neatly bound papers. "I have read your history in Catrina Rossi article. Dr. Kristin Stefsdotir was you mother. This belong to her."

Scrawled across the top of the document in his mother's neat handwriting was: *First draft copy for preliminary review by Drs. Marsh and Camponolo.*

CAMPI FLEGREI—PREVENTION OF CATASTROPHE IN EUROPE AND THE MEDITERRANEAN. *Detailed Prediction of Eruption, submitted by Dr. Kristin Stefsdotir and Dr. Reginald Pyper...*

Riccardo pointed at the papers. "Instead of listening to your mother and this man Pyper, who can tell them how to save thousands of people from a terrible death, these two decide to shut them up."

"Damn you for keeping that," Hilda mumbled.

"Quiet!" Camponolo growled.

Riccardo scowled down at Camponolo. "You sunk this boy's yacht, so it is only fair we give you an option to replace it. Other option is we drop you all into sea, feed sharks. First option sounds a little better: You will sign over the ownership your yacht to Jeff Kingston for one euro and we put you in the wooden rowboat with food and water. What do you say?"

Camponolo leaned forward, *"Io ho del denaro."*

Riccardo snorted. "I don't want your money."

Camponolo nodded resignedly. *"Sì, è tuo.* The yacht, it's yours."

"Go to pilothouse," Riccardo told Jeff. "Find yacht registration. Write out bill of sale. Camponolo will sign. Marsh will witness."

It took only a few minutes to find the registration in the pilothouse and write out a bill of sale. When Jeff returned to the deck Riccardo, pistol drawn, had it signed and witnessed. He handed it to Jeff. "You still think Campi Flegrei will erupt?"

Jeff nodded. "With my phone I can read the Naples monitoring instruments and tell you what's happening under the city."

Riccardo handed over the phone and waited expectantly as Jeff scrolled through a few screens.

"This does not look good," he said. "Look. See this map of the Naples Volcanic Area? Each one of those tiny groups of markers are called leveling networks. Anchored in solid rock, they are monitoring stations. They are positioned around the Naples area to measure the vertical movements of the earth's surface. This shows that for the past thirty-six hours there have been intense episodes of surface uplift around the caldera. This indicates that the likelihood of an eruption is still increasing."

Riccardo took the cell phone from Jeff and looked northward. "We will turn the yacht around. Return to the marina. If it erupts, you think we have tsunami?"

"Yes."

Riccardo looked at his men. "*È ora di andare,*" he said. Then he turned to his prisoners. Over objections from the still bound-up pair, Riccardo's men carried the two down to the lower deck where the rowboat had already been put in the water. The two were placed on board, one in the stern and one in the bow. The men attached the chains from the cement blocks to the captives' ankle ties, then they threw in a bag of food.

Hilda's voice wavered. "How do we free ourselves?"

Riccardo smiled. "No problem. Knife in food bag."

"And where is our water?" Hilda complained.

"Ah yes, your friend the deputy mayor will provide this!" Riccardo nodded to his men who were up on the deck above. "Stay clear of center. Here he comes now!"

From above, two of Riccardo's men flung the mayor down into the rowboat. The concrete block chained to his feet hit first, crashing down into the middle of the little boat, cracking through the floorboards.

Water began flooding in.

"*Del'acqua* for Dr. Marsh." Riccardo laughed. "You think it is fair to tell part of the story, lie about other half. Now is your turn to get only half truth. Our families all die at Lake Fusaro!" Switching to Italian, he continued to shout as the two boats slowly drifted apart.

Jeff watched in horror. "My god," he objected, as the boat's occupants, still bound hand and foot, screamed for help. "You can't—"

"Ah, but I can," Riccardo growled. "My wife and children die yesterday in Lake Fusaro eruption. No warning. Only reassurance all was safe. Too late the *cane bastardo* evacuate the city. Those three responsible for our family dying. Now, they die too."

"But the courts, couldn't they have convicted them?"

"You think they get where they are without help?" He laughed bitterly and pointed to his chest. "We convict," he said. "They pay."

Jeff watched seawater gushing up inside the boat. Hilda Marsh began wriggling to the food bag. Turning her back to it, she began searching frantically through the bag. "I've got the knife!" she yelled. "Move over with your back to me! I'll cut your bonds!"

The mayor whimpered in terror. Camponolo lurched past him in the rising water and twisted, holding his bound hands back toward Hilda. "Do it!"

Choking and cursing, Hilda struggled with the knife. Camponolo suddenly came up with his hands free.

"Buon, buon!" Camponolo yelled. He reached down, grabbed a concrete block and heaved it over the side. The chain rattled after it, dragging the deputy mayor feet-first into the water. Camponolo turned to Hilda, who was thrashing about, trying to slice at her bonds and keep her head above the rising water.

"Antonio, help me! Cut me loose!"

Camponolo reached into the water near her feet.

"Here," she cried. "Take the knife!"

Straining, Camponolo heaved another concrete block out of the boat. Jeff's stomach lurched; Hilda's screams were silenced as the chain dragged her under.

Camponolo reached down near his own feet, tugging at the bonds. Riccardo put a hand on Jeff's arm. "Leave him to die," he said. "The knife went with the woman, and his little boat will sink before he saves himself." He turned and left.

Jeff was alone on the lower deck.

"*Ragaaaazzzzzzo!*" Sunbeams reflecting off the water obstructed Jeff's view of the little boat, but he heard the spine-chilling shout from Camponolo. "We have your girlfriend and her mother and sisters, *ragazzo!* If my men do not hear from me in twelve hours, they will kill them all!"

... seismic profiles of undersea portions of Campi Flegrei show massive rock fracture at points of maximum uplift...

CHAPTER 20

Friday, June 26, morning
"Stop the yacht!" Jeff ran up the stairs. "Turn around! Go back! Go back!" By the time he reached the pilothouse, the yacht was speeding shoreward. "You must turn around," he shouted. "He's got Anita and her family! Camponolo's the only one who can tell me where they're being held prisoner! Turn! Please turn!"

The man at the wheel shook his head. *"Io non capisco Inglese."*

Jeff picked up the field glasses and focused them in, but was unable to pick out the boat among the waves. "He's the only one who can tell me..." He looked at the man at the wheel imploringly. *"Girare! Girari!"*

The man shook his head again.

Jeff rushed down to the salon and found Riccardo. "Camponolo's men have Anita and her family! You've got to go back!"

Riccardo shook his head. "No. I will not turn back. You will have the yacht when we are back to the Gaeta marina, yes? Now leave! I must make calls."

A shudder enveloped Jeff as he checked his watch. He had until nine tonight, maybe less—

"Oh God, Anita!" The rowboat would have swamped

by now. He couldn't see it against the glare of the rising sun. How could he find Anita and her family? They had to turn back!

Jeff's stomach sank. It may be too late anyway. Camponolo had probably drowned by now. He left the salon and tried to calm himself. There must be another way to find them. What was he missing? He went to the rail and watched the green Italian countryside drawing nearer. Think Jeff, think!

Riccardo's men had left the salon, so he went inside. He must find something, some clue that would expose where Camponolo's people were holding the Arneils.

After hours of travel on smooth pavement, the van was bouncing on a dirt road. When they'd stopped for gas Anita had hoped to get a chance to call for help, but one of the kidnappers stayed with them, pointing a gun in their direction, while the other fueled up. He disappeared for a few minutes, returning with a few bags of take-out food.

Although her hands were tied, she used the jostling motion of the van to try to wriggle her phone from where she'd stashed it. She thought she was having some success when the van slowed, turned, bounced hard for a few seconds and then came to a stop.

The kidnappers climbed out and opened the side door, waving them out of the van. Cramped and stiff, the women stumbled to the ground. From there, they were shoved into a shed.

One of the kidnappers, Diego, brought in the bags of food and set them on the wooden floor of the shed, then cut their wrist straps while the other, Francisco, held the gun on them. Diego pointed to a bucket in the corner and made a rude gesture with his groin.

"Toilet?" said Anita.

He nodded. The door banged closed, and they were left alone in the dark.

Anita tugged out her phone and dialed the cell number Jeff had given her. She groaned.

"Lines are still clogged," she whispered, holding the phone up to give them a bit of light.

Sandra shook her head. "Everyone's probably trying to call right now," she said, leaning forward to open the bags of food. She passed a package to Cheryl, who made a face.

"Better eat it," said Janet, taking her share. "You might not get any more."

Cheryl nodded glumly.

"Hold on," said Anita. She turned the phone and pointed it at the take-out menu stapled to the food bag. "Maybe this will get through." She punched a few buttons and clicked *send*. "Quick, girls. Get your food. I need to hide this again." She deleted all evidence that she'd sent the photo, deleted the phone's history, stashed it, and tried to choke down some food.

She had to figure out a way to get them out of here. So far every plan she'd come up with seemed likely to end with someone she loved getting killed.

Riccardo came into the salon, sat down and studied Jeff. "We leave you at the marina, Kingston. You tell no one of what happened this day. Our families die because of those murderers. They get what they deserve."

Jeff nodded and put his fingers to his lips. "Your secret is safe with me. I must find Anita."

"Something interesting just now on the radio," Riccardo said. "There is worldwide warning about Naples Campi Flegrei eruption. International volcano center in America is receive, how do you say... information from a new source. This source shows Flegrei, it is erupt... and very soon. Cruise ships and foreign peoples are to leave from Eastern Mediterranean."

"Information from a new source?" Jeff frowned. Was it the data Giovanni sent direct to Florida?

No, it couldn't be. They'd had those same data feeds from Campi Flegrei for years.

Riccardo placed the cell phone and battery, the Beretta and the keys to the yacht on the table. "Good luck to you, Jeff Kingston."

After Riccardo left, Jeff snapped the battery into the cell phone and tried to call Anita. All lines were busy; he couldn't reach any of the numbers he tried. He got up and went back out on the deck. What the hell was he doing? He had no time to go on a wild goose-chase looking for them. He had a far more important mission to finish and very little time left to finish it… a mission that may save millions. Perhaps hundreds of millions.

Tangling with Camponolo had almost cost him the opportunity to detonate the explosives.

He secured the yacht and walked up to the hotel. The clerk took in his bloodied nose and disheveled appearance. Jeff ignored his concern, booking the room for two more nights. He pointed to the television behind the clerk. "What's the news out of Naples?"

The clerk picked up the remote and switched to an American news channel. The screen showed a mass of people still fleeing the city; according to the news tape along the bottom, officials hoped to have the city cleared within another forty-eight hours.

Jeff shook his head. Well, no way on God's green earth he was going to just sit around waiting. With another two days until he could detonate the explosives, he had to do something to find Anita and her family. If Camponolo was telling the truth, he only had… he glanced at his watch.

Shit.

Where could he have taken her?

He snapped the battery into the cell phone. No message, no email, nothing from Anita to show which way she might have gone, where they'd caught her, how long they'd had her. Should he risk keeping the battery in the cell phone? Camponolo hadn't been working alone.

The phone buzzed in his hand. A message—from Anita! A photo of a take-out menu? What the—oh, of course! He swiped the screen to enlarge it, zooming in on the address. Strada Statale 577, L'Aquila AQ, Italy.

He considered calling the number back, but realized he'd probably just succeed in alerting her captors. Shutting off the cell phone, he pulled the battery, stowed it and the Beretta in the backpack with the rest of his stuff, locked the door of his hotel room and took a taxi to the nearest car rental agency.

Four hours later, Jeff had found the restaurant, a highway outpost just west of the junction with 690. He ordered a coffee and a sandwich to go, then used the restroom. When he came out, he was pleased to see that the take-out bag had an identical menu to the one in the photo.

He took the bag to the rental car and waited in the deserted parking lot. Two cars went by, and a young couple on bicycles. Half an hour later, the coffee was gone and he was considering getting another when a dusty Fiat pulled into the parking lot.

A man got out, went inside, and reappeared moments later with four take-out bags of food. Jeff waited for the Fiat to pull out of the lot, then followed.

The car headed east to the junction of 690, then turned south. Realizing the driver could be watching for a tail, Jeff passed the junction and then wheeled around, turning onto the 690, fingers crossed that he hadn't lost the Fiat. He needn't have worried. Just past the junction a cloud of dust billowed from a side road off to the right; a bit further up the hillside, the Fiat was climbing a switchback.

Jeff followed. Within a few miles he spotted a fence line, then an open gateway. Between a cabin and a small shed, dust was still settling around the Fiat. Jeff backed the rental around a corner and parked. He slipped between the strands of barbed wire and crept forward through the bushes, ducking when the man emerged from the shed. As he watched, the man reached through the Fiat's open window and retrieved a take-out bag, then went into the cabin.

Wood smoke wafted from the cabin's chimney, and Jeff approached cautiously. The door stood partly open; inside, the man stood feeding a small wood-burner. The take-out bag sat on the nearby table.

Jeff slipped past the cabin to the shed. Its door was secured with an iron hasp. The padlock hung open but laced through the hook to prevent the door being opened from the inside. Jeff removed the padlock, but as he opened the door its hinges squealed.

From the cabin came the sound of a chair being pushed back. Jeff ducked inside the shed. "It's Jeff," he whispered.

Behind him, the man was at the shed door. Through the crack around its jamb, Jeff watched him reaching for the hasp. He slammed the door back into the man, sending him off balance, his rifle firing harmlessly into the air. As the man tried to bring the rifle down into firing position, Jeff stepped in close and gave him a judo chop to the neck.

Dropping the rifle and gasping for air, the man turned and staggered back to the cabin. Jeff grabbed the weapon and followed, slamming the rifle butt into the back of the man's neck and sending him to the floor. The kidnapper fell forward, sending the table flying into the wood burner, knocking it over. As the metal chimney collapsed, soot and smoke billowed into the cabin.

Jeff left the man choking and writhing in pain and ran to free the women in the shed.

Sandra Arneil was already outside with Cheryl and Janet. Jeff looked behind them. "Where is Anita?"

"Jeff, thank God you found us," said Sandra. "They took Anita away in the van about half an hour ago."

"Are you three okay?" Jeff asked.

"We're sore and tired, but unhurt," Sandra said. "They jumped us at the Abruzzo airport, dumped us up here."

"They?"

She nodded. "There were two. One took Anita—"

There was loud *poof* from the cabin, and a flash of light as flames erupted inside. Jeff stepped through the doorway and grabbed the kidnapper by the ankles, hauling him out and dumping him unceremoniously on the ground.

"What is your name?" Jeff asked.

The man on the ground gave him a defiant look.

"The other guy called him Diego," said Janet.

"And that guy's name was Francisco," said Cheryl.

Jeff grinned at them, then glowered at Diego. "Where did they go? Where did they take the young woman?"

"Dov'e mia figlia?" Sandra demanded.

The man, still choking, answered hesitatingly.

"He doesn't know," Sandra translated, holding the two girls close. "Before they took Anita away, they got a call. God knows how they managed to get through; Anita tried and tried to call you, but all the lines were busy. Was it the photo she sent you that—"

Jeff nodded. "They got a call?"

"Yes. Camponolo told them to take Anita somewhere, he doesn't know where. He thinks it was a ferry terminal."

Jeff frowned. "Camponolo? Are you sure?"

Sandra nodded. "They were talking about how Camponolo was picked up by a fishing boat after some kind of mishap at sea."

Jeff glared at the injured kidnapper, reached down and checked his pockets, retrieving a phone, the keys to the Fiat, and a pocket knife.

He dragged the man into the shed.

"Are you going to lock him in?" asked Janet.

"That's what he tied us up with when he went for food," said Cheryl, pointing to a container of tie straps.

"Then he tied us onto those hooks so we couldn't get up and kick the door open," said Janet.

"Otherwise we'd have been long gone," nodded Cheryl, glaring fiercely at the kidnapper.

"Well, I think that's what we'd better do to him," said

Jeff. After securing Diego, he handed Sandra the padlock. "Climb into the car while your mom locks up," he told the girls. In a low voice he said to Sandra, "Tell him that if he follows us, I will kill him."

Backing the Fiat out onto the road, he waited for Sandra to join them, then drove the short distance to where he'd left the rental. "Take my rental and drive to Paris," he said, unlocking it passing her the keys. "Do you have money for fuel?"

Sandra shook her head. "They took my purse."

He peeled off some euros and held them out to her.

"We have no passports," she said. "They took them from Anita at the airport. I'll have to go back… but where? And Keith is…"

Jeff leaned forward to take Sandra in his arms. "I am so sorry about Colonel Arneil," he said, hugging her for a moment. Then he released her. "Anita didn't get all of her strength from her father's side. I know you three will do everything in your power to get each other to safety."

The girls nodded solemnly, and Sandra swallowed, smiling at them.

"Go to the nearest military base and explain your situation," he suggested.

Sandra Arneil squared her shoulders. "Yes. Yes, that will work."

As the girls settled into their seatbelts, Jeff pulled his backpack from the floor on the passenger side and got out a cell phone. "I picked up a couple of these along the way," he said. "I know they're not much good right now, but you might need one at some point. If you think you're being followed after you've used it, pull the battery—I think that's how they've been tracing our movements. We'll find you by calling NATO." He copied the cell's phone number onto a corner of the map the rental agency had given him, tore it off and tucked it in his wallet. "Spin around and follow me back to the pavement. We'll be here." He drew an X on the map, then gave it to Sandra.

She nodded.

"From there, just focus on getting the girls to safety. I'll find you as soon as I have Anita."

Sandra squeezed his hand. "Thank you, Jeff. Find my daughter."

"I will. You can be sure of that."

On the drive back in the Fiat, Jeff developed a plan. The previous day, Camponolo probably expected to set the *Signora Luisa* on a planned course before leaving the Gaeta marina. He'd had a destination in mind when he put out to sea with Hilda Marsh and Benvenuti; it would still be in the ship's computer. Now, rescued by a fishing boat, Camponolo may still be on his way to that location. That meant the *Signora Luisa* would still have a course setting that may take him directly to both Camponolo and Anita.

It was a hunch but it seemed like a good one. And it was the only one he had. Heading down to the Marina where the *Signora Luisa* lay berthed, he had a sudden concern. What if Camponolo had returned to Gaeta and taken the yacht? But his fears were short-lived. Even in the dark, he could see the yacht was still there.

He approached the yacht carefully, did a thorough search of the craft, and decided he was alone. In the pilothouse he turned on the lights, went to the master computer and brought up the yacht's course settings.

He checked against the map. Savona, well up the coast—almost at the French border. He did a map search: there was a ferry terminal serving the island of Corsica.

Jeff crossed his fingers, hoping he was right. He checked the VolcanoWatch feed: ... *seismic profiles of undersea portions of Campi Flegrei are showing massive rock fracture at all points of maximum uplift...*

Trying to ignore the sick feeling at the pit of his stomach, he picked up the yacht's hand-held remote control and was about to back the yacht out of the marina when he had a thought. Whoever was transporting Anita was communicating with Camponolo by phone. What if there was a way of interjecting himself into that communications loop? Although the kidnappers had a half-hour lead from the cabin, they had a long way to go to Savona by land — they couldn't possibly have arrived.

And he had Diego's phone. What if he had him drive Anita to a different location, away from Camponolo?

He checked the kidnapper's phone log. There were numerous calls to "F" from "D." He checked the number in the contacts. Francesco.

It was worth a try. Using an online translator, he composed a brief text message: F: CHANGE OF PLAN. CAMPONOLO SAYS BRING GIRL TO YACHT SIGNORA LUISA. ANZIO HARBOR. 06:30 ALIVE. CONFIRM. D.

After a tense half-hour, a reply finally popped up. CONFIRMED.

"Yes!" Jeff yelled. "Yes! Yes! Yes!"

Saturday, June 27, early morning
With the *Signora Luisa* handling well in the rough waters of the approaching storm, Jeff was nosing into the Anzio harbor. On the cliffs above Anzio beach, the famous Tor Caldara Tower sat like a small sentinel on a headland. In the harbor, choked with fishing boats, he steered in near the ferry terminal and stopped the vessel without setting anchor. Throttling the diesels down to idle, he used the translator to practice several Italian phrases and waited.

This was too easy. It would never work.

A motor launch approached carrying three people, a man and two women; the one in the center was clearly Anita. As they approached the yacht, Jeff went to the rail, motioned them aft and hurried down to the deck where they could board easily. As the motor launch drew close, Jeff could see amazement in Anita's eyes. Her hands were bound and she looked tired but unharmed.

"*Voglio parlare a Camponolo,*" the man said.

"*Più tardi. Il ragazza!*" Jeff pointed at Anita, motioning her aboard. When one of the men made a move to board, Jeff waved him off. "*Il ragazza,*" he repeated authoritatively pointing to Anita.

The man stepped back to allow Anita to move forward. Jeff reached out and caught her, dragged her aboard, and shoved her toward the inner stairway, yelling sternly, "Up! Go!" As soon as she reached safety he used the hand-held controller to push the diesels up to full throttle. The yacht plunged forward, almost swamping the motor launch in its heavy wake.

"*Stai attento!*" the woman hollered while the man yelled a stream of oaths. "*Che cos'è questo?*"

Jeff retreated up the aisle, onto the stairway, following Anita to the upper deck. "Sorry for the rough treatment!" Hurrying past her to the pilothouse, he turned the craft out toward the open sea.

Anita, breathless, followed. "My God Jeff! Did you find Mom and my sisters?"

"Yes. They're free, and your mom was determined to get them safely to the nearest military base. Come, I'll untie your hands. Are you okay?"

"Yes, I'm okay. Are they following?"

"No. They looked utterly confused. They turned back toward the shore. If I were them, I'd be running from Camponolo."

"How did you get his yacht?"

"I'll explain later."

"But how did you…"

Jeff freed her hands, looked into her beautiful green eyes, and hugged her to him. "Are you sure you're okay?"

"Yes." She rubbed her wrists behind his back, hugging him. "But Jeff… Dad is gone…"

"I'm so very sorry about your father." He held her for a moment, sharing her pain.

"It hasn't really sunk in yet."

"What about you," he said. "Did they hurt you?"

She shook her head. "They were too worried about their families back in Naples to pay much attention to us. I'm shaken, but okay. Are you sure Mom and...?

"I put them in a rental car, with some money for gas. They'll be fine. As soon as we can, we'll track them down and let them know you're okay."

"Oh, I'm so relieved! Jeff... about Dad. It's devastating. I wish he had listened about not flying over the Lake Fusaro area. The NATO folks said the helicopter was over the eruption and disappeared in the cloud of... They don't believe any of the..." she looked at the deck and sucked in a breath, "... any of the remains of those killed will ever be recovered." Swallowing, she held out a hand. "If you'll lend me your phone, I'll go below and try to find Mom."

"Start with this number." He dug the scrap from his wallet. "If you don't get an answer, leave a message to let her know you're okay. Then call NATO. They're sure to have some kind of family reconnect system set up by now." He watched her go below.

A while later she returned. "You reach your mother?"

She brushed tears away, nodding. "NATO's helping them get new passports, and they've arranged for a couple of soldiers to take Mom and the girls directly to Paris. From there, they'll fly to London."

"How did they nab you?"

"They were covering all the major airports, looking for you and me. And Jeff, after being with those members of the dreaded C-2 for several hours, listening to them talk, without them knowing I could understand Italian—it was absolutely amazing. They thought they would be instructed to kill us. They spoke openly about Camponolo's role in an elite group within the C-2 called the *Corrado* which means 'bold counsel.' The group wields total power over Italy's bloodiest Mafia."

Jeff rubbed his eyes. "We were lucky today. They didn't see through my ruse."

"Yes. And wait until you hear the rest! If you thought my life was in danger before... well, before you and I were just like a thorn in Camponolo's big toe. Now, when they find out I've escaped their custody—with the information I've learned in the last few hours? I'll be on the C-2's most wanted list! You are looking at a dead woman Jeff. In fact, now that you've rescued me? We are the walking dead!"

Jeff stared at her, his head spinning. "Anita, can you tell me later?" He gestured for her to take the helm, then bent to his backpack and started pulling the batteries out of the cell phones and laptops. "Take us out to sea a ways and cut the power. Drift for a couple hours. I have nothing left. I've only slept two hours in... I can't remember. I have to crash and regain some strength." He went into the salon, collapsed on the divan and closed his eyes.

… massive magma source centered at a depth of 2.8 to 3.2 km beneath the Bay of Pozzuoli and the City of Naples…

CHAPTER 21

Saturday, June 27, noon
After taking the *Signora Luisa* out to sea and allowing her to drift for a while, Anita sat in the pilothouse listening to the yacht's motors idle softly while the ship rolled and pitched in the advancing storm. Here on the Tyrrhenian Sea it was raining hard. She wished she'd had more time to talk with Jeff, but he was obviously exhausted. While he slept, she grew increasingly nervous. As it grew closer to noon she held their bow into the advancing storm and considered waking him.

She checked the radio; the volcanic eruption at Lake Fusaro had ended. Ash was no longer falling on Naples, but the whole Mediterranean was being evacuated for fear of a Campi eruption, and concern was growing that the warnings had come too late.

Finally she went into the salon and roused Jeff. "I'm sorry to wake you, but…"

He rose unsteadily to his feet, "How long have I been out?" He looked disoriented.

"A bit over three hours. I'm sure you need more sleep but… come one, one of us should be at the wheel." Taking his elbow, she guided him back to the pilothouse and took the wheel again, making sure the bow was into the wind.

He glanced at his watch. "Holy shit, time is slipping away. The storm has worsened, huh?"

"The wind is getting up. Looks like a blow."

They surveyed the ocean around them. "Okay," Jeff said. "You had something to tell me."

She studied him for a moment. "Jeff, do you recall our discussion about the International Earthquake and Eruption Prediction Center in Orlando, and how they saw absolutely no evidence that Campi was about to erupt?"

"Yes, it's ridiculous. None of the world's leading scientists seem concerned."

"Well, there is a reason for that. Those scientists around the world have not been seeing the true data from Campi."

"The hell you say!"

"The direct feed volcanic data, the VolcanoWatch stuff that you see on the screens of Giovanni's Naples data collection center, is true data that's transmitted to their Com Unit on the floor below. Unknown to Giovanni and his little group of dedicated scientists in the monitoring center, the data they transmitted downstairs has, for several months, been doctored before it was re-transmitted externally. That's because the Com Unit has been run by hand-picked people selected by Dr. Camponolo on authority of the C-2 leaders… the Corrado."

Jeff was speechless for a moment. "But why? Why would they do that?"

"Camponolo and the Corrado have known for some time that the supervolcano is about to erupt. They wanted to keep it from the world so that the real estate prices in southern Italy wouldn't tank. Over the past several months, they have been selling off all of their southern Italian real estate at great profit and moving their families to South America."

Jeff shook his head. "A bloody master deception!"

"Yes, and very lucrative. From what I overheard, I gather they've sold off almost a billion euros worth of real estate in the past few months. And thanks to people in high places, they've done it under the radar."

"Un-bloody-believable!" He was quiet for a moment. "That explains my conversation with Giovanni. I asked if he phoned the scientists around the world to tell them Campi Flegrei was threatening to erupt. He said they were not allowed to do that, that they were only to transmit Campi data to the Com Unit."

"So, then, how did Michael get the correct data?"

Jeff stopped short. "Yes. How did Michael access the truth from the Naples monitoring center?" He nodded with a wry grin. "You know what Michael did? He was a whiz at computer stuff. I remember him telling me he'd hacked into direct feeds from the Naples monitors so he didn't have to register as a user and pay the fees."

"He mentioned that to me too," Anita agreed. "So he got the direct, un-doctored data by hacking into what they were sending downstairs. And that solves the mystery of how a third-year earth sciences student could predict accurately when the PhDs couldn't."

"But how did Camponolo stop the other honest Naples scientists from revealing the truth to their counterparts around the world?"

"From what I could gather, those scientists were fed the same erroneous data, not the real data. For the past few months Camponolo kept their Com Unit off-limits."

"But there are phone calls, conferences. Surely someone would have—"

"I don't know, maybe Camponolo controlled the travel budgets," Anita suggested. "He was very powerful. It was, as you say, a masterful deception."

"Well, the truth was right there all the time, staring us in the face and we didn't see it."

"They deceived an entire population and put them at horrendous risk." Anita paused. "And our friend Dr. Hilda Marsh was up to her eyeballs in it too. She was scouting properties in South America for the C-2 to purchase."

"Camponolo killed her."

"He did?"

Jeff nodded. "Tossed her overboard, with an anchor tied to her feet, like she was nothing." He filled her in on Riccardo. "Last I saw, it looked like Camponolo was going to drown too. He killed Marsh and the deputy mayor just to save his own skin."

"Maybe he didn't trust them."

"Maybe, but at the time it just looked like ruthless self-preservation."

Anita powered up the engines and swung the wheel around, bringing the yacht into a southern heading. She knew where they were going and she knew that Jeff did, too. "There would have been no evidence of their crime," she said. "It would have been destroyed in the eruption along with any witnesses, who would have been amongst the millions of dead."

"Yes. But now many of those witnesses are alive, leaving Naples and heading for safety."

"Their strategy must have changed a few months ago," Anita continued. "For years, they were protecting the tourist industry and vibrant economy of the area. But then, when they realized that Campi was actually about to erupt, they initiated this… this horrific crime."

"Unforgivable criminal arrogance," Jeff agreed. "So that couple that delivered you, they divulged all this—they will be desperate to silence us. If they don't, they'll be murdered by their own leaders for their indiscretion."

"And not counting Camponolo, it sounds like there's eleven in the Corrado. Here, I've listed all the names I can remember." She scratched out Marsh and Benvenuti and passed him the piece of paper. "And there's only two of us." She looked at him, serious. "So, we are the walking dead and we have to stick together."

He nodded slowly. "We do."

"By the way, I wish now I had listened to your advice and stayed clear of airports with Mom and my sisters."

"Yes, but Anita, think about it! If you hadn't been captured, we might never have found out why they did this, and exactly who they are!"

"Yes."

"Just think! Your kidnapping was the key to all this! After the eruption no one may ever have figured out why the VolcanoWatch data wasn't accurate. The whole system would be seen as unreliable."

"My kidnapping *and rescue*. If not for you I'd be dead by now. So would Mom and my sisters. We owe you—"

"Oh, my god," he interrupted. "They will be tracking us. There's GPS on the yacht."

She grinned. "I thought of that. So, let's go where they'll least want to be. Besides, if I'm right about who stole the explosives from the NATO storage, and about what he did with them, we probably have to go back there anyway."

Jeff stepped up close and placed a gentle hand on her shoulder. "I'll go and make our lunch. You have the ship." And he disappeared into the salon.

After making a meal and sharing it with Anita in the pilothouse, Jeff put the battery in Diego's phone and found a new text message. He passed the phone to Anita.

"C has left Italy," she translated. "C not aware we lost the Arneil woman at Anzio. Must keep it that way. Arneil woman with Jeff Kingston on C's yacht. Both now our top 88 priority. Leave communication with C to me. Confirm you understand and meet me usual place tonight. F"

"I guess you were right," he said. "Camponolo is alive and likely gone to South America. These guys are our assassins now."

She smiled. "I've set our course straight for the supervolcano."

"We have to lure the kidnappers into Naples if we are to have any chance at all. They'll be intent on a quick kill."

Clenching his fist in determination, Jeff looked at Anita. They'd have to come up with a very simple plan and kill all of Camponolo's remaining crew quickly. It would probably be a suicide mission for him, but at least it would give Anita a chance to break free of all this. What if... Yes! Eliminate the group of eleven quickly and at the same time detonate the Vesuvius high explosives. He probably wouldn't live to see if it would subdue the supervolcano, but so be it.

He waited until she left the pilothouse. On the computer, he set a course to Corsica that Anita could use to sail away to safety. He then wrote a brief note and hid it in the map case. At the appropriate moment he would tell her where to find it.

Anita returned.

"Want to take the wheel, or would you rather check the yacht for weapons? Camponolo is sure to have some on board."

"I'll start a search," she said. "It's blowing up something awful, isn't it?"

The yacht was beginning to roll and pitch more violently as the storm worsened, so he increased the speed. She came and stood beside him.

He raised his voice. "Once more into the breach my friends... once more! Let blood... let blood be your motto! Slit their gizzards!" Enjoying her reaction, he added, "King Richard III attacking the Turks."

"Did he win?"

"He did. That is, I think he did."

"Okay, King Richard, what is our plan."

"Later, good lass, later. I'm still thinking." He couldn't tell her. She would see it was a suicide mission for him and balk at it.

On the voyage down the Italian coast, they saw smoke from burning buildings but, during the lull in volcanic activity, the heavy rain and wind seemed to be clearing the area of ash. They examined the weapons and ammunition

Anita found during her search. Although now they were heavily armed, he didn't plan to use the weapons. There were other ways to kill rats.

By mid-afternoon they were crossing the Bay of Pozzuoli. Directly above Campi Flegrei, bubbles of hot gasses burst up from the depths carrying the pungent odor of sulfur into the air. The sense of impending disaster was so strong they could actually taste it.

Anita stood at the rail in the storm, staring down into the depths. "This is the closest to the feeling of dying I've ever had," she called out. "Think, in a matter of hours, perhaps minutes, perhaps seconds…"

"We'll sail straight in and find moorage right under the shadow of Mount Vesuvius," Jeff yelled back. "Then we'll leave a few clues as to our whereabouts."

She came into the pilothouse. "So when do I get to hear our plan?"

"We're close to that deserted dock over there. It's protected from the wind. Let's pull in and tie up. Then I'll explain."

With a crew of only two, they had difficulty securing the yacht to the wharf in the high wind, so pulling back out into the bay with their bow to the elements they sat under power riding out the storm. Anita made coffee in the galley and rejoined Jeff in the pilothouse.

"So?"

"Well, here's our plan… as far as it goes." He told her about planting the high explosives in Vesuvius and his plan to explode the volcano into an eruption, hopefully easing the pressure on Campi Flegrei and preventing a full-scale eruption.

"My God Jeff, the whole thing is so far out, it's beyond… it has so little chance of success!"

"Got a better idea?"

"Well okay… but now, how are we going to kill our potential assassins?"

"They must be all taken out together and quickly, so

stragglers can't alert Camponolo and get the whole C-2 after us." He found a close-up map of the Vesuvius cone on the ship's computer, showing the Via Observatorio winding up the mountain and ending just below the crater. Then, tracing the bicycle trail around the mountain side, he pointed to a tiny square spot on the map. "This is a small building. In it is the deep probe down into the throat of the volcano with hundreds of high explosive charges that I can set off with my cell phone. We must lure the Corrado to that building, thinking that we are in it."

Anita frowned. "And how are we going to see when they're in the building… and if we are up there, how are we going to escape such a horrendous explosion?"

"I haven't figured that part out yet," he lied.

She was thoughtful a minute. "How long do you think it will take Diego to get out of the shed and back in touch with the rest of them?"

"A day or two, with luck on our side. Why?"

"You've got his phone."

Jeff nodded slowly. Damn, she was smart. He dug in his pocket and gave her Diego's phone. She texted a brief message and without translating or sending it, showed it to him. "What about this?"

ARNEIL WOMEN FREED BY KINGSTON. I AM CAPTURED. TAKEN TO NAPLES. AM WITH KINGSTON AND ARNEIL WOMAN IN SMALL BUILDING ON SIDE ROAD TOP VESUVIUS JUST BELOW CRATER. HELICOPTER TO FLY THEM OUT SOON AS STORM CLEARS. HURRY. D.

Jeff laughed. "That should work. Translate it to Italian and send it! You're a brain!"

"You realize we'll probably only get the ten."

He nodded. "We can probably take Diego if we have to. He'll be a lame duck on his own."

"Wait. Before we send this, what's your next step in this strategy?"

"I'll go up there and wait for them. When they are all in or near the building I'll activate the explosives inside the deep probe pipe with my phone. Then I'll get the hell out of there."

She tipped her head forward and gave him a "tell me another" look. "Don't bullshit me Jeff. You'll die in the process. It's a suicide mission!"

"I think it's do-able. There is no other way to be certain all ten of the C-2 die at once."

"We better get off this yacht before they get here."

"Yes. They'll be here and likely start up the mountain before the storm lets up. Let's get the local weather before we take her in to that wharf and tie up."

In the salon Jeff tuned in the local news channel. "… and British Press reported this morning that most of the City of Naples and surrounding areas have been evacuated. Fortunately, following the earthquake, the ash fall from the Lake Fusaro eruption was blowing out to sea, enabling a skeleton police and emergency presence in the city. Now, as a major storm pummels Naples, the wind and rain is reported to be washing much of the ash away. The evacuation of the city is extraordinarily good news. If the Campi Flegrei caldera erupts tomorrow as the young Americans Jeff Kingston and Anita Arneil have predicted, over three million may have died in the city and surrounding area. And on that note, when Lake Fusaro erupted just as Kingston and Arneil predicted, many forgot their reservations about the young geology students and began evacuating. We have received many reports that Naples City Administration had ignored repeated…"

Jeff turned to the weather channel:

"… has been the first summer storm of the year and has caused considerable flooding across parts of Europe. Now over the central Mediterranean, strong winds have left a path of destruction across central Italy. By tomorrow the storm will weaken as it crosses the…"

He turned the set off and returned to the pilothouse. "Soon we'll meet our adversaries," he said. "By this time tomorrow we'll be dead or congratulating ourselves on a successful Vesuvius eruption. From there it's in the hands of the gods."

Anita searched his face. "You were going to die up there after enabling me to sail to safety. I saw on the ship's computer where you charted a course for Cagliari, Corsica. That was for me. And I dug around until I found the note you planned to leave me."

He looked at her fondly for a moment. "It seemed the only way to give you a chance."

She put her arms around him. "I'm staying. I'll take my chances with you."

He realized she had made up her mind and when she did that... well, you didn't argue with her. "Okay Anita. Together we'll do or die." He held her close for a long moment while the yacht bucked and rolled in the waves.

… the caldera floor will collapse into the larger magna reservoir and cause a four mile wide explosion of magma to atmosphere…

CHAPTER 22

Saturday, June 27, evening
As the wind subsided somewhat, Jeff and Anita were finally able to get the *Signora Luisa* tied up at an unoccupied ship-refueling dock. After grabbing supplies and stuffing them in a backpack with the weapons, as an afterthought, Jeff went to the pilothouse and retrieved the field glasses.

They scrambled onto the wharf and hurried along the jetty toward the shore. Directly above, Vesuvius's cone-shaped dome rose like a sentinel scowling down on the town of Herculaneum perched on the cliffs just ahead.

As the rain continued to pelt down they jogged past several vessels tied up along the dock. Just beyond, Jeff eyed a large tanker truck parked beside a fuel shed.

"That will do," he said, motioning to the abandoned tanker. "We need a vehicle to get up to the top of Vesuvius."

"But Jeff! That's an eighteen wheeler with a sixteen-wheel pup trailer!"

"Probably empty. Beggars can't be choosers. Let's see if we can break in and find a set of keys."

"Maybe you won't have to."

Jeff followed her gaze. A man was sitting in an office next to the shed. He looked up from his reading as they went in.

"*Siamo qui per il camion,*" Anita said.

The man got up, retrieved a ring of keys from the wall, gave them to Jeff and said something in Italian that he didn't understand but that made Anita laugh.

Once outside, out of the office, shivering and soaked by the rain, Jeff looked at Anita. "I didn't get all of that."

"He said he was glad to see us. Herculaneum and the whole area has been evacuated. He's the last one to leave, and said it's about time you showed up."

"That's very good news. What made you laugh?"

"He said no monkey business in the truck—it's a rule. It was funny." She gave him an impish grin. "But maybe he had a good idea there."

He glanced at her, thinking she was just kidding around and keeping things light. If she had only known how much he would have loved to crawl into the big rig's sleeper cab and cuddle. No point having expectations beyond that; he knew her reputation and respected her for it.

They climbed up into the cab, thankful to get out of the rain, and studied the interior of the tractor unit. He started the diesel, let it run for a bit, found the wiper controls and released the brakes. With a roar and a burst of diesel smoke from its twin stacks, the big unit was soon pulling away and up onto the road and into Herculaneum.

Having to gear way down on the first steep slope, Jeff realized he had been wrong. The rig was fully loaded with fuel and it would be touch and go for it to make the steep grade up to the crater rim.

"I've got an idea," he said. "The first older vehicle we see that looks like we can quickly hot-wire it, I'll stop and we'll commandeer it. You can follow me up the…" Pulling over, he applied the air brakes. "There!" He grabbed a screwdriver from the truck's glove box.

"What?" Anita asked, but seeing Jeff was already half way out of the truck, she got out and followed him to a beat-up old Fiat parked beside the road.

He was already inside jimmying the ignition when she

got there. In no time, he had it running. "Quick, before someone comes! Follow me!" Running back to the tanker, he released the brakes, pulled out and passed her. Watching his mirrors to be certain she was following, he turned up onto the Via Vesuvio and geared way down, urging the big rig to crawl slowly up the curvy mountain road.

He realized Anita would be angry. He had no time to explain his plan to her. Or perhaps it was just that he didn't want to tell her.

He slowly negotiated the switchbacks on the wet pavement. With each mile it became more difficult to keep traction and prevent a stall. "Just another quarter mile," he muttered. "That's all we need." Did he dare gear down once more? There was no choice now; he was stalling out on the steep grade. He double-clutched down into the lowest gear, almost stationary now, just inching along. The big diesel groaned, black smoke billowing from its twin pipes. "Come on baby, you can do it."

The bridge was in sight now. "Just make it to that bridge baby, to the bridge!" The last hundred yards took the longest and the drive wheels were beginning to spin. When the tanker was half way across the bridge, Jeff pulled over to the right-hand curb and cranked the wheel left. The machine turned sluggishly. When it completely blocked the road Jeff jammed on the air brakes, leaving it stalled.

He shut it down. Grabbing the backpack with their supplies and weapons, he jumped out. Anita, a few dozen yards behind, stopped the Fiat. He ran down to her and hopped in.

"Turn around. Head down about a hundred yards. There's a bicycle trail off to the left. Stop and pull in there until we're out of sight of the road."

"Damn it, Jeff!"

"Here," he said, pointing.

She swung into the bicycle path and coaxed the Fiat around a bend and beyond sight of the road. Stopping, she stared at him. "By the speed you were going the truck and trailer was loaded, right?"

"Right. It was too steep. I was about to spin out."

"But why block the road? What now?"

"Grab a weapon from the bag and load it. Now we wait. But first let's check Diego's phone and see if we can figure out how close they are." He turned the kidnapper's phone on and checked messages. There was one, sent hours earlier. He handed it to Anita.

"Unable to contact you," she translated. "All to meet at Naples headquarters at 07.00."

"Here's the plan," Jeff said. "The Corrado should be coming to stop us, before we escape by helicopter at the building near the summit, right?"

She was busy loading a clip into her weapon. "Yes, when the storm stops. But why block the road at the bridge?"

"Because under that bridge are four high explosive charges, and if we can get all our bad guys on the on the bridge, I can detonate it by dialing a number."

"A number…"

"Yeah."

She stared at him. You could have told me the plan."

"I was figuring it out as I went along."

"Why are there explosives under the bridge?"

"I thought I'd need them to stop someone from following me, if I have to go up and detonate it manually."

She glowered at him. "But what if someone else dials those numbers before you?"

He'd thought of that. "The chances of that are one in ten million," he said. And if they did, they would have just been advancing the inevitable. He rubbed the steam off the inside of the windshield. "The rain is letting up. I think it's beginning to clear. We have to get to that rise over there, where we can see the bridge." He dug the field glasses out of the bag and opened the door. "Come on!"

They scrambled over the wet rocks to a rise where they

could observe the bridge. He gave her the glasses. "What do you think?" The sun was just going down, and dark shadows had begun to appear.

"We don't need these. We're awfully close. When that tanker goes up…"

"Yeah, maybe we should get back a bit."

"Too late. Hear that? They're coming."

Three cars rounded the curve and came to a sudden stop just short of the bridge. They counted. Ten men got out of the cars and advanced cautiously onto the bridge.

Jeff began dialing the trigger number on his phone. With his finger on the last digit, he hesitated.

They were all around the tanker now; one man was getting in the cab.

"Get down."

They ducked down behind the rocks. Still he hesitated. She looked at him. "What are you waiting for?"

"I'm not sure I can do this."

She looked at the phone in his hand. "It's kill or be killed. Do it."

"Ten lives… ten lives at the tip of my finger…"

She reached over and touched his finger ever so gently. They looked at each other, feeling the horror of it but knowing it must be done. She pushed lightly.

A shock wave accompanied the horrific explosion. As they peeked over, a ball of fire had shot skyward sending fire and debris raining down around the area. The bridge was gone. So was the tanker.

"Holy Jesus…"

They watched for a moment as the wreckage settled and the smoke cleared. Anita stood and began running down over the rocks to the Fiat shouting, "You drive." Jumping in, Jeff backed out onto the road and headed down the switchbacks.

Neither spoke as they drove back through the city, toward the *Signora Luisa*. Finally, Anita muttered something under her breath.

"Diego?" he said.

She nodded.

"Think he'll tip off Camponolo to unleash the rest of the C-2 on us?"

"Not likely."

He looked at her.

"Diego was responsible for losing the people they kidnapped," Anita said. "I think he'll just fade into the woodwork."

"I think you're right." Jeff grinned. He'd been thinking much the same thing.

He turned his thoughts to Vesuvius. Hopefully they still had time to set off the explosives before Campi erupted. They could set a course for the outer islands, perhaps Capra Island in the Tyrrhenian Sea, before detonating it. But there was really no need to. The Vesuvius fallout would go due east with the strong winds—if it even erupted—and they would be fine in the bay.

But if Campi erupted there was no place to hide anywhere in the central Mediterranean; they would be better off right at ground zero.

In that case, how many lives would be lost downwind? A million? Two million? Ten million?

Everything hinged on his mother's belief that there was a common magma chamber. Of course, diverting the Campi magma to Vesuvius would be impossible if she was wrong. As he thought about it, he knew his diversion strategy was likely doomed to failure.

"When will you set off the explosives?" Anita asked.

He looked at his watch. "It's dark now. We should wait another three hours to make certain everyone has evacuated safely. We'll set it off at first light. Soon as we get to the outer islands."

"Do you think it will...?"

"It better," he said. "It bloody better."

"So if Vesuvius erupts, how long before we know it's successful in stopping a Campi eruption?"

Jeff shrugged. "Several days. Perhaps weeks."

"Why don't we go out to the very center of Campi Flegrei? Right out there," she pointed. "Dead center over to caldera. Why don't we just sit out there and see if Vesuvius will erupt? Why don't we defy the monster while we set off Vesuvius?"

"Defy the monster…"

"We're toast it if erupts in the next few hours anyway. The tidal wave will take us. There's no way to travel inland to escape fast enough. Out there would be the ultimate thrill, Jeff! The ultimate living on the edge!"

"I knew you embraced danger, but…" he hesitated. "And you're right about a Campi tidal wave. We could go to the airport and see if there's a small plane."

"The engine would be full of volcanic dust from Lake Fusaro. Besides, the earthquakes may have damaged the runways. Even if you could find a still-fly-able small plane, we'd be—"

He held up a hand and nodded. "You really want to defy the monster?"

She nodded, holding his gaze. "At least until we see if you can get Vesuvius to erupt."

He considered. She knew the odds of escaping this were about zero if Campi erupted. Still, it would take real guts to be out there.

"So be it!"

Back on board the *Signora Luisa,* they took the yacht out into the Bay of Pozzuoli in the darkness, and about three miles from shore they stopped dead center over the caldera. Standing in the moonlight, looking back at the shore and the beautiful old buildings of the once vibrant city, Anita wondered, "How many people have stayed, do you suppose?"

"Some have. Like us, they're defying the monster."

"I can understand it now. Why people have stayed all these centuries and lived with the threat. It is a beautiful city, full of wonderful, caring people…"

They sat listening to geysers of hot gasses shooting up all around them. The smell of sulfur filled the air. It was a dangerous, eerie place—the last place on earth anyone would want to be. Still they waited silently, lost in their own thoughts as finally the approaching sunrise brought on the first light of day. Jeff checked VolcanoWatch. ... *the caldera floor will collapse into the larger magna reservoir and cause a four mile wide explosion of magma to atmosphere...*

Sunday June 28th. Perhaps one day to Armageddon.

Out on deck, Jeff took out the cell phone and dialed the Vesuvius trigger number, pausing with his finger over the last digit. "Care to join me in this?"

They stood close and looked up at the distant peak of the volcano. She placed her finger gently over his. They looked at each other briefly and then turned their gaze back to the crater at the top of Vesuvius. Then, in unison they pressed.

A narrow stream of flame shot high into the air. As they watched, waiting, a rumble from the underground explosion reached them. The stream of fire dispersed.

Then, nothing.

They looked at each other.

Jeff shook his head and looked at the deck. "Well, we didn't get our Vesuvius eruption," he said. "It was worth a try, but I suppose it was a long shot."

Anita looked into the dark water, her hand over her face. The acidic, sulfurous air was burning her nose and throat. "I know what's going on under us. I wonder what the rest of the world is thinking."

"Giovanni gave CNN International a direct connection with the unmanned Naples Volcano Monitoring Center. Let's check CNN Atlanta online, see what they say."

They went below and found the station, waiting as it aired several commercials before returning to an interview with a scientist.

"Data from the the Campi Flegrei caldera indicates it should be upgraded to stage eight," said the scientist.

"And that means…" prompted the interviewer.

"It will erupt within hours."

"Here's live feed again," the interviewer continued. "That yacht we showed you earlier is still there. We'll try to get you a telephoto shot—tell me, Dr. Johansen, do you think they're scientists? Thrill seekers?"

Jeff pointed. "Look. That's us out there!"

The scientist shrugged. "More likely the latter. They seemed interested in the minor Vesuvius eruption that occurred just a few minutes ago, but I can't imagine what scientists would be doing at such a dangerous location at this time."

Anita couldn't suppress a grin. "I'll bet Camponolo has recognized his yacht out here."

Jeff nodded, reminded that Camponolo and his Mafia friends were very much alive and would be far away from here by now, likely in the safety of South America. If he lived through this, he would kill them for what they had done here.

For the first time in his life he needed revenge. He felt bitterness… a need to rid the earth of these cruel, malicious criminals who would trade the deaths of millions for personal financial gain. They were monsters, not unlike those of the Third Reich.

"I guess we better figure out what to do next," he said.

"We'll talk about it in a minute," Anita said, heading down the stairway and into one of the washrooms.

Jeff followed her below, entered one of the staterooms and lay back on the bed. What should they do? Their best course of action, now that Vesuvius was not going to erupt…

He felt something. What was that, the wind? He half rose from the bed and called out to Anita, who was likely still in the end washroom. "Did you feel someth—?"

A sudden shock. Had Vesuvius erupted? He jumped up and looked out a porthole.

The whole side of the Vesuvius volcano had lifted out

and was sliding down over Herculaneum and into the sea. A wall of water was rolling toward them.

"Tsunami!" he screamed. "Look out, Anita! Vesuvius has—"

The yacht pitched sideways, rolled over, flung him against the wall, now the ceiling, now the floor, now the wall again. With an enormous crash, something came smashing down through the ceiling. As it struck him, the rolling stopped. They were upright again. Something pinned him. Pain. Heat.

Try to breathe... breathe... Everything faded to gray, then to black.

... Vesuvius began erupting unexpectedly at 04.53 hrs on June 28th...

CHAPTER 23

Sunday, June 28, morning

The woman looked down at him with brown eyes; friendly eyes. Who was she? Her image was fading... fading...

The old woman had a calm about her. Was she an angel? Was he dead? Her image was fading again...

Now her face was above him. She was speaking, but he couldn't hear her. Was he deaf? Was he dead? He must be dead; he could feel nothing... nothing...

The old woman... she was trying to move him. But why?

She was there again, speaking to him. He couldn't hear her. He must try to speak. Where was Anita? Yes, Anita... why couldn't he speak? She must go and help Anita...

He was awake now... he was twisted somehow. His legs were... above him. He could see one. It was bruised an ugly purple. He tried to move it. Where was his other leg? His body was down there below him... in the water... yes... in the water. But then why was his leg above him?

The old woman, where had she gone? Had she gone to help Anita? Good. Darkness closed... he must stay awake. Where was Anita? She was in danger. The boat had rolled... Was Anita safe?

"Anita," he croaked, "are you..." Gray again. Black.

"*Risvegliare.*" The old man had a deeply lined face. He had blue eyes. He could hear the man speaking but his voice seemed far away. "*Non spostare.*"

"English," Jeff whispered.

"Ah, English. Not to move," the old man said. "We get you out."

"No. Find the woman," he whispered. "She was with me... Anita."

"Not to move!"

"Where are we?"

"Washed up on shore. We get you out. Not to move. Stay still."

"Look for a woman. Her name... is Anita..." It was coming on again, the blackness.

Jeff opened his eyes. The room was barren, nothing on the walls or ceiling, just cracked white plaster. He tried to move his head to the left; pain. To the right; more pain. He was lying on a floor. The door was open. He could see outside. He was looking down at the water from a hillside, high above. Beside the open door, high grass waved in the wind.

Where was he? How did he get here? There had been an old woman. An old man. He tried to move his arms. One moved and the other....

He settled back down. Don't panic. Explore the logic of it. He wasn't in a hospital; he was lying on the floor of an old building. He could feel a mattress with his right hand... yes, a mattress.

He tried to rise up but pain stabbed both sides of his chest. Broken ribs? Probably. He could see a black bag with silver instruments beside it on a table in the corner. He felt his face with his hand. His nose was itchy. He rubbed it. An incredible stabbing pain ran from his nose clear into his brain. Now he was gasping for air, unable to breathe, he was passing out... blackness.

"Risvagliare. Risvagliare!"

He opened his eyes. An old man looked down on him. Jeff opened his mouth to speak. Nothing, no sound came from his effort to whisper. Then a faint croak, "English."

"Ah, yes, English. Wake up, but do not speak. You were in a boat wreck, young man. Washed up by the tsunami, injured. I am a retired physician. My wife and I live here on this headland, surrounded by the sea. The tsunami has washed away my dock, taken my boat. We have no way to get you to the hospital, so we have carried you here, to this hut."

Jeff tried to whisper. "Vesuvius erupted?"

"Sì, yes."

"There is a woman... a woman in the... she was with me..."

"No, young man; there was no woman."

"There is a woman. Anita. Go back to the wreckage. You must find her!"

"You have told us. We have searched the wreckage."

Jeff closed his eyes. "Go back. The last stateroom. At the back. She is in there."

"I am sorry. No woman. We searched twice."

"Thank you for helping me. Where is the yacht?"

The old doctor looked at him but said nothing.

"The boat... the boat... where is it?"

"Nearby. The wave threw it up onto the rocks."

"How far from here?"

"A hundred meter."

"Please. Look again."

The old doctor shook his head in frustration. "Your arms and legs are badly bruised, but no fractures, other than your ribs and, perhaps, a concussion. You must rest quietly. My wife has gone home to make you some soup. I will bring it to you. Rest quietly." He looked at Jeff, shook his head again and left the hut.

Jeff sat up with difficulty, ignoring the stabbing in his chest, then slowly got to his feet. Staggering to the door, he looked out. Vesuvius was erupting, a huge cloud rising to the sky. The wind was from the west, taking everything east and away from the city.

He stared at it. "We did it, Anita, but will it work? And where are you?"

The hut was fifty feet above the water, perched on a sloping rocky cliff. Three hundred feet away, jammed in against a rock outcrop, was what was left of the *Signora Luisa*. The yacht lay on her side, high above the present water level, the keel facing him, the pilothouse crushed, the bow gashed open and the first deck jammed against the rocks.

"Holy!" he whispered softly. The wave must have been fifty feet high.

Dizzy now, he was beginning to pass out. Grabbing onto the door frame he waited until it passed, then began hobbling toward the wreckage. "Anita," he called out, but his voice was weak. Nearing the boat, he tripped and fell onto the rocks. Pain shot though him. He got up and staggered on. "Anita…"

He crawled up onto the edge of the deck and could see where the old folks had cut through a crumpled stairway to get to him. Squirming down through the hole, he dropped into the belly of the beached wreck and down the wall of the lower corridor in the darkness. A flashlight would help. He tried to remember. Where had the door been to the second stateroom?

It would be on the left. Above him. Having difficulty breathing, he stopped and rested.

"Anita!" He climbed up and through an opening. The crushed stateroom was illuminated by a gash in the hull. The place was a shambles. There was no sign of her.

"Anita!"

Nothing.

"Anita! Where are you?"

He climbed down out of the stateroom, removing some debris in the darkness, including his backpack. He tossed it aside and found the door of the washroom at the very end of the stern section. It was jammed shut. "Anita, are you in there?"

He had nothing to pry the door open with, so with his hands together, he stood sideways and ignoring the pain in his chest, smashed an elbow against the door. The warped door bounced open. The washroom was empty.

"Oh my God, Anita! Where the hell are you?"

Picking up his backpack, he crawled out of the wreckage and looked out at the sea. Had she drowned out there? Frantic, he began climbing down to the beach. Maybe she had gone for help. "Anita," he yelled. Still nothing. Leaving his backpack behind, he walked up the beach. It soon came to an abrupt end, cut off by rugged cliffs plunging straight down into the water. He painfully retraced his steps, walking in the sand in the opposite direction.

Were those footprints in the sand?

She was lying motionless on her stomach, her arms flung out as if reaching for something. He hurried forward and felt for a pulse. Relief flooded over him; it was strong and regular. He whispered in her ear. "Anita! Can you hear me?"

No response. He hesitated. She had been walking; he could see her tacks in the sand. He rolled her face-up. "Anita! Can you hear me? How badly are you hurt?"

"Jeff?"

"Yes."

"My head hurts," she whispered. "Maybe con... con..."

"Concussion?"

"Maybe."

"Broken bones?"

"No." Ignoring his pain, he lifted her gently, held her in his arms and began limping back toward the hut.

"I... I couldn't get you out," she whispered. "I was going... for help..."

"Hey!" The old doctor was down the beach, calling to them. "Hey there!"

"Bring us water," Jeff called. "I've found my woman!"

She tugged on his shirt. "My woman?"

"Hey, I'm a caring colleague... It wasn't meant to be possessive." He looked down at her. "Still got a bit of spunk left, have we?"

She didn't answer but, arms around his neck, she hugged him closer.

The doctor ran up, carrying Jeff's backpack. "How can I help?"

"I can carry her okay, but I'm light-headed. Steady me if I lose my balance."

"We take her to the house," said the doctor. "Up this way."

Climbing cautiously, propped up by the old doctor, Jeff made his way up a winding trail to a small villa perched near the cliff top. Built of heavy timbers with white stucco walls, the house commanded a sweeping view of the bay, and in the opposite direction, the Island of Proceda.

The doctor's wife ushered him through the door and showed him to a room, where he lowered Anita to the bed. "I will care for her," the doctor said. He motioned to his wife. "Maria has made soup. You go with her, rest, eat."

He followed the old woman to her kitchen. Exhausted from the climb, he sank painfully into a chair. "Thank you for rescuing me, Maria... Mrs. ..."

She smiled. "Aquino. You both very lucky."

"Yes."

She brought his soup. "My husband say you are stubborn young man. We are glad you found her." She told him how the wave slammed into the island, how they had pulled him from the wreckage of the yacht, but were not able to carry him beyond the shack.

She continued talking, but Jeff wasn't listening. As he brought Anita into the house he had seen a look in her eyes. She had a raised bruise on the side of her head and he knew it was very serious.

He had to get her to a hospital.

The old doctor came into the kitchen. "I am almost certain she has depressed skull fracture. She needs immediate attention of a neurosurgeon and fully equipped operating room. I do not even have an IV here to give her liquids. Even if we could get over to Proceda Island, we do not have an operating room or neurosurgeon there. Blood and fluids are building pressure against her brain. These first hours, they are critical. There is no time."

"Do you have anything that will float? A raft? Anything?"

"No. And you would need power to move out against these currents."

"Can I use your phone?" Jeff asked.

"We have no phone on the island," said the doctor. "That is why we live here."

Jeff unzipped his backpack and pulled out the cell phones, checking each one in turn, knowing it was futile. They were all soaking wet and unusable.

He went in to where Anita lay. "I need your phone. I'm going to check your pockets." He squeezed her hand but there was no response; she was unconscious. He patted her slacks pockets; there was no telltale outline of a phone. He looked at her, feeling panic. Dropping to his knees, holding her limp hand, he whispered, "Oh, God—what can I do? She's going to die here."

An idea. He turned to the doctor. "I'm going down to the wrecked yacht. Come with me. I'll need your help."

They climbed down to the wreck and Jeff went around the stern of the vessel to the lower deck that was wedged against the rocks. "There should be an inflatable Zodiac in here, with an outboard. If there is one… and if it isn't too badly damaged…"

After several tries, they pried the hatch off and were relieved to find a Zodiac. Carefully avoiding the sharp rocks, they carried it to the beach, inflated it and checked the outboard.

"Okay," Jeff said, feeling faint. "I'm going to carry Anita down here. Somehow I'm going to get her to the Naples hospital. Maybe there is still a neurosurgeon in the hospital. It's our only hope."

After climbing back up to the villa, Jeff dumped his backpack and stuffed his passport and wallet into his pocket, along with what was left of the euros. Then he wrapped Anita in a blanket and lifted her from the bed. "I'll send someone to rescue you two," he told the old couple, grimly. "And thank you. We owe you."

The old folks followed him, concerned as he climbed down, carrying her to the raft. Although almost passing out, he placed Anita in the Zodiac with care, started the outboard and pushed off. It was dusk now and the fiery eruption from Vesuvius was lighting up the sky. Looking back, he saw the old couple waving as he pulled away.

Tears streamed down his cheeks as he spoke to Anita's still form. "We're going straight back over Campi, Anita. I'll get you to a neurosurgeon. Oh God, woman, I love you! Don't leave me now!"

As he rode at top speed across the waves he could see only darkness along the shoreline ahead. Had the tsunami swept everything away?

Suddenly he was praying unabashedly. "God, let there be someone over there to help us to get her to the hospital. Please God, hear me."

… the diameter of the resurgent dome continues to expand…

CHAPTER 24

Sunday, June 28, evening

Crossing over the five-mile-wide caldera in the half light, Jeff had time to think. The chances of there being a neurosurgeon at the Naples hospital in the evacuated city were all but impossible. He could lessen that risk if there was an emergency phone on the Zodiac.

There was, but the batteries were dead. He checked Anita's pulse. She was not going to make it.

His dread turned to resolve. He needed help from somewhere—but where? He had prayed. Would God have heard him?

As he approached the coast he found that the tsunami wave had taken out the wharf at Pozzuoli so he beached the Zodiac. With Anita unconscious in his arms, he climbed up over the washed out shoreline to the road. There, a car pulled up, its headlights illuminating him in the near darkness. It stopped. On its door was written in large letters, POLICIA.

The cop rolled the window down. *"In difficoltà?"*
"Sì. English?"
"Non."
"Woman injured… uh… *donna fertiti."* Jeff frowned, trying to remember. "Hospital… *Ospedale."*

The cop got out to help.

As Jeff got Anita into the police car he said, "She needs a neurosurgeon."

"Neurosurgeon?"

"Sì. Can you call *ospedale* and have neurosurgeon in to meet us?"

"*Neurochirurgo. Sì!*"

Jeff climbed into the back seat with Anita and cradled her as the cop put the siren on and burned up the road, calling into his handheld microphone for a neurosurgeon.

"Thank you, God—thank you! Now if only there's still a neurosurgeon..."

The city was deserted. The winds had carried the ash away and except for detouring around several quake-damaged roadways the cop was making good time. It was dark now and only a few streetlights were on, but ahead a large building was fully illuminated.

The cop pulled up to an emergency entrance which was jammed with injured people waiting to be seen.

"You are all very brave to stay and help people," Jeff said, taking Anita gently out of the car. He thanked the cop and rushed past everyone, through the double doors, past Emergency, down a long corridor to where two white-clad men were entering an elevator. "Wait!"

The men turned, one holding the door. "Operating room." Jeff said, entering the elevator. "I think we have... a neurosurgeon... waiting for us." The small space seemed to be making him dizzy.

One of the men stepped forward and looked at Anita's bruised head. "Floor five," he said, punching the button and then holding out his arms. "Give her to me."

"No." Jeff shook his head. "Show me where to go."

"I'm a doctor. And you look like you both need one." As the elevator door opened on five, Jeff staggered against the elevator wall. Both doctors moved quickly to keep Anita from falling.

"*Medica sala operatori! Fretta,*" he heard one say.

Good. He could let go now. He tried to keep standing

as they took Anita from his arms but everything was going black. Slipping down the wall to the floor he could only see the doctor's feet as they left the elevator. "Help her live, God…" Then everything faded out.

A strange weight kept him from moving. He forced his eyes open and was surprised to see only a sheet. Heavy sedation was keeping him immobile.

He managed to flag a nurse and asked about Anita.

The nurse didn't recognize her name, but scurried off, returning with another nurse who explained that Miss Arneil had survived yesterday's surgery and had been transferred to the intensive care unit at Avanzato Vita Suporte in Rome. He would not be able to visit because of the strict security for that ward. The nurses were thrilled to have the famous Americans in their hospital, but Mr. Kingston would also be transferred out later that day.

As soon as the nurses left, Jeff disconnected his IV tubes, found his clothes in the closet next to the bed, and began searching for the exit.

If his Vesuvius strategy was right, it would take days to confirm that Campi Flegrei was not going to erupt. Each hour that passed without an eruption would be positive, but it may take weeks for the supervolcano to go quiet. Anita was safe for the moment, and he intended to keep her that way. Camponolo had vast resources at his fingertips, resources he could use to destroy them. With what he and Anita knew about the C-2 leader's Naples deception, Camponolo couldn't afford to leave them alive. There was no choice; he must destroy Camponolo if either he or Anita were to have a future.

Down a long hospital corridor he stumbled into a vacant nurse's station. In it was a phone. Pulling a water stained card from his wallet, he called Moe Labouef.

Waiting for Moe in the Hotel Raganelli bar, Jeff checked VolcanoWatch on his new cell phone. *The diameter of the resurgent dome continues to expand...* Damn it! He turned the phone off.

"*Bonjour*, Jeff."

"Hi, Moe!" He got to his feet, wincing, and wrung the Frenchman's hand. "It's good to see you!"

"Yes, yes. Let us have an ale and lunch! I cannot wait. I have learned all about Camponolo's treachery. And I have an idea." They sat and enjoyed a glass while Jeff brought Moe up to date. Then over lunch they focused on their plan. Both were intent on ending Camponolo's life. If they could take out some of C-2's new leadership with Camponolo, all the better.

Jeff studied his friend. "It's not going to be easy, Moe. And we could get killed for our trouble. You certain you're up for this?"

"*Absolument, mon ami! Absolument!*" Moe smiled. "I have already sent my cousin, a beautiful young woman, to Brazil. Able to speak fluent Portuguese as well as Italian and French, she has obtained employment as a servant in Camponolo's new villa. She will help us, *mon ami*." Jeff's shock must have showed. "Ah. Her family died in the eruption. So you see, she will do what she will do."

They decided going to the Italian or Brazilian police or INTERPOL would be useless.

After they made reservations on the next flight to Rio de Janeiro, Jeff visited a nearby Bank of America. Flush with funds, they did some carefully planned shopping and headed for Rome's Leonardo de Vinci Airport. By late that evening they were airborne.

Anita opened her eyes. She was in a bed and hooked up to a monitor. A feeding tube ran up her nose. Another dripped a clear liquid from an IV bag into a tube attached to her arm. A monitor placed on her finger pulsed her heart beat. Beep. Beep. Beep. The nearby portable defibrillator looked ominous. Her head ached. She reached up to brush her hair back only to find her head had been shaved. On the right side, an area was particularly sensitive. She ran her finger over it. She could feel a plastic-like covering over stitches.

Slowly she began making sense of it. The yacht had crashed onto the rocks. Unable to free him, she had gone for help but had collapsed on the beach. He had found her, picked her up in his arms and carried her.

What was his name? His image was clear—her man—but what was his name?

A nurse appeared. She must speak to the nurse. The nurse was already speaking. *"Qual è tuo nome?"* She couldn't understand her.

She tried to speak. Nothing—she could make no sound. What was his name? He had carried her—her man—what was his name? She closed her eyes again and drifted.

"Qual è tuo nome?" The was woman leaning over her. She was young and dark haired. *"Qual è tuo nome?"*

What was the woman saying? ... *nome* ... name. Italian. She wants to know my name.

What was his name? Her man—his name was... ahh... Jeff! Yes, God love you, Jeff! But she must not say his name; no, no no. His name was a secret and so was hers. But, why?

The nurses came and went. A doctor visited. Time to figure it all out. Time slipped by. Three days passed—maybe more. Each time she awakened again, a little more came back. Maybe she could talk coherently now. She was feeling stronger.

One day as she lay with her eyes closed half asleep she was jarred awake.

"Anita! It's Catrina Rossi."

She recognized Catrina instantly. "Hello Catrina."

"How are you feeling?"

"Fine. Like it's time to get out of this place. Campi Flegrei... has it...?"

"No, that monster is still in its den." There was warmth in Catrina's friendly smile, but her lined face betrayed a worried look. "Are you sure you are okay, Anita?"

"Yes. Don't say my name. Where is my friend?"

"Ahh. You mean Jeff."

"Don't say his name!"

"My dear, you must not worry. The staff here already knows your name. You are in Rome, in a large hospital. I had great difficulty finding you after your transfer from Naples. There is heavy security. Only those with your mother's permission are allowed to come into your room. You are safe here."

"Do you know about my friend?"

"He left the Naples hospital—no one knows where he has gone."

"How did you find me?"

"I was at the Naples hospital that night covering a story when your friend brought you in. He carried you right past us all. He wouldn't put you down until he..." She paused. "I sniffed a great story so I found out everything that happened. Are you able to understand? Do you want to know what I found out?"

"Yes. Tell me."

"Well, you waited to see if the stolen explosives would cause Vesuvius to erupt. You got caught in the tsunami, after the eruption, and your yacht slammed into the rocks on the Presidia Island promontory. The old physician and his wife stopped looking for you, but your badly injured colleague began searching for you..."

When she finished telling the story she ended it with, "He must love you very much, my dear. I think from what he did that night, if he could, he would die for you."

Anita was silent for a long moment. "Are you planning to print our story?"

"It must be told, my dear."

"If you do, it may result in us both being murdered by the Mafia or sent to prison."

"You really think so? Everyone will be on your side; you will both be honored."

"How be I give you another story, an even better one you can use in its place?"

"Ah, nothing can match your story."

"This one will. It's about the greatest deception ever. I'll tell you about it but you must only print one, not both stories. Do you agree?"

"I am intrigued. Of course, I agree."

Catrina pulled out her recorder and began making furious notes as Anita told the story of the C-2's massive criminal deception and real estate fraud, providing plenty of names and dates. "If you check the real estate sales in the last few months, you will find what I say is true. They were trading the lives of the people for financial gain."

Catrina nodded. "I will exchange this story for yours. I must go now, my dear. When I get done with this, all hell will break loose. Thank you for it. Good luck to you. I admire you both... as would all the people of the Mediterranean if they knew your story. But do not worry, my dear; they never will."

After Catrina left Anita closed her eyes. It had all come back now—everything. Catrina's story had filled in the blanks from when she passed out on the beach. Jeff would be coming for her; she knew that. She had a good idea where he had gone. Until Camponolo was dead, they were on borrowed time. But now Catrina had the information, names and events that could sink the C-2 leaders. That is, if any of them were still in the country.

She must find a way to tell Jeff that she was in love with him. She didn't want it to end up the same way it had for his father and mother.

Maybe after they graduated they would get married. It was okay to dream. Many of her dreams had not come true and maybe the supervolcano would end this dream too.

She must recover quickly and be ready to leave when Jeff came for her.

Anita sat up as Catrina swept into the room, picked up the remote and switched on the television. "Watch," she said breathlessly, skimming through the channels. "Oh, drat. We've missed... no. Here." Leaving the television on a news station, she turned the volume up.

The doctor, who had recently relocated here from Naples, was killed, along with fourteen high powered businessmen, also from Italy, many of whom had been implicated in a recent exposé by Italian journalist Catrina Rossi. Local police say that while the rest of the property had unusually strict security, there was no expectation that anyone could ever come up from the cliff face.

This appears to have been a targeted attack, as the explosives were detonated at around 1:40 a.m., when all staff had been told to leave by one of Camponolo's newly hired employees, a woman the police would like to speak with as soon as possible.

In other news, the recent eruption...

Catrina clicked the television off, grinning. "I thought you should be the first to know."

On the flight back to Rome, Jeff relaxed in his seat. Going over his struggle to save Anita and marveling at the way it turned out, he realized God had been with him. It was the only plausible explanation. The chances of the police car being there on that dark dirt road—the one that picked them up that night—the chances were one in a million, but there it was, on the little-used side road right above where he landed on the beach.

Coincidence?

No. Impossible.

The cop had to have been lost. There was no reason for him to be down there. He smiled. It seemed Michael was right. Perhaps he had a spiritual side after all.

The loudspeaker crackled. "This is your captain speaking. In ten minutes we will be landing in Rome…"

In the taxi from the airport into downtown Rome, he realized how anxious and excited he was. He hoped she'd be happy to see him. Well of course she would be; she was probably bored stiff. Only Catrina Rossi had been allowed to visit. Her sisters had chicken pox and were quarantined in the States, Sandra too, until the girls recovered.

It was too early for hospital visiting hours, so he booked a suite at the Capannelle, a four star hotel near the city center. After checking in he did his exercise routine, took a long shower, dressed in new clothes and placed the new outfit he'd purchased for Anita in a travel bag.

In the bedroom he looked at the king sized bed, wondering if he should have specified twins. He had to have a place to bring her. Their flight to New York didn't leave until the following morning. He knew her rules: wedding ring first.

There was a large divan in the suite's living area. He could sleep on that.

At 10:00 a.m. he bought a dozen white roses and hailed a taxi for the medical center.

On the third floor, he walked down the long corridor to a nurse's station.

"Do you speak English? My name is Jeff Kingston, nurse, I'm here to…"

"Come with me, young man. She has been waiting for you."

He was taken to a large pavilion where several patients sat in wheel chairs. On an outside patio several patients sat in deck chairs enjoying the morning sun.

The nurse pointed. "Over there…"

"Thank you."

He clutched the roses. She looked pale but terrific. Her head had been shaved—there were no bandages, just a slight scar from the surgery. He bent down beside her chair. "You look terrific!"

She turned, a smile lighting up her face. "Jeff!"

"I brought you some flowers." He set them in her arms, tears coming to his eyes. "You look so very beautiful! I'm just so happy to see you. It was just such a... such a close call. To see you getting well... it's... it's... just..."

She got to her feet and set the roses on the chair, then turned to put her arms around him.

He kissed her cheek, feeling the softness of her against his chest. "Are there any nagging problems?"

She stepped back. "No. I'll be good as new. No memory loss. That's a very good sign, they say. I see you cut your hair. You look yourself again. And you... you were successful."

He nodded grimly. "He will never threaten the Italian people or us ever again."

She nodded thoughtfully, "We had no choice but to end it this way did we?"

"No."

"I'm glad it's over. Now we have to wait to see what Campi Flegrei does."

They walked out to the edge of the hospital sunning area and looked out at the City of Rome in all its historic grandeur.

"We should have realized," he said, "that when Vesuvius erupted, to be out there on the bay was lunacy..."

She laughed. "We were tempting the monster—remember?"

"Yes." He gazed at her. "My! You look so good! A bit pale, but really good. You realize I'm in love with you, don't you? They told me at the desk I can take you out of here." He pulled his phone from his pocket. "I want to show you something."

She moved closer and looked. It was a newspaper article from the English-language edition of the *Observatorio Romano: Yesterday the Thera volcano in Greece slowed its eruptive activity and, amazingly, the Vesuvius eruption seems to have ended at 5 a.m. this morning. The greatest news however, is that Vesuvius's dreaded big brother is no longer threatening millions. Campi Flegrei, has been downgraded to a Stage 4, not expected to erupt for months; experts hope, for eons. And while Aetna is still active, all evacuation orders have been rescinded.*

The citizens of Naples and all those in the Mediterranean who have been forced from their towns and cities can now begin returning to their homes.

He showed her another from the Associated Press. *Twelve years ago deceased volcanologist Dr. Kristin Stefsdotir appears to have "got it right" about the two volcanoes threatening Naples. The world renowned scientist set forth the opinion that Vesuvius and Campi Flegrei shared a common magma chamber. Now, observing the behavior of the two volcanoes it would appear she was correct...*

Anita looked up and smiled. "We got them all to safety; then we put our doomsday monster back to sleep. And we survived it all, didn't we?"

"We sure did. And we had Divine help."

She raised her eyebrows.

He grinned. "I never could have saved you alone. Now look at this headline in *The European*, English edition."

Anita scanned the headline. MONSTEROUS CRIMINAL DECEPTION by Catrina Rossi.

"Gee, great headline," she said, grinning at him.

"So! I figured it was you behind this!"

"I traded Catrina our story for this one. Ours will never be written."

"You are truly brilliant!" He shook his head in admiration. "Now read the end."

Unfortunately it is believed the perpetrators of this heinous crime, whose motive was to sell billions in real estate, have fled Italy to Brazil, a nation which does not have an extradition treaty with Italy. It is therefore probable that those responsible will never be punished... She was silent, looking at him.

"I got them all, Anita. The whole bloody bunch."

They stood for a while in silence looking out at the city. "I'm glad you are safe and it's over," Anita said at last.

"We should celebrate." They walked along the patio rail, examining the flowers in planters and the lush greenery. She stopped and faced him. "And what was that comment you shoehorned into your greeting? Something about being in love with me?"

"I am, Anita! Totally!" He hesitated and then placing his hands gently on her shoulders he looked into her eyes. "Will you...?"

"Will I what?"

"Will you marry me?"

"Yes," she said, "but after our graduation."

"But that's a year away. I was hoping... I mean I know you need a ring and all and..."

"Think you can wait that long for an old fashioned girl?"

He looked deep into her eyes, feeling the excitement of the moment, yet understanding the deep significance of her question. He didn't hesitate. "If it means we can spend the rest of our lives together, of course I can!"

She kissed him again. "There is a way of expressing how I feel right now," she said, "about everything we've accomplished together... and about what we've just decided to do with our lives. In Italian it is *felicità totale!*"

"Total happiness," he grinned. "Yes! And is there an Italian word for euphoria?"

She laughed, hugging him. "Yes, it's pronounced the same way but spelled differently, e-u-f-o-r-i-a." Her kiss was long and lingering. "You feel it? *Euforia!*"

"Yes," he said, "*Euforia.* What a fantastic Italian word!"

An excerpt from The Garibaldi File

Epilogue

Five years later
Awakened at 3:30 a.m. by the sound of multiple sirens, Doctor Jeff Kingston, a Seattle-based Volcano Scientist and Coast Guard Reservist, grabbed his iPad and checked the Major Emergency channel.

The quake under British Columbia's coast registered 8.2 on the Richter scale, with its epicenter located at coordinates 50°80'24" N, 123°18'09" W under Princess Louisa Inlet.

Jeff squinted at the screen. The map showed it centered just north of the city of Vancouver, Canada, and the quake epicenter was seven miles inland, in a coastal valley perilously close to the dormant Mount Garibaldi volcano.

Although a damage assessment is not yet in, preliminary reports indicate the tsunami swept southward sending a thirty-foot wave down both sides of Texada Island through Georgia Strait, into parts of Vancouver and Victoria and then into Seattle.

While the tsunami could have been highly destructive, it occurred during low tide and resulted in little damage along the Washington coast.

"So why wasn't I called?" Jeff muttered.

We are still awaiting word, but this earthquake will have caused considerable damage to buildings and infrastructure in those British Columbia cities. Little damage is expected in the

Seattle area. A tsunami warning had been issued for both the Canadian and U.S. West Coast. However, because the wave reached Vancouver in seven minutes and Seattle in twenty-three minutes, there was little advance warning.

Jeff frowned. Everyone knew the dreaded "Big One" was coming somewhere along the west coast, but it was surprising that this large earthquake had occurred seven miles inland.

He double-checked the map for the location of the earthquake's epicenter. Its proximity to the towering Mount Garibaldi volcano just fifty miles north of Vancouver was troubling. Presently dormant, the massive volcano was at coordinates 49°51'02" N and 123°00'17" W, a scant eleven miles east of the quake's epicenter. Was Garibaldi coming to life?

While he pondered the situation, a more troubling event appeared on the screen:

Northeast of Vancouver there is breaking news. In the rugged inland coastal mountains, a landslide in the Fraser Canyon at a Hell's Gate, possibly triggered by the earthquake, has completely blocked off the Fraser River at a point about one hundred and thirty miles northeast of Vancouver.

Jeff checked the internet. North America's fifth largest river system, the Fraser discharged 27 cubic miles of water into the Pacific Ocean annually, along with 20 million tons of sediment, draining a vast watershed area of 85,000 square miles of British Columbia's interior. Communities above the slide would be seriously impacted as the trapped water rose.

He studied the waterway further and brought up details on Hell's Gate. At the point the slide was reported to have come down, the river was being forced through a narrow canyon only 115 feet wide at the rate of 200 million gallons per minute. No wonder they called it Hell's Gate.

He got up and pulled on his clothes.

On a Coast Guard Reserve helicopter training flight into the Coastal Mountains near the Canadian border, he had flown over a vast scene of devastation. In 1965, the Hope Slide had dumped pulverized rock, mud and debris into the valley, to a height of two hundred and eighty feet, as a mountain-side collapsed onto a busy highway. The cause of that slide had likely also been seismic activity.

He considered the impact of the new slide. If the river remained blocked for, say, six months before the slide broke free, it would back up into a massive lake. A sudden release would see some 14 cubic miles of water hurtling down the Fraser Canyon onto British Columbia's heavily populated Lower Mainland area, likely wiping out several Fraser Valley cities as well as parts of Metro Vancouver, and further endangering the 2.5 million people already dealing with this massive earthquake.

He pulled up a map of the area. Starting from the east, downstream from the slide, the first to be washed away would be the town of Hope, then the cities of Chilliwack, Langley, Fort Langley, Maple Ridge, Surrey, Pitt Meadows, Coquitlam, Burnaby, Delta and much of metropolitan Vancouver. All of it could be swept out to sea if a high debris-filled slide gave way and released what could amount to a two-hundred-foot-high torrent of destruction.

"Unthinkable!" he breathed.

He returned to his concern about Mount Garibaldi. Unlike American volcanoes, which were all heavily monitored, neither the Government of Canada nor the Province of British Columbia had any monitoring instruments in this volcanic area. Ridiculous, given that Mount Garibaldi is one of the dangerous coastal "ring of fire" volcanoes. There was no way of knowing if an eruption could trigger a flow of melted glacial ice, lava and debris down through Pitt Lake, into Pitt River and across the heavily populated area. There were no hazard warning systems, no way of notifying the residents of such an event.

His phone rang, and he glanced at the display: Ted Stoles, the Situation Commander at Military Emergency Response in Seattle.

"Good morning, sir," he said.

"You can drop the 'sir,' Jeff. I'm calling from a private office. Good morning."

"Why wasn't I called, Ted?"

"Because we don't need you for Coast Guard duty, Partner. We need you up in Canada. You've already seen the reports?"

"Yes. You want me in Canada, huh?"

"Yeah, Canada. I've just come from a meeting. We've been talking to the Canadians. We want you up there."

"Okay. The aftermath could be horrific, Ted. The slide would have taken out both intercontinental railways and Highway One in the Fraser Canyon. They may have liquefaction in the Fraser Valley. That whole valley delta, if I recall, is filled with deep layer sediment from eons of the river…"

"Yeah. But it's the volcano hazard we need you to focus on, Jeff. You remember our field trip up to the Garibaldi volcano when we were undergrads?"

"Sure do. That was the last field trip Michael Lundquist took with us."

"Yeah. Look the Canadians will be dealing with the disaster. There's going to be a major impact on the State of Washington from all this. Perhaps as many as a couple million Canadians cut off, trying to escape down through our state. They won't be thinking about the possibility—"

"Yes. Of the Garibaldi volcano coming to life. It could present a hell of an added hazard, Ted, and it was sitting practically square on top of that big son-of-a-bitchin' quake. I'm on it."

"Good man! Check it out fast, Jeff. Over two and a half million good folks are in trouble up there. We will be too if this gets any worse… Look. We're expecting another big quake off our own west coast. I'll notify the Canadian federal and provincial government authorities when you are ready to leave. I'll email you the government contacts and get you a budget charge account. You better take someone to help you deploy ground instruments from the helicopter. And take another geoscientist with you to help deploy ground monitoring instruments. Someone who doesn't shrink from risk or danger. Can you think of anyone? Someone you've worked with before?"

"Yeah," said Jeff. "I know someone."

"Good. I'll reserve a helicopter for you from the base. We are short of pilots. You'll have to jockey this one up there yourself. We'll name your mission the Garibaldi File."

About the Author

G. D. Matheson began writing after his retirement from management in the North American forest industry. A student of global challenges that may face us in this century, Matheson folds a pending Mediterranean catastrophe into a gripping story of danger and intrigue. He and his wife Norma live in British Columbia's Okanagan Valley.

Made in the USA
Charleston, SC
03 June 2014